BEST LOVED FOLK TALES OF INDIA

India is a treasure-trove of folktales born out of the customs and traditions of the country. Sometimes these tales are retold in its different regions, while imparting the local flavour to them. The mobility of the folktales can be attributed to the pilgrims and travellers journeying from one part of the country to another. They rested at night in *dharamsalas* or inns, often attached to temples, where they mingled among themselves and with the local people.

More often than not, folktales are passed on from grandmother to grandchildren so vividly that they are impressed in the listener's memory forever. They are delightful and fascinating to the young as well as the old. The same story even when heard repeatedly does not lose its interest as it appeals to the fantasies, the make-beliefs and the primitiveness in us.

These beautiful folktales of India were on the verge of extinction when a project of compilation of 21 volumes consisting of folktales of different regions was launched by Sterling. The *Best Loved Folktales* have been gleaned from the larger collection.

P.C. Roy Chaudhury during his thirty-nine years of service with the Bihar government which he joined in 1927 re-wrote fifteen District Gazetteers and the story of the 1857 movement in tribal areas. He was adviser to His Majesty's Government in Nepal, and the governments of Orissa and Rajasthan on gazetteer work. His publications include Jainism in Bihar, Folktales of Bihar, Folklore of Bihar, Inside Bihar *and* Temples and Legends of Bihar. *He was Editor-in-Chief at Gandhi Peace Foundation and his study of Gandhi is recorded in* Gandhi's First Struggle in India, Gandhi the Man, Gandhi and His Contemporaries and Gandhi and International Politics. *He has written critical biographies of C.R. Das, C.F. Andrews and Edmond Privat.*

As General Editor, Roy Chaudhury was associated with the twenty-one volumes of the series Folktales of India. *He also compiled the* Folktales of Bangladesh *and* Folktales of Thailand *published by Sterling.*

Published by
Sterling Publishers Private Limited

BEST LOVED FOLK TALES OF INDIA

Edited by

P.C. Roy Chaudhury

A Sterling Paperback

STERLING PAPERBACKS
An imprint of
Sterling Publishers (P) Ltd.
A-59 Okhla Industrial Area, Phase-II,
New Delhi-110020.
Tel: 6313023, 6320118, 6916165, 6916209
Fax: 91-11-6331241
E-mail: ghai@nde.vsnl.net.in
www.sterlingpublishers.com

Best Loved Folk Tales of India

ISBN 81 207 1660 4
First Edition 1985
Second Revised & Enlarged Edition 1994
Reprint 1995, 1996, 2001

Published by Sterling Publishers Pvt. Ltd., New Delhi-110 020.
Printed at Print India, New Delhi-110064.
Cover design by Narendra Vashishta

To
Mothers and grandmothers
over the generations
who so lovingly passed on
these tales to us

PREFACE

India has a legacy of rich and varied folklore. While research in ancient and modern history has been directed in recent decades more to the political shifts, little notice has been paid to the culture-complex, traditions and social beliefs of the common people. The sociologists should pay a good deal of attention to the customs and beliefs of the people and to changes therein through the ages. They have rather neglected the study of folklore which gives an insight into the background of the people. There has always been an easy mobility of folklore through pilgrimages, *melas* and fairs. The wandering minstrels, *sadhus* and *fakirs* have also disseminated them. People of the north visiting the temples of the south and vice versa carry their folk tales, songs, riddles and proverbs with them and there is an inconspicuous integration. The *dharmasalas, musafirkhanas* and the *chattis* (places where the pilgrims rest and intermingle) worked as the clearing house for the folk tales, traditional songs and riddles. That is why we find a somewhat common pattern in folk literature of different regions. The same type of folk tale will be found in Kashmir and in Kerala with slight regional variation. These stories were passed on from generation to generation by word of mouth before they came to be reduced to writing.

Folklorists have different approaches to the appreciation of folklore. Max Mueller has interpreted the common pattern in folk literature as evidence of nature-myths. Sir L. Gomme thought that a historical approach is best for the study of folklore. But Frazer would rather encourage a commonsense approach and to him, old and popular folk literature is mutually interdependent and satisfies the basic curiosities and instincts of man. That folklore is a vital element in a living culture has been underlined in recent years by scholars like Malinowski and Radcliffe Brown.

It is unfortunate that the study of folklore in India is of recent origin. This is all the more regrettable because the *Panchatantra* stories which had their origin in Bihar had spread through various channels almost throughout the world. As late as in 1859, T. Benfey held that there is an unmistakable stamp of Indian origin in most of the fairy tales of Europe. The same stories with different twists and settings have come back to us through Grimm and Aesop and the retold stories delight our children. That India has neglected a proper study of the beautiful motifs of our folk tales is seen in the fact that the two large volumes of the *Dictionary of Folklore, Mythology and Legend* published by Messrs Funk and Wagnalls and Company of New York have given a very inadequate reference to India.

What is the secret of the fascination that the folk tales hold for the old, the young and the very young? The story is often repeated but does not lose its interest. This is due to the satisfaction that our basic curiosity finds in the folktales. The tales through fantasies, make-believe and credulous acceptance helped the primitive man to find an answer to the mysteries of the world and particularly the many inexplicable phenomena of nature around him. Even a scientist finds great delight in the fairy tales like the one about the moon being swallowed, causing lunar eclipse. Through folk tales man has exercised his imagination and in turn folk tales have helped arouse the curiosity of the people. In spite of the scientific explanation of why earthquakes take place, the old, the young and children are still delighted to be told that the world rests on the hood of a great snake and when the snake is tired it shakes the hood causing an earthquake. Among the Mundas, an aboriginal tribe in Bihar, there is a wonderful explanation of the constellation Orion. The sword and belt of Orion, the Mundas imagined, are an appropriate likeness to the plough and ploughshare which the supreme *Sing Bong*a God first shaped in the heavens and then taught people on earth the use of the plough and the ploughshare. It is further said in the Munda folk tale that while the *Sing Bonga* was shaping the plough and the ploughshare with a chisel and a hammer he observed a dove hatching its eggs at a little distance. The *Sing Bonga* threw his hammer at the dove to bag the game. He missed his mark and the hammer went over the dove's head and hung on a tree. The hammer corresponds to the Pleiads which resemble a hammer.

The Aldebaran is the dove and the other stars of the Hyades are the eggs of the dove. Any illiterate Munda boy will unmistakably point out these constellations.

There are stories linked with seasons. The wet season and the hottest month are associated with the ripening of crops or the blossoming of trees or the frequency of dust storms and stories are woven round them. But nothing is more satisfying as a folk tale than the explanation of the phases of the stars, the moon and the sun. A Munda would point out the milky way at the *Gai Hora*, i.e., the path of the cows. The *Sing Bonga* God leads his cows every day along this path—the dusky path on the sky is due to the dust raised by the herd. The dust raised by the cows sends down the rain. A story of this type can never fail to sustain interest in spite of all the scientific explanation of the astral bodies.

The 'why' and 'wherefore' of the primitive mind tried to seek an answer in the surrounding animal and plant kingdom. Animals are grouped into different categories according to their intelligence and other habits. The fox is always sly while the cow is gentle. The lion and the tiger have a majestic air while the horse is swift, sleek and intelligent. The slow-going elephant does not forget its attendant nor does he forget a man that teases him. Monkeys are very close to man. The peacock is gay while the crow is shrewd. The tortoise is slow-going but sure-footed. The hare is swift but apt to laze on the road. These characteristics of the common animals are acceptable even today. Similarly, a large and shady peepal tree is naturally associated with the abode of the sylvan god. The thick jungle with its trees and foliage is known to be frequented by thieves and dacoits. Any solitary hut in the heart of the forest must be associated with someone unscrupulous or uncanny. These ideas are commonly woven into stories and through them the primitive mind seeks to satisfy the eternal why and how of the mind. Folk literature is often crude and even grotesque. The stories of the witches and the ogres fall in this category. There is nothing to be surprised at that. Scientific accuracy should never be looked for in folk tales although they are a very good index of the social developments of a particular time.

The last source of the folk tales is human society itself. The elemental moorings that are at the root of human society are sought to be illustrated in folk tales. The day-to-day life of the common man finds its full depiction in folk tales. Parental love, family happiness, children's adventurous habits, love and fear of the unknown, greed, etc., are some the usual themes of folk tales. The common man yearns for riches and comforts beyond his reach. He dreams of riches, princes, kingdoms, and finds satisfaction in stories and fantasy. Men love gossip and scandal. Women cannot keep secrets, children will love their parents, a mother-in-law will always think the daughter-in-law needs to be told what to do—these are some of the basic ideas that make up much of our daily life. The folk tales are woven round them and whether fantastic or with a moral undertone they only reflect the day-to-day life, the joys and sorrows of the common man.

Unknowingly, the folklorists bring in the religious customs, beliefs, food habits, modes of dress, superstitions, and thereby leave a picture of the culture-complex of the region and its people. A tribal story does not picture a king riding a large, white, foaming horse followed by hundreds of other horsemen going for a *shikar*. It will describe the Raja cutting the grass and bringing back a stack of it to feed his cows, but a folk tale more current in urban areas will have large palaces, liveried-servants, ministers and courtiers in the King's court. The very fact that the folk tales have woven man, nature, animal and plant creation together shows the great flight of imagination and singular development of mind. Introduction of moral lessons or any dogma was not deliberate but an after-thought and came in as a very natural consequence. The time and the origin of the stories are widely different. It is here that the sociologists and the anthropologists are useful. As life is different in rural and urban areas or is chequered so is folk literature diversified, as it must be, being a replica of life.

These beautiful folk tales were almost on the point of disappearing when a few pioneers, mostly foreign missionaries and European scholars, looked into them and made compilations from different parts of India. Our present generation of grandmothers know very few of these tales. The professional story-tellers who were very dearly sought after by the old and the young, not to speak of the children, have almost disappeared from India. The film industry and the film songs pose a definite threat to folklore.

The work for launching the project of publishing a compilation of 21 volumes consisting of the folk tales of different regions was entrusted to specially selected writers who had an intimate knowledge of their regions. The regional elements of the stories have been preserved as far as possible. The stories have an elemental involvement about them and they are expected to appeal to the child and its parents. We expect the reader to experience the atmosphere of different regions after reading the various folk tales. We want him to have an idea of how Kashmiri folk retire in wintry nights with the *Kangri* under the folds of their clothes to enjoy gossip. We want him to appreciate the splendour of colours in the *sari* and the flowers that are a must in Tamil Nadu.

We want him to know the stories that are behind some of the famous temples in the South such as the Kanjeevaram temple and the story about the construction of the famous Konarak temple. We want him to enjoy the stories of the heroes of Gujarat, Punjab and Rajasthan in their particular roles. We want the reader to have an idea of the peace and quiet of a hut in the lap of the Kumaon hills. We want the reader to enjoy some of the folk tales of Bengal and Bihar that have found wings to other parts of India, and to appreciate the village life with its *Alpana* and *Bratas*, at the same time get to know the customs and manners of the Santhals, Garos, and other tribes inhabiting NEFA and Assam.

The publishers wanted to present a miniature India in this collection of folk tales of the different regions. The best loved stories were gleaned from the twenty-one volumes and it is hoped the book will fascinate the reader and give him a glimpse of India through her wonderful folk tales.

P.C. Roy Chaudhury

CONTENTS

FOLK TALES OF ANDHRA PRADESH

Andhra Pradesh

Andhra Pradesh (Capital: Hyderabad) is the fifth largest state in India in respect of both area and population. It has an area of 275,068 sq km and a population of 66,304,854 (1981 census). The density is 241 per sq km and literacy is 45.11 per cent.

The state is surrounded in the east by the Bay of Bengal, in the south by Tamil Nadu, in the south-west by Karnataka, in the north-west by Maharashtra, in the north by Madhya Pradesh and in the north-east by Orissa. It forms the major link between the north and the south of India.

Telugu is the language of the State while Urdu is also spoken by a large section. There are a number of rivers, the principle being Godavari, Krishna and Tungabhadra. There is a coastal line of 982 km with a good potential for development of fisheries.

The racial history of the Andhras can be traced back to the remotest antiquity. Vedic, Puranic, Buddhist and Greek literature refer to the Andhras. Andhra or Telugu is one of the important Dravidian languages. Its literature and tradition are much influenced by Sanskrit and Prakrit.

The history of Telugu folklore is as old as the history of the Telugu language and culture. The Telugu folklore is rich and represents the culture of Andhra more vividly than Telugu classical literature. As a matter of fact it has drawn sustenance from the life of the Telugu people. It echoes the religious movements, heroic deeds, stories of saintly persons, customs and traditions of the people.

1
THE EVIL SPIRIT

THERE lived a Brahmin named Sanubhuti in the village Vinnakota. He was very poor and lived on alms. His wife was quarrelsome and suffered from an itch. She would cook and eat the rice which her husband brought. The poor husband ate the leftover food, if any, and cleaned the utensils. Daily she made a rope with which she used to beat her husband at night. That was the only way to relieve the itch in her hands. Thus poor Sanubhuti lived with her in misery.

Once a rich man sent Sanubhuti on an errand to a distant village which took ten days. Meanwhile his wife kept ten ropes awaiting his arrival. His return journey was delayed and her hands started itching severely. As it became unbearable, one night she took all the ten ropes and went outside the village. There was an old fig tree. She beat the trunk of that fig tree with the ropes till they broke one after another. This gave relief to her hands.

Often Brahmarakshasas[1] live on fig trees. On that fig tree a Brahmarakshasa lived from time immemorial. The Brahmarakshasa had to bear all the pain of the fig tree subjected to the beating. As the pain became acute the Brahmarakshasa left the tree wailing loudly.

He saw Sanubhuti returning home with his begging bowl and other things. The Brahmarakshasa encountered him and enquired his name and whereabouts. Sanubhuti told him his name and the name of his village. Thereupon the Brahmarakshasa told Sanubhuti that a woman from that village had severely beaten the fig tree on which he lived and that he had

1. An evil spirit of the other world.

to run away in great pain. He wondered how Sanubhuti could live in a village where the terrible woman also lived. Sanubhuti knew him to be a Brahmarakshasa and slowly spoke in fear:

"My Lord! The shrew who beat the fig tree which you made your home is none other than my own wife. She beats me thus nightly. Look at my back; how raw it has become." Saying so Sanubhuti showed him his back with hard skin and marks of beating.

Pitying the poor Brahmin the Brahmarakshasa said, "Why do you live with her in spite of the beatings from her everyday? Why don't you leave her and go away? What pleasure do you derive from her? I could not withstand her beating even for one day and how is it that you bear it everyday, and why are you in a hurry to go to her carrying on your head the heavy loads?"

Sanubhuti replied, "Sir, I am carrying on with her, bearing her beating everyday because she cooks for me. I am a poor wretch. I don't have any relatives. What am I to do?" Saying so he wept bitterly.

The Brahmarakshasa who devoured human beings like a cruel tiger, took pity on Sanubhuti and said, "O poor Brahmin! Don't weep. Don't go home, do what I say. There is a city called Vanadurga nearby. It is ruled by a king named Durgadatta. He has only one daughter. I will possess her. Yielding to no exorcists, I will sap her blood and make her a skeleton. You come there after some days and throw out a challenge that you would drive away the devil and cure her. After you take a promise of some villages as endowment and presents from that ruler you try to cure her. Come close to her and tell her in her ear that you are the Brahmin living under the fig tree. Then I will leave her. You will become a rich man and marry a fine woman."

Sanubhuti prostrated before the Brahmarakshasa and extolled him with lavish panegyrics and abused his wife. The Brahmarakshasa, pleased with the praise, went away. Instead of going home Sanubhuti went to another village.

On the same night the Brahmarakshasa possessed the princess. With a loud shriek she jumped out of her bed. Startled, her husband too woke up. When he asked what had happened to her, she jumped over and began biting him. He escaped somehow and informed her parents. When the parents came, she attacked them also, groaning loudly and gnashing her teeth. They took it to be an evil spirit and locked her up. Day by day she became emaciated, shunning food and sleep. The king thought she would die soon. Her parents, her husband and all the inmates of the royal palace were terribly grief-stricken.

At that time Sanubhuti came to that city. Everybody in the city was talking about the dangerous condition of the princess. He went to the palace and informed the guards that he would cure the princess. They took him to the king. Seeing the ragged form of Sanubhuti the king did not believe that he would cure the princess. Sanubhuti challenged him and said that he was ready to stake his life if he failed to cure her. The king, then, took his challenge seriously and at once gave in writing an endowment of a dozen villages and many gifts. Thus assured, Sanubhuti asked the king to show him the princess. The king accompanied by a dozen attendants led Sanubhuti towards the room where the princess was locked up. When Sanubhuti was unlocking the door the king warned him not to enter the room without equipping himself properly, lest he should face a serious attack from the devil. Sanubhuti smiled and said he did not require any equipment and ritual and then entering the room closed the door behind him. He saw a heap of broken mirrors and lamp globes, torn cushions and ruined canopies.

When the princess saw Sanubhuti nearing her slowly, she shrieked loudly and picked up the leg of the bedstead to attack him. Folding his hands in panic Sanubhuti said, "My Lord! I am the Brahmin living under the fig tree. I came here as you commanded. The king has granted me a dozen villages and rich gifts. See this document. By your grace my poverty has disappeared." Hearing Sanubhuti's words the Brahmarakshasa possessing the princess said, "I did all this in order to make you rich. I am glad you have become rich. Now you marry another woman and enjoy life. I will leave this princess. But listen to me. Brahmarakshasas take pleasure in possessing youthful princesses. I will go and possess another princess. If you are invited to cure her, don't accept. If you disobey my order I will kill you. Be careful." Saying this the Brahmarakshasa left the princess and disappeared, blowing the roof of that palace

The princess lay motionless on her bed as soon as the Brahmarakshasa left her. Sanubhuti opened the door and came out smiling. The king who was waiting outside the room asked

Sanubhuti eagerly whether the evil spirit was driven away. Sanubhuti told the king to go in and see for himself. The king and his men slowly entered the room. When accosted, the princess opened her eyes slowly and asked for food, in a feeble voice. Her mother came and fed the princess. By good nursing and attention the princess recovered.

The king, his relatives and other officers of the state, praised Sanubhuti as a god and showered extraordinary honours upon him. The king granted him double the number of villages he had promised earlier. He gave him big houses and performed his marriage with a good Brahmin girl from the family of Rajapurohitas. Sanubhuti started leading a peaceful life of opulence.

After six months another king from a neighbouring kingdom, Ratnapuri, wrote to Durgadatta that his daughter possessed by some evil spirit was suffering and not only defied all efforts to cure but also killed three conjurers. He requested Durgadatta to send the famous Sanubhuti to cure his daughter and promised to grant any rewards he wished. He also sent a palanquin to fetch Sanubhuti.

Durgadatta called Sanubhuti, read out the contents of the letter and requested him to go to that place to cure the princess. This, he said, would spread his fame in other regions also. Sanubhuti with a sinking heart said meekly, "My Lord! Exorcism is not an easy task. I had to bestow the merit of my long time penance in order to drive out the Brahmarakshasa from your house. If I attempt once again I lose all my merit of penance and also the other world (Punyaloka). Please excuse me for my failure to comply with your orders." But Durgadatta pleaded and persuaded him to go there as that king was his close relative. He also promised that he would never send him again on similar missions.

Sanubhuti had to accept. On an auspicious day he left for Ratnapuri in the palanquin sent by the king. During the journey he thought to himself, "Alas! I am going there to drive out the Brahmarakshasa as if I am capable of doing so. The Brahmarakshasa has already warned me not to go over there. If I transgress his orders, he will kill me. I should have told the truth to the king. I have put on a false show unnecessarily. Except *Ashtaksharimantra* I know nothing. Only Providence should save me."

Sanubhuti was given a rousing reception when he arrived and was led to the palace with great pomp. The conjurers who were already there in the palace surrounded Sanubhuti and asked him about the method of sorcery which he followed and whether he wanted any equipment for rituals. But Sanubhuti required nothing. He simply asked them to show him the room where the princess was lying.

The king led the way. Alone, with stubborn fortitude, Sanubhuti entered the room slowly and closed the door behind him. On seeing him the princess jumped shrieking to attack. Sanubhuti with folded hands said, "I am the Brahmin living under the fig tree. As usual I have come to pay my respects to you." Then the Brahmarakshasa possessing the princess said, "You wicked fellow! Have you forgotten my command? Did I not tell you not to come here? Not satisfied with the wealth that I caused to be given to you, you have greedily come here once again to drive me out. I will do away you in a minute."

Pretending fear, Sanubhuti replied, "My father! How can I defy your word, you who have done so much good to me? I am in a calamity. As I do not know how to overcome it I have come here to seek your advice. I was very happy all these six months after you favoured me. But fortune never allows a man to live in peace forever. Somehow my first wife came to know that I was favoured by you and had all the fortunes bestowed by King Durgadatta. She loaded all the 180 ropes (which she made daily to beat me) on the carts and reached my place. I was perplexed. Now I have come running to seek your help. You saved me from her at that time. I implore you to save me from her now also. I am your slave, kindly protect me." Saying this Sanubhuti prostrated himself before him.

The Brahmarakshasa shivered in fear when he heard Sanubhuti's tale. Then he said, "O Sanubhuti! I can never forget her beatings on the fig tree. You say that she came to your palace with cartloads of ropes. Will she remain there? Or will she follow you knowing you have come here? First of all let me know her whereabouts."

Sanubhuti replied, "Sir, it seems she possesses foresight. Without enquiring of anybody she came to my place. Now she might have started following me. I think she might have come to the outskirts of this city also. Kindly show me some way to escape her rage."

The terror-stricken Brahmarakshasa said, "Suffer your fate alone. You have to bear it because you have married her. But I must save my skin first. I will run away to some islands far away, so that she may not come to me." Saying so the Brahmarakshasa left the princess and blowing up the roof of that house flew away.

The impossible can be accomplished by tact. Sanubhuti thanked God for the trick which came to his mind at that crucial moment. He came out of the room and told the king and his men that he had cured the princess. The king bestowed on him many gifts and arranged a grand farewell. Then onwards Sanubhuti lived in happiness and peace.

2
THE DEAD RAT

In the city of Ujjain there was a young merchant named Madananka. He lost his father when he was in his teens, so it was his mother who brought him up with great affection and love. Unfortunately, he turned out to be a vagabond. His mother hoped that he would become normal and settle down if he was married and so she found a suitable girl and they were married. But Madananka became worse.

One day he absconded from his house, deserting his mother and pregnant wife. His mother grieved for him. The daughter-in-law, after some time, gave birth to a son. He was named Ratnanka. Though poor, Ratnanka was brought up with affection and care and given a good education.

One day when he was ten years old his grandmother said to him, "My lad! Your father left all of us in misery. We two women have brought you up with what little money and jewellery we had. Now we don't have anything to fall back upon. You are quite grown up, so you take up some business to eke out a living. In the neighbouring village there is a well-to-do merchant named Yakshadatta who lends money to the poor but capable persons. You go to him, explain to him our condition and borrow some money so that you can start some business for our livelihood."

Following the instructions of his grandmother Ratnanka went to Yakshadatta. At that time Yakshadatta, the rich merchant, was taking a stroll. Knowing him to be Yakshadatta, Ratnanka approached him and said, "Sir, I am a poor merchant boy. My father deserted us before I was born. My grandmother and my mother have brought me up with great difficulty. We have heard of your fame and generosity in helping people of our community. I request you to lend me some money for business and I promise to repay the amount soon."

Hearing Ratnanka, Yakshadatta laughed, looked around and pointing towards a dead rat lying on the street said, "Lo my boy! That dead rat is the capital which I can lend you. You take it away and do some trade with it. To an intelligent man it will fetch millions and even if I give millions to an unintelligent man it will be of no use." Ratnanka thought for a minute and then took the dead rat as a favour from Yakshadatta. He made a cup out of a leaf and placed the dead rat in that cup. He carried it through streets crying, "A rat for sale!" One merchant who was taming a cat in order to get rid of the rats that were a menace in his shop, purchased that dead rat as prey for his cat and gave him a handful of bengal gram.

Ratnanka took the bengal gram home and soaked it in water. Next morning he added some salt and pepper to the soaked and swollen bengal gram, took drinking water in an earthen pitcher, went outside the city and sat under the shade of a tree. That was the place where the woodcutters with heavy faggots of fuel wood on their heads would take rest everyday while returning from the forest. Ratnanka waited there till late and offered each woodcutter some bengal gram and cold water. The hungry and thirsty woodcutters, pleased with Ratnanka's service, gave him two pieces of firewood each. By evening the pieces piled up into a big heap which Ratnanka sold away for two rupees in the city. Out of the two rupees Ratnanka gave one to his grandmother towards savings and with the other rupee purchased a Kuncam[1] of bengal gram. Out of this he soaked one kilo everyday and sat under the same tree with cold water. In this way he collected many cart-loads of fuel within a month. Fortunately, there were incessant rains for ten days and as a result there was a scarcity of firewood in the city. The firewood which Ratnanka had collected fetched him a hundred gold coins. With that money Ratnanka opened a firewood stall and began dealing in timber. From timber to cloth, from cloth to grain and from grain to diamonds, his business progressed rapidly. Within a couple of years Ratnanka became one of the leading merchants in that city.

One day Ratnanka got a rat made with gold, weighing one kilo. Its eyes were made of rubies, ears of sapphires and it had a diamond chain round its neck. It was kept in a silver trap and

---

1. A measure, about 14 kilograms.

carried in a procession with pomp. Ratnanka was leading the procession. When he reached the residence of Yakshadatta he asked the procession to halt. Hearing the band and the noise of the procession, Yakshadatta came out of his house and enquired what all that pomp and hub-bub was about.

Ratnanka addressed Yakshadatta thus: "Sir, I became a millionaire by your grace. Two years back when I came to you for a loan you gave me a dead rat. Your wise sayings and the capital which I borrowed from you made me a rich man. Now I have come to repay your debt in the shape of a golden rat. Kindly accept this as a symbol of my gratitude."

Yakshadatta was amazed to hear his story. He was very pleased with the intelligence and gratitude of Ratnanka. He thought that a clever boy like Ratnanka alone was suitable to marry his lovely daughter. On an auspicious day Yakshadatta gave his daughter in marriage to Ratnanka and from that time onwards Ratnanka lived happily with his grandmother, mother and wife. He kept the golden rat in the silver trap hanging in front of his shop to remind him of how he became rich. Though he became the richest merchant after inheriting the property of his father-in-law yet he never forgot the poor woodcutters. He made arrangements for supplying bengal gram and cold water free to the woodcutters of that city.

FOLK TALES
OF
ARUNACHAL PRADESH
AND MEGHALAYA

Arunachal Pradesh
Meghalaya

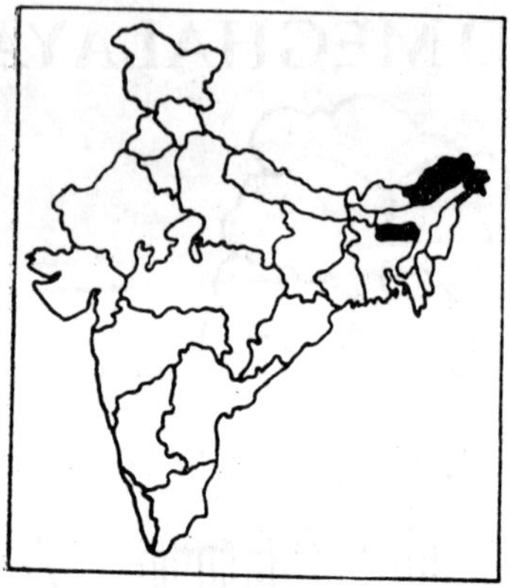

Arunachal Pradesh: A Union Territory with its capital at Itanagar is one of the most picturesque tribal areas in India. It covers an area of 83,743 sq km with a population of 858,392, the density being 10 per sq. km. and literacy 41.22. It is an area noted for its greenery, tall evergreen forests, high and rugged mountains and silvery meandering rivers.

Arunachal is wild and elemental, so are its people. There is music all around, the music of the stately forests with winds rustling in their ferocity, the music of the gurgling, angry waters of its innumerable rivers and rivulets, the music of the icy howling winds piercing through the cruel mountain passes, the instrumental and vocal music of its people along with dance unravished and untainted by modern civilisation.

She has a long border with China, Tibet and Burma. The five areas of the state have various ethnic units. The vast Arunachal tract has been marked into broad cultural divisions, the habitat of tribals who are Buddhist by religion, and include the Sherdukpens and the Monpas; the second cultural area stretches from the west to the east, from Sepla in Kameng and through the greater part of the Subansiri, Siang and Lohit district. The population here has varied traditions, but with basic affinities with other tracts.

Nearly half the population of Arunachal Pradesh is engaged in agriculture. The traditional method of agriculture, *Jhumming*, is a kind of shifting cultivation by burning the forest and throwing in the seeds on the ashes. The territory has rich fauna, flora and avi-fauna. Musk deer, lesser panda, clouded leopard, mountain goat, elephants, bisons and tigers are commonly found in the forests.

Numerous languages and dialects are spoken in this region.

Meghalaya: Literally 'the abode of the clouds' (Megha-clouds, alaya-abode) is an autonomous unit. The population of the State is 1,760,626 with a density of 78 per sq km, spread over an area of 22,429 sq km. The literacy is 48.26 per cent. The State is surrounded by Bangladesh, Assam, West Bengal and Tripura.

The capital of the State, Shillong, is situated in the centre of a high plateau. The highest peak in the state is Shillong peak which is 9,450 ft. high. A number of rivers, none of these navigable because of their rocky beds and swift currents, abound in cataracts and waterfalls, The Cherrapunjee Mawsynram belt in the northern slopes of Khasi Hills has the distinction of having the world's heaviest rainfall, with an average of 1,270 centimetres per annum.

Meghalaya is a region abounding in scenic beauty. Waterfalls and mountains, lakes, rising peaks and billowing hills, meadows, valleys and rushing rivers combine to make a dream-come-true for the tourist. Dance, music and sports reflect their way of life. Festive sounds of merry-making echo from hill to hill revealing the pulsating life of the tribal people. These simple folks are jovial and hospitable.

The exclusive tribal state of the Khasis, Jaintias and the Garos is a mountain region. The three tribes who had settled in these hills are very ancient. The Khasis and Jaintias are held to be a remnant of the first Mongolian overflow into India. The Khasi language is believed to be one of the few surviving dialects of the non-Khmer family of languages in India today. They believe in God and in good and evil spirits. The older generation, although conservative, do not mind their children becoming converts to Christanity and other faiths.

The majority of the people depend on land for their livelihood and practise *Jhumming* or shifting cultivation. Forests and forest products are the chief resources of the State.

Principal languages of the state are Khasi, Jaintia and Garo.

3

TELL NO SECRET TO A WOMAN*

An old Shingpo once told his son a very old truth.

Said he, "Son, if you have any secret, don't tell it to any woman. You must also not plant any thorny tree at the gate of your house."

The son decided to test the advice, which the old man had given him. And so, he took a wife. He also planted a thorny tree at his gate.

One morning, he secretly took a dog with him to the woods and cut it up. He buried the dead dog and then smeared the knife with the dog's blood, and returned home. He told his wife, "Hey! I have cut up a man. See this knife, do you want any more proof?"

The wife gasped with fright and cried out, "What, you have killed a man! Now the king will kill you also. I am not going to live with you anymore."

And so saying, she went off to see the king, and told him that her husband had killed a man.

The king sent out two guards to catch the man and bring him into the court.

The guards went into the man's house and caught him.

Shingpos always wear turbans. They consider it humiliating to go about bare-headed.

As the guards were marching the man out, through the gate of his house, his turban was caught in the thorny tree which he had planted and it came off.

At this, the words which his father had said about not planting any thorny tree at his gate, flashed across his mind, and he heaved a sigh.

---

* A Shingpo folktale

When he was produced in the court, the king demanded, "You have killed a man. Is it true?"

The man replied, "No, sir, I haven't killed a man. What actually happened was this. My father had told me that I must not tell any secret to any woman. I decided to test the warning. So, I quietly took a dog into the wood and cut it up. I also smeared the knife with the dog's blood. On coming home, I showed the knife to my wife and told her that I had killed a man with it."

The king sent his own men to find out what had actually happened. His men came back and told him that what the man had said was correct. Thereupon the king set the man free, but banished the woman from his kingdom as a punishment.

The king took a great liking to the man for his intelligence. As a reward he gave him one of his own daughters in marriage.

Shingpos have a custom of giving dowry in a girl's marriage. The king followed that custom and gave a large dowry and a lot of presents to his daughter.

4

A CUNNING SHINGPO*

A SHINGPO had a buffalo. The buffalo used to graze in the king's garden and destroy the crops. The king, therefore, one day warned the Shingpo:

"Hey, look here. I am afraid, I have to kill your buffalo."

The Shingpo replied: "If you kill the buffalo, then please keep the skin for me."

The king killed the buffalo and kept the skin for the Shingpo. The Shingpo called on the king and brought the skin home. He dried the skin very carefully.

One day, he went out, taking the dried skin with him, and climbing a tall tree, he sat there and waited quietly.

Soon after there came a blind man and a deaf man. These two men started to divide some money under that tree. The Shingpo who was quietly sitting atop, began to beat the dry buffalo skin. When the blind man below heard the noise, he got frightened and fled. Seeing him running away, the other man who was deaf, also took to his heels, leaving behind the bag of money. The Shingpo then got down from the tree and took all the money and left the place.

He informed the king who had killed his buffalo that he had earned some money by selling the skin. He said to the king:

"You did not dry the skin well, so I got a small amount of money."

When the king asked the Shingpo if that much amount was the price of a buffalo skin, he said, "Yes."

The king killed all his own buffaloes, dried their skins very carefully, and sent them off for sale. But nobody was willing to buy the skins.

---

* A Shingpo folktale.

The king then came to realise that the Shingpo had played a trick on him, and so he (the king) thought out a plan to catch the Shingpo and kill him.

One day the king caught the Shingpo, put him in a big cage and hung the cage on a tree right over a deep pool of water. His plan was to keep the cage hanging thus for a few days and then drop it into the water.

When the cage with the Shingpo in it was thus hanging from the tree, one day a man passed by that place on a horse. He became curious when he saw the Shingpo in the cage and asked him what he was doing in the cage.

The Shingpo told the man that all the people wanted to make him their king but he did not want to be a king, so, they had kept him shut-up in the cage. The Shingpo, then very cleverly talked the man into the cage and himself got out and rode off on the man's horse.

After a few days the king's men cut the string from which the cage was hanging and it dropped into the water drowning the stranger.

After that, the Shingpo appeared before the king and said: "Because your men did not throw me into deep water, I got only a horse. If they had thrown me into deeper water I would have got elephants as well as horses."

The king believed the Shingpo. He got some cages made and put himself in one of them and the other chiefs in the other cages and had all the cages hung over deep waters.

The Shingpo then let all those cages with the king and all his chiefs fall into the water and be drowned.

After that, the cunning Shingpo himself became the king.

5

THE STORY OF ANIMAL SACRIFICE

FORMERLY the people of the Naga tribe lived in the mountain called "Insai Sira".

In olden days even animals could talk like human beings. Men and animals lived separately, but when they fell ill, the same medicine was used to treat both. The medicine was so good that it could even bring the dead back to life. So, neither men nor animals ever died. As a result, men and animals filled the land.

As the number of human beings increased, the area under cultivation also extended and the animals had nowhere to graze. In whichever direction animals went in search of grass, they met with paddy raised by men. Thus unable to find grass to eat, animals became very cross with men and they began to eat up the foodcrops men had grown. The men told the animals not to do so. But the animals did not listen. When the animals went on destroying the crops, men had nothing left to eat and they began to starve. Human beings then approached the medicine man and made complaints against the animals. The medicine man also got very annoyed with the animals for the wanton destruction which they were causing. He decided that he would no longer treat animals if they fell ill. Whenever any animal went to see the medicine man, he sent it back giving various excuses.

So whenever animals fell ill, they died for want of medicine, and their number decreased. On the other hand, the number of human beings went up as they continued to receive medicine, and none of them died of sickness. The animals decided to take revenge on men. All the birds and beasts got together and discussed how they could possibly destroy all the herbs from which the medicines were prepared for men. They decided that they would destroy all the grass and plants either by eating them up or by trampling, then those herbs and plants with which the medicines were prepared, would also be destroyed, for, no one except the medicine man knew the exact medicinal herbs. The animals began to crush under their feet any plant or creeper which came their way. After destroying all the plants and creepers of that mountain, the animals moved to another place. Those among them who would not move, stayed behind.

Now, as no plant or creeper was left, the medicine man was unable to prepare his medicine. And so, if anyone was ill and came to him for medicine, he had to go away disappointed. A large number of men began to die, and many others left the mountain and went away to live at other places.

When many people died and many others left the place because he could not give them any medicine, the medicine man decided that it would be useless for him to live, he killed himself. Before he took his own life, the medicine man told the people that he was leaving this world because the animals had destroyed all the medicinal herbs.

After the death of the medicine man people reasoned thus:

"The animals have eaten up all the medicinal herbs and they have thereby become immortal. If therefore we sacrifice them and offer their meat in the name of our people when they fall ill, then those sick people also must get well."

Therefore, whenever anybody fell ill, some animal was killed and its meat was offered for the recovery of the patient. The Nagas observe this custom even today and they sacrifice dogs, pigs, cows, buffaloes and fowls whenever anybody falls ill.*

---

* The district of Tirap where the Tangsas live adjoins Nagaland. This folk tale is popular in Nagaland also.

6
NAMSANG PUJA*
(WORSHIP OF THE MOUNTAIN GOD)

IN OLDEN days the Naga tribe lived on the mountain called *Mu Bum*. A very large number of people lived there. There were not less than a thousand houses there. The people kept themselves busy in cultivation and they lived happily. After cultivation was over, the grown-up boys and girls held dance and music parties and drank *"Ju"* (Rice beer). They knew only merry-making and never worshipped any god. Grief and sorrow were unknown to them.

While they were thus living merrily, free from all worries and anxieties, one day all of a sudden, they heard a rumble in the interior of the mountain. They were terrified. As the sound grew louder, the mountain began to tremble. Masses of dark clouds filled the whole sky from one end to the other. Rain followed by hailstorm came down pouring like a river in spate. The people were frightened. They knew not whither to go or how to save themselves.

An old man of the village had dreamt the previous night that another very old man came to see him and said that the god of the mountain was angry with the villagers, because they were busy in merry-making and had ignored him completely. The old man of the dream advised that the villagers should, therefore, sacrifice animals to please the angry mountain god. But the old man of the village did not believe in the dream nor did he speak of his dream to anyone. Now when the mountain started to tremble and hail and rain came down ceaselessly, the old man told the villagers of the dream. Nobody listened to him. They arranged many dances

* A Nokte folktale.

and music parties in the hope that by doing so they would be able to save their lives. But instead of stopping to shake, the mountain began to quake even more. Ultimately one side of the mountain slid down and buried under it many houses, along with a large number of men, women and children. Then the villagers offered pigs and chickens to the mountain god and prayed to him.

As soon as they did so, the rumblings in the mountain stopped. Landslides, rain and hails stopped too. Since then they began to make offerings of pigs and chickens to the mountain god.

The Nagas, in many regions, even now worship the god of mountain by sacrificing animals in his honour once every year.

7

THE STORY OF A LIAR*

LONG, long ago there lived on a mountain a tiger, a pig and a man. The man and the tiger were good friends. The tiger felt very tempted to eat the pig. One day, the tiger pounced upon the pig. But the pig was a large, hefty animal. Besides, by wallowing in the mud and basking in the sun days on end, his body was covered with a dry, thick layer of hard mud. The tiger, therefore, could not bite the skin through the thick coat of mud. The pig always kept himself ready to repel the tiger's attack. When the two were thus always engaged in deadly fights, sometimes the tiger found himself at the mercy of the pig. Even then the greedy tiger did not stop attacking the pig.

At last, when he failed to kill the pig, the tiger asked his friend, the man, for advice. The friend thought over the matter and said that if the tiger attacked the pig before it had a chance to wallow in mud and bask in the sun early in the morning, he would be able to kill it quite easily.

Following his friend's advice, the tiger set out early in the morning, and attacked the pig and killed it.

After slaying the pig, the tiger went to his friend and gave the news with great pleasure.

On hearing the news, the friend made a plan to pinch the whole of pig's meat for himself. He cut out a branch of a thorny *Kutkura* tree to use it as *Kandh-mari* (a balancing bar to be carried on the shoulders). He took care to remove all the thorns from that end of the stick which he decided he would carry on his own shoulder, and left the other end, with the thorns intact, for the tiger. He tied the dead pig tightly on the stick. Immediately before

---

* A Tangsa folktale.

he and the tiger lifted the load to place it on their shoulders, he warned the tiger saying, "My friend, it is a terribly big pig, our shoulders may therefore pain when we carry it. But we must bear it. We must not groan in pain. If we groan, then the meat will become bitter." He ended by saying that he would carry the pig only if the tiger would agree that he would not groan.

Otherwise, said he, "It would be far better not to take any trouble at all rather than eat some bitter meat."

He reminded the tiger that if the meat became bitter, then all the efforts which he (the tiger) had made for such a long time would come to nothing. The tiger gave his word that he would not groan.

The place where the man lived was quite far from the spot where the tiger had slain the pig. The two friends went along towards the man's house carrying the pig on their shoulders. When, after going some distance, the man began to feel that the pain was becoming too much to bear, he said to the tiger, "Mind, you must not groan. Go on bearing it."

For fear that the meat would turn bitter, for some distance the tiger ignored the sharp pain which he was getting from the thorns of the *Kandh-mari.* At last the pain grew unbearable, that he forgot the fear that the meat would turn bitter and he quickly threw the *Kandh-mari* down and cried out "Aah" in pain. At that his friend reminded him of the agreement. He pretended to be cross and said that he was not going to take any more trouble simply to eat some bitter meat.

"You said 'Aah' and all the meat has become bitter. After taking all the trouble to get some nice meat, we shall now have to eat only bitter meat." Thus, pretending to be angry he led the tiger with the pig to his home.

After reaching home, and before cutting up the pig, he sent the tiger away to fetch water with a bamboo tube that had a hole in it. The Nagas do not use buckets or earthen pots. They use hollow bamboo tubes with open necks and closed bottoms to carry or store water in them. They live on high rocky mountains where ponds or wells cannot be dug. They collect their drinking water either from springs or small streams which may lie far down their villages. It takes time to walk down to the spring or stream and climb back to the village carrying water-filled bamboo tubes on their backs. The tiger of our story too had to go a long way to fetch water.

When the tiger was thus away, his friend dressed the pig but hid the meat away. He picked some *vekoori* seeds (a kind of very bitter berries) and made a curry out of them. He then roasted some of the meat on a few sticks for his own meal and kept them tied up to the back of his bottom and sat waiting for the tiger to return.

After returning about half way, with the bamboo tube filled with water, the tiger found that there was not a drop of water left in the tube, and so, he walked back to the spring, filled the tube again and started climbing homeward. After coming about half way, he found that the tube was empty again, and he went back to the spring and filled it. But it became empty again and again. When he was going to the spring again, he heard a pigeon singing on a tree:

"The tiger goes off to fetch water in a tube which has a hole in it, while his friend is busy hiding away the pig meat in the woods."

When he heard this song, he flung away the bamboo tube and dashed back to his friend's home.

After the tiger's return, his friend sat down with him and began to eat the bitter curry which he had cooked with *vekoori* seeds.

While eating the curry, the man said, "The meat is bitter, because you did not listen to me. It is a sad thing that after taking so much trouble one has to eat only bitter meat. Now we can do nothing better than cut flesh from our own buttocks and eat it." And so saying he took out his knife and began to cut off slices of the meat which he had kept concealed behind his buttocks and ate them.

Seeing that his friend was merrily eating meat, which he had carved out of his own buttocks, the greedy tiger too felt tempted to carve out flesh from his own buttocks and eat it. So he borrowed a knife from his friend and began to graze it on his buttocks. But when he felt the pain, he came to realise that his friend was simply cheating him.

He got cross and rushed at the man. The man took to his heels. While he was fleeing, he kept thinking how he could possibly destroy the tiger. He reached a well. Entering it, he remained there pretending that he was guarding it.

The tiger, who was searching for him, found him there and yapped:

"After making me cut my own buttocks, you are now hiding in this well like a coward? Be ready to die."

When his friend heard this, he feigned surprise and mumbled out that he had not asked anyone to cut his own buttocks. He told the tiger that since his father had asked him to guard the well of his grandfather's animals, he was there simply keeping a watch on it. He added that there was a large number of animals living down at the botom of the well. When he heard of the animals, the greedy tiger became anxious to have a look at them. He could not recognise that it was his tricky friend. He took him to be a different person and asked for his permission to have a look at the animals.

The so-called guard of the well, however, replied that he could not give permission without asking his father first. The tiger pressed him for permission. The man felt unable to turn down the tiger's request. So he walked off some way from the well to ask his father, and there he asked in a loud voice:

'Hi Dad, the tiger wants to have a look into the well of our animals, shall I let him do it?"

He then replied as if it was his father who was replying, and said: "Okay son, but tell him that he will be able to see the animals only if he leaps into the well."

As soon as the greedy tiger heard this he thought that when the man returned to the well, he (that is the tiger) would be able to see the animals, but he would not be able to eat any animal, and it would be great fun if he killed one or two animals and ate them before the man arrived. So deciding, he took a leap into the well. Let alone kill any animal and eat it, he was lucky the well was not very deep. He climbed out of it with great difficulty. The tiger recognised only then that the other man was none other than his old friend. So, after escaping from the well, he again went in pursuit of the fellow.

After covering some distance, the man rested under a tree, on which there was a large beehive.

The tiger found him there and warned him saying that one may escape after cheating once but one cannot go on cheating for ever and hope to escape.

The man again pretended to be unable to understand what the tiger was saying and said that he did not see any reason why he (the tiger) should be cross with him. But, he added, if the tiger had any desire to eat, he (the tiger) had simply to tell him as a friend and he (the man) could then get him an order from *Chikyaa* (the king of gods). Pointing to the cluster of bees, he said that *Chikyaa* had asked him to guard that gong and see that no one touched it. "If any one beats this gong," he added, "he will get any kind of meat that he wishes to eat. And I have been guarding this gong for over a decade now."

When the tiger heard the man talking about meat, he totally forgot all that had happened before and decided that instead of making an enemy of the man, he had better please him and beg for some meat.

So deciding, the tiger in all humility told the man that he would like to beat the gong and asked him to forget and forgive him for what he had said.

The deceitful friend, pretending to go to see *Chikyaa* for permission, went some distance and shouted to the tiger, "Look, you can get meat to eat only if you beat the gong with all the strength in your body."

Hearing this, the tiger's mouth began to water and he beat the hive with all his might. But instead of eating any meat, he himself got nearly killed by the bees, and he fled for his life through the woods and somehow made his escape. The foolish tiger became furious at the roguishness of his friend, and rushed off to find and kill him.

In the meanwhile, the friend reached a distant off spot and there he made a seat of nails with the sharp ends pointing upwards and sat beside it. The tiger traced him there and roared out:

"You cheated me and then bolted off like a coward. So you are now sitting here. Wait, instead of eating pig meat, today I am going to feast myself on human flesh."

But the friend did not let the tiger finish what he was going to say and interrupted him, "Now you tell me, is there only one man in this world? There are so many men who are living on this earth. One man may be a rogue. But it does not mean that all other men are, therefore, also rogues. Besides, I did not have any tiger as a friend. In fact, I have never seen a tiger before."

He tried to assure the tiger that it was only now that he had seen a tiger for the first time in his life. Ever since he was born, he had never in his life obtained even a grain by deceiving anybody, he said. He was sitting here only because *Chasa* (Creator) had asked him to watch the stool. It was impossible not to obey God who is the Creator, he said. He warned the tiger that he was going to tell *Chasa* that he (the tiger) was threatening him. He said that he (the tiger) had insulted him and he would tell *Chasa* to hold a *bichar* (an enquiry) and punish him (the tiger). The tiger got terribly frightened. He admitted that he had done a wrong unknowingly. He begged to be forgiven.

When the friend saw that the tiger was greatly scared, he described the powers the stool possessed. The man said,"If anyone just sits on this stool of *Chasa*, it will fly him across to the spot where his enemy is living or hiding, and enable him to catch the enemy. It (that is, this stool) can reach any place in a moment, however distant it may be. Let alone catching a human being, it can enable one to catch even god *Mangya*. That is why *Chasa* has asked me to watch this stool lest someone sit on it."

One hearing it, the tiger came to the conclusion that far from killing the man and eating his flesh, he himself would be slain by this man. The tiger thought, 'Since this fellow is put in charge of a stool that belongs to Chasa, he cannot be an ordinary mortal.'

Then the tiger begged the man for permission to sit on the stool. He reasoned within himself that if he was allowed to sit on the stool, it would enable him to destroy his foe and he would be able to kill animals without making any effort and eat them.

But the man who was pretending to be guarding the stool, would not by any means let him sit on the stool. The tiger related in detail how a friend of his had stolen a lot of meat by deceiving him and put him to a world of troubles. And he added that if he came back after destroying that friend through his help, he would remain his lifelong slave.

Hearing the tiger say this, the guard of the stool laughed within himself and told him that it was all right, and he would ask *Chasa* to permit him (the tiger) to go, and destroy his friend-enemy and come back. And so saying he told the tiger to stand near the stool and went some distance away and shouted from there:

"The stool will take him to the place where his enemy was living in an instant, if only he sat down upon the stool and pressed it very hard with all his might."

As soon as he got the permission, the tiger sat down on the stool with a big thud and with the strength of seven bulls. But instead of scurrying through the sky, he nearly got himself killed by the nails that pierced his bottom. It did not take the tiger long to realise that the man was really his old friend who had fooled him and none else. He felt very ashamed and small for trying to be too cunning by trusting the words of such a sly fellow and for bringing himself into such a fix.

He pulled himself out from the stool of nails with great difficulty and with a body all drenched in blood he again stormed off to find the man.

While he was thus pursuing his friend, he did not get even a drop of water to drink, let alone any food to eat. Thirst and hunger added to the pain he had from the piercing of nails and doubled his anger. While he was chasing the man, the tiger said to himself that he would not relent even if God Himself came down and begged for his life.

On the other hand, the friend went a long way off and there he remained seated with a pot of poisoned water in front of him. Seeing him, the tiger, whom thirst and hunger had driven mad, accosted him and said, "My friend, there is no pardon for all that you have or have not done for me. All my suffering will vanish only after I have drunk the blood from your chest. However, although you are now my enemy, once you were my friend too. So better remember God now before you die."

On hearing the tiger say so, the friend said: "Well, if you must kill me, then do so. But I shall consider my life worthwhile even if I die, only if you would drink a drop of water offered by me. I should then know that my friend would kill me only after listening to my request simply because once you were a friend although you have now become my enemy."

The tiger thought, "Well, it's not a bad idea. Let me have a drink first and then eat him in comfort." And thus thinking he agreed to drink water.

The friend offered him the water and pretended to be praying.

The tiger who was very thirsty, gulped down the entire pot of poisoned water. As soon as he had finished the last drop, his throat started to burn and he died.

After destroying the tiger in this way, the friend returned home and made a hearty meal of the pig meat.

FOLK TALES OF ASSAM

Assam

The name is derived from *Ashama* which means, without a parallel. The reference is to the natural beauty, wildlife, mighty rivers and dense forests.

Its capital is Guwahati. The State language is Assamese. The present area is 78,438 sq km with a population of 22,294,562. The density is 284 per sq km. and literacy 53.42 per cent. The State is bound by Bhutan and the Himalayan ranges in the north, Arunachal Pradesh in the north-east, Nagaland, Manipur and Burma in the east, Bangladesh, Tripura and Meghalaya in the south and south-west and West Bengal in the west. Rainfall in Assam is the highest in the world.

Rich in mineral wealth, it has abundance of mineral oil also. Tea cultivation and handloom weaving are the principal occupations of the people. Only a few decades back, an Assamese girl could not find a groom, unless she was an expert in the craft of handloom weaving. Owing to her geographic position, Assam has many ethnic units.

Assam, has a rich folklore comprising ballads, tales, dances and music. The Assamese name for oral tale is *Sadhu Katha*. The word is derived from *Sadhu*, meaning a merchant. Obviously, the wandering merchants were a good source of folk tales. The tribes in Assam have made a distinct contribution to Assamese folklore.

The people are intensely bound to their culture and tradition. Basically affectionate, pragmatic and eclectic they do not want to be swept off their feet by cultures from beyond the frontiers.

8
THE LEGEND OF JAYAMALA

THE northern portion of the Goalpara district in Assam lies at the foot of the Bhutan hills. Tearing through the dense forests of the Bhutan hills runs down a stream. At the foot of the hills on the bank of this stream in Goalpara there lived in olden days a Brahmin, Jayanath, with his comely wife, Jayamala.

Jayanath was a priest. He performed Durga Puja, Lakshmi Puja, Kali Puja, *Upanayan* (sacred thread ceremony), marriage rituals and other sacred rites to earn his livelihood. His wife *Jayamala* spun *Poita* (the sacred thread worn by a Brahmin) on her spinning wheel. The Brahmins in the adjoining villages bought all the sacred thread she spun. What they earned was enough for their limited needs. They could save some food which Jayamala gave to the deers, pigs, goats, cows and birds like woodpeckers and snipes. Occasionally even some wild elephants would come and share the food. The wild creatures were friendly to this couple and in return they brought them oranges, plantains, jackfruits, mangoes and pineapples, *arum (kachu), dhenki sak* and bamboo shoots for food. Jayamala's affection for the wild animals and her devotion to her husband were her pleasures of life.

The smooth tenor of their life was soon lost. Jayanath's services were called for conducting the last rites of a well-to-do Brahmin. This brahmin had only a daughter who was very ugly, lazy, spoilt and extremely selfish, and so nobody married her. The Brahmin's widow felt helpless with such a daughter and implored Jayanath to marry her. Jayanath, as he was fond of his wife, first spurned the proposal. But as the girl would inherit all her father's property he could not but yield to the widow's wish for the greed of money.

Jayanath brought *riha, khonia* and *mekala,* woven of *muga* and *silk,* a pair of bangles, earrings and necklace for his bride and a large pot of curd, some molasses and big *mahseer* fish.

In the evening he and the Brahmin's daughter were bathed solemnly. Next morning, the wedding was to be celebrated and the girl was woken at daybreak. Some curd was put on her forehead and she wore the dress brought by Jayanath and was ready to welcome him. Jayanath was then seated on a wooden stool at the entrance to the Brahmin's house and was smeared with sandalwood and crowned with flowers.

He was led inside the house. A portion of the courtyard was fenced with slit bamboos. There the sacred fire was lighted with mango wood, and rice, flowers and ghee were offered to the fire by Jayanath himself as he was a Brahmin. The priest then tied the thumbs of Jayanath and the Brahmin's daughter with *Kusha grass,* and *mantras* were chanted. Jayanath and the Brahmin's daughter were declared husband and wife. He returned to his hut with his rich, proud and selfish wife. Jayamala was hurt and shocked to see her husband married to another girl. She looked at them tearfully and went back to her hut.

In a few days Jayanath's second wife had a *temahala* (three-storeyed) mansion built for herself and Jayanath beside the humble hut. The big house was full of life as there were many servants and maids and sentries. Jayamala with a broken heart watched the prosperity of her husband and his growing love for his second wife. The second wife would never allow Jayanath to see Jayamala. Jayamala was assigned the job of bringing water from the river, and that was what she still lived for. For, while she filled the gold *Jhari* of her rich husband, they would look at each other. That was the only link she had with her husband.

In return for her service, the maids gave her a handful of rice in a brass plate at the end of the day. But Jayamala hated to touch this food. She lived on the fruits and roots brought to her by the animals ever since her husband remarried. With the plate of rice in one hand, the gold *jhari* in the other, and a copper pitcher on her head, she would go walking through the forest to the river giving the rice away to the birds and animals she came across and when she reached the river bank she sat there and thought about her sad life. Tears rolled down her cheeks and mingled with the river water.

The elephant king often came to drink water from this river upstream. He came with his herd of elephants, drank water from the river and played in the water. One evening he found the water salty and tasteless as he waded through and reached downstream.

He asked one of his companions, "The water upstream is so tasty, how is it that it is salty and tasteless downstream?"

The companion replied, "Your Majesty, a beautiful girl sits at the *ghat* every evening. She weeps and her tears mingle with the river water. The salty tears make the water downstream tasteless."

The elephant king was moved to learn this and swam up to the girl. Jayamala had just taken up the copper pitcher on her head, the gold *jhari* in her hand, and was about to go back to her hut. The elephant king stood in her way. He heard her story and asked her to leave the cruel world of man, join him in the kingdom of elephants and stay there as his queen. Jayamala did not readily agree. But she could not get much chance to think because a sudden surge of the river roaring like thunder swept away her small hut and her co-wife's big house all at once. Jayamala stood dumbfounded when the elephant king lifted her up on his back.

Then the elephant king passed through the deep forests of pine, sal and simul, think bamboo thickets and groves of betelnut and reed interspersed with jackfruit and orange trees. The whole place was filled with the sweet scent of the wild roses and *kapauphool*. Thus the elephant king went on for seven days and seven nights till he reached his kingdom at the foot of the Bhutan hills.

The milk-white palace of the elephant king was standing there, carved out of ivory, and inside it was the throne of ivory. The elephant king went in and placed Jayamala on the throne. The beautiful Jayamala looked like a golden doll on the ivory throne. Thousands of elephants trumpeted and bowed before the new queen. The elephant king took his new queen on his head once again and arrived at a miraculous waterfall with his herd of elephants. They went through a pass. The waterfall flowed in seven streams of seven colours. The elephant king put the water of the seven streams in seven jars and poured it over the new queen's head and lo! she changed into a beautiful young female elephant. The copper pitcher on her head turned into the elevation on the forehead and the old *jhari* changed into her trunk. The elephant king announced in his jubilant voice, "Hereafter we shall serve you and your word will be our law." The queen led the herd of elephants back to the elephant land.

Till this day in the Goalpara district of Assam you will find many herds of elephants, each of them always led by a she-elephant.

9
TEJIMOLA

IN ANCIENT times there was a merchant in Assam. He had two wives. The elder one had a daughter named Tejimola. The younger one had no child. Tejimola's mother died when she was a small child. Her stepmother brought her up. She did not love Tejimola, but as she was the only child in the family her father was very fond of her. The stepmother looked after Tejimola only to please her husband.

When Tejimola was eleven, her father took her to a rich man's daughter of the same age. They made good friends.

Tejimola's father was a merchant and he had to go to many places to sell his goods. At that time there were no roads and journeys had to be slow. The merchants went to the markets with a number of men, bullock-carts and guards. The voyages by river were also a hazard as there were pirates. Once he had to be away for six months. He felt very unhappy as he had to leave his only daughter behind. But he could not do otherwise. He called his wife and said, "I am going out on business leaving Tejimola under your care. Look after her and love her. She is my beloved little child." Tejimola's stepmother agreed silently to do so.

She was happy that she could now torture Tejimola as she liked. But why should she stop at torturing her? She could even kill her if she liked. Yes, she would kill her anyhow. If Tejimola was married, at the time of her marriage her father would give her a large dowry. But if she died all this money would be saved, and her stepmother would send all this money to her mother.

Poor Tejimola! As soon as her father's barge left the village her stepmother tried to find faults with her. She would beat her hard for the slightest offence.

She was suffering much when fortunately, one of Tejimola's friend's marriage was settled. It was to take place on the following day. Tejimola wished to attend the wedding party and to stay with her friend for three or four days during the wedding. Her friend was very eager to have Tejimola near her at the time of her marriage.

The stepmother allowed her to go. She even discussed eagerly about the dress Tejimola would wear at the wedding. Tejimola was surprised to see such a change in her. The stepmother asked a number of people as to which *Riha* would go well with which *Mekhala*. She had a lovely *Riha*, a splendid *Mekhala* and a gold embroidered *Khonia*. She told Tejimola, "*Aitee* (my girl), put on these when you are in your friend's house. I shall now pack them and give the packet to you. If you wear them now, they would be dirty for the wedding party." She made a packet of this *Riha*, *Mekhala* and *Khonia* and gave it to Tejimola. Had poor Tejimola known what was in the packet, she would not have accepted it. Her stepmother had placed a mouse in between the *Riha* and the *Mekhala* and some cinders in the *Khonia*.

When she was about to arrive at her friend's house Tejimola very gladly opened the packet. She imagined herself as one of the best dressed girls in the wedding party. But alas! all her hopes were lost. The *Riha* and the *Mekhala* were bitten to pieces and the *Khonia* was dirty and burnt at places and smeared with ashes. She was scared to death. What would she say to her stepmother? She sobbed loudly. The servant who escorted Tejimola to her friend's house was also puzzled. She took another *Riha* and *Mekhala* from her friend and attended the wedding.

When Tejimola returned home her mother asked her about the dress. She was trembling with fear and could say nothing. She dropped the packet and stood sobbing. Her stepmother scolded her and beat her very cruelly. But she did not stop at that. She took Tejimola to the *dhenki* (rice pounding tool). She would have to put rice into the hole and her stepmother would pound it. While pounding with all her might she crushed Tejimola's right hand. Tejimola wept hard but was ordered to put paddy and her mother, with all her might, crushed her left hand also. Tejimola cried miserably but her stepmother ordered her to put rice in the hole with her left foot. She was now ordered to push paddy with her right foot and the stepmother crushed her right foot also.

Poor Tejimola now lost her hands and feet but her stepmother pounded rice with still more force and crushed Tejimola's head hard, with the result that Tejimola died.

Her mother buried her under the eaves of the rice pounding room. Some days passed. The neighbours asked about Tejimola. They had not seen her for a long time. Tejimola's mother told everyone that she had gone to her friend's house.

One day an old woman asked for a pumpkin from Tejimola's stepmother. She replied that she had no pumpkin creeper in her garden. The old woman took her to the garden. She saw a pumpkin plant just where she had buried Tejimola. She was pale with fear. She did not touch the plant herself. She told the woman, "Well, pluck as many pumpkins as you like." As the old woman was about to pluck a pumpkin the pumpkin plant sang, "Do not pluck my fruit, oh, old mother. I am Tejimola. My father is away. My mother killed me and buried me here." The old woman was shocked and told Tejimola's mother what she heard. The stepmother uprooted the plant and threw it away in a distant corner of the garden.

After some days a party of cowboys came to Tejimola's mother and asked her for some shaddocks. She told them that she had no such tree in her garden. The cowboys took her to the garden and showed her the tree. She saw it standing on the spot where she had thrown the pumpkin plant. She permitted the cowboys to pluck as many shaddocks as they liked. As soon as the cowboys touched the tree it sang, "Brother cowboys, do not pluck my fruit. I am Tejimola. My father is away. My mother crushed me to death and threw me here." The cowboys repeated to the stepmother what they had heard. After the cowboys went away she cut the tree and threw its branches into the river.

Tejimola's father was coming home after finishing his business. His barge was heading towards his home. He saw a very nice lily plant floating in the river. He thought he would give it to Tejimola. As soon as he touched the lily plant it sang very sadly, "Father, father, don't pluck me. I am Tejimola. Mother has crushed me to death."

Tejimola's father understood everything. Still he wanted to verify the truth. He took on the palm of his left hand a little bit of the betel he was chewing; on the palm of his right hand he put a *laroo* (sweetmeat) and he said, "If you are my Tejimola be a *salika* bird and eat the betel from my hand. If you are not my Tejimola take the *laroo*." Soon a *salika* bird came and perched on his heft hand and ate the betel. He put the bird in a silver cage and brought it home. When he reached home he asked his wife about Tejimola. She told him that Tejimola had gone to her friend's house. The merchant then took a *gamcha* and told the *salika*, "If you are my Tejimola be in human shape and put on this *gamcha*." As soon as he uttered this Tejimola came out of her cage in her human shape, a lovely little girl, and put on the *gamcha*. Her father clasped her to his bosom. The stepmother was driven away by the merchant. The little girl lived happily everafter with her father.

Riha is a six cubit long piece of cloth usually woven of *rhea* thread. It is folded breadthwise and cut and sewn. It is worn from the waist downwards.

Mekhala is also a six-cubit-long piece of cloth folded lengthwise. It is worn from the waist to cover the upper portion of the body reaching the head. It serves the purpose of bodice blouse and everything. Borders are designed upon it.

Khonia is a scarf woven out of cotton or muga thread. Sometimes lovely borders are woven. This is worn over the *Mekhala*. In Assam it is necessary for every woman to know how to weave. Weaving is not a job confined to a particular community as in Bengal. In Assam in every household the women spin the thread and weave the cloth for the use of the family.

10
QUEEN KAMALA KUORI

ONCE there was a king in a certain area in Assam. He loved his people and did all that was possible to protect them. His subjects were also very loyal. The king led a happy life with his devoted queen Kamala Kuori.

But alas! happiness does not last forever. It is like a dew drop on a leaf. There happened to be a severe drought in the country. The fields were parched. There was not a jot of verdure anywhere. People and cattle were dying of thirst and hunger. The king was very anxious to save his people. He engaged some people to dig a wide and deep tank. The tank was deep but where was the water? It was dry. The digging was done deeper and deeper but there came not a drop of water from it. The king was lost in thought. The people gave up.

At this time, the king had a dream, that he would be able to save his people, and water would come in the big tank but he would have to sacrifice his beloved queen.

The king woke up. He struggled in his mind. On one side there was the queen, his loyal and devoted wife and on the other were his subjects; to protect them was his sacred duty. What could he do? He told queen Kamala Kuori about his dream. She heard it, and was silent for a while, then with tears in her eyes, said, "King, I must sacrifice myself for all these people, who are like my children. I know you will never be happy without me, but let me go."

The king stood on the bank of the tank. The people were full of grief and suspense. The queen bade goodbye to the king and stepped into the hollow of the tank and lo! there was water—cool, clean, transparent—oozing out.

The king cried out to the victim,

"O lady of myheart, Kamala,
How much is the water?"
"O lord of my heart,
To my ankle is the water."

The water rose up still higher. The king asked again,

"O lady of my heart, Kamala,
How much is the water?"
"O lord of my heart,
To my knee is the water."

The water rose up higher. The king asked again,

"O lady of my heart, Kamala,
How much is the water?"
"O lord of my heart.
To my waist is the water."

The queen went forward and the water rose up still higher. The king asked with a tear-choked voice,

"O lady of my heart, Kamala,
How much is the water?"
"O lord of my heart,
To my neck is the water."

The queen went further ahead and now the water surged higher. The king asked with tears rolling down his cheeks,

"O lady of my heart, Kamala,
How much is the water?"
"O lord of my heart,
To my head is the water."

The faint voice of the queen was heard and the beautiful queen Kamala Kuori was lost in deep waters forever. The king and the subjects mourned her loss. She is still remembered for the sacrifice she made for the well-being of her subjects.

11
THE STORY OF TENTON

FATHER went to plough the field. Mother went to transplant the seedlings of paddy, and sister went to catch fish. There was nobody in the house except Tenton. He had been asked to stay back because his sister's husband was to come. His parents told him again and again to receive his brother-in-law respectfully.

When the brother-in-law arrived at the gate of their house, he said, "Hullo, is your father in?" Tenton thought, 'Look at him, he does not know how to address his superior. He says "Your father". Why, he should have called my father *Deota*.' He replied, "Father has gone to pierce the *patal* and make the earth upside down." The brother-in-law asked again, "Where's your mother?" Tenton thought, 'The audacity he has! He does not say *ai* when he refers to mother,' and answered, "She has taken seven days old *Painta*[1] and gone to revive the dead."[2] And no longer waiting for another question Tenton said further, "And sister has gone to filter the sea for precious gems." The brother-in-law felt insulted and went away immediately.

At dusk the parents returned home. When they heard that the son-in-law had gone back the father was in a fury and beat Tenton severely and turned him out of the house.

Tenton was not worried. He roamed about here and there. After some days he made friends with two thieves. One night he broke into a house with his friends. The thieves collected the booty and slipped away. Tenton knocked against a drum and

---

1. *Painta* is cooked rice put in water to keep it fresh longer.
2. To revive the dead—when the seedings are collected for transplanting they look dead and dry and after transplanting regain their freshness.

when it produced a sound he began to play on it. The inmates of the house woke up by the loud sound and caught him. They decided to take him to the king's court.

On their way they came across a man who was very annoyed with his bullocks. He shouted, "I wish somebody would finish them with one blow." Tenton instantly took him at his word and killed the bullocks with just one blow. This was beyond the imagination of the owner and in great anger and grief he tied Tenton with a rope and joined the first party to charge him before the king's court.

As they were going they found an old woman. She was selling bananas and shouting,

"Give me a pice to have a bunch,

Then give me a kick and go on your way."

This she said only to attract people by a piece of quaint humour but Tenton, true to his nature, took a bunch of bananas from her, gave her the pice and a kick also. She was angry and said she must have justice and started for the king's court.

Though Tenton was dragged to the king's court by three parties, he was not perturbed at all. His answers were ready for the charges against him. For the first charge against him he replied, "Is there a thief so foolish as to beat upon a drum in a house where he comes to steal? I searched for some *Chira* (Parched rice) which I needed very badly." The Tamuli Phukon, minister to the king, was fully satisfied with his explanation and remarked, "His words are worth a hundred rupees."

Then Tenton was given the second charge and asked to reply. To this he said, "I did not do any wrong. The man invited someone's help to finish his unruly bullocks and I did only what he wanted someone to do." The Tamuli Phukon agreed and observed, "His words are worth a thousand rupees."

To the third charge against him Tenton defended himself boldly. He said, "I did exactly as the woman wanted me to do. How should I know that she did not mean what she said?" The Tamuli Phukon was much impressed with Tenton's intelligence and observed, "His words are worth a lakh of rupees."

The king acquitted the boy of all the charges. Tenton went out of the king's court with a glint of mischief in his eyes.

A few days passed. Tenton went to the king's court. No, Tenton was not tied with a rope and dragged into the king's court by someone. He went there on his own. "A word is a word," he reminded the minister. Yes, the minister owed him a hundred, a thousand and a lakh of rupees. He must pay the price which he declared for the intelligent words of Tenton. The king could not ignore the claim of the boy. He gave him the money.

Tenton filled two baskets with the money. But he was not a boy to go away silently. He stood at the door of the minister in a heroic pose and shouted, "If one gives me a good and satisfying meal one gets all this wealth." You must be wondering why he shouted like this. Well, you will see what he gained by this peculiar venture now.

Tamuli Phukon had a young and beautiful daughter called Champa. Champa had a maidservant on whom she counted on much. She wished that her mistress should get all this money and so she persuaded Champa to invite Tenton for a meal. Champa granted the wish of her favourite. She cooked delicious dishes and invited Tenton to a meal. She placed a seat for him, bathed him and fed him with her own hands, and after the meal she gave him *pan* and *supari*.

Now Tenton had no excuse to break his promise. So he gave all the money to her and went back to the king. He said to the king, "Oh king, will you kindly allow me to put some questions?" The king smilingly assented. Then Tenton asked, "My lord, who is it that places a seat for someone and asks someone to take it? Who is it that bathes and feeds someone with her own hands? Who is it that keeps someone's money?"

The king answered readily, "Why! It must be the wife! But what does it mean?"

Tenton said with a grin, "My lord, please ask the Tamuli Phukon's daughter." The king understood everything.

The Tamuli Phukon was beside himself with rage. His foolish and greedy daughter had been trapped by this mischievous boy. The king told him that he could give his daughter in marriage to this boy and calmed him, saying, "Tamuli Phukon, this is a clever boy and he will make a nice husband for your Champa."

Tenton became the son-in-law of Tamuli Phukon. The king made him a Tamuli next in rank to his father-in-law and he lived happily ever after.

12
THE STORY OF THE SIX BROTHERS AND THEIR NEPHEW

ONCE upon a time somewhere in the Mikir Hills, there lived a widow. She had a son. She was anxious to bring up her son well and asked her brothers to help her. She had six brothers. But far from helping her to rear up the small boy they were very jealous of him. The boy was cleverer and handsomer than his uncles.

The boy had only one thing to call his own. That was a calf. The calf had a glistening body and you cannot imagine how plump it was. The boy was very fond of it. He used to feed the calf and tend it with loving care. The six brothers did not like this. One day they killed the calf.

The boy was very clever. He took off the hide of the calf and cut off one of its legs. He went to another village with that leg. There he came to a Brahmin's house. While nobody saw him, he buried the leg in a corner of the house. Then he went to the Brahmin and asked him, "Respected sir, how is it that there's smell of beef in your house?"

The Brahmin angrily retorted, "You fool! How dare you talk such sacrilege! Let a tiger eat you. Don't you know this is a Brahmin's house? Wicked fellow, I challenge you to find it out. If you can't find out any beef from my house, let my curse turn you to ashes." The boy meekly replied, "Well, let me search," and he pretended to search.

After a short while he presented the leg of the calf to the Brahmin, smiled with a flash of mischief and said, "Sir, you challenged me, now see whether this is anything but a cow's leg." The Brahmin felt very angry because if his neighbours would see it, he would be an outcast. After a little thought he decided to take the Mikir boy into confidence and whispered to him, "My boy, don't let anyone know about this. I'll give you a *Man-thing* (bag) full of money." He gave him the money and the boy went away.

The boy felt very glad. He had never seen so much money in his life. He ran to his mother and said, "Mother, go and bring the rice-measuring pot from my uncles." She went and brought the pot. As soon as the widow was gone, her brothers talked among themselves. "It's really a mystery. They are so poor. What'll they do with the rice measuring pot? Let one of us go and secretly find out what they are doing." And they sent their younger brother. He hid himself behind the fence and saw that the mother and the son were measuring a large amount of money. He came back and reported, "The boy has brought a large heap of silver coins and they are measuring it with our rice measuring pot. Really, it is hard to believe my own eyes."

When the widow went to return the pot, her brothers told her, "Go home and send our nephew. We have some urgent work with him."

When the boy went to his uncles they asked him, "Where from have you brought so much money? You borrowed the pot to measure money, is it not? It's no use hiding it from us, you'll be in trouble." He promptly answered, "There's nothing to hide. It's the price of the beef. When you killed my calf I cut it into pieces and went to the next village. The people there swarmed around me as soon as they got the smell of beef, and so all the beef was sold in a few minutes. They told me that I had too little a quantity of beef and they needed more. Their appetite for meat seemed so much that perhaps they would have eaten me if I had not promised to bring more beef for them, immediately. What shall I do, uncles?"

The six brothers thought this was a chance for earning some money and asked him, "Well if we take some beef for them, will they buy from us?" "Surely," the nephew replied, "and you have many cows, you can kill all of them and sell the beef. Perhaps you'll get so much money that it'll be difficult for you to carry."

They did not lose any time at all. They killed all their cows and took big bags of beef on their backs and were ready to go for selling it. Their nephew gave directions to that village where he had been and advised them thus, "The head of this village is a Brahmin. Just as you step into the village shout like this, 'Who's there to buy beef?' and there'll be a throng of people around you."

The six brothers went to the next village and started hawking beef loudly in the village of the Brahmins. A number of people were chatting in that Brahmin's parlour who was cheated by their nephew. All of them called the brothers in a chorus, "Yes, we'll buy beef, come here," and as they entered the outhouse of the Brahmin these people caught the six brothers and flogged them. The brothers fell at the feet of those people and asked for their forgiveness. The Brahmins let them go after warning, "You are too bold. You have come to sell beef in a village of Brahmins. This is a good lesson for you to remember for your whole life. We hope you'll never come again."

The six brothers came out of the village with their limbs aching. On their way home the eldest said, "This boy has cheated us in a very nasty manner. Let us take revenge on him. We'll set fire to his house."

This was an act congenial to their nature and all the brothers agreed. As soon as they reached home they set fire to their nephew's house very secretly. The hut was turned into a heap of ashes in no time. The poor widow and her son became homeless. The boy wove huge baskets of cane with much trouble, and filled these with ashes. Then he advanced towards a far off village. He found that the people of this village had been suffering from acute eye-trouble and could not see anything clearly. When the boy entered the village the villagers asked him, "Stranger, why have you come here?" The boy answered, "Brothers, I heard that all of you are suffering from sore eyes. I could not wait when I heard this, so I have brought some miraculous medicine." They felt grateful to him, and brought a lot of money and took the ashes to fill his baskets with the money they brought. The boy told them, "But there's a rule for the use of this medicine. Unless you go by this rule it'll not be of any use. Don't apply it on your eyes, as soon as you get it. When I shall start for my village and go some distance and shout, 'apply', all of you apply it at once on your eyes."

In this way, the boy used his wit and earned two bagfuls of money in lieu of the ashes. When he went out of sight the patients shouted, "Shall we apply the medicine now?" He replied from a distance, "Wait a little, don't be too hasty, then all will be futile." He shouted these words, till he crossed the boundary of the village. When he reached a safe distance, he shouted, "Now rub it deep into your eyes." The patients rubbed the ashes deep into their eyes. And you can imagine what effect the miraculous medicine could have had on their eyes! Their eyes were bleeding and they were mad with pain. They talked among themselves, "This is how the Mikir boy has cheated us. Well, if he dares to show his face again we will tie his body tightly and thrash him well."

The boy reached home and again sent his mother for the rice measuring pot. The uncles were surprised. "Perhaps he has got some hidden treasure," they observed. They could not resist themselves. They came to their nephew, and asked, "Wherefrom have you brought so much money, dear?" The orphan replied, "It is the price of the ashes of my house to which you set fire. The people of the village where I went to sell the ashes were telling me repeatedly, 'We want more ashes, we want more ashes!' But my hut was very small and I couldn't get much ashes from it. If you burn your huts you'll get a large amount of money and then perhaps you'll be able to build a thousand huts like the ones you have. And you'll need some porters to carry the money."

The brothers consulted among themselves. They decided that such a chance should not slip by. They set fire to all their huts immediately. The fire spread and consumed all the big huts. They all turned to ashes. Their neighbours thought that they were mad. However, ignoring everybody, each of the brothers took a huge bag of ashes on his back and started his journey on the meadowy track. They were bent under the weight of the ashes but they did not mind it as they thought about the money they would get out of it. Suddenly their nephew approached them running and said, "Go to the village where the people have sore eyes and hawk your ashes there." When they were hawking ashes there, the villagers invited them inside. As they came in, the six brothers were tied from head to foot with ropes by the villagers who then rubbed the ashes deep into their eyes. They were almost blinded. Besides, they were severely beaten. Thrashing the brothers to their heart's content, the villagers released them. On their way home, the brothers discussed among themselves, "This devilish boy has given us so much trouble. He has made us burn our houses and we have been flogged for selling ashes. We must take revenge on him. Let us reach home. We'll put him in an *Ingchin aru* (iron cage) and throw him into the river."

They caught the boy when they came home and put him into an *Ingchin aru* and took him to the jungle on the bank of the river. They rested there and thought, "This boy will go down the stream presently. He'll not be able to slip away from us now. Let us go and take some rice."

When they were away, a prince from another kingdom who was out hunting, came near the cage and saw the lad in it. He was taken aback and asked him, "What's the matter? How is it that you have been left in this dense forest in an *Ingchin aru* with your hands and feet tied?" The boy replied, "I have a maternal uncle's daughter. You can't imagine how beautiful she is. But as my ill luck would have it, my maternal uncles are pressing me hard to marry her. I have selected my own bride and my answer to them always is, 'I will never marry her. You are my *Ong* (uncles), I shall never allow you to be my *Ong-hi* (father-in-law).' But they would not listen to me. At first, they coaxed me, then they flogged me and when they could not persuade me by any means they thrust me into this cage and brought me here. I don't know what they'll do with me." The prince said, "If I marry her, then will the problem be solved?" The boy answered, "Then you'll have to enter this cage and wait till my uncles come back." He remained silent for a while and said, "When they return they'll ask you, what else have you got to say? Tell them, 'Throw me into the river, that'll be better.' Then if they tell you something more, say 'Yes, I am ready.' "

The prince felt glad and said, "I shall remember you for long." The boy said, "But it can't be so easy. If you go into the *Ingchin aru* in that princely dress and ornaments of yours they'll find out who you are. Take me out. I shall give you my clothes. Wear them and enter the cage."

The prince opened the door and the boy came out and changed his garments with those of the prince and the prince entered the cage in the shabby clothes of the Mikir boy. The boy advanced towards the village.

The brothers finished their meal and came back. One of them put his mouth on the cage and asked,"What else will you to say?" The prince, as taught by the boy, answered "It would be better if you throw me into the river." "Then it'll be no fault of ours," said the brothers and hurled the caged prince into the river. The prince was going down rapidly into the river. "What's the matter?" he thought. "Am I to marry the princess who belongs to the kingdom of death?"

The six brothers ran home with a peaceful mind. They thought that by this time their nephew must be dead.

As they reached home they saw a godly looking prince walking in the courtyard of their sister. How beautiful was his dress! And his ornaments dazzled their eyes. They came near their sister's house and saw that this was nobody else but their nephew. They were wild with envy. They thought that the *Arnam Atooms* (evil spirits) were pleased with the boy. A boy thrown into a river and still alive! Had anyone ever come across such an incident? Perhaps, he had gathered much wealth from the *patalpuri* (the kingdom of the god of death). They grew curious about the land of the dead. They went to the boy and asked him, "Child, we threw you into the river because you told us to do so. You must have been around the nether world (*patalpuri*). But how could you come back so soon? We are very eager to know how you went there."

The boy opened the story with an air of seriousness, "You threw me into the river and I went down slowly where only *Arnam Ketha* knew. Suddenly a *palki* (sedan car) stopped near my cage and out came a number of armed guards. They showed much respect to me and opened the cage. They told me, 'Sir, your grandparents have sent this *palki* to take you to the kingdom of the death-god. Kindly take your seat in it.' I was scared but I thought that since I was already dead, why should I worry? Then the bearers of the *palki* swam and reached the kingdom of the death god. I got down from the *palki* and saw a big house before me. Out came granny and gandpa. They caressed me and at the time of return they gave me this dress and ornaments and said, 'Child, we are very eager to meet your uncles, tell them to come soon, for once.' They also gave me a knife wrought with gold and said, 'Perhaps your uncles will remember us when they see this knife'." The boy showed the knife of the prince to his uncles and went on with his story. "Then the bearers of the *palki* left me at the bank of the river. You should go there very soon, otherwise grandpa and granny will be very sorry."

The six brothers said, "Well, we understand it all, but how to reach that place?" The boy replied, "It's not very difficult. Bring an *Ingchin aru* for each of you and come with me to the bank of the river. Then each of you go into your own and I shall throw you into the river, one by one. Then three pairs of *palkis* will come and take you straight to the *patalpuri*."

The six brothers went home quickly and brought six *Ingchin arus*. They went with their nephew to the bank of the river and each one of them went into an *Ingchin aru*. The boy tied them tightly inside the *Ingchin arus*.

He threw his eldest uncle first into the river. As soon as the cage was cast in the river there were a lot of bubbles on the water. The nephew shouted, "Look, look, granny has given so much *harpo* (rice bear) to the uncle that he has become tipsy and is vomiting like anything." His uncles, when they heard this, felt still more eager to reach their brother in the *patalpuri*. Each of them burst out of his cage, "Throw me first, throw me first." Then the nephew cast all of them into the river and went home with relief.

His aunts saw him alone and asked him when his uncles would return home. The boy replied, "Why do you worry? They'll meet grandpa and granny after such a long time and they won't leave the uncles so soon. They have just now started drinking, then they'll eat good dishes and they'll dance and sing; so they'll be there long."

The wives of the six brothers kept awake for four nights but they did not return. They apprehended some danger and asked the nephew, "What's the matter, child? How is it that your uncles haven't returned yet?" The boy said, "They'll come soon." The six wives spent some more sleepless nights and asked the boy again, "Why haven't your uncles returned? We are terribly afraid that some evil has befallen them. Go and see what has happened." The boy now replied carelessly, "Don't talk uselessly. Do what you should; place a plate of rice for each on the *Nok-Sek*."[1]

His aunts then realised what ill luck had come to them. The village echoed to the cries of the six widows.

The uncles who had ill-treated the son of their widowed sister were given early death by *Arnam Kethe* and their widows were left on this earth to lament over their death.

---

1. It is the custom of the Mikirs to give food to the dead. *Nok-Sek* is a place in the kitchen where they put food for the dead.

13

RUPATYLLI

If you have the opportunity to snatch a holiday and go to Laitkynsew or Mahadeo peak in the Khasi Hills you will find a river shining in the sun. It seems that a glittering silver necklace of a beautiful shape has been laid on the plain. The river has a fascinating name Rupatylli. Rupatylli in Khasi language is the name of a peculiarly shaped silver necklace commonly worn by the bonny buxom Khasi girls.

The river has a story which is fondly repeated till today. The story relates to the ancient time when the world was created.

The god of the Shillong peak had two daughters who were twins. Like all twins, they were very fond of each other. They grew into lovely young girls. One day they were playing on the Shillong peak. The Shillong peak was beautiful with its rich downs rolling along and dotted with pines standing straight like comely, slim women, with the wild flowers weaving a pattern in red, blue and mauve. But the undulating plains of Sylhet lay stretched before the eyes of the twins. They looked very inviting and suddenly the twins took it into their heads to run a race to the plains of Sylhet.

So the sisters Ka Iam and Ka Ngot took the shape of two rivers Umiam and Umngot and leapt from the peak and flowed towards the plains of Sylhet. The shy and unassuming Ka Ngot was by nature demure and petite. Ka Iam was more dashing, showy and enterprising.

The river Umngot chose an easy track. She meandered through a long, but soft bed and reached the plains of Sylhet. There she has been called "Shengurkhat". She went across Chhatak town and reached Dewara. She looked around to find her sister Umiam but in vain. She was, naturally, in a very joyful mood. She realised that she was going to win the race. She meandered slowly in a long and semicircular way like a shiny silver necklace. The people who were on the hills saw this lovely semicircle of a river gleaming in the sun and they shouted in joy, "Rupatylli! Rupatylli!" Since then she has been called Rupatylli at Dewara.

Umiam, with her adventurous nature, took a difficult route through gorges and rocks. While Umngot was covering her long but soft track at ease, Umiam was leaping from one hill to another and lost much of her energy in the hazards.

Thus, much time was lost when she reached Dewara. She found her sister Umngot smiling in the shape of a silver necklace. As she had lost the race she wanted to hide herself. She broke herself up in five streams-Ka Umtong, Ka Torasa, Ka Pasbiria, Ka Kumarjani and Ka Dewara.

Both the rivers Umiam and Umngot have their sources close to the Shillong peak. The Khasis offer their *khub-lei* (worship) to the river Umngot before they cross it as she had won the race. It is often seen that there is a party of Khasi men and women assembled on its bank. The young smiling Khasi women with rosy cheeks and in colourful dresses bring the offering of orchids, rhododendrons, azaleas and wild roses. They adorn their hair with the honey scented *Kapauphul* (Aerides odoratum) of delicate colour and beauty. They dance to the beat of drums, their feet moving in rapid and short steps encircled by the Khasi men who participate in the dance in manly and long strides.

14

THE STORY OF THE GODDESS KAMAKHYA

KAMAKHYA Devi's temple near Guwahati in Assam is very well known. This goddess is worshipped daily by thousands, many of whom come from beyond Assam. It is said that goddess Kamakhya grants the wishes of the persons who worship her with devotion. But earlier there was no goddess Kamakhya and her temple at that place. It was a desolate place.

People who live in the Garo Hills district of Assam and its adjoining places are called Garos. The Garo Hills district is to the north of Mymensingh in East Pakistan.

In ancient times the Garos lived in a country called Mandalae. They were prosperous. They lived in large villages. They built big and high houses for themselves and magnificent temples for their gods and goddesses. They were ruled by kings and chieftains.

The Garos were once suddenly attacked by wild, cruel and vast number of men from the north. They defended themselves with all their might but their enemies were much larger in number and had more weapons. So the Garos were defeated.

A certain division of the Garos settled in a country called *Salaram Mithdaichak.* There was a woman among them called Nunui Nanokhi, also called Noini Mechik. She had with her an image of a goddess named Phojou. Phojou means the goddess-creator who causes living beings to be born, seeds to sprout, flowers to bloom and mature into fruits. She always carried this image on her head.

An Assamese king Lila Sing reigned there at that time. He was extremely cruel and wicked. He was so heartless that he used the Garos as beasts of burden. The good natured Garos could not go on bearing all this cruel treatment. They waged a war against the king. There were leaders such as *Gume, Roti, Asal, Jarin, Domepa, Jirik, Sakso, Wasang, Athu, Badingring, Boriding, Kepesa, Jajang, Silma* and *Rothang* who fought bravely against King Lila Sing.

As usual in a war, the people were living a very disturbed life. The houses were destroyed. There was no food. Dead bodies of the soldiers were scattered here and there and many were going away in search of a new place to settle. Nunui Nanokhi was also escaping with her children. The children were tired and hungry. They were crying aloud. To pacify them she put down the image of Phojou on the ground and rested a while on the way.

After a while she wanted to resume her journey and stretched her hand to lift the image of the goddess Phojou. But the image was hard fixed on the spot. She tried hard to take it away but in vain. She realised that the goddess wished to stay where she was. She performed her *Krita* (worship) by sacrificing one of her goats and offering wild flowers to the goddess.

The goddess Phojou remained for ever at the place where Nunui Nanokhi placed her and her worship has been going on for ages. The Garos call this place *Salaram Mithdaichak* which means the sanctuary of the past. People other than the Garos call it Kamakhya. Soon Kamakhya Devi became the most popular deity in Assam.

FOLK TALES
OF
BIHAR

Bihar

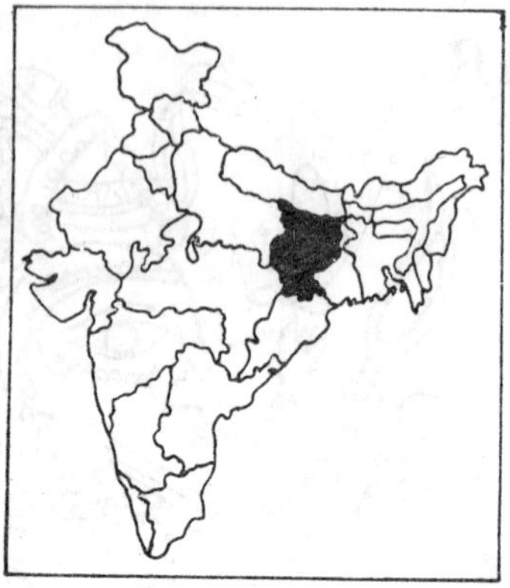

The state stretches from the Himalayan foothills in the north to Orissa in the south, in the east from West Bengal, touching Madhya Pradesh and Uttar Pradesh on the west. It has an area of 1,73,877 sq km, with a population of 86,338,853 and density 497 per sq km, literacy 38.54.

The state capital is in Patna. The State language is Hindi and the other main languages are Urdu, Bengali, Mundari and Santali. Hindi language in all the three dialects, Bhojpuri, Maithili and Magalu, has rich literature.

Bihar is the cradle of Jainism and Buddhism. She has a glorious past as the ancient relics strewn throughout the State indicate. The word Bihar is derived from *Vihar* which means a monastery. The State has a large number of places sacred to the Hindus, Muslims, Buddhists, Jains and Sikhs.

The folklore of Bihar is rich and variegated. The Adivasis, Mundas, Oraons and Santals have their folk tales, dances, festivals and music. Bihar had a class of professional story-tellers, particularly in Mithila and Bhojpur areas. They used to wander from village to village and narrate stories in verse and prose. The Mithila Raja and most of the large feudal lords in Bihar appointed *Bhats* or singers whose duty was to entertain the people with folk tales. That class has disappeared now.

15
VIR KUMAR

A YOUNG man, Vir Kumar, lived in Bihar in bygone days. He belonged to the caste of *Ahirs*. The *Ahirs* are milkmen by profession. They rear the cattle for milk and milk products like *dahi* (yoghurt), *makkhan* (butter), *khoa* (soldified milk) and *ghee* (melted butter).

In those days much of the land was dense forest. There were tigers, wolves and other wild animals in the dense forest. The lofty trees like the *sal, neem* and the banyan were in abundance. The *Ahirs* grazed their cattle in one of these forests daily. They were a class of brave and strong people. Vir Kumar was their leader.

All was going well when some cattle suddenly fell ill and died. They found no reason for the calamity. As Vir Kumar was the leader, people came to him for advice. The deep jungles were inhabited by witches. Witches had evil powers through which they would destroy men and animals. They practised their witchcraft in the thick of the jungles. Vir Kumar suspected that the witches were responsible for the death of the cattle. On *Sohrai* night (the night of the new moon) he took a *lathi* (stick) and arrows and went into the deep forest. It is believed that on this night all the witches assemble.

As he stood under a *Gular* tree he saw the witches. They had parched lips, shrivelled fingers and big white protruding teeth on their blackened faces. Their eyes were like glowing pieces of coal. They were tall and thin with dishevelled hair flying around. They shed their *saris* and were dancing nude with broomsticks in their hands. The brave Vir Kumar was not daunted by this strange sight and he took away their clothes. They implored Vir Kumar to return their *saris*. Vir Kumar refused till they agreed not to cast an evil eye on the cattle. They threatened to kill him. But he was firm in his decision.

Finding no alternative through witchcraft, they summoned twenty-one tigers with ferocious eyes and wide open jaws. The tigers quickly tore the body of the brave man into pieces. Within moments the entire forest rang with the savage laughter of the witches. Barring the earrings and yellow *dhoti* which too was soaked in blood and the weapons, nothing remained of the solid body of Vir Kumar. Next morning his kinsmen went searching for him and found all those remains.

Vir Kumar became a legend and has been worshipped ever since as a hero. Ballads and pastoral songs are sung in his memory throughout Bihar.

In Palamau district of Bihar on every *Sohrai* of the year a pillar is raised in his memory at the village of the *Ahirs* and *puja* is offered.

16

THE STORY OF KARUA CHAUTH

KARUA Chauth is observed on the fourth day of the dark fortnight in the month of *Kartik* (November). All married women observe the fast till moonrise and pray for the well-being of their husbands.

There is a legend associated with this vow.

The day was at its close. Chanda, the beloved sister of seven brothers, did not know how it was to feel hungry. Her parents and brothers were all ready to make her comfortable at any cost. This was the first time she was observing Karua Chauth fast after her marriage. She passed half the day playing dice, a quarter was passed chatting, but the last quarter was very trying. She felt weak and hungry. Her youngest brother was unhappy to see her tired and said to their mother: "Mother, *Jiji* (elder sister) is feeling hungry. Give her something to eat." Mother said, "She is observing a vow and she can't eat till moonrise."

He went to Chanda and tried to keep her in good mood by telling her jokes but still it was a long time before the moonrise. The eldest brother looked at Chanda and said to mother, "Mother, shall I show her the moon?" "How can you? You are not God," said the mother.

The brother fixed a lamp on a tree and partially covered it with the foliage and showed it to the mother. The mother said, "This is not a matter for a joke, this is a vow and she is not a child that she should be impatient with hunger. She will be going to her husband's house tomorrow and she should not break a vow meant for the well-being of her husband." But he did not listen to his mother and showed the false moon to Chanda. He gave her fresh and dried fruits. As she took the first bite she found a hair in her mouth; at the second bite of the fruit she got a small piece of stone in her mouth and as she was taking her third bite a messenger from her father-in-law's place came with the message that her husband had been bitten by a snake. Her hand stopped midway. It was a bolt from the blue. She went to her mother. She could not shed tears out of modesty. Her legs were trembling. She said to her mother, "Mother, may I go?" Her mother was dumbfounded. "Yes, child," was all she could manage to mumble and burst into tears. She hugged her daughter and said, "Child, entreat everyone you meet; who knows who will take pity on you and bless you?"

Chanda touched the feet of everyone she met on the way but nobody could bless her that she should be happy in her married life. She gave away her necklace to an old beggar woman and the beggar woman blessed her that her brothers and nephews would live long.

Chanda's mind ran to her husband's home.

When she had gone there earlier as a bride the house had welcomed her, the *shehnai* had played *Raga Basant* and there was light and fragrance of flowers all over the place. But now nobody greeted her. She entered the house with a heavy heart when her elder sister-in law came to receive her. She touched her feet. The sister-in law blessed her saying: *"Bhabhi seli saputi ho. Burhi suhagan ho, peli patiyo raj kare, Dudho nahao, puton phalo, Bhai bhatije ke kherhe bass."* (Sister-in law, be cool tempered and mother of sons; be dear to your husband, enjoy the bliss of family life till your hair go grey. Let there be riches and many people around you. Let there be a village full of your brothers and nephews.

Chanda felt that she had got whatever she had wished for. Somebody called: "Sunaina! Sunaina!" Sunaina replied, "Mother, *Bhabhi* has come." The mother said, "What shall I do with that ill-fated woman? She has lost her happiness and fortune." And she began to wail. But Chanda touched the feet of her mother-in-law. She was taken to her dead husband. Many of the *Sanpere gardu* (Those who can extract the venom from the body after snake-bite) and doctors were called but to no avail. The pulse was felt. The heartbeat was felt. If there was life, there was hope. His hands and feet were cold. These were massaged with musk. But nothing happened.

Chanda had some idea that a man bitten by a snake might come to life if his body was kept for a year. So she implored everybody not to cremate the dead body. As she was so unfortunate and pitiable she was allowed to keep her husband's body. Her mother-in-law hated to see her so she would send a spoonful of mustard oil and a bit of *gur* (crude sugar) to her daily. Chanda would light the lamp with the oil and throw the piece of *gur* in a corner of her room. She would sit with her husband's head on her lap day and night. She would make his bed everyday with a banana leaf and covered his body with another.

She became very thin but her face was lit with heavenly glow.

One day she saw from the terrace that women were returning after a bath in the river. They were dressed in their best and made up with *Solah-Singar* (all the 16 items of a woman's make-up.) One of them told her, "This is the day when you lost your husband last year." 'Shall I observe the vow today?" Chanda asked. One of the ladies said with a grimace, "You may if you like." There was an old mendicant woman amongst them, who said to Chanda, "Observe the vow and fast today without taking even a drop of water. If you do so, you can get back your husband tonight. The goddess of love will come in the guise of an old woman seven times. These old women will torture you but you are to fall at their feet and implore them. It is they who can bring your husband back to life." Chanda touched the feet of the old mendicant woman. She washed her house thoroughly. She burnt incense and scattered flower petals. She decked herself like a bride. She tinged the parting of her hair with vermilion and put a bindi on her forehead. She wore new bangles. She bathed the body of her husband and changed his clothes. At night one of the old women came and said:

Karua le, karua le,
Bir piyari karua le,
Bap bhai ki khatti khani
Karua le, karua le,
Dhaule narha, dhaule sari
tera janam jaiyo
Karua le, karua le
Adhure chand khani
Karua le, karua le.

(Observe the *karua*. You are the beloved of a hero. You are enjoying the earnings of your father and brother. You'll have to spend your whole life in white garments, as a widow if you eat again before the full moon rises).

Chanda touched her feet and implored her for blessings but she pulled away her feet and said that her sister would come and bless her.

Thus came six old women one after another. They repeated the same thing and went away in the same manner. Now the seventh old woman was to come. Chanda was waiting breathlessly to meet her. Each moment seemed like an age to her. At last the goddess came. She said:

Karua le, karua le
Bhaiya piyari karua le
Bap-bhai ki kamai khani
Karua le karua le
Dhaula marha, dhauli sari
Karua le, karua le
Adhure chand khani
Karua le, karua le

(You have eaten before moonrise, so you wear white garments like a widow, your brothers pamper and feed you. You had better observe *karua*.)

As soon as the goddess appeared Chanda covered her neck with garlands and fell at her feet. But she pushed the girl forcibly and her head knocked against the door. Blood was oozing profusely but she did not leave the feet of the goddess. She said, "Mother, either bring him to life or let me die. I can't live like this."

The goddess relented and she cut her little finger and dropped the blood on the dead body of Chanda's husband.

Immediately he sat up and asked Chanda, "When did you come? Why didn't you wake me?"

Chanda coyly stood in a corner. He embraced her affectionately. He had been defeated by her on the last *Karua Chauth* in a game of dice; this day he challenged her for another game. She did not have the energy to play but she could not refuse. While Chanda was playing with her husband the maidservant came with the daily quota of mustard oil and *gur*.

She went back and reported to Chanda's mother-in-law that she saw Chanda playing dice with a stranger. The mother-in-law did not believe it and hastened to see for herself. When she found her son alive she was very much surprised. Chanda and her husband touched the feet of the mother. She blessed her daughter-in-law saying, *"Burhu suhagan ho, dudho nahao, puton phalo."*

17
TILAMANJANI KUMARI

In ancient days a Brahmin in Mithila had two wives and two daughters. The daughters were called Tilamanjani and Carabhusako. Tilamanjani lost her mother when she was a small child. Carabhusako's mother was alive. But she did not like her stepdaughter Tilamanjani as she was beautiful and good-natured while her own daughter Carabhusako was ugly and ill-tempered.

The stepmother would sometimes order Tilamanjani to grind wheat for the whole day and would give her a piece of *chapati* and a little *dal* at the end of the day. Sometimes the stepmother would order her to bring water from the river in the scorching heat of the mid-day. More often than not she would be given the food left by others in their dishes.

But the news went round that Tilamanjani was beautiful. One day a barber visited Tilamanjani's father and proposed her marriage to a king.

The Brahmin was not very rich and he hesitated to accept the proposal but his wife was very eager. The marriage was settled and the Brahmin visited the king to perform the *Dhanabatti* when they both brought a handful of paddy and mixed it up and divided it between themselves. The king sent the bride's dress or the *Kanwai*, a brocade silk sari, with ornaments for the bride. He sent a *tiara* and *mangtika* for the head, *mala* and *hansuli* for the neck, *jhumka* for the ears, *anant* for the arms, *pahunchi* and *balas* for the wrist and *punjeb* for the feet.

The house of the Brahmin was illuminated and the *marhwa* was decked with flowers. The musicians were playing the *shehnai* but alas! poor Tilamanjani was the unhappiest in this house, because though her marriage was settled, the crafty stepmother put a magic root in her ears which tuned her into a bird and shut her up in a cage.

The king wore a *sehra* on his face and he had not seen his bride before; so when he was married to Carabhusako in place of Tilamanjani he could not detect the fraud. The king put the vermilion at the parting in the bride's hair; they sought the blessings of the family deity Shiva and became husband and wife.

On his return to his palace with his new bride the king found out that she was ugly. She did not have the eyes of a startled deer as he had heard. She didn't have the complexion of liquid gold as he was told. She did not have thick long black hair touching her ankles as he was informed. Besides, she was selfish and ill-tempered. She always demanded good clothes, food and ornaments from the king. She never showed her love for the king. The king was very unhappy and disappointed with his new bride.

Meanwhile, when the marriage ceremony of her daughter with the king was over, the stepmother set Tilamanjani free. Tilamanjani, who was now a small bird, migrated a long way and reached the kingdom where her stepsister Carabhusako had come as the queen. Tilamanjani flew around the king's palace saying:

Tilamanajani phirathi dari dari
Carabhusako bhogthi raj
Dhana ehi rajake kahi aurhi
Jeth sali sang karthi bilas.

While the king held court, the bird would be singing these verses. When the king rose in the early morning, bathed and stood on the roof to pay his respects to the sun-god, the bird would hum this tune.

The king grew curious and sent his retinue to catch the bird.

The bird looked lovely—a parrot with a coat of fresh green, a ruby-red beak and a big tail. The king held it in his own hands and while it tried to struggle out of his hands the magic root came out of its ears.

And to his joy and astonishment the king saw a paragon of beauty standing before him. A bashful, charming, young girl in tears. The king listened to her story and called Carabhusako and asked her why had she cheated him. Carabhusako could not raise her head in shame and fear. She was taken to a forest and deserted there for ever by the order of the king.

The king and Tilamanjani, thereafter, lived for one hundred years in great joy.

18
THE GREATEST FOOL

FOUR fools, who were friends, were travelling together. They were tired and stopped under a pipal tree to rest. They belonged to the four castes—Brahmin, Kshatriya, Vaisya and Kayastha.

Another man also came to rest under the same tree. He bowed to them.

The friends quarrelled among themselves on the point as to whom the man had saluted. Munshiji (the Kayastha) said, "He has courtesied to me." Panditji (the Brahmin) said, "No, he has bowed to me." Singhji (the Kshatriya) said, "No, he has saluted me." Sahaji (the Vaisya) said, "In fact he saluted all of us. If you have any doubt, go and ask him. *Hath kangan ko arsi kya?* (Why should one look at the bangle on one's hand from a mirror)?"

Singhji burst out: "Oh you brags! Who cares for you? I am a Rajput and enjoy the birthright to salutes."

When they could not decide, they asked the man who had bowed.

The man was clever enough to realise that these were utter fools. He said, "I have really saluted to the greatest fool among you. And let me see who has that glory. You are to prove who the greatest fool is." Each one was very eager to show that he was the most foolish. It was decided that one by one each would come, tell a story proving his foolishness.

The Panditji put his turban properly on his head and began, "I shall tell my story first. It was a dark night in the month of *Bhado* (August.) My wife had gone to her father's place with the children. I was alone. A thief broke into my house. I was roused by the noise. I remembered that I should see the *Patra* (calendar) to find an auspicious moment to challenge the thief. I consulted the calendar and found that the auspicious moment was on the night of the full moon and that the present moment was a very inauspicious one. So I remained silent while the thief stole away everything.

"On the night of the full moon the sky was clear. The auspicious moment had come. I came out of my room and shouted, 'The thief! The thief!' at the top of my voice.

"The neighbours assembled to help me. A man was returning home with some money he had earned in the town. With the help of the neighbours he was caught.

"In the morning when the king was in his court, he heard the case and asked me: 'Is he the thief?' I hesitated. 'When did the theft occur?' the king asked. I replied, 'The theft occurred about eight or nine days ago. I lost everything.'

'Then why did you shout after so many days, on the night of the full moon?' the king asked. I said, 'Your Majesty, I had consulted the calendar; this was the first auspicious moment for me after all these days, since the night of the theft.'

"The king angrily said, 'You fool! Clear out of my sight.' The other man was released.

"So I have been certified by the king himself as a fool. If you don't believe, let us go to the king."

Now it was the turn of Sahaji. He said, "How can you be a greater fool than me? Hear my story. It was the night of *Diwali*. I performed the *Lakshmi puja* and put all my money on a plate and sat beside my wife. One must gamble on the *Diwali* night. The gambling on the *Diwali* night is a means to get the forecast for the following year. I told my wife that I must go out to gamble. She said, 'Why should you go out at this time of the night? Let us gamble between ourselves.' Then we touched each other's hands and promised that the one who spoke first would lose the game. After sometime we retired to our beds.

At midnight a thief slipped into our room. We were awake. But who would speak and lose the game? We were silent and the thief collected everything we had and left. But he was very greedy and returned. Now he snatched away her *Hansuli* when she shouted, 'Please speak, we have lost everything, now I'll have to lose my honour.' I said, 'You have spoken, you have lost the game.' She shouted, 'Let the game go to hell, everything is already looted and now I am going to lose my modesty.' We were quarrelling thus when the neighbours came to see what had happened. When they knew everything, they said that we were fools, because we were quarrelling while our house was being looted. Tell me, who is the greater fool?"

Then it was the turn of Singhji. He said, "I was sitting on my balcony and enjoying a *hookah* (hubble-bubble). I saw a Kabuli (an Afghan) coming riding on a good horse with a load of blankets. I stopped him and asked whether he would sell the horse. He answered, 'Yes, I shall sell, but you will not be able to pay its high price. Only a king may purchase this horse.' I asked him the price. He said, 'One thousand rupees.' I said, 'It's all right.' I ordered him to tether the horse to a rod. I took five hundred rupees out of my pocket and requested him to come for the remaining amount after selling the blankets. The Kabuli went away.

"He came after two days. I borrowed money from the money-lender at a high rate of interest and paid some money to the Kabuli. I promised to pay the rest after a week. He shut his eyes for a moment and said that the week was over and demanded the money. I could not collect even hundred rupees with all my effort; so I sold the horse to the Kabuli for hundred rupees and paid him that money as the price of the horse. I thought I had come out clean. But whosoever heard this said I was a first rate fool."

Then Munshiji said, "It is now my turn to prove my foolishness. Of course I am still not sure whether what I did was intelligent or foolish. It was the rainy season. The rivers and canals were full. All of a sudden a message came from my father-in-law that my mother-in-law was very ill. There was no hope of her survival. If we wanted to see her we should reach there immediately, so I started out for my father-in-law's house with my wife and children. There was a river to cross. My wife said, 'Let us take a boat to cross the river.' I said, 'What nonsense are you talking? I'll have to find out a boatman and depend on his pleasure to take us across—what is the necessity of all this? I know how to measure the depth of water. If it is not much we'll cross the river without the help of a boat.' I entered the river, and found the water only ankle-deep. I proceeded, till my knees were under water. I went farther and the water came up to my thighs. Further on the water reached my waist and then it was up to the chest. I told by wife, 'There's nothing to worry, the water is a little above the knees—as I have found out by my formula of measurement; so let us cross it.' My wife did not understand me. I was very angry. I am an accountant by profession and she spends her life in the kitchen; so who is she to question my measurement? I shouted at her and commanded her to come into the river with the children. As soon as they reached the middle of the river the children were drowned; in trying to save her children, my wife also lost her life; but I was sure that my measurement of water was correct. When I saw them all drowned I could not make out what was wrong. I again measured the water and the result was the same. I am still puzzled:

"Lekha jokha, jyon ke tyon
Larka Larki dube kyon?

(While the measurement was always the same, why were the children drowned?)"

The newcomer who had saluted, smiled and gave his opinion, "Munshiji is the greatest fool. There could be no doubt. The rest of you only lost your property, he lost his family due to foolishness. Who will not bow to him with respect?"

The four friends were satisfied with the verdict of the saluting man. Happily they resumed their journey.

19
ORIGIN OF PATNA

PATNA is the capital of Bihar. There is a legend relating to the name Patna.

In the city of Kosambi, there lived a Brahmin named Bhumideza. He had two sons. They were called Kusa and Bikusa. Kusa married Pramati and Bikusa's wife was Sumati. They were daughters of sage Sarvasidhi. Kusa and Bikusa were poor so they went abroad to seek a fortune with their wives.

After a few days when they could not get any job or money they fled leaving their wives asleep in a jungle. When Pramati and Sumati woke up they wept at their misfortune.

Parvati and Siva were passing that way. Parvati took pity on the poor women and implored Mahadeva to do something for them. Mahadeva prophesied that Sumati would have a son who should be called Putra. And whenever Putra would rise from a sleep a shower of thousand gold coins would come from his head.

The prophesy came true. As the child woke up from his first sleep a thousand gold coins fell from his head. The mothers thought that the money was stolen from someone and out of fear they left the place. But wherever they went the same miracle occurred.

They were alert and found out the truth. They went to Kasi and settled there. Putra, it is needless to say, grew into a very rich man and was generous in charity.

People from all corners of the world came to receive his bounty. Kusa and Bikusa lived in Karnataka begging from door to door. They heard of Putra and came to receive alms from him. Sumati saw them from the balcony of her mansion and recognised them. They were received with great respect and led a happy life from that day.

But Putra's father became jealous of him. He was a boy of sixteen. Bikusa sent two *chandalas* to Putra. They said to him that he ought to offer *puja* to the goddess Vindyasani, to whom his mother owed a pledge which she had made before his birth. Putra verified the statement from his father and he supported the *chandalas*. The *chandalas* pretended to be the *pandas* of the goddess who would take him to the temple.

The innocent boy was taken into a dense forest and the *chandalas* disclosed to him their conspiracy. Putra was mortified to learn that he was about to die. But the executioner's sword fell from his hand on every attempt. As they could not kill him they spared his life in return for a large amount of money.

The boy was alone in the wilderness. He climbed a banyan tree at night without knowing what to do.

Two demons Sankata and Bikata climbed the same tree. But they promised not to harm Putra. They requested him to act as a judge in a dispute between them. They were the sons of a demon called Karibak. Karibak once pleased Mahadeva and obtained three gifts from him. The first was a pair of shoes on wearing which a man could travel thousands of miles in a moment; the second was a bag out of which would come handfuls of jewels whenever anybody put his hands in it, and the third was a rod by which rotating it overhead one could build a magnificent city. Karibak was dead now and his two sons were quarrelling over the possession of these three things. Putra was requested by them to decide who was to inherit these three wonders.

Putra said to them, "Go and touch the lofty *sal* tree which you see ahead. Whoever will come back first and pick these things up will inherit them."

As they were running, a voice from heaven said to Putra, "Wear the pair of shoes and fly to Sinhal dwipa (Ceylon)."

When he landed at Ceylon he met a Brahmin in white robes sitting at an altar under a tree. He spoke to Putra and prophesied that he would be married to the princess Patali, the daughter of King Pataleswar who reigned in Ceylon then.

The young man took the clue and he secretly visited Patali at night in her chamber and disclosed his identity. The girl was ready to accompany him wherever he would go. Putra put on his shoes again and within moments reached a place on the south bank of the Ganga, north of Gaya, east of Sonbhadra and west of the Punpuna. Narada visited him here and ordered him to find a city with the help of the rod. Putra obeyed sage Narada and named the city Pataliputra by combining his name with his wife's. He later conquered many kingdoms and became a renowned and valiant king. Meanwhile, his mother passed away broken-hearted.

Putra's son Kusum succeeded him and renamed the city Kusumpur. King Kusum had a son called Patan and a daughter called Patna. Patna did not marry and lived the life of a *brahmacharini*. She was worshipped as a *devi* after her death and she is still the deity presiding over the city which is now called Patna.

FOLK TALES OF GUJARAT

Gujarat

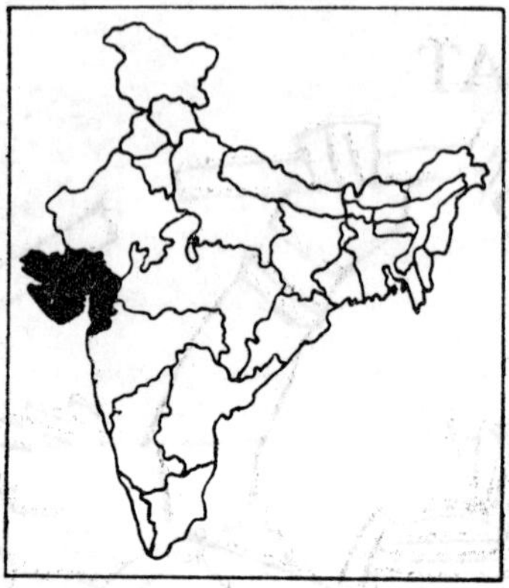

Gujarat is situated in the north-west corner of India. It is bordered in the north-west by Pakistan, in the north by Rajasthan, in the east by Madhya Pradesh and in the south and south-east by Maharashtra.

The state capital is in Gandhinagar. It has an area of 1,96,024 sq km with a population of 41,174,060, density of 210 per sq km and literacy 60.91 per cent.

The early history of Gujarat is lost in antiquity and is intermingled with myths and legends. But later periods saw this state as part of the great Mauryan and Gupta empires. Gujarat passed under the Muslim rule by the end of the thirteenth century. As a result the state evolved a happy synthesis of Hindu and Muslim cultures.

The major industry of the state is textiles.

The principal language of the state is Gujarati, and Hindi is commonly understood and spoken. The language of the people is rich in literature and folklore and has absorbed the legends and myths from across the borders.

20
THE HEROES OF GUJARAT

THE camel plodded slowly, leaving its footprints in the thick layers of dust on the uneven roads. The night was dark, and the camel driver and his passenger sat quietly looking at the countryside. They were coming from Dholka. They stopped near a deserted temple of Shiva and the traveller told the driver to rest. "Let us stop here under the trees. You give the camel some water and feed it. I have to go to the village, and will return soon; but do not worry about me if I am delayed."

The traveller did not want to be recognised, so he carefully tied a scarf around his beard, pulled down his turban to hide his forehead, and covered himself with a white cloth. He was richly attired, he carried a dagger at his waist, and slung around his shoulder was his sword. Slowly he proceeded towards the village. All round lay destruction. Qutb-ud-din had ransacked and plundered everywhere. He sat down on a stone parapet and looked sorrowfully around him, recalling the past beauty. A herd of buffaloes was being driven home.

It was dusk, and the cattle were moving quietly. He went to one of the shepherds and asked, "Where is the house of Devraj Patkil?" The shepherd pointed out the house, and the traveller walked with them, till they reached the house.

Softly, he went inside. The wind had blown off the lamp. The traveller went in and hid behind a big water jar. A woman was standing before the fire making some *rotis* from *bajra*. She was a Rajput, and the years of hard work had not in any way lessened her beauty. The flames of the fire danced on her face. He wanted to call out to her. It was after many years that he was seeing her again, but he changed his mind and decided to wait.

Soon he heard the sound of horse's hooves, and Devraj Patkil came in. His wife called out to him, "Come and eat, the *rotis* are hot."

"Where is Viru?" he asked.

"He must be playing," she replied.

"I will wait for him," Devraj said, "I cannot eat without him."

From what the traveller saw and heard, he was deeply touched. He had come to the house with the sole intention of killing Devraj Patkil, because the woman was his wife, and Viru his own son. But now he did not know what he should do. He was surprised to see the love and devotion Devraj had for Viru, who was not his own son. "Go and bring Viru, then I will eat," Devraj told his wife.

She went out calling "Viru, Viru." Devraj sat quietly deep in thought. Suddenly looking up, he saw a shadow on the wall. He shouted, "Who are you?" The traveller stood up, and removed the scarf from his beard and the white cloth with which he had covered himself. "You do not recognise me. My face is scarred from many battles."

"Lavan Prasad!" exclaimed Devraj.

"Yes, I am Lavan Prasad. I came here to kill you and take my wife and son back, but I am defeated seeing the love and care you give them both. She had always wanted a peaceful life. My mind is at peace and I must go." Saying this he returned the sword into the scabbard and was ready to leave. Devraj said, "Stay and eat with me and see your son."

"I will stay, but do not tell anyone who I am," said Lavan Prasad.

They sat in the darkened courtyard, and the woman came in pulling Viru by the hand. "He did not want to come. He is getting so strong, I can hardly lift him these days. At night he will not sleep until I tell him stories of war and chivalry," the mother said. Viru was a big, handsome boy, and with tears in his eyes his father looked at him and touched him on the head.

After finishing his food, Lavan Prasad prepared to leave. They walked together to the gate. "Patan has fallen," Lavan Prasad said. "Make my son a brave boy, and when he is old enough send him to me at Dholka." With these words Lavan Prasad returned to the temple of Shiva and mounted his camel. "Gujarat will be rebuilt," he told the camel driver. "My son is growing up and getting ready."

After spending the night at Viramgam, Lavan Prasad mounted his camel and continued his journey to Patan. Soon he came to a village. Near a pond a family was standing, a mother with six children. A horse was tied to a tree. The woman, a widow, was dressed in a very old red sari, which had been patched at several places. Her arms were bare of bangles. Her three sons were going on a journey. "Have you said your prayers?" the mother asked them. "Obey your guru, and look after yourselves." The eldest of the three boys was called Lunig. He was sickly, and was interested in sculpture and painting. Vastig and Tejig followed. They were going to school at Patan. "Do not worry about us mother, we will soon be men," the boys replied. They spoke to their sisters and asked them to help their mother with the grinding of the wheat, in fetching water from the well and told them to look after her. "The sun is rising, and there comes a woman with a water pot on her head. All good omens; now begin your journey." The eldest boy Lunig mounted the horse, while the other two walked behind. The mother watched with tears in her eyes until they were out of sight.

Lavan Prasad had been watching this little drama and he came up to the woman and asked her, "Are those your boys? Where are they going?" "To Patan, to study with a guru," she said. He spurred his camel and soon caught up with the boys.

"Where are you going boys?" he asked them. "We are going to Patan to study literature and sculpture, reading and writing," they said. Lavan Prasad laughed at them saying, "Learn literature, but do not learn sword fighting, *lathi* fighting and self-defence. All this is forbidden in your religion. You are Jains, and you cannot kill—so learn sculpture." Lavan Prasad glared at the boys, and they who had never seen anyone like him before, ran even faster, to keep up with his camel, and to talk to him. "You should learn how to protect and defend women; all you will learn is to wear a red *teeka* on your head and bow to your priest in the temple." The boys were getting angry and said to Lavan Prasad, "We are not going to a temple but to Kumar Deo's Ashram to study." "Will they teach you how to wrestle, how to fight with a dagger, and sword play, and how to use a bow and arrow?" "We do not know," one of the boys said, "but if they do we would like to learn." "No, no, do not learn; this kind of education will make you like me: brave in battle but poor, without any money. You will not be able to hang lamps outside your house like all the rich people do in Patan," said Lavan Prasad. He continued, "If you study, and learn to write Sanskrit, you will be given honour in the court of the king. Your Sanskrit verses will please the king even if he does not understand what you are saying—even if you abuse Gujarat." The boys were really angry by now and one of them picked up a stone to hit Lavan Prasad. But he went on teasing them saying, "You are *Baniyas*; perhaps you will teach the kings of Patan to observe *ahimsa* and they will never fight."

Many years passed. Tejig (Tejpal) and Vastig (Vastupal) grew into fine men. Tejpal went to Dholka where he owned a grocer's shop. But he kept himself fit with fighting and the practice of archery. Vastupal became a scholar. He was very wise and able and became a minister in the court of the king.

As this story comes to an end, Gujarat was ruled by Lavan Prasad at Patan. In Dholka, Viru, son of Lavan Prasad, was on the throne. Lavan Prasad sent for Tejpal to lead an army against the enemies of the king. He became a General. Gujarat flourished under the rule of these men.

•

21
THE SON

THE village of Chalala was the home of Apa Devat, a notorious robber chief. As the story opens, we see him sitting in council, surrounded by the Kathis of the village One of the men offers him tobacco, the best and most expensive, saying in flattering tones, "Only Apa Devat can do justice to this tobacco." Another man presents him with a *hookah*, inlaid with silver and gold work. Then someone else offers him a red banner for his horse. All these gifts are accepted with a quiet smile. Apa Devat looks around, twirling his moustache and thinking no end of himself.

Among the crowd, a little aloof, sits a Kathi from another village. He watches all this and very quietly asks the man sitting near him, "Since when have the Kathis begun offering gifts and flattery? Who is Apa Devat?" The man answered saying, "Apa Lakha, you are still a boy. Your village has not been plundered by his horses and men. If this had happened to you, you would have offered him the best mangoes from your trees." Apa Lakha shook his head and replied, "No, no, I will never offer anything out of fear to anyone. It would be better if my mangoes are eaten by the birds. We Kathis are born equal." Apa Devat heard the last few words and cried out angrily, "Who is this who speaks such rash words? Come out and speak up."

"I am Lakha. All Kathis are equal. I am distressed to see my fellowmen offering you gifts out of fear. You should be ashamed to accept what they give you." Apa Devat was angry, and he said to Lakha, "Build a fort around your village to protect it, for, I will come and destroy you." Lakha said, "You are welcome. I am the owner of a small village, and cannot afford to build a fort, but I will be prepared to meet you, and will receive you with honours." Apa Devat accepted the challenge. In the meantime an elder member of the group fell at his feet asking him to pardon the words of Lakha, saying he was young and hot-headed and did not know what he was saying. But Lakha was not afraid and said to Apa Devat, "I repeat my invitation. Come when you like. The sword belongs to him who wears it with honour." Saying this he mounted his horse and rode away.

The name of Lakha's village was known as Lakhapadar. It stood on the banks of the river Shel. The water flowed over big, black rocks, gurgling happily. The soil was rich and flowers bloomed everywhere. Peacocks roamed around in the fields and sat under the shade of the banyan trees with their beautiful tails spread out. Fish swam in the sunlit water of the pond. The villagers had built a "gowmukhi" near the banyan tree, and everyone drank the fresh clear water. The people of this village were happy, brave and kind.

When Lakha returned to the village he told his people what had happened, and asked them to keep themselves in readiness for the visit of Apa Devat. Months passed, and Apa Devat did not come. Everyone thought that either he was afraid or had forgotten about the challenge. One day Lakha had to leave the village and go to Chalala on some business. He remained out for the night. On that very night Apa Devat and his men plundered the village of Lakhapadar. The villagers put up a brave fight with their spears but they were powerless against the band of fierce robbers on their swift horses.

After Apa Devat had ransacked the village, killing many, he went to the house of Lakha, and called out to him, "Kathi, come out. It was you who challenged me. Why do you hide now?" His wife, hearing these words, came out and said, "Apa Devat, if Kathi had been here, he would have met you on the opposite side of the river Shel. He would never have hidden from you." Saying this she went inside.

All this time, Heerbai, the fifteen-year-old daughter of Lakha, was standing near the door, leaning against the pillar of the house. She saw the fierce look in the eyes of the robber chief, the blood-stained spear in his hand, and watched the horse on which he sat, foaming at the mouth. But she was not afraid. Suddenly Devat saw a litle colt grazing in the shade of a tree. It was a very beautiful animal. So Devat thought he would take it away and show the surrounding villages how he had defeated Lakha, and also got a new colt. He got down from his horse and rested the spear against a tree, and bent down to untie the colt. Heerbai realised that this was her only chance to save the honour of her father, and she must not lose any time. In a flash she picked up the spear and with all her strength plunged it into the back of Apa Devat, thereby pinning him down to the ground.

In the meantime the robber gang, thinking their leader had gone ahead, left the village and rode away towards the forest, where they were supposed to meet after the raid.

The news of the plundering of his village had by now reached Apa Lakha. He was ashamed and unhappy, and did not want to return to the village. He felt that it was he who had brought trouble to his own village, and he had not been there to protect it. Meanwhile, Heerbai had sent a messenger to her father asking him to come home immediately. He realised that his daughter must have a good reason to send for him, so he rode home as fast as he could.

When he reached home, his daughter took him to the garden and removed the white cloth with which she had covered the body of Apa Devat. Apa Lakha was astonished, and overjoyed. He blessed Heerbai, and touching her on her head said, "Everyone says I have only a daughter; but today, through your courage and bravery, you have proved that you are also my son."

FOLK TALES OF HARYANA

Haryana

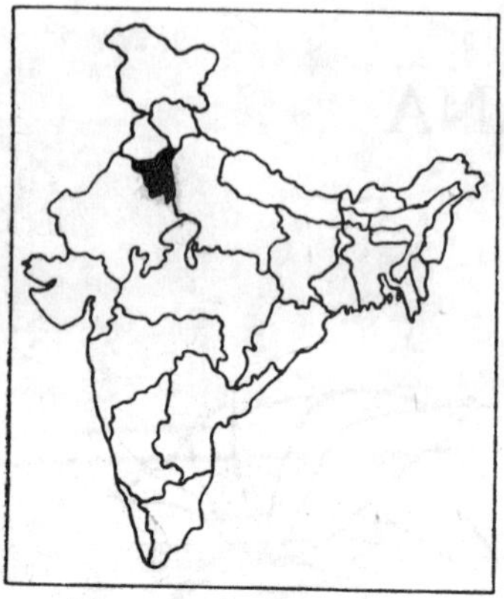

Haryana state, born on November 1, 1966, has an ancient heritage. The people of the state are sturdy, joy-loving and persevering. Haryana has produced many heroes in the past and has always been a popular area for recruitment to the armed forces. The word "Haryana" is derived from two words, 'Hari' (God) and 'Ayana' (Vehicle) and means the abode of Gods.

Haryana's social and cultural history is intimately associated with many famous *rishis*, heroes and legends. Kurukshetra in Haryana, saw the battle between the Kauravas and the Pandavas, chronicled in the *Mahabharata*, and it was here that the *Gita* was preached by Lord Krishna to the wavering Arjuna. Panipat, where India's political fate was once decided, was the scene of the three battles, in Haryana.

Haryana has a rich treasure of folklore, orally carried on from generation to generation. Folk tales are an integral part of this folklore.

Some of the folk stories and legends were later reduced to writing and preserved in the form of verses called *raginis* and they were converted into *swangs*, i.e., plays. Haryana is full of temples, monuments and landmarks connected with legends and historical events.

The state has an area of 44,212 sq km with a population of 16,317,715; density 874 per sq km and literacy 55.33 per cent. The capital is in Chandigarh, which is also the capital of Punjab State and the headquarters of a Union Territory of the same name. The main occupation of the people is agriculture. The State language is Hindi but the people of the State speak a dialect called Haryanvi.

22
THE TRAVELLER'S STORY

FOUR friends lived in a village. Their names were Ramu, Shyamu, Bansi and Biru. All these friends were in the habit of concocting and repeating tales.

Once, while coming from the weekly market, they rested in a *sarai* (rest house). There they saw a traveller wearing very fine clothes. The four friends decided to cheat him of his clothes.

They approached the stranger and engaged him in a conversation.

"Where are you coming from, sir?" they asked.

"Please let me know who you are," said the stranger.

"I am coming from a merchant village," said Ramu.

"My house is deep in the forest full of wild animals," said Shyam.

"I have my house near the river," said Bansi, "which is very long and difficult to cross."

"And I live on the top of the highest hill near by," said Biru.

The traveller said that he was coming from a distant land after trading for many years. Ramu said, "The night is long. Let each one of us tell a story. The one who tells the most unbelievable story will win. Others will be obliged to obey whatever he says." The traveller agreed.

Having made the traveller walk into the trap the four friends winked at each other as if to say, 'The old fool! How we have trapped him.'

First Shyamu started: "Immediately after I was born my mother asked my father to pluck some plums for her from the tree in front of the house. My father refused saying that the tree was too high to climb. So she asked all my brothers, but they also declined. I gently slipped out of my cot, climbed the tree, plucked the plums and placed a basketful at the kitchen door. My mother was very happy to see them there not knowing how they had come. She ate as many plums as she liked and distributed the rest to the neighbours."

Shyamu waited for comments from the traveller but he only nodded. It was Ramu's turn. "When I was a week old," he said, "I went for a stroll in the forest. I found a tree there loaded with ripe tamarind. So I climbed up. I had as much tamarind as I wished to eat. I did not know how to climb down. So I went to the village searching for a ladder and leaned it on the tree and climbed down."

After completing his story he also looked hopefully at the stranger for comments, but again he only nodded. Then Biru started his story. "I had my first adventure fairly late. When I was a year old I chased a rabbit but to my surprise when the rabbit went into the jungle it turned into a tiger. So I told the tiger, that if he intended to eat me it would not be fair because I had actually chased a rabbit and not a tiger. But he sprang on me. So I caught his jaw and tore him into two pieces."

Bansi was sure that this story would surely impress the old fellow. But no, the man was just nodding with not a flicker of doubt on his face. Defeated at heart they rested their hopes on Bansi. "Last year," said Bansi, "I took a boat and went fishing. There were other fishermen also but none of us could get a single fish. I left the boat and dived into the river. Down I went and after three or four hours I touched the bottom. Then to my horror I came upon a fish as big as a huge monster swallowing all other fishes. Before it could see me, I charged and gave it a mighty blow with my fist. The fish was dead. As I was hungry, I made a fire and roasted the fish, and ate it all by myself. Then I floated back and told the other fishermen of my adventure."

The traveller nodded again in appreciation of the story and did not utter a word that the story was absurd. Crestfallen Biru's companions also nodded.

Now it was the traveller's turn. He cleared his throat and began.

"Some years ago I had a cotton farm in which there was one big tree, bright red in colour. For a long time the tree was bare without any branches or leaves, but after sometime it grew four branches. On each branch there came a bud which blossomed into a flower and later a big fruit was formed. I plucked the fruit but when I cut it open, a young man jumped out of the fruit. Since the four young men grew in my farm they were my slaves."

His listeners nodded. The traveller continued, " I put them to work on the farm. I soon discovered that they were very lazy and would not work until I gave them a good beating.

"One day I had to go to another village and on my return I found that they had run away. Since then I have been looking for them. How lucky I am that I have found you four at last! Young men, you have to come back to my farm. You know that you are my slaves."

The four young men looked disbelievingly at each other. They were completely outwitted and cornered by the traveller. If they said they believed him, then they had to become his slaves and if they disbelieved saying the story could not be true they had to fulfil his demand. Therefore they said that he would have his wish. The traveller said, "I do not want to have you at the farm. Give me your clothes." The young men quickly stripped and gave their clothes. The traveller made a big bundle of them and walked away.

23
THE MISCHIEVOUS HELPER

A JAT lived in a village. He needed a helping hand for his farm. But everybody demanded exorbitant wages, so he had to go without one.

One day he came across a stranger who was in search of work. The Jat asked him what he would like as wages. The stranger replied, "Please do not bother about the wages, I am prepared to work for food and clothing." The Jat was very happy and agreed. But the man said, "Sir, there is only one condition. I play one prank once a year. Only if you agree to this you may engage me as a servant." The Jat thought that it would be impossible to get a cheap servant like him, so it would be better not to lose him. As for mischief, he could be on his guard. So he employed him. The man worked very well. The farm prospered. The Jat began to thrive. He had enough leisure also and was so happy and contented with the new hand that he almost forgot about the talk of mischief.

Five or six months passed smoothly. One day the helper thought, 'Now I should play some mischief with the Jat.'

The Jat's sister-in-law and brother had also come to stay with them; the stranger decided to do something that day.

He approached the Jat's wife and said, "Good lady, your husband is ill and may not live for long. No cure is possible. If you do not believe me just try this. You lick his back when he takes his bath in the evening. You will find its taste salty."

Then he reported to the Jat and said, "Sir, your wife seems to be losing her mind. Beware of her."

Next he went to the Jat's sister-in-law and said, "Your brother-in-law seems to be cross with his wife. I expect he will give her a sound thrashing this evening. You must keep close by."

After saying all this the stranger disappeared quietly.

The Jat returned in the evening from the farm. He asked his wife to prepare water for his bath for in Haryana it is usual for the wife to get water for the husband's bath. While her husband sat without his shirt, she was tempted to test what the servant had said, so she went near him and licked his back. The Jat jumped up crying, "O! she is really insane, and now she wants to bite me." Stick in hand, he rushed at her. Now the sister-in-law had already informed her husband about the servant's talk, so he was already there, prepared for the occasion. He pounced upon the Jat and snatched his stick. There was a fight. Hearing the noise the neighbours gathered there. When the whole thing was talked about, it became clear that it was all due to the mischief played by the helper. A search was made for him. But he had already disappeared. The villagers had a good laugh.

24
THE JAT'S MELONS

THERE was a king who was keen to know how his subjects were living. He used to move about in plain clothes with his prime minister to do this.

During one such trip the king went very far. He was very hungry and thirsty. He saw a Jat's garden full of tempting melons. The king asked the Jat if he would sell the melons.

"No," replied the Jat, "they are not for sale."

"Then what will you do with them? Surely you will not eat all these melons yourself," said the king.

The Jat replied, "They are for the king. I am going to present my melons to the king."

Now the king and his minister were in plain clothes. The Jat did not recognise them. The king was a bit disappointed by the Jat's refusal to sell him the melons. In disgust he said, "You are sure to present these melons to the king?"

"Yes sir," replied the Jat.

"And supposing he does not accept them?"

"Then he can go to hell," the Jat said bluntly.

The king did not say anything. After some time the Jat visited the king with the melons. He recognised the king.

The king said, "Well farmer, you have brought these melons for me?"

"Yes, Your Majesty.'

"And supposing I do not accept them?"

"Then sir," replied the Jat shyly, "you already know the answer."

The king had a hearty laugh at the ready wit of the Jat and he gave the Jat a handsome reward for the melons.

25

THE FOOLISH COBBLER

AXE in hand, the cobbler climbed up a tree to cut some firewood. He seated himself at the outer end of the thick bough and started cutting it from the other end. Just then a Brahmin happened to pass that way. The Brahmin said, "O fool, what is this? Are you not wanted by your family?"

"Why, sir, why are you so uncharitable in your remarks?" asked the cobbler.

The Brahmin replied, "Don't you see that you are cutting the same branch on which you are sitting? I wonder how you can escape falling down!"

"You mind your business," said the cobbler.

"All right, go ahead then," said the Brahmin and went his way.

No sooner had the Brahmin left him than the cobbler dropped down with a thud. He got up and hastily ran to the Brahmin and said, "Sir, I did fall down as you had said. You can certainly predict future events. Tell me one thing more. When shall I die?"

The Brahmin laughed and said, "Bravo! Cobbler, you are a fool after all. Anyone could see that you would fall down. There was nothing to predict about it."

But the cobbler held his feet and said, "No, sir, you do know everything. Why don't you tell me when I am going to die?"

To get rid of him, the Brahmin pulled out a thread from his shawl and putting it round the cobbler's wrist said, "You will die the moment this thread breaks." The cobbler was convinced. On returning home he related the story to his wife. He wore the thread with great care. One day the thread snapped while he was taking his bath. He started weeping aloud. His wife came running and asked, "What has happened to you?" she asked.

"Do you not see the broken thread? I am dead now."

His wife said, "No, you are not dead. You are alive."

"What a fool you are! Did I not tell you that the Brahmin had predicted that I would die when the thread breaks?"

Hearing his loud crying the neighbours also gathered. They enquired what the matter was. He said, "Friends, I have died. Now you may take me to the funeral pyre. A dead body should not be kept long in the house."

His friends prepared a bier and laid him on it and took him towards the burning ground. On the way the funeral party met a stranger. The stranger asked them if they would tell him the way to a certain village. The mourners said that they did not know it and were not in a position to help him. Hearing them the cobbler sat up and said, "Listen, when I was alive, that village was towards the north." Upon this the people put him down and ran away. The cobbler was much surprised. But he came back home. His wife greeted him. The cobbler was at last convinced that he was not dead.

FOLK TALES OF HIMACHAL PRADESH

Himachal Pradesh

Himachal Pradesh is a land of mountains and snow, lush green forests, swirling streams, captivating lakes, verdant dales and emerald meadows. The people are simple, sturdy, joy-loving and hard working. The women love colour and mirth and are as hard working as the menfolk.

There is a rich legacy of folk tales. Much of the folklore has grown around the deities and demons. Himachal Pradesh is known for its colourful fairs which provide recreation and marketing places for a happy and joyous people who love to dance and sing.

The state language is Hindi. Its capital is in Simla. The state has an area of 55,673 sq km, and a population of 5,111,079, density of 92 per sq km, literacy 63.54 per cent and sex ratio 988 females per 1000 males. The state is bound by Jammu and Kashmir in the north, Punjab in the west, Haryana in the south, Uttar Pradesh in the south-east and Tibet in the east.

Seventy-five per cent of the people are engaged in agriculture and industries absorb a small number. A variety of agro-climatic conditions make it an ideal region for growing many kinds of fruits.

26
RAJA BANA BHAT

LONG, long ago Bana Bhat ruled over Kangra. He was an ideal and simple king. He earned his own living by making ropes and selling them at a fair price. He got the name of Bana as *bana* means *rope* and *bhat* means to distribute.

He had a very faithful and religious wife named Mehto. She did all the household work and drew water in an earthen pot from a well near the fort early in the morning. During her leisure she used to spin and both she and the king wore handspun cloth only. Raja Bana Bhat stayed in a hut near the fort.

All his subjects were very happy. The people did not pay taxes and had plenty to eat.

A big fair was held in Kangra. Men, women and children in very large numbers came to see the fair, made purchases and sold their wares. They put on their best clothes for the occasion. Once the king and the queen also went to see the fair in their usual dress. They moved among the men and women freely. There were no bodyguards, no servants, no pomp and show. Those who had seen the king before only could recognise him. A merchant and his wife came to see the fair. He was the richest man in Kangra valley. The merchant's wife had a necklace worth nine lakhs of rupees (navlakha). People were curious to see the necklace and wherever they went people followed them.

The king and the queen also met the merchant and his wife. They stood there for a little while and started talking. The merchant's wife talked to the queen. She was very proud of her necklace. She was haughty even when she talked to the queen. The queen felt rather small for not having a necklace. She wanted to have a similar necklace.

The next day when the king returned home after his work he found the queen very sad. This went on for quite a few days. One day the king asked the queen why she was sullen.

The queen was silent for some time and then said, "I am fed up with my wretched life. We are the king and queen but we have to toil for our bread the whole day. I have no ornaments to wear and we lead a very miserable life. Unless and until I get a necklace worth nine lakhs of rupees I will not have any mental peace."

The king was very sorry to hear this. He kept on explaining to her the reasons for leading a simple life but nothing seemed to have any effect on her.

Finally the king taxed his subjects to collect the amount and got the *navlakha* necklace made. The queen wore the necklace in the morning and admired herself in the mirror.

When the king returned from his work he was very tired and had fever. He called the queen and asked for some water. The queen came near the king and found that he had high fever. She sat near him. He asked for more water. She took the pitcher and tied its neck with a rope and dropped it in the well. But to her utter surprise the pitcher melted away as soon as it touched the water. She felt very sorry. She realised the reason for her not being able to get water as she had lost her simplicity. She threw away her necklace and wore a simple dress and took another pitcher. Only then could she fill it with water. By the time the queen returned with the water the king had died.

The queen wept bitterly and went mad and died a few days later.

Kangra, which was once upon a time a prosperous region, became poor after the death of such a king. Even now the people of Kangra recall Bana Bhat and feel that the poverty of the area is due to the queen discarding her simplicity.

27
LABOUR AND GOLD

LORD Shiva and Parvati have many devotees in Himachal Pradesh. There are many temples built for Shiva and Parvati. The hill people always refer to Parvati as a goddess of kindness.

One day while Lord Shiva and Goddess Parvati were on their journey back to their abode, Parvati said to Shiva, "Lord! You are very cruel and seldom take pity on the suffering human beings. You ignore their prayers. There are many people on the earth who are not even getting enough to eat."

Shiva on hearing her, said, "What has happened now? Who is suffering?" Parvati did not miss this opportunity. She pointed out to a beggar on the ground and said that he was very poor and something should be done for him.

Shiva explained to her why many people suffered like that on earth. This was the result of *Karma* (action) and they were all reaping the fruits of their own actions of this life or of the past.

But Parvati was insistent and requested that the beggar be helped. Lord Shiva then dropped a golden brick in the beggar's way.

The beggar had a bag on his shoulder. He was walking back home brooding over his poverty. He thought that if he did not die before he got old, then he would soon be blind and would have to lead a miserable life. He wanted to experiment how he would manage as a blind man. He started walking with his eyes closed and so passed the golden brick without seeing it.

Goddess Parvati was watching. She was very disappointed when the beggar passed the golden brick without noticing it.

Lord Shiva, with a twinkle in his eyes, told Parvati, "You see, your poor beggar did not even look at the golden brick. So do many opportunities flit by a man without being utilised. It is only good actions that bring a reward. Do you realise that?" Goddess Parvati nodded although in her heart she had great pity for the beggar.

28
BUDDHINATH

In Himachal in the olden days a man could have more than one wife. As a matter of fact it was often taken as a mark of affluence if a man had more than one wife. This is a story of how a man managed to win seven girls with his intelligence

In Kurmanchal there were three brothers. The eldest could produce six bags of rice in a very small plot of land. The second was capable of milking any cow and get one maund of milk. The third brother who was very intelligent composed songs and sang them. Their names were Siddhinath, Riddhinath and Buddhinath. Siddhi means a person will always be successful. Riddhi means a person will always be self-sufficient. Buddhi implies intelligence.

All the three bothers were just as they were named. The youngest brother preferred isolation, so his brothers took him to be a fool and called him Buddhunath which means a fool.

The three brothers had to buy some pulses, oil, etc. For this purpose they had to go to Almora. There were actually two roads leading to Almora. One was a shorter route and the other longer.

Siddhinath started for Almora taking the shorter route. After covering a long distance he came across a betel shop. The shopkeeper spoke to him very affectionately and offered him tea. Siddhinath took the tea. The shopkeeper then said that he would narrate an incident which he would have to admit as true. Otherwise he would cut his nose and ears. Siddhinath accepted the condition thinking that it would not be difficult for him to nod. The shopkeeper then said, "I have an ox which has five horns." Siddhinath then said, "It is possible. In our own village a lady gave birth to quintuplets. Your ox has five horns. It is all nature's wish."

The shopkeeper then said, "One horn will go to the Himalayas and bring snow and ice. The second will go down the deep sea and bring rubies and pearls. The third will go to Kabul and bring all kinds of dry fruits. The fourth will go to Bengal and bring mouthwatering *Rasagollas* (a kind of sweet famous in Bengal). The fifth will go to Delhi and bring antiques."

The shopkeeper had not even finished his narration when suddenly Siddhinath said, "It is true that you may be having an ox having five horns but their horns could never do such unusual acts."

The shopkeeper then called his son and asked him to cut his nose and ears. Siddhinath begged to be excused. He surrendered his money and his possessions but the shopkeeper did not leave him. He cut his nose and ears and left him.

Siddhinath hid the stubs of his nose and ears in a towel and came back home. Siddhinath told his brothers that dacoits had cut his nose and ears but spared him his money.

Riddhinath, who heard his brother's story, thought of taking revenge. He started on his journey. He also took the shorter route. He also met the same shopkeeper. Riddhinath also lost his ears and nose and returned home.

Buddhinath who was the youngest brother got ready to go to Almora. Both his elder brothers allowed him to go. Buddhinath took the shorter route and approached the same betel shop. The shopkeeper started narrating the story. All the time while listening to the story Buddhinath was looking inside the kitchen. He saw seven ladies busy grinding yellow turmeric. Buddhinath kept on nodding his head. When the shopkeeper finished his story, Buddhinath said, "Uncle, I also have a story to tell. If you say 'no' any time I will cut your nose and ears. Do you agree to the condition?"

The shopkeeper agreed to the condition. Buddhinath said, "We were seven brothers. All of us were married and each one of us had a pretty wife. We were all very proud of them. One day a gusty wind came and all the wives were blown away."

The shopkeeper said, "All this is possible. Your pride in them snatched all of them from you."

Buddhinath then said, "But, uncle, I am seeing all of them here. Please tell me whether it is correct or not?"

The shopkeeper was in a fix. If he said 'Yes' he would have to lose his daughters-in-law. If he were to say 'No' then he would have to lose his nose and ears. The shopkeeper gathered courage and said, "Well you must be able to recognise all of them." Buddhinath said, "Well, their hands were yellow."

The shopkeeper said, "The hands of my daughters-in-law are fair." He called all of them and asked them to show their hands. The hands of all of them were yellow.

The shopkeeper was very much puzzled. He called all his sons and told them everything. They told their father to give away his daughters-in-law and that they would marry a second time. The sons were not in favour of their father losing his nose and ears. Buddhinath brought the beautiful ladies to his house and lived happily with all of them.

The shopkeeper spent the remaining part of his life in *Hari Kirtan* (singing in praise of God).

FOLK TALES OF KARNATAKA

Karnataka

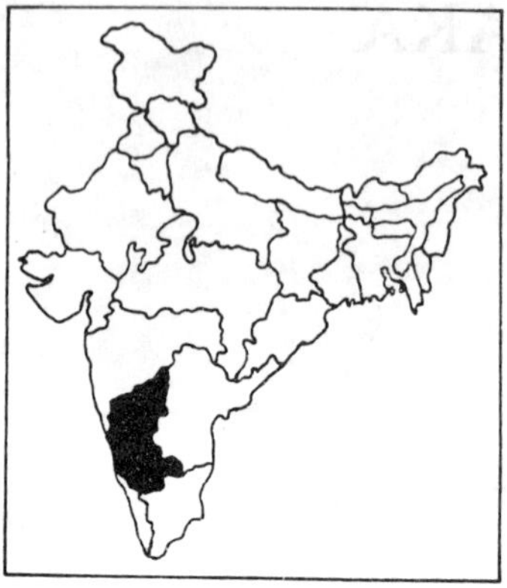

Karnataka is the eighth largest state in India, both in area and population. The principal state language is Kannada. Its capital is in Bangalore. It has an area of 1,91,791 sq km with a population of 44,817,398, density 234 persons per sq km, literacy, 55.98 per cent.

Karnataka is situated on the western edge of the Deccan plateau and has for its neighbours Maharashtra and Goa in the north, Andhra Pradesh in the east and Tamil Nadu and Kerala in the south. In the west it opens out on to the Arbian Sea.

The history of Karnataka goes back to the days of the epics. The capital of Bali and Sugreeva, 'the Monkey kings' of the *Ramayana*, is said to have been Hampi in Bellary district. Vatapi associated with sage Agastya, is Badami in Bijapur district.

Karnataka is predominantly agricultural. The state is rich in mineral resources. It accounts for 85 per cent of the raw silk produced in the country.

The people are highly cultured, traditional and love the indigenous folklore.

29

FORTUNE AND INTELLIGENCE

A MOTHER had two sons named Fortune and Intelligence. They met a poor man who brought firewood from the forest daily and sold it in the bazaar. Even if he was ill for a day he would lose his daily gruel.

Fortune said to his brother Intelligence: "Look brother! You rule over the whole world by giving people education and intelligence. What would happen to this man tomorrow, when he would be too old and weak to work?" Intelligence replied, "Brother Fortune, you must help the poor man by giving him luck." It was finally decided that Intelligence should try to help him first.

Intelligence gave him a gold pendant which was worth three thousand rupees. He told the poor man, whose name was Kencha, "Build a house for a thousand rupees. Spend another thousand for your marriage. With the remaining thousand rupees you could buy all the things you need for your house. Stop selling firewood from today." Brother Fortune was watching all this and smiled quietly to himself. The poor man Kencha took the pendant and left for the village. He felt thirsty. He kept the pendant on a stone slab near a pond and drank water. As the pendant was glittering in the sun, an eagle taking it to be a cobra, swooped down, picked it up and flew away.

Kencha felt very sad. He resumed his occupation of cutting and selling firewood. Brother Fortune said to his brother Intelligence, "This is very unfair. You should not snatch away what you have given." Brother Intelligence replied, "He is very proud. He lost what I had given him as a gift."

Brother Intelligence gave Kencha some gold. He told him, "This would fetch you five thousand rupees. If you spend it properly you would no longer be a poor man."

Again the poor man went out. He felt thirsty on his way to the village. He did not risk losing the gift this time. So he kept the gold in his pocket. But as he bent over the pond, all the gold fell into the water. "How unlucky I am," he told himself. He had lost the day's wages also. He went begging to a couple of houses and got a handful of rice to eat. The next day he returned to the forest to cut firewood.

This time brother Intelligence gave him a pot full of money. The poor man ran straight to his house without stopping anywhere on the way. But as he was very hungry and thirsty, he fell down unconscious near his doorstep. An old woman who was passing by stole the pot.

Both the brothers were surprised to find Kencha again cutting firewood the next day. Brother Fortune told his brother Intelligence, "You gave him riches thrice. But he could not keep them. Let us not give him any more riches today. Just follow me."

Again they approached him. They asked for the price of each bundle of firewood. He demanded twelve annas. They gave him the money and told him, "You buy rice for four annas, get salt and chillies for another four annas. Buy vegetables with the remaining four annas."

The poor man spent only ten annas on provisions. As he was returning home, he saw an old woman selling fish. He bought a big fish with the remaining two annas. As he made a very good bargain he felt very happy. He wanted to cook the fish first. As he had no firewood in the house, he went out to get some. There was a neem tree right in front of his house. As he was cutting a branch, he saw something glittering in the eagle's nest on the tree. He climbed up to the nest and saw that it was the gold pendant which he had lost.

He was overjoyed. He took it and shouted, "At last, I got you back." The old woman who had stolen his pot of money was living in a hut on the other side of the tree. She heard his shout of joy. She thought that he had seen the pot of money in her hut, when he had climbed to the top of the tree. She returned the pot of money to him, saying, "I have not touched even a paisa in the pot." The poor man, Kencha, lived happily after that.

Intelligence realised that without Fortune he could not get very far.

30
THE FOOLISH VILLAGERS

ONE day, in the village Periyapatna, seven-year-old Rama was digging in the kitchen-garden to plant some bean seeds. He was a dutiful son always trying to help his widowed mother as much as possible. As he was digging, he found an earthen pot full of money in the ground. He ran to his mother and gave her the pot in great excitement.

His mother bought a buffalo with the money. She asked Rama to take it out for grazing. After sometime he fell asleep under the shade of a tree. While he was asleep, the buffalo strayed into the field of the village chief, Byre Gowda. Byre Gowda was a very short-tempered man. He ordered his servants to kill the animal.

The mother scolded Rama for his carelessness. She went to the village-chief and apologised to him. She begged to have the hide of the dead buffalo. She dried it in the sun for a few days.

One day Rama set out to the market in the neighbouring village to sell the hide. As he had started late in the afternoon, darkness fell soon. He climbed a mango tree and sat on it quietly with the hide.

After sometime three thieves came with three trunks full of sarees, dhotis and money. They wanted to rest for a while under the mango tree before proceeding to their own village. One thief said, "Somebody had told me that a ghost lived on this mango tree." On hearing this Rama made a thumping noise with the hide on the branch of the tree. The thieves were alarmed. Rama then dropped the buffalo hide in their midst. The thieves were terrified and ran away leaving all the loot under the tree.

At dawn Rama got down and brought all the things home. When the other farmers asked him in surprise how he had got them, he replied, "I took the buffalo hide to the fair. I got money, sarees and dhotis in exchange for it. There is a great demand for buffalo hides."

Some farmers killed their buffaloes and took their hides to the market. But nobody wanted to buy. They came home disappointed and angry. In anger they decided to burn Rama's house. Rama overheard their conversation. Quietly he shifted to a neighbour's house with his mother, taking all his belongings with him.At night the angry farmers set fire to his hut.

In the morning Rama collected all the ashes and filled them in three sacks. He hired a donkey and loading the sacks on its back, he announced that he was on his way to the market to sell them. All the people laughed at him and called him a big fool. On the way, it became dark and he halted under a tree. After sometime, a jeweller came that way from Arasikere with three bags. The jeweller asked Rama, "Who are you? What have you got in the three sacks?" Rama replied, "I have small pearls in them. I am on my way to Bhadravati where there is a big demand for small pearls." The jeweller said, "I have big pearls in my bags. I will take them to Mandya to sell them."

It was then decided between them that Rama should sleep first, while the jeweller kept watch over the bags. Later, the jeweller slept, and Rama was guarding the treasure. The cunning Rama quietly exchanged the bags.

In the morning, both of them parted and went their ways and Rama returned to his village with the pearls.

On hearing this, some foolish farmers burnt down their houses and collecting the ashes took them to the Arasikere market. As they were sitting on the roadside with heaps of ashes in front of them, a breeze blew the ashes all over the market. All the people who were in the market got angry and drove away the farmers.

The angry farmers got hold of Rama and beat him up. The king of Mysore heard the story and summoned Rama to the court. Rama told his story. The king called the farmers of Periyapatna and scolded them for their foolishness. As he was very impressed with Rama's cleverness he gave his daughter, the princess Vishalakshi, in marriage to him. Rama and his mother lived in the palace happily ever after.

31

PRINCESS LAKSHMI—THE DEVOTED WIFE

LONG ago there was a king in Bangalore who had a daughter called Lakshmi. She was married to Prince Krishna Raja of Mysore.

Some months after the wedding there was a drought in Mysore. Both the king and the queen died in despair. The people drove out the prince and his younger brother Narasimha Raja.

The two of them moved to another city. They did some odd jobs and lived as poor labourers. Princess Lakshmi insisted on joining her husband Krishna Raja but her parents opposed the idea as they did not want their daughter to live like a labourer's wife in poverty. But Lakshmi was a devoted wife. She knew that she should not desert her husband in poverty.

The parents offered her some money and jewels to take with her, but she refused everything. She took only a handful of rice and some *haldi-kumkum* as auspicious symbols from her mother's house. The parents sent her away to her husband in anger and disgust.

Princess Lakshmi did not grumble about her poverty or ill-luck. She kept house for her husband happily. Though a princess, she went to work on the paddy-fields.

Once the queen of the city was bathing in the pond in the palace compound. She had removed her necklace and kept it on the steps of the pond. A playful cat picked it up and dropped it in front of Lakshmi's hut. The necklace was worth seven thousand rupees.

When Lakshmi saw the necklace lying at her doorstep she thought to herself, 'Oh God! The queen has lost a precious jewel.

If I had only wanted, I could have brought hundreds of such precious pieces with me from my palace. Now why should I want somebody else's jewel?'

The king's guard began searching all over the city for the lost necklace. Finally they found it lying near Lakshmi's doorstep. Both the king and the queen were very impressed by Lakshmi's honesty. They sent the guards back to bring Lakshmi and Krishna Raja over to the palace.

Lakshmi and her husband were treated very lovingly for three days at the palace as royal guests. When they were to take leave of the royal couple, the king offered some money to them. He said, "You can ask anything you want from us." But Lakshmi replied, "No, sir! I seek only God's help. If I have done anything good at all, I am sure to get it."

Lakshmi used to do her *puja* till late at night daily. Bhagyalakshmi or the Goddess of Fortune wanted to test her devotion. On the first night, she came as an old woman begging for food. Lakshmi happily gave the old woman her own meagre meal. The next night, the goddess put on the form of a sick man, shivering in cold. Lakshmi willingly gave away her only blanket.

The goddess needed no further proof of her devotion. She showed up before Lakshmi in her true form. The people of Mysore again welcomed their former prince as their king and Lakshmi as their queen.

Thus Lakshmi was rewarded for the devotion to her husband and faith in God.

FOLK TALES OF KASHMIR

Kashmir

Kashmir has always been a rich storehouse of folktales. Situated in the northern part of India, this beautiful valley is protected by high mountains and difficult passes. The inhabitants in the past had thus, to fall back on their own resources to keep themselves busy and amused. With winter come its long snowy nights. The men retire early into their homes. As they warm themselves with the Kangri (an earthenware bowl of live coal, held in a frame of wickerwork and slipped under their voluminous gowns), they weave beautiful and fascinating stories. These stories, handed down from generation to generation by local bards, reveal the flight of imagination of the village-folk, of their acute common sense and of their practical acceptance of things. Kashmiris have changed little over the years. They have retained their culture and their arts and crafts.

The language of the state is Kashmiri. Dogri, a dialect, is spoken in Jammu and the surrounding areas. Both Kashmiri and Dogri are enriched with folklore and songs. Kashmir has Srinagar as its summer capital and Jammu as the winter capital. The area is 2,22,236 sq km and has a population of 7,718,700,literacy 26.17 per cent.

Tourism is the major industry in the state. The economy of the state is largely agrarian. Horticulture and forestry constitute the next important sector of the economy.

32
THE CAPTAIN OF THIEVES

THE Kashmiri pandit was deeply worried. His one and only daughter had passed the marriageable age and yet he was unable to get her married. This was not because there were no bridegrooms. On the contrary proposals for her hand had steadily come in, for she was, like all Kashmiri girls, fair and pretty. In fact the pandit did not have the money to marry his daughter off. The pandit's extravagant forefathers had always maintaind a big palatial home with lots of servants. There were also large *marals*[1] of paddy land. Important festivals like the Shivaratri had always been celebrated on a grand scale and on the New Year's day there had always been new clothes for every inmate of the house. The basement of the ancestral home was said to be full of treasure-laden chests.

But whatever his financial condition, he had not dared to reduce the pomp and show his forefathers had maintained for fear of the ridicule of the neighbours. Most of all he feared the ridicule of Sunder, once a friend but who now had become worse than an enemy. How had such a thing happened? Once Sunder had asked for the loan of a large sum of money. The pandit had tried to explain his inability in the best possible way but Sunder had taken it as an insult. Forgotten were all the years of friendship as he vowed to avenge the insult. From thence on he never spared any chance of belittling the pandit. The latter thus kept well out of his way.

This did not deter Sunder. He wished to see the pandit's position further degraded. How could this be done? Whilst he thought over this, one of his servants came to his aid. He said,

1. A measure of land.

"Master, I know the captain of the thieves. Employ him to rob the pandit clean. That will be the end of the pandit and of his big ancestral home."

The captain of thieves was accordingly employed. He was known throughout the land for his cunning and daring. People feared the very mention of his name.

The pandit was of course not aware of this mean plot. One night as he lay down to sleep, his wife said, "It is time you thought of your daughter's wedding. What is the reason for postponing it every year?"

The pandit realised that the time had come to reveal to his wife how poor they really were. He replied, "Rightly have you asked why I am not getting our daughter married. The truth, dear wife, is that I do not have money for the purpose. For the past few years I have been spending far above my means to keep up the dignity of the family. The position now is that I see no way of getting or earning enough to run the household. How then can I provide for a daughter's marriage?"

The wife could also see no way out and she cried, "Oh whatever will happen! O, that I had lived to see the day when poverty would be our lot!"

She wept bitterly. The pandit was deeply moved and before he could check himself, he was also weeping. He felt as though his heart would break.

This pathetic scene, which had taken place in the privacy of the bedroom, had been witnessed by an outsider. He was the captain of the thieves, who had sneaked into the house with the intention of committing theft that night. He was shocked at all that he had heard. He had been tempted by Sunder to rob the pandit under the belief that the ancestral home of the victim was full of treasure. He realised now that he had been falsely led. Anger flared up within him. He finally thought out a way by which he could make his journey worthwhile. Waiting patiently till the pandit and his wife were fast asleep, he slipped out of the house.

The next day Sunder waited eagerly for the captain of the thieves to report of the theft at the pandits's house. The man not only failed to turn up, but, to his horror, Sunder found that he had been robbed of every piece of jewellery and gold and silver coins in the house.

The next morning when the pandit's wife awoke, she was surprised to see a bag lying by the side of her pillow. It had definitely not been there the night before. On opening it she found a heap of gold and silver coins. Over these was a slip of paper on which was scrawled, "The captain of thieves leaves behind a small present for your daughter's wedding."

33
THE PEARLS

BHOLANATH, a Kashmiri farmer, was in misery. His rice field lay parched and the rich fruit trees had dried up. A severe drought had hit the fair valley of Kashmir and there was no food anywhere. People begged from door to door. Vultures crowded the skies. The *Kashmir-zannạt puzir* or the Kashmir equal to paradise, became a land of the hungry and the dead. Bholanath peeped into his wooden granary. It was empty. He picked up a bag and left the house wondering where he would get grain to fill it up. Who would give him even a handful of grain when there was hardly any?

On the way he met a hermit. Bholanath was indeed looking so miserable that the hermit asked, "Son, is there anything I can do for you?"

Bholanath spoke of his hopeless state to the hermit and asked expectantly, "Sir, can you help me in any way?"

The hermit replied, "In my hut, which is in the forest bordering the village, lives my daughter. Go to her. She will solve all your problems."

With great hope in his heart, Bholanath went to her. When she heard his story, she started weeping. Large drops of tears fell from her eyes, but as they fell to the ground, they were changed into priceless pearls. When a heap had collected she gave them to him and said, "Sell these pearls to buy food."

Bholanath thanked her profusely and hurried off to the market but when he tried to sell the pearls he found that no one was willing to buy them. All the people asked him the same question, "Where have you got such priceless pearls from?" They looked knowingly at one another and asked, "Till yesterday you were a poor man. From where did you suddenly get all this treasure?"

To make matters worse they led him to the king and said, "Sir, the man has suddenly acquired a big treasure of pearls. It is for you to judge from where he got them."

The king questioned him and Bholanath told him the whole story. The king found it difficult to believe. He said, "Take me to the girl to see whether her teardrops really change into pearls such as these."

Bholanath and the king went to the hermit's hut. When the girl heard of the reason of their visit, she refused to come out to meet the king. Instead she wept and when her tears changed into pearls, she sent them to the king. The king, greatly impressed, asked the hermit for his daughter's hand in marriage. The hermit, happy that his daughter would become the queen of Kashmir, gave his consent. Arrangements for the wedding were made and the king and the hermit's daughter were married in the hermit's hut. The next day, the king left for his capital with his bride.

The bridal procession went along the Jhelum river and entered a thick forest. It had become dark and so the royal party camped for the night. At midnight, when everyone was asleep, the personal maid of the bride gagged and blinded her, took off her ornaments and clothes and locked her up in a wooden box. She bribed some men to throw it into the river. Then she dressed her own daughter in the bride's clothes and ornaments and put her in the bride's place.

The wooden box went floating along, dashing against stones and rocks. It was a sturdy one and no harm came to it. A woodcutter who had come to the forest to cut wood, saw it floating. He became curious and dragged it ashore. When he opened it he was aghast to see a beautiful girl inside it. She was unconscious. He gently carried her to his hut. It was when she regained consciousness that he discovered that she was blind. He was a childless man and he took good care of the girl. He soon nursed her back to health. He was pleasantly surprised to find that whenever she wept, her tears changed into big glistening pearls. She would collect these and give them to him saying, "Father, sell these and buy things for the house." She was indeed very grateful to this man who had not only saved her from sure death but who had also looked after her as his own child.

By and by, the woodcutter became a rich man. He left the wooden hut in the forest and moved into a large rambling house.

Fruit trees surrounded it and in season, they were ablaze with the brightest colours. There was also a vegetable garden and two wooden granaries, which were well stocked with grain. The vegetable garden outgrew its fences and spilled itself on the wayside. The wood-cutter's *pheran*[1] and *pyjamas*[2] were now made of the finest cloth in the land and he donned a brightly embroidered cap. He bought beautifully embroidered clothes for her. For her ears, he bought large earrings studded with precious pearls and a matching necklace for her neck. He served her with the most delicious and nutritious food and soon her glowing health made her look more beautiful than ever. But there were times when she was sad and would sulk and brood. This would make the woodcutter sad and he would say, "Daughter, you have never told me how you happened to get inside the wooden box. Who is responsible for the evil deed? Is there no way of getting back your eyesight?"

"Oh, father, you ask too many questions. I cannot answer all of them. All I can say is that my eyesight can be restored."

"Tell me how this can be done and I will spare no pains to do as you say."

"Take a handful of pearls and go to the palace. Bribe one of the queen's maids to get for you the eyes of the queen's personal maid. If I wear those eyes, I will be able to see again."

The woodcutter did as he was told. One of the royal maids, her eyes round with wonder at so much wealth, agreed to do the job. When the maid was asleep, she expertly took out her eyes and gave them to the woodcutter, whilst the bag of pearls she slipped into her pocket. The woodcutter ran home and gave the eyes to the blind girl. She put them on and cried, "Father! I can see everything."

The woodcutter soon became a millionaire and the news reached the king. He summoned the woodcutter and asked, "From where did you, an ordinary woodcutter, get so much wealth?"

At first the woodcutter was reluctant to say anything but when the king threatened to punish him if he did not speak the truth, he told him the sad story of the blind girl. The king was

---

1. Long coat.
2. Long pants.

quite disturbed to hear that her tears turned into pearls whenever she wept. His queen, who was the maid's daughter, had never given him a single pearl. The king ordered the woodcutter to bring the girl to him. She told him her whole story. The king was happy to get back his bride and he declared a week's holiday for celebrations. The maid and her daughter were given the punishment they deserved. They were hanged.

34
SHABRANG

ONCE a king of Kashmir went on a visit to a neighbouring kingdom. Here the princess of the land was very beautiful, more than anyone he had ever seen, and he wished to marry her. He proposed to her, "Will you become my queen and return with me to my kingdom?"

The princess agreed, and then she said a very stange thing, "I have always wanted to marry someone like you so that one day my son could marry your daughter."

The king did not understand her words. They sounded meaningless to him. He married the princess and together they left for the capital of Shergarhi. But, strange as it may seem, once the king was there, he ceased to take any interest in his new queen. He never visited her palace nor did he send messengers to inquire about her welfare. The new queen did not like this and at the earliest opportunity she went back to her father's palace.

Months passed but no news or inquiry came from the king. The new bride became the mother of a bonny little boy. He was dark and so he was named Shabrang, the colour of night. The mother refused to intimate to the king about the birth of the child.

As the boy grew up he was given instructions in various subjects fit for a prince. But along with this his mother also wanted him to become an expert thief. Why it should be so, she refused to disclose even to her parents. So she engaged a veteran thief who was notorious in the trade. The prince set down to study the art as was the wish of his mother. It was not long before the tutor said that the prince had become an expert thief. Calling Shabrang to her, the mother said, "Son, today you are fit for the job for which you have undergone such rigorous training. A couple of months after my marriage, your father deserted me. I had vowed at that time that I would avenge the humiliation I have suffered at his hands. This is what you are to do. Go to Shergarhi and enter the king's service. Then commit such daring burglaries that will baffle both the king and the police, till out of sheer helplessness the king will be compelled to announce that if the thief surrenders himself, he will be married to the king's daughter, the princess. When this occurs, acknowledge the thefts but do not accept the marriage proposal. Send word to me and await my arrival."

With these words of advice, she sent him on his mission to Shergarhi. It did not take Shabrang long to make friends with the palace-guards. Wherever he went, the people admired his handsome face and muscular build. They whispered to one another, "Who is this handsome stranger?"

Soon Shabrang secured a place among the king's guards. Then one night he committed his first theft and hid all the stolen goods in a hole under a *chenar* tree. He covered up the hole with great care. This theft was followed by half a dozen more burglaries, each more daring than the previous one. The police were baffled and the citizens were frightened. Who was the man whose burglaries were daring and cunning, they wondered. They had neither seen nor heard the likes of it before. No one ever suspected Shabrang, for, every morning at the stroke of the clock, he was back at the palace, looking as fresh as anyone after a good night's sleep.

The king was rather disturbed at these daring thefts. Never before had his kingdom been harassed like this. He reprimanded the policemen for lack of efficiency in their ranks. This rebuke hurt them to the quick and one of them volunteered to patrol all the streets of the capital in an attempt to catch the thief.

Night came and everybody went to sleep. All was quiet. Only the crunching of the policeman's boots could be heard echoing in the stillness of the night. He was walking along the outskirts of the capital when he heard a kind of noise as though someone was grinding corn. In the darkness, he saw the flickering of a lamp and in its light he saw a woman grinding corn. He walked impatiently towards her and asked, "Why are you grinding corn so late at night?'

"Sir," replied the woman, "I could not do any work as my child was ill. He is asleep now, so I am here."

"Have you seen anyone pass this way?"

The question seemed to frighten the woman. She asked nervously, "Why, have you seen anyone? A man came last night and stole wheat from my wooden granary. I am sure he will come for more today."

"Good," said the policeman. "I will await him here and capture him when he comes."

"But, sir, he will flee the moment he sees your uniform. The best arrangement would be for you to wear my clothes. You can then sit in my place and pretend to grind corn. When the thief comes you can immediately capture him."

The policeman accepted the proposal and donned the Kashmiri woman's clothes. He then sat down in her place to grind corn.

The next morning, news of more burglaries, committed the night before, spread through the capital. The king, apart from feeling more worried, was also wondering where the policeman had disappeared. Nowhere in the capital could he be found. At last after a long search, he was found in the outskirts of the city dressed in a woman's dirty clothes, grinding corn. He could have died with mortification when he was brought before the king.

For the next two nights, two senior police officers went out in an attempt to catch the elusive thief, but they too met with the same fate. The king now was at his wit's end. The thief had not only committed burglaries of the most daring nature but had also made fool of his officers. "Your Majesty," urged the courtiers, "the thief must be made to stop his burglaries if anyone is to remain in the capital."

What was the king to do? Day and night he tried to think of a way out, till at last he reached a decision. The people were taken aback when they heard of it. The king had it drummed through the streets and lanes of the capital that he, the king, would give his daughter in marriage to the thief if the latter came forward and vowed never to commit a burglary again.

A huge crowd collected before the palace the next day to see if the thief would surrender himself. Who was he, they wondered. The people whispered and wondered as the minutes ticked by. A drummer came up to the gates and once more announced the proclamation of the king. Shabrang, who was standing in the crowd, walked out and stood before the king.

"What have you to say?" asked the king.

"Your Majesty, I am the thief who has committed the burglaries," said Shabrang and to prove his words, he took the king to the *chenar* tree under which he had kept all his loot. Among them was the policeman's uniform.

True to his word, the kind offered his daughter in marriage when Shabrang vowed that never again would he commit any theft. Shabrang, at the king's offer, said, "I shall send for my mother. She will do the needful."

His mother came as soon as she heard of the royal proposal. The king welcomed her and renewed his proposal. Shabrang's mother said, "Shabrang can no more marry the princess than a brother can marry a sister."

"How is that?" asked the king, much surprised at her words.

Shabrang's mother related how the king had married her years ago and had later deserted her. She also reminded him of her words, "I have always wanted to marry someone like you so that one day my son can marry our daughter," which she had spoken when he had proposed to her. The king remembered the past and was happily reconciled to his queen. Shabrang was welcomed by the king and the people and was accepted as the heir to the Shergarhi throne.

35
HOW THE CLIENT OUTWITTED THE LAWYER

As THE lawyer worked feverishly among the high piles of files in front of him, he heard an apologetic cough. He looked up wearily to see a man of the most humble appearance standing near the door.

"Come tomorrow," said the lawyer and returned to his files.

The man, wringing his hands, stood where he was. He was the picture of misery. He sobbed and said, "Sir, please do not send me back. I am in great need of your help."

"Come in," said the lawyer and the man came in looking very relieved. He said, "Sir, I have heard what a great lawyer you are. Your name is known throughout the *maraz*, the southern valley of Kashmir. It is said that you can win the most difficult cases for your clients. Sir, I had once been a farmer but I have changed my profession and now own a small shop in Pampur. Business was dull so I had to take loans from a moneylender. I have been unable to pay back even a small portion of the sum borrowed, with the result the interest on the loan has increased so much that it is now more than the sum borrowed. The moneylender has brought a case against me. What shall I do? I do not have the money to pay back the moneylender just now or in the future."

The man's flattery had made the lawyer feel happy. He said, "Do not worry. The moneylender will not be able to do you any harm. I may even free you of the loan; but as you know, my fee is high. I must be assured of payment before I can accept your case."

"Of course," replied the man, "that is assured."

"Then meet me at the court a week from today."

On the appointed day, the man went to the court. Here he found his lawyer and the creditor with his lawyer. The man avoided the eyes of the creditor as he took his seat in the crowd. The judge arrived and the men walked into court.

First the creditor took the stand. He went into detail about the amount of money he had lent to the shopkeeper, which the latter had failed to repay. "He has no intention of repaying the sum," added the creditor.

Then the shopkeeper took the stand and the judge asked, "Do you wish to say anything?"

The man looked blankly at him and then looked down at his own *patawa* or leggings. With much effort he said, "*Zafran.*"

The court was startled at this strange reply. The lawyer was puzzled at the queer behaviour of his client. His forehead wrinkled up in deep thought, then quick as lightning, he rose to his feet and said to the judge, "Sir, this man has not taken the large sum stated by the creditor. He had taken only 50 rupees and not the 150 of which he is charged."

The man, all this while, had been repeating the word *zafran* over and over again. The judge demanded, "Why does he repeat the word *zafran* over and over again?"

"Sir, this man once owned a large field of *zafran* on the saffron plateau of Pampur. Last year the field was full of the rich purple blossoms of *zafran*. These blossoms had turned the dry plateau of Pampur into a rare and wonderful garden. The perfume of the flowers had filled the air of that region. Then a forest fire burnt the whole crop of *zafran* to the ground. The man never recovered from the shock and that is why he keeps repeating the word *zafran* to himself."

The judge was quite touched by the sad story. The man was indeed rolling his eyes in a painful manner as he repeated the word *zafran* to himself. He was set free and the loan struck off his name. The lawyer was a happy man that evening as he waited to receive his fee from his satisfied client. The latter came with the same blank stare he had in the court. The lawyer rubbed his hands in satisfaction and said, "See how easily I won your case. Give me the fee and go home in peace."

The blank look had not left the face of the shopkeeper. In a dull voice he said, "*Zafran.*"

"O forget that game. It is all over now. Come, give me my fee."

"*Zafran,*" repeated the client.

"Do you mean to say that you are trying to dupe me as you had duped the judge?" asked the lawyer in shocked tones, but the word *zafran* was all that he could get out of the man. He realised that for the first time in his career he has been outwitted by a client. He bowed his head in defeat and the shopkeeper went home.

36

THE FOOLISH KING

LONG time ago, before Shergarhi became the capital of the kings of Kashmir the fairyland of Kashmir was ruled by many kings, each living in his own city. In one such city, there came a group of *fakirs*.[1] They liked the city, for it was as beautiful as a picture. There was a broad track with a grassy border, bound by a rippling stream and shaded by large walnut trees. This was the time of *har*.[2] It was a delight to watch the farmers as they harvested acres and acres of cultivated land, terraced squares and crescents of rice, maize, sesame and amaranth fields.

The *fakirs* found one thing queer in this village. Everything was sold at the same price. This meant gold was as cheap as coal and saffron was sold at the same price as salt. This state of affairs greatly pleased one of the *fakirs*. He said, "This is a fine place to live in. We can eat the best food at a nominal price. Let us rest here awhile."

"No, no," said the leader of the group. "If everything is bought and sold at the same price then justice, too, is probably bought and sold here. It is dangerous to live in such a place. Let us make haste and depart."

But the first *fakir* would not hear of it. As the leader failed to persuade him, he was left behind whilst the others moved out of the city. As ill-luck would have it, a daring theft took place that very night. When the king heard of it, he ordered that any stranger who was found in the city, was to be caught and hung for the burglary. When the men saw the strange *fakir*, they caught hold of him and accused him of the theft. Though he strongly

---

1. Holy Men.
2. Harvest.

denied having anything to do with the theft, no one listened to him. They dragged him to the king, who gave one look at the robust body of the stranger and ordered him to be executed the next day. He was taken away and thrown into prison.

The innocent man was in tears. Why, oh, why had he not listened to the wise advice of his chief and left the queer city with its queer ways? He sobbed and wrung his hands in helplessness at his miserable fate. He sent a message to his chief about his sad plight.

The day of the execution dawned and the people thronged the market square where the *fakir* was to be publicly hanged. The hangman was there in his black mask and awaited the arrival of the king. The chief of the group of *fakirs* arrived in haste and was seen whispering to the condemned *fakir*. He said, "When the king arrives, I wll go to him and beg him to hang me instead of you. Everytime I say this, you must forcefully say, 'Sire, do not allow such a thing, hang me.' "

Though the *fakir* could not understand how such a thing could save him, he piously put his faith in his patron *Pir* or saint and nodded. The king soon arrived in his gilded carriage. As he alighted, the old *fakir* ran forward and fell at his feet, sobbing, "My lord, do not hang this unfortunate man. He has an old mother to look after. What will become of her when he is no more? I am old and my days are numbered. Hang me instead, you will be doing a kind act."

Hardly had he finished speaking when the condemned *fakir* cried, "Sire, do not allow such injustice, hang me."

The chief of the *fakirs* repeated his request, not once, but at least half a dozen times, giving various reasons. Each time, the condemned *fakir* played his part by protesting vigorously. The king looked in wonder from one to the other as they spoke. He was surprised and could hardly find his voice. Both the men were willing to die. But why? Not being able to understand the situation, he called the two *fakirs* and taking them aside, asked them, "What is the meaning of all this? Why are you both willing to die? It is natural for a man to save himself, but both of you seem eager to die. Explain yourselves properly."

The older *fakir* said, "My lord, if you have the sacred books of the saints read to you, you will find in them that this is the most asupicious day to die. The man who dies today, will surely find a place in paradise, no matter how great a sinner he may be. But this is a great secret known only to a few."

The king had always been worried about how to get into paradise and had been performing various ceremonies for a long time, all with the hope of getting an undeserved entry into the desired place. Being rather gullible, he was delighted to hear the *fakir's* secret and immediately believed it. Turning to the crowd he cried, "My dear people, as the holy books say this day is the most auspicious day for dying, I have a great desire to relinquish my life today. I hereby order you to hang me instead of these innocent men here, so that my soul may go to heaven."

Well, the king had always been obeyed, no matter how foolish his orders were. So his people promptly took him and hanged him before he had any chance to change his mind. The *fakirs*, blessing their stars, disppeared as fast as their legs could carry them.

FOLK TALES OF KERALA

Kerala

Kerala is one of the smaller states tucked away in the south-west corner of India. Malayalam is the state language with a very rich legacy. With an area of 38,863 sq km and a population of 29,011,237 the state is almost bursting at the seams with a density of 747 per sq km. Literacy at cent per cent is the highest in the country.

The people are highly intelligent, progressive, persevering and possess a high degree of common sense and a sense of humour. Rice, spices, tapioca, fruits, cashewnuts and onion are the main crops. Keralites are outgoing and are found in every part of India and probably in every part of the world.

Their wit, love for tradition, dance and music are reflected in their folk tales.

The backwaters form a specially attractive and economically valuable feature of Kerala.

37

THE ABSENT-MINDED SON-IN-LAW

A YOUNG man went to his mother-in-law's house, leaving his wife at home.

The mother-in-law received him with great joy, as is usual in our country.

Among the many delicacies placed before him, he liked *kozhukkatta* best. This is a typical Malayali cake. It is a round ball two inches in diameter. It is very tasty, being made of rice, with coconut and sugar stuffing.

The son-in-law liked it very much. He had never seen it before. He asked for its name and was told that it was a *kozhukkatta*.

He was sure that his wife could make it. She was a born cook, and had been well taught by her mother to make nice things. But she had never made him a *kozhukkatta*.

"Do you like it?" asked the mother-in-law.

"Yes," he replied.

"When you reach home, you ask my daughter to make it for you. She knows its method of preparation."

So, when he walked back home, he repeated to himself all the way, *kozhukkatta, kozhukkatta.* But unfortunately, he had to cross a narrow stream. He jumped across, saying *thitthey,* which is a Malayali cry. He forgot *Kozhukkatta* and went on repeating the word *thitthey,* until he reached home.

When his wife greeted him, he said, "Do you know, your mother gave me *thitthey* cake. I liked it very much; your mother said that you know how to make it. Do make it now and let me have some to eat."

The girl stared. She had never heard of *thitthey* as anything but an exclamation. She asked her husband what he meant. "I mean *thitthey* cake," he said, "Your mother told me that you know how to make it, so do not pretend that you do not know."

But the wife pleaded ignorance, and the husband got angry. "You will not do what I say, then I will make you. Take that," he said, and gave her a few blows on her arms. The poor girl began to cry, saying, "You cruel beast! My arms have swellings like *kozhukkattas* on them. Look at them!"

"Oh! it is *kozhukkatta,* not *thitthey*. I am sorry, please make some *kozhukkattas*."

So the wife made a few *kozhukkattas* and made her husband happy.

38
THE CLEVER GOLDSMITH

PONNAPPEN was a very clever goldsmith. He was clever not only in his art, but also as a thief. It was known that wherever he touched gold, a little of it would stick to his itching palm.

Viswan Namboodiri wanted to make a gold necklace for his daughter. Ponnappen was asked to do the work, who promised to do his best. Knowing how clever Ponnappen was, the Namboodiri specially engaged a servant to watch over him. He did the work in an outhouse of the Namboodiri's house, the latter's servant watching him all the time. In the evening he would leave, after giving the gold into the servant's hand. The latter would weigh it and make sure that there was not the slightest loss.

The work was finished. It was a lovely ornament. The Namboodiri was anxious to see it, and ordered that it should be brought to him. So it was being taken to him, wrapped in a piece of silk, the goldsmith walking in front, the servant behind.

On the way to the Namboodiri's house, there was a brook. Unfortunately the necklace fell into the water, when they were crossing it. The goldsmith immediately jumped in and recovered the article, and went on to the Namboodiri's house.

Reaching the house, they put the ornament before the owner. He was very pleased, and paid the goldsmith and also gave him a present. He congratulated his servant, who had watched over the work so well, and gave him a present also.

But their joy was short-lived. Two weeks later, it was found that the necklace had taken on a dirty grey colour. Nobody could understand how it had happened. They did not know what the goldsmith had done on his way back. He had gone down into the brook again, and taken something out of it. It was the real gold ornament, while the one he had presented to the owner was made of brass, so well polished as to look like gold. He had made it and hidden it in water. When the real gold necklace had fallen into the brook, the goldsmith had taken out the brass ornament. It had been done so cleverly that even the astute servant had been deceived.

39
THE LITTLE CHILD'S DILEMMA

"If I tell the truth, father will kill mother; if I say nothing, he will eat dog's flesh." This is a common saying in Malayalam, to indicate a dilemma. There is a story behind the origin of this saying.

Ramu was a very ill-tempered man, and usually came home drunk. His wife found her married life very unhappy. One afternoon, Ramu brought home some mutton, and asked his wife to make a tasty curry with it for his evening meal. He then went out, and the woman went to the kitchen to bring a plate and a knife, leaving the piece of meat on the verandah.

When she returned, she saw that a dog had just finished eating the meat. She was terribly upset and afraid. She took a stone, and threw it at the dog, hitting it on the head. The animal fell dead.

She had an idea. She cut the dog to pieces, washed the meat, and made a nice curry of it. When her husband came home, she set it before him, with rice. Their little daughter had been a witness to all this. She said, "If I tell the truth, father will kill mother, if I say nothing, he will eat dog's flesh."

Ramu was intrigued by the child's words. "What does she mean?" he asked his wife. The poor woman, trembling, told him the truth. Ramu, however, was in a good mood. He enjoyed the humour of the situation, and did not punish his wife. But he turned the incident to his advantage later, and used to taunt his wife for attempting to make him eat dog's meat.

40

THE MAN WHO CAUGHT THE LEOPARD BY THE TAIL

THERE is a well-known saying is Malayalam, about catching a leopard by the tail. When anyone is in a mess, of which he cannot rid himself, he is said to have caught a leopard by the tail. This is based on the following story.

Once upon a time there was a clever merchant in a village. He used to take his goods to a distant market, sell them there, and return to his own place, before nightfall. He was returning one afternoon when a terrible thing happened. A fierce leopard sprang at him, from a nearby thicket, with every intention of eating him up. There was no chance of escape. But the merchant, with great presence of mind, caught hold of its tail, and began to run round it, as it tried to attack him. The animal could not get at him, because he was holding fast to the end of its long tail.

This strange circus went on for sometime. The merchant had a purse full of money, tied to his waist, but in the struggle it got open, and a large number of coins fell on the ground.

A man came along that road, and saw what was going on. "What is this?" he asked the merchant. "Why do you go round the beast in this way?"

"Oh, can't you see?" said the merchant. "This is a magic leopard. It drops gold and silver when you pull its tail. I got some. Have a try, if you like. But I must have what I have earned."

The newcomer, a simpleton, jumped at the chance of making some easy money, and received the gift of the leopard's tail from the merchant, with thankfulness. The latter gathered up his money and gold coins, and quickly got away.

FOLK TALES
OF
MADHYA PRADESH

Madhya Pradesh

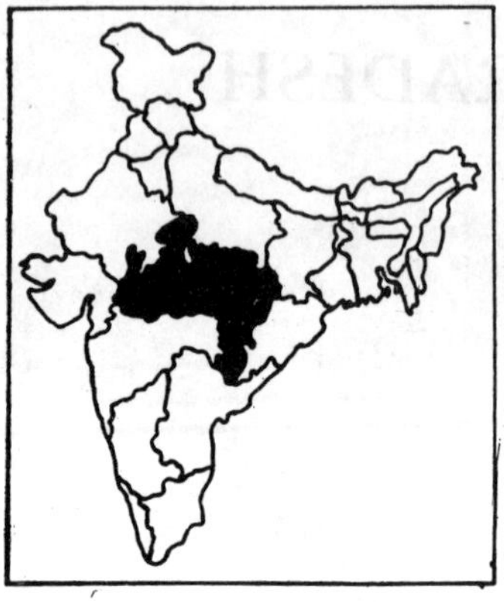

Situated in the centre of India, Madhya Pradesh has an area of 4,43,446 sq km; population 66,135,862; density 149 per sq km and literacy 43.45 per cent.

Madhya Pradesh has remained one of the poorest states in the country.

The State is bound by Uttar Pradesh and Bihar in the north and north-east, Orissa in the east, Maharashtra in the south and Gujarat and Rajasthan in the west. The capital is in Bhopal. The main languages in use are Hindi (State language), Urdu, Marathi, Marwari, Gujarati, and Sindhi. Despite the diversity in spoken dialects, the people have remarkable similarity in cultural and religious beliefs. The main rivers are Narmada, Mahanadi and Tapti.

Madhya Pradesh presents a panorama of people from aboriginals to scholars, producing a variegated folklore.

The State has the largest population of Scheduled Tribes and Scheduled Castes. They constitute one-third of the population. As a result it is very rich in folkart forms, be it music, dance or crafts.

41
THE CLEVER DAUGHTER-IN-LAW

ONCE the daughter-in-law of a merchant went to fetch water from a well which was at the far end of the village. No sooner had she pulled out a bucket of water than four travellers appeared near the well.

One traveller said to her, "I'm thirsty, will you kindly give me some water?"

She hesitated a little, primarily because she was not fully clothed, and secondly, there was no tumbler for water. She, therefore, thought of some excuse for not giving them water at the well. So she put a question to him, "May I know who you are?"

"A traveller," replied the first man.

She asked again, "There are only two travellers, which one are you?"

The man could not answer. The daughter-in-law, on finding him perplexed, said, "Unless you answer my question I'm afraid I will not be able to give you water." Saying this she poured the water in a pitcher and pulled another bucket.

Just then the second traveller came forward and requested her for some water. The woman asked him the same question, "Who are you?"

"I am a poor man," said the second traveller.

"There are only two poor persons, which one are you?"

The second traveller failed to answer the question and he also did not get water from her.

The third man turned up. He was also questioned like the other two. He called himself an illiterate. The daughter-in-law said, "There are only two kinds of illiterates, which one are you?" The question confused him.

Lastly, came forth the fourth traveller. He said that he was a fool. The woman immediately asked him which one of the two kinds of fools he was. He too could not answer.

The woman finished her task and lifting up the pitcher she said, "If you all are thirsty, come along with me to my place. There you will get water." The travellers followed the daughter-in-law to her house.

On reaching home the daughter-in-law first placed the pitcher on its stand and thereafter, dressing herself properly came out to the verandah with a tumbler full of water. She gave water to all the thirsty travellers who resumed their journey after quenching their thirst.

Her father-in-law, the merchant, had seen all this from another verandah. He thought to himself, 'My son is not here and his wife brings outsiders to the house. This is not good. I shouldn't remain quiet when things like this happen before my eyes. Something must be done immediately. *One's boil cannot be cured by one's own hands.*'

Thinking so, the merchant went to the king and related the story about his daughter-in-law's behaviour. The king summoned the woman through a guard. When her mother-in-law came to know about this, she was terribly disturbed and asked, "Oh! my daughter-in-law, did you have any quarrel at the well?"

The fair lady simply nodded her head. Then she went to the guard and rquested him to go and ask the king whether she was being summoned as a daughter-in-law or as a daughter.

After sometime the guard came back with a palanquin and said that she was being summoned as a daughter-in-law. So she sat in the palanquin and went to the king.

"Why did you call the four men to your house when your husband was away?" enquired the king.

The woman explained, "To give a glass of water to a thirsty traveller is the duty of a housewife. When I went to fetch water, I was scantily clothed. I couldn't have given them water at the well with so little clothing on. So I found a way of bringing the travellers home by asking them puzzling questions. My questions were such that they were unable to answer."

"What were your questions?" asked the king.

The woman repeated the questions. The courtiers and the king failed to answer them. The king requested her to tell the answers.

The woman said, "In my opinion the answer to my first question is that there are only two travellers—the sun and the moon. The answer to my second question is that the cow and a daughter-in-law are the only two creatures who could be classified as poor. To the third question the answer is water and food. They go to everyone like the illiterates do." Continued the woman, "When the fourth man said that he was a fool, he was blank when I asked him which of the two fools he was."

"Do you mean that there are only two types of fools?" asked the king with curiosity.

"Yes, very much," replied the daughter-in-law.

"Who are they? Tell me quickly," asked the king eagerly.

The woman said: "If you forgive me then only shall I answer the question."

"Don't hesitate to answer in the court."

"There are two fools at the moment. One is my father-in-law who reported against me in the court without finding out the facts, and the other is the king who without considering the daughter-in-law's social honour called her before the court."

On hearing this the king was nonplussed but in his heart of hearts he was full of praise for the woman.

42
JEWEL THIEF

In a village there lived a rich merchant. When he grew old he divided his property amongst his four sons: to the first he handed over his moneylending business, to the second he gave his grocery shop, to the third a cloth shop and to the fourth, the youngest one, he gave his high yielding fields. All of them were farsighted and diligent. They made good fortunes through their inherited property.

One day the rich man called them and said, "My sons, now that my days are nearing, I wish that you always continue to be united and remain faithful to each other. May your interest grow in your jobs. But you know, I may go any moment. I have called you to disclose a secret. Below the legs of my cot you will find your jewels which you shouldn't forget to take into your possession after my death. But mind, the jewels should be taken out when you are all present and only then should you have one each."

A couple of months later the old man passed away. The four brothers made up their minds to take out the jewels. They assembled in their father's room. The piece of ground under the legs of the cot, on which their father used to sleep, was dug out. But to their surprise they found only three jewels. They looked at each other. Where was the fourth one? They were sure about their father's statement. They thought that the missing jewel must have been taken out by one of them as no other person besides them was aware of the precious stones.

They were now keen that the jewel be traced out and the name of the culprit remain a secret as it might cause embarrassment to him and hatred amongst them, moreover their father's soul would be pained in heaven.

They gave full thought to the problem. Finally, they decided to seek the help of the wise king whose kingdom was miles away from their village. The king was known for his justice. On reaching his kingdom, the four brothers, sought his audience and explained the purpose of their visit. They said: "O great King, we expect from you that

Mal paiye apno chor na janyo jaye
Preet reet din din badhe, kije soi upaye.

We should get back the jewel, but the thief should not be made known to us. Do something in such a way that our affection may grow day by day.

The king patiently heard them and said, "Friends, for today you had better stay at my guest house. Tomorrow I shall look into the matter."

They were led to the guest house where they were served with all kinds of food. While enjoying the food one of the brothers commented, "Though it is royal food, the flour used in the cake appears to be spoiled by blood."

That very moment the second brother uttered, "The *ghee* too is stale."

"To me the milk used in the food seems to be tinged with human milk," said the third brother.

The fourth added, "I sense the *pattals* (leaf-platters) too are made out of leaves spoiled by cowdung."

One of the attendants was listening to their conversation. He went to the king and conveyed to him all that he had heard. The king became furious over the comments made by the brothers. He summoned them in his presence and also called the *bhandari,* the storekeeper. He asked the brothers, "Is all that you said about the food true?"

The eldest brother replied, "Since you are interested to know, my lord, it would be better if you enquire into the matter thoroughly."

First of all the supplier of the flour was called, who said that he had nothing to say as he had purchased the wheat from Chunni farmer.

Chunni farmer was summoned into the court. With folded hands he said, "My lord, when the harvesting was being done, a wild boar happened to come there. I killed the animal over the heap of threshed wheat. I'm sorry I couldn't manage to put aside the portion of the wheat which had bloodstains." The first comment made by one of the brothers came out true.

Now it was the turn of the *ghee* seller who revealed that he had bought the *ghee* from a sweeper, who might have collected it from leftover leaf-platters.

The king felt much embarrassed when he came to know this.

Then the milkman was asked about the milk he had supplied. He replied, with a guilty expression on his face, "Sir, kindly forgive me! I accept, it was my mistake. I had kept the milk-pot near a *gwalan** feeding her child. When the child took a little turn in her lap, some of the milk dropped into the milk pot from her breast. I assure you it will never happen again."

The king kept silent. Lastly, the leaf-platter supplier was called before the king. He too admitted the fault.

All the four brothers' comments were found to be true. The king and the courtiers were amazed at the remarkable sensitivity of the brothers. After a little pause, the king said, "Brothers, you are so sensitive, clever and wise that I wonder why you don't find the culprit yourselves. I think I would not be able to solve your problem. It is better that you should go to the king of Dharampur, who would certainly help you to your satisfaction."

The brothers arrived at Dharampur. The next morning they saw the king and related to him the purpose of their visit. They further requested him that the judgement should be given in such a manner that their relationship should not be strained.

The king of Dharampur had already heard about these brothers. He thought that it would be wise to test the intelligence of the brothers before solving their problem. The king ordered a pot. Its mouth was closed. The king said, "First tell me what kind of a thing is in the pot?"

The eldest brother took the pot in his hands and shook it. "There is something of a round shape," said the eldest brother.

The second brother said after inspecting the pot, "Yes, it is spherical and its colour is red."

"It's of course, roundish and red in colour, but it has seeds in it," said the third brother.

The youngest brother said, "Ah! it is a pomegranate." Immediately after saying this he banged the pot against the ground and broke it into pieces. There was indeed a pomegranate

* Milkmaid

in it. The king was surprised to find the brothers so intelligent. He requested them to go to Swarngarh.

So the brothers started for Swarngarh. On their way the elder brother said, "It seems that a lame camel has passed this way."

"The camel had only one eye," said the second brother.

The third brother said, "One of his teeth was missing too."

"I think a pregnant woman was sitting on the animal," said the youngest brother.

Along with these brothers there was another traveller, who was their guide. When they reached Swarngarh, the guide said that he would go and meet the king and fix up the appointment. As a messenger from the king of Dharampur, he went to the king of Swarngarh and narrated what he had heard the brothers say on the way.

The king called the brothers and asked them, "How did you come to know that a one-eyed, lame camel, having a broken tooth and a pregnant woman sitting on its back passed that way?"

The eldest brother said, "Your Highness, on the road I saw that three of the footmarks made by the camel were very clear. The impression of the fourth was not so distinct as the other three. So I assumed that the animal was lame."

"When I saw," said the second brother, "that the camel had eaten the grass from one side of the road only, I presumed it must be one-eyed."

The third said, "And where he had eaten the grass, a patch of grass remained untouched. This gave me an impression that the animal had lost one of its teeth."

The youngest brother said, "Of course, I said that there was a pregnant woman sitting on the animal. I came to know this when I saw some hand marks of the rider on the ground where the animal took rest."

Listening to this explanation of the brothers, the king of Swarngarh said, "Well it will be difficult for me to trace out the jewel thief amongst you. You had better go and meet my daughter who lives in Dhara Nagari. She will be able to help you."

They proceeded towards Dhara Nagari. There the daughter of the king of Dhara Nagari used to give judgement from behind a curtain. For the judgement she sat in a balcony of the palace. There was a big drum at the main gate of the palace. Those who wanted to have any judgement came and beat the drum.

As soon as the sound of the drum was heard the princess of Swarngarh came out and sat in the balcony behind the curtain. The brothers said, "We are four brothers. As you know we want to remain united and do not want to have any friction amongst us, please do something in a manner that

Mal paiye apno, chor na janyo jaye
Preet reet din din badhe, Kijie soi upaye.

The princess of Swarngarh listened to them, patiently and then said, "Well, I will try to do my best to help you. But you have to stay here for a fortnight."

The brothers agreed to stay there. The princess asked them to stay separately without having any communication with each other so long as the jewel was not traced. She had in fact put them under vigilance.

Next day she called the eldest brother and narrated the following story to him.

In a town there lived a king. Between his son and the son of his divan there was good friendship. One day both these young friends decided that they would send their respective wives to each other on their first night. Whosoever was married first was to observe this promise. After all, this would make their friendship closer, they thought.

After some years the prince was married. His wife came home. He remembered what he had promised to his friend. He told his wife about the promise the two friends had mutually made. The newly-married woman followed her husband's wish. She left the palace and set out to meet the divan's son. After she had gone a little distance she met a gang of robbers. They stopped her and tried to snatch the ornaments which she was wearing. The prince's wife requested the thieves, 'Listen, you are like my parents. Please listen to me. I am the wife of the prince and I am going to meet the divan's son. This is my wedding night. Let me go there to fulfil my husband's promise. On me return I will gladly hand over all these ornaments to you."

The thieves discussed amongst themselves. One of them said that as the prince's wife was the daughter of a big man, she might deceive them. The other one said that it would be foolish of them to let her go. But the chief of the gang said to her, "Well, you may go, but keep the promise when you return."

The bride proceeded further. It was midnight. The divan's son was waiting for her. As soon as he heard her footsteps, he came to the door to welcome the young woman. He said, "Welcome, my sister!" The bride entered the room. The divan's son presented her a new dress and some ornaments. "This is just a small present from a brother to his sister. Kindly accept this," said the man. He then served her good food. He touched her feet when she started to go back.

The bride on her way back met the thieves. "Lo, I have come back. Here are my ornaments." Saying this she bagan to take off the ornaments one by one. Tears came to the eyes of the chief of the thieves. The other members of his gang were also astonished to see jewellery worth lakhs of rupees come to them without any effort. But the leader of the gang asked her not to remove the ornaments. He said, "Daughter, you have called us parents. How could we take your things now?" Instead, he presented her a diamond necklace and allowed her to go.

The bride arrived at her palace and narrated the whole incident to the prince.

After telling this story, the princess of Swarngarh asked the elder brother, "You have heard this story. Now tell me, what do you think of the prince, the divan's son, the bride and the thieves?"

The eldest brother replied, "I think they were honest persons. The prince sent his wife to his friend because he was true to his word. We rarely come across such people. The bride is again commendable. She followed her husband's wish. She went to his friend's house on her wedding night because she wanted her husband to keep his word. The son of the divan was equally faithful. Seeing a young girl in his chamber, he treated her like his sister. The thieves too were very good. They did as good parents generally do. They did not take the ornaments worth lakhs of rupees. They were wonderful. I consider them truthful and honest."

The princess called the next brother. She related to him the same story and got a similar reply from him.

The third one also gave the same opinion.

Lastly, the youngest brother was summoned. The princess told him the story and asked him to give his comments about the characters. The youngest brother reacted differently. He said,

"Well, if you ask my sincere comment I should say that the prince was a fool. To send one's own wife at midnight to a friend's house was absolute foolishness. To hell with such a promise! The bride too was of a loose character. That is why she did not hesitate to go out at midnight to another man's house. And the divan's son, he was no less a fool. He left the young woman untouched when she came to him. The thieves were again equally stupid not to avail of the opportunity."

The princess heard the comments of the youngest brother and came to the conclusion that he was the culprit. She said, "So you are the person who has stolen the missing jewel. Take it out and give it to me immediately, otherwise I will teach you a lesson which you will never forget. Hurry up, give me the jewel."

The youngest brother first hesitated to accept the charge. But he soon realised that he would not be spared if he did not give the jewel. He took out the precious stone from his pocket and gave it to the princess.

The princess had already collected the other three jewels from the three brothers. She got the missing one also. She then called all the four brothers and gave them one jewel each.

Thus, the jewel thief was traced, but nobody came to know who he was. All the brothers got their gem and continued to live happily.

FOLK TALES OF MAHARASHTRA

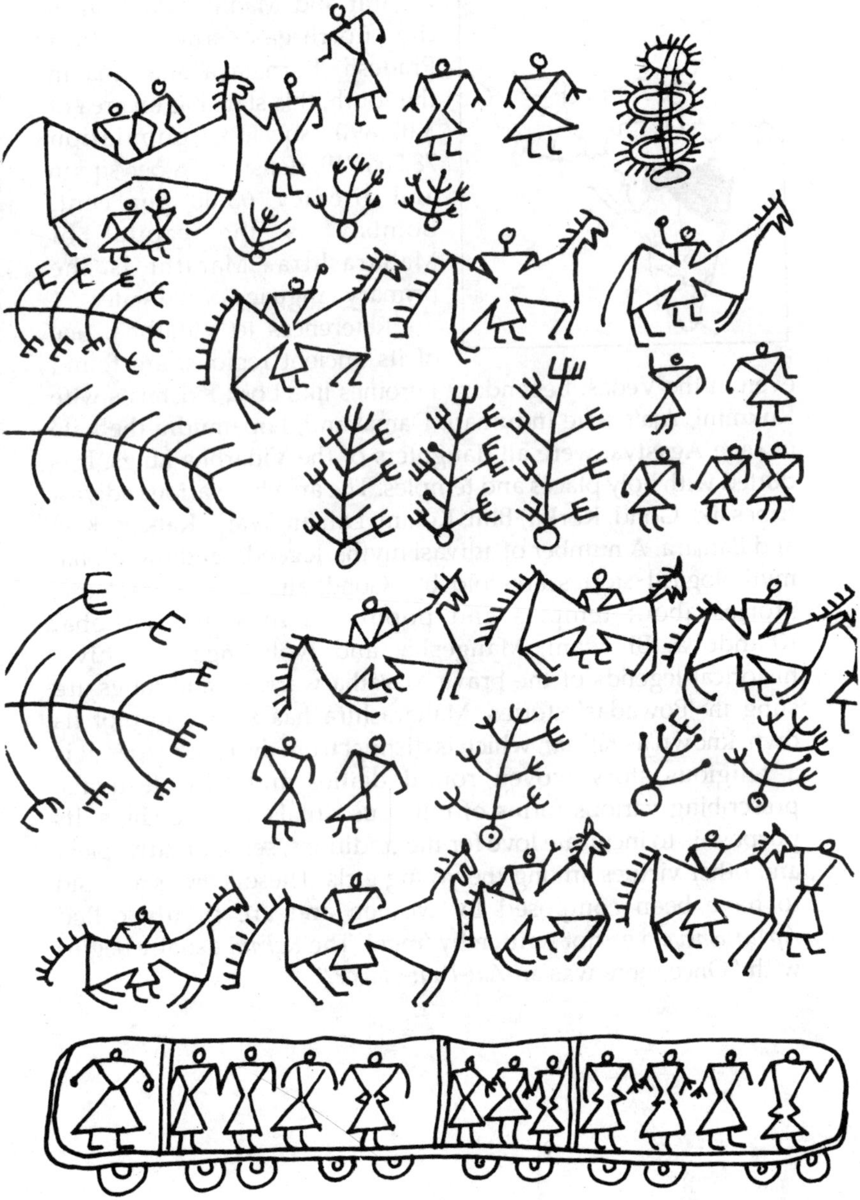

Maharashtra

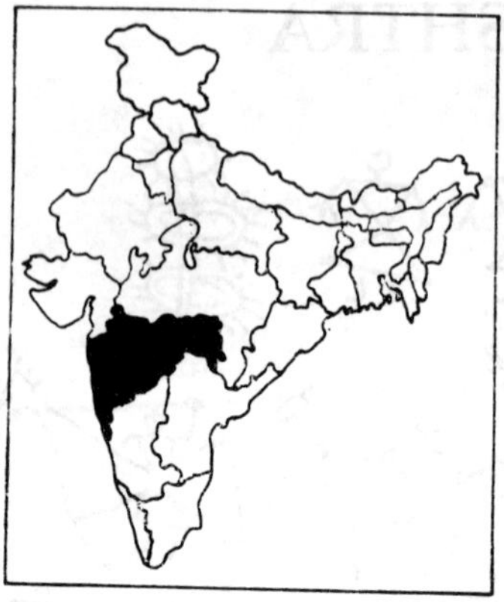

With the Arabian Sea in the west, Gujarat and Madhya Pradesh in the north-east and Andhra Pradesh, Karnataka and Goa in the south, this state has an area of 3,07,690 sq km, population 78,706,719, density 256 per sq km and literacy 63.00 per cent. Bombay is the capital of Maharashtra. Marathi is the primary language of the state.

References to Vidarbha, one of its ancient regions, are found even in the Vedas. Legendary heroines like Lord Krishna's wife Rukmini, Aja's wife Indumati, Damayanti, Lopamudra the wife of sage Agastya, were all daughters of the Vidarbha kings. It is dotted with holy places and temples. The area has various adivasi tribes like Gond, Korku, Bhil, Kolam, Laman, Warli, Katkari, Koli and Banjara. A number of adivasi myths, legends, and traditional mythological stories are told by 'Gondhalis' and 'Kirtankars'. Stories about temples and popular deities like Vithoba, Khandoba, Bhawani, Mangesha, and Jyotirlingas of Shiva, historical legends of the brave Maratha warriors and kings are sung in 'Powadas' stories. Maharashtra has a speciality of its own, known as *Kahani*, which is distinct from the other types. It is a religious story woven round deities and their festivals, prescribing various forms of religious rituals and worships. Its purpose is to inculcate love for the traditions, sense of duty, piety and other virtues among the young girls. These *Kahanis* are said to have been composed by women and are rightly called *Apaurusheya*, i.e., not written by 'men'. The *Kahani* usually begins with "Once there was an *Aat-Paat-Nagar*."

43
THE INCOMPARABLE ARCHER

Soon after the coronation of Shivaji as *Chhatrapati,* a capital complex was built at Raigarh with three hundred spacious buildings, a temple to God Jagadeeshwara and a huge tank. The tank, named *Kushavarta,* was full of varieties of lotus Kartik when Shivaji and his mother Jijabai saw the tank abloom with beautiful blue, white and red lotus flowers.

The mother said, "The holy day of *Vaikunta Chaturdashi* is very near, Shivaba."

Shivaji replied, "Yes, Masahib, I have heard that it was on that day that God Vishnu worshipped God Shiva with one thousand lotus flowers. When he fell short by one flower, he made it up by offering one of his eyes."

"It is my desire," said Jijabai, "that I should worship God Jagadeeshwara with a thousand white lotus flowers from our tank on that day." Shivaji assured her that he would see to it.

But Jijabai wondered how it could be done. "It is not as simple as you think. For this *Pooja* I want fresh and pure flowers, not only unsmelt, but also not made impure by the thought of the *Pooja* in the mind of the man who plucks them. But when anyone gathers the flowers, he will be inevitably thinking of the *Pooja* to God. As soon as he touches the flower, he will have unknowingly offered it to 'Him' in his mind. So what I then get for my *Pooja* will be nothing better than the impure, second-hand flowers already mentally offered."

Shivaji realised the difficulty. It was not possible for his mother at her age to gather a thousand flowers by herself, and if he had to get them plucked by another person, he could not find a way out of the difficulty.

Next day Shivaji summoned his court and confronted them with his mother's wish and her predicament. They heard Shivaji solemnly but none could suggest a solution.

At last a young man rose and said, "Your Majesty, it is my humble request to you to see how I use my skill to gather one thousand white flowers untouched by hand with stems of the same lengths."

Everyone was curious to know who this rash young Maratha was. Someone in the court identified him as Vikram Dalvi of the Maharaja's personal bodyguard.

Shivaji warned him, "Vikram, you know what you have said. You will have to stand by every claim you have made. Otherwise, there will be harsh punishment."

On the appointed day, at sunrise, Vikram came to the tank with a bow and a thousand arrows. Shivaji, his mother and members of the royal family as well as all the courtiers had come out of curiosity to see how Vikram honoured his commitment.

After touching the feet of Jijabai and Shivaji, he laid himself flat on the ground. Then estimating the distance and length of the stem, He started felling white flowers with bow and arrow. One arrow, one flower. His arrows fell like rain. His concentration was so intense that he was oblivious of everything around him. He was only seeing the exact spot of the stem where the arrow had to pierce it.

When all his one thousand arrows were used up, he went in a boat and picked up all the flowers with a pair of tongs. He also collected all the arrows which were floating on the surface of the tank.

Shivaji praised his performance, but what Jijabai said was more to the point. "Vikram's concentration was so good," she said, "that he was not aware of anything except a particular point on the stem. Neither the thought of *Pooja* nor God could have touched his mind."

Vikram requested Shivaji to check if the flower stems were of the same length. Shivaji asked one of his officers to measure the lengths of the stems. He reported that they were of the same length. Everyone, including Shivaji and Jijabai, were amazed at the wonderful performance.

Shivaji publicly honoured Vikram by placing a gold and emerald necklace round his neck himself.

44

HOW PARVATIBAI OUTWITTED THE DACOITS

In the middle of the last century, areas on the outskirts of Maharashtra were full of thugs and dacoits. They used to raid the villages, terrorise the people and take away their valuables. The police could not protect the people. The people had to defend themselves by forming their own groups. But many times they fled from their homes to save their lives.

A notorious dacoit chief spread his activities, from villages to the nearby towns. He had now become so bold that he used to send advance intimation to the people as to when he would raid and which houses he would loot. If an effort was made to remove the valuables from the houses or call the police, the victims had to face more severe reprisals. There was thus no way out but to allow oneself to be plundered or offer whatever resistance one could by mustering men who were ready to fight. But the dacoits would always succeed in the end.

On day a rich man named Bapurao received word that his house would be attacked that night. He was also given the usual warning, "If you try to deceive by removing the ornaments from your house or inform the police, you will be given a blood-bath."

Bapurao turned pale when he heard it. He had a big *haveli* and a brigade of servants working in his house. His coffers were full. He was afraid, but his wife Parvatibai was a courageous and clever woman. When he broke the news to her she asked him, "What do you propose to do?"

"Surely I am not going to yield to these plunderers! I will collect men from the town and along with the servants give them a fight. What do you think?"

"I think there is no use giving an unequal fight. After all, the dacoits are better armed, and more used to fighting. They will overpower you in no time."

"But what else can we do?" asked Bapurao.

"I think we should outwit the dacoits by some plan," said Parvatibai thoughtfully.

"But how? Should we hide your jewelbox somewhere... say in the dung-heap in the cattleshed?"

"Let me think," she said, "till then you do whatever you think proper. I will fight them in my own way. Don't worry."

Bapurao felt a little reassured and he went about the town in search of men to help him, while Parvatibai sat a long time thinking. Soon it was evening. Bapurao came back and told his wife, "I have collected some twenty men. We will hide in the woods near the village border and attack the dacoits before they can enter the village."

Saying this he took four servants and several weapons and went away.

It was now dark and the whole village was silent.

Parvatibai then called her maidservants and the two cooks and ordered them, "Prepare a royal meal for fifty persons. Time it in such a way that it should be ready to be served hot by about midnight."

The servants were surprised but they went their way and set to work. Parvatibai supervised the preparations. When the meal was almost ready and the plantain leaves and seats for fifty persons were laid for supper, she put on a new sari, and except the *mangalsutra,* took off all her ornaments and arranged them in a tray along with her other jewellery. She then sat waiting.

When it was midnight she heard the distant noise of horses' hoofs and sabre-rattling. Soon the noise grew louder. Suddenly there was a loud knock on the door. Her heart almost stopped beating, but the next moment, wearing a calm and eager expression on her face, she hurriedly went to the door and opened it. Before her stood a large man with a ferocious look, a naked sword in his hand.

Parvatibai was scared but with courage she said sweetly, "Come in, brother. Please do come in."

The dacoit was taken aback by this address. But before he could open his mouth Parvatibai said, "I have been waiting for you and other brothers since I received your message this morning." The dacoit stood staring at her, surprised at this unusual welcome.

"Please come in. And don't waste time. Wash your hands and feet. The supper is ready. Have a hearty meal before you do your work."

The dacoit-chief was still hesitating. But she made them sit on the seats and ordered the servants to serve them hot food. While they were eating, she personally attended to each one and pressed them to eat some more, and not feel shy. When they finished their supper, she brought the plateful of ornaments and placing them before the dacoit-chief told him, "Brother, this is all that I have got, but I have kept back only one piece for myself." She indicated towards the *Mangalsutra* on her neck and said, "It is a sacred marriage token which I wear for the long life of my husband and I pray that you should spare it."

The dacoit-chief could contain himself no more. With emotion in his voice he said, "Of course I will spare it. We have eaten your salt and we are never unfaithful to those whose salt we eat. What's more, you have called me brother and given me a brother's welcome. From today you are my sister and I will see that no harm comes to you."

Saying this he returned the plate of ornaments to her and ordered his fellow-dacoits to bring her husband in who was lying on the roadside along with others tied hand and foot. He then set them free and departed.

The villagers were greatly surprised when they heard the story next morning. Since then no dacoit attacked Parvatibai's house, and even today her story is narrated to children.

45
A BHIL STORY OF CREATION

THE Bhil* God—Bhagwan—created the earth and on the earth he created two human beings, a male and a female. They lived as brother and sister and were very happy. They were kind and generous to other creatures. The brother went out to work, while the sister fetched water. While going to the river she would take rice with her and feed it to the fish. This went on for a long time.

So the queen fish Ro, very pleased with the girl's generosity, one day asked her, "Maiden, what reward do you desire? If you have thought of anything, tell me. I shall fulfil it."

"I have thought of nothing," replied the girl.

So the queen fish told her, "Through water and rain the earth will soon be turned upside down. Ask your brother to make a cage, and keep pumpkin seeds with you. When it begins to rain you and your brother should step into the cage, taking the seeds and water with you. Also do not forget to take a cock with you."

Very soon it began to rain, slowly at first, then in torrents, as if the heaven and earth had merged together. For days, the brother and sister floated in their cage, with the seeds, water and the cock with them. At last the rain stopped, the deluge subsided and they found their cage perched on a rock. Soon their cock crowed.

And they heard Bhagwan speaking, "Thus have I turned the world upside down. Has anyone survived? I can hear the crowing of the cock."

The Bhagwan himself went to find out. When he saw the cage, he enquired, "Is anyone inside?"

The girl answered, "We are inside—my brother and I."

---

* The Bhils are aboriginals and have their own culture.

Bhagwan found in the cage the two young people in their prime of life. He asked them, "I have destroyed the whole world. Who warned you of the deluge and gave you advice to make such a cage? You must explain the mystery to me."

The girl replied, "It was the fish Ro who instructed me."

Bhagwan called the fish and asked, "Was it you who brought the knowledge to these two?"

"Oh no, Lord Father, not I," protested the fish.

But when Bhagwan beat the fish, she finally confessed, "Yes, Lord Father, I did it."

Bhagwan was very angry. He said, "Had you at once confessed the truth, nothing would have happened to you." And saying this he cut off its tongue and threw it in the water. Since then the Ro fish have remained without a tongue.

Then Bhagwan looked at the girl and the youth and was pleased with them. He turned the girl's face to the east, the man's to the west. He again made them turn and face each other. Then he asked the man, "Who is she?"

The man, when he looked at the girl, was aware of a very strange feeling in his heart. He replied, "She is my wife."

"Who is this?" he asked the girl, and she too, conscious of a new feeling, said, "He is my husband."

Then God made them man and wife.

Thus this couple started the human race.

46
GODDESS LAKSHMI'S ROCK

In the city of Hyderabad there is a shoulder-high piece of massive rock jutting out of the earth. It is commonly known as Lakshmi's rock. In Marathwada, which was formerly a part of Hyderabad State but now in Maharashtra, there is a legend about this rock.

In olden days Hyderabad was known as Vasumoti Nagar. At that time Hyderabad, though the capital city of Nizam's dominions, was not such a big city as it is now. But by the standard of those times it was quite a big town. Under the Nizam's benevolent rule the people were happy, particularly in the capital city. Nobody was poor. Even poor people could afford to feast on *puran-poli** and other delicacies on festival days. It was a common belief that Goddess Lakshmi (Goddess of wealth) was staying in the city as the guardian angel of the dominion.

Later when sin and evil became rampant, she, in anger, decided to leave the city.

At the site where the present Char Minar stands, there used to be a sentry-post. Everyone had to pass through the post, whether going out or coming into the city. One day the sentry saw a tall and beautiful lady of a noble family coming towards him. She was attired in a Maharashtrian nine-yard green *sari*, green *choli*, with green bangles on her wrists, a big *sindur* mark on her forehead, a pearl nose-ring, and silver anklets on her ankles. The sentry thought this was unusual. He could not understand why a lady of a high family should want to go out of the city alone without any escort. Since it was the king's order that no one should be allowed to leave the city without his permission, the

---

* *Puran-Poli* is a sweet pancake and highly prized delicacy in Maharashtra.

sentry respectfully asked, "Madam, do you want to go out?" She replied, "Yes."

"But no one can leave without the king's permission," said the sentry. "I will go and ask the king. But you must remain here till I return." The lady nodded her assent and said, "Yes, I will," whereupon the sentry left for the palace.

The sentry ran to the king and narrated the story. He sought his permission for the lady's exit. The king was puzzled. He could not make out who the lady could be. He was a very intelligent person. After deep thought he was convinced from the description of the lady that she was none other than Goddess Lakshmi leaving his kingdom.

When the sentry asked again, the king said nothing but chopped his head off with his sword. Everyone in the court was astounded. No one could understand. The poor sentry had committed no fault. Why did the king cut off his head? One courtier summoned courage and asked the king, to which the king explained, "It is the Goddess Lakshmi leaving our kingdom. Since she has promised to stay at the sentry-post till the return of the sentry, I made it impossible for him to go back. Had the sentry returned, Lakshmi would have left our kingdom and with her our wealth and prosperity. Gods are true to their words. Lakshmi will be waiting for him at the spot. Let us all go and see for ourselves."

When the king accompanied by his prime minister and noblemen went to the spot they saw the lady waiting there. But as soon as she saw the party approaching, she disappeared into the earth. A big piece of rock shot up in the place where Lakhshmi was standing.

This rock, known as Lakshmi's rock, still stands and is worshipped.

FOLK TALES OF MANIPUR, MIZORAM, NAGALAND AND TRIPURA

Manipur

Mizoram

Nagaland

Tripura

Manipur is a picturesque area. Songs and dances form an inseparable part of the life of the people. The population mainly comprises the Meitos with 29 tribes and subtribes under the generic name of Kukis and Nagas. The state has an area of 22,327 sq km, population 1,826,714, density 82 per sq km and literacy 60.96 per cent.

Manipur lies on the north eastern boundary of India, south of Nagaland. Burma lies to its east and south, Mizoram to the south-west and Assam to the west. Imphal is the capital city.

Manipuri is the principal language. Each tribe has its own dialect. Forms of Vaishnavism is the springboard of the religion which has given the great Manipuri dances. The Manipuri culture is variegated because of a large number of ethnic groups compressed into a small area and the natural exposure to the different environs. The folklore and traditions are highly interesting and show sensitivity to the regional religious impacts.

Mizo Hills was a district of the Assam province before it became Mizoram, a Union Territory. The principal languages are Mizo and English. The capital city is Aizwal. Mizoram occupies the north-eastern corner of India.

The Mizos comprise a variety of tribes—the Lushais, Pawis, Paihtas, Raltes, Phangis, Hmars, Kukis, Maras and Riangs. These tribes are also found in the neighbouring areas of Manipur, Tripura, Burma and Bangladesh and show aggressive hostility at the slightest provocation. Other tribes in the region are the Chakmas and Tipras.

Among the Lushais the percentage of literacy is 86 per cent. It is due to the pioneering efforts of the Christian missionaries that the average literacy is 81.23 per cent. Christianity is the main religion.

The Mizo folklore is yet unexplored though it has been tapped at the fringes. The dances, songs, tribal traditions and stories are fascinating. The area is a paradise for the anthropologists but under the influence of Christianity much of the traditional lore has been lost.

Nagaland: The state of Nagaland is a narrow strip of mountainous territory between the Brahmaputra Valley of Assam and Burma. It is bound by Assam in the west, Arunachal Pradesh in the north, Burma in the east and Manipur in the south. Kohima is the capital city. The State has an area of 16,579 sq km, population 1,215,573 and literacy 61.30 per cent. There are 1,096 villages and almost every village has a school.

English is the official language of administration and education. Nagamese language is largely used. The Christian missionaries had spread Christianity and English education to the remotest villages.

A picturesque country with some minerals and forestry, it has few large industries but has its own cottage industries. The main tribes are (who are the most advanced and educated of all the other tribes) Angami, Sema, Lotha, Rengma, Chakhesang, Sangtam, Konyak Chang, Phom, Yichangar, Kuki, Khemungan and Zeliang.

Although agriculture is the mainstay of the State only a little more than one-third of the total area is cultivable. The folklore of Nagaland is still largely unexplored. The tales, music and dances, arts and crafts are unique and popular outside the State also.

Tripura became a full-fledged State only in 1972 with Agartala as its capital. The area is 10,486 sq km, population 2,744,827 and density 262 per sq km and literacy 60.39 per cent. Bengali is the State language. Tipra is the spoken language of the inhabitants. The Tipras are colourful, gay people, fond of singing and dancing. Some of their folk tales are superb. Handloom products and cottage industry of Tripura are famous. Tea along with natural gas and some minerals sustain the economy of the State. The gay abandon of the people and their fondness for *jhumming,* i.e., burning forests and putting seeds in the ashes, has affected the forestry and general economy of the area. With Bangladesh in the north-west, west and south and Assam and Mizoram in the north-east, Tripura is naturally exposed to political and cultural impacts from regions beyond. The tribes of Tripura have a strong affinity for the tribes beyond the borders, that is, Bangladesh, resulting in immense similarity of folklore and culture.

47

LAIKHUT SHANGBI

ONCE upon a time there lived a small family of two children and their parents. They were very poor. The man had to work for others to feed the family. Sometimes he had to go to work far away from his home and he would not return for two to three days. When he was away, his wife was very afraid. But she never let the children know of it.

At that time there was a belief among the people that an evil spirit called Laikhut Shangbi roamed about at night in the form of a woman with a pair of long hands and if it found that there was no adult male in the house, it would enter the house or push its long arms through holes of the walls, grab anybody found inside, pull him out and run away. The people were, therefore, terribly afraid of this spirit and as soon as the sun set, they used to remain inside their homes at night.

One day it so happened that the father was away at work and Laikhut Shangbi also decided to call at his house. Laikhut Shangbi called out from outside asking the mother if the father was in. The mother panicked but she did not lose her head. She immediately replied that her husband was at home. Hearing this, Laikhut Shangbi got terrified lest the man came out and killed it. So it took to its heels as fast as it possibly could. Laikhut Shangbi, however, did not give up. It visited the same house on the following three nights also and demanded to know if the father was at home. Getting the same answer it fled again.

On the fifth day, however, the father was back and the mother was very happy. She told him how Laikhut Shangbi had attempted to enter the house and how she had bluffed it away each time. They discussed how they could possibly destroy Laikhut Shangbi. It was decided that if Laikhut Shangbi called again when the father was also at home and it enquired if he was in, then the mother should tell it that he was out.

As expected, Laikhut Shangbi came that night and put the same question. The mother pretended great panic and replied in a trembling voice that she was afraid, her husband had gone out to work at a distant place and he was not coming home that night. Laikhut Shangbi was overjoyed at the information and it gloated in the thought that now it will be able to kill the whole family and make a nice meal of them. So thinking Laikhut Shangbi gleefully thrust her long hands into the house through an opening and played them around to catch hold of the victims. The mother kept herself and the two children huddled in one corner which Laikhut Shangbi's hands were unable to reach easily. All this time the father was quietly waiting with a long sword in his hands and as Laikhut Shangbi was moving its arms around searching for the family, he hacked off one of the hands with a stroke of his sharp sword. It sent Laikhut Shangbi into a wild scream which aroused the whole village and it fled as fast as it could, never to return again. Laikhut Shangbi never troubled the people again and they lived happily, for which they remained ever grateful to the father for his courage and to the mother for her presence of mind.

48
HUMILITY AND PRIDE

Two Pawi brothers, Liando and Thalsial, were very poor and the village chief ill-treated them. They were always ordered to do various chores for the village. The two brothers submissively obeyed.

Once the whole village left for hunting in the forest. All the adults have to join in such hunts. The two poor brothers also joined but they were at the rear of the party while the village chief and the rich folks led.

On the way they crossed a stream in the jungle. They saw something like a bridge that spanned the stream and all of them but the two brothers crossed the stream by walking over that.

While moving on the bridge, the brothers realised that it was really a huge and fat python that had gone to sleep. Pythons have a long spell of sleep at a particular time of the year. The brothers rushed to the party that had moved ahead and gave them the good news.

The party returned. The python was cut into pieces. The brothers were given the stomach with entrails, considered to be the worst part of the meat. The brothers brought the stomach part to their hut. At night when they chopped the stomach, they found valuable jewellery in it. Evidently the python had eaten up some women who were wearing jewellery.

They kept their secret. Sometime later the village chief's elder daughter fell in love with Liando. The village chief did not like that poor Liando should marry his daughter. He demanded a big bride-price. Among the tribals of that area the bridegroom has to pay bride-price at the time of marriage.

Liando paid the bride-price by giving a portion of the ornaments. Everyone was surprised but nobody knew the secret of the brothers.

Once an old man passing through the village wanted shelter for the night. The brothers offerd him shelter and food for the night. The old man was pleased and accepted their hospitality.

When he was leaving the next morning, the old man told them that he was the chief of the neighbouring village and asked them to pay him a visit. The brothers visited him after sometime.

Lessia, the chief of the neighbouring village, presented them a lame female *mithun*. The brothers did not protest when a lame *mithun* was being given. They thanked their host profusely and sincerely for the gift and left.

To their amazement, they found the female *mithun* giving birth to a *mithun* calf every month. Very soon the brothers had a herd of *mithuns*. Now *mithuns* are like cows much valued and a man having a herd of *mithuns* was considered a very rich man.

The village chief now himself offered his second daughter in marriage to the yonger brother, Thalsial. Thalsial refused but the elder brother agreed. Thalsial did not want to marry a girl from the proud and rich family of the village chief.

The brothers showed that humility in a man is an asset while pride is a drawback.

49

THE FAIRY AND THE HUNTER

SOMETIMES fairies from heaven come down to earth for sports. Particularly they love to swim and bathe in a clear pool of water.

Kut is an important festival in Mizoram. Once some fairies had come to bathe in a pond. A young man hurrying to join the Kut festivities saw the fairies and hid himself behind a big oak tree.

The fairies dumped their clothes in a heap and got into the water. The young man rushed and took away the clothes of one fairy. The fairies were frightened, gathered their clothes and flew away. The fairy whose dress had been taken could not fly.

She appealed to the young man and said, "I will give you plenty of *shikar* everyday if you want. But do not shoot any animal with a white face as I ride on such animals." The young man was happy with the boon, returned her clothes and she flew away.

From that day the young man hunted plenty of animals and became the object of envy.

But he soon tired of hunting. He developed a dislike for killing animals.

He prayed for the fairy. The fairy appeared again and on hearing him took away the special gift. He became a normal hunter again.

Excess of anything loses its pleasure.

50
THE STORY OF NORBOO

THERE lived a woman in a village who had a son. His name was Rokepoo. The mother and son passed their days in great hardship. When Rokepoo saw that other people had land, cattle and houses, he too wished to cultivate land and possess what others had. He always used to potter around other people's fields, but no one ever cared for him. So, he spent his time sadly walking around the fields or sitting on the river bank and he did not know how he could fulfil his desire.

At that time, the villagers left for many far flung places for trading.

One day, while Rokepoo was sitting beside the river and thinking what to do, two traders passed by him. He heard one of them saying, "Horns are in great demand in that village where the people wear tails on their bodies. They buy any horn to make musical pipes."

The news filled Rokepoo with hope that at last he would be able to fulfil his dreams. He remembered that they had an old, rotten horn lying in the house, and he thought of taking it along to sell.

He went home. He said to his mother, "Mother, I wish to take away that bison horn. If I can sell it, then I should be able to buy a cattle or two with the money."

His mother replied, "My son, you and that horn are my life. Now if I lose both, how shall I live?"

But Rokepoo did not change his mind. He reasoned, "If a man cannot live like a man, then of what use is any property? The rich save their money to live happily, to spend when the need arises, and to provide for necessary things when they are in difficulty. My father also left this horn to be used when I am in difficulty."

Thus arguing, he decided that he would not listen to his mother's dissuasion and he left with the horn. His mother looked out as far as she could see him.

As he was proceeding, he painted gay pictures of his future days. Thought he, "I shall sell the horn and with the money I shall get, I shall buy two bullocks, I shall buy some land also, and I shall plough the land with those bullocks and then grow paddy, and so on and so forth."

As he was thinking, he began to sing.

He also thought, "If I can't sell the horn, I won't come back home. A man should set an aim and then achieve it. I must be able to cultivate my own land."

Thus thinking and marching on, he reached a village. There he settled down under a tree to spend the night.

As soon as it was morning, he entered the village.

Seeing him and the horn of a bison, the villagers were very excited. The word went round that "A rich trader has brought a costly and beautiful horn which will make an excellent pipe."

A wealthy villager bought the horn for four pieces of silver mohurs. Rokepoo was very happy and headed for home. He had come a very long way from home for the first time, and so, on his return journey lost his way and landed in a strange village.

In that village all the people armed with bows, arrows, knives and spears, were chasing a cat to kill it. Rokepoo felt very sorry for the cat. When he asked the people why they wanted to kill the cat, they said: "This cat eats up everything in the village. Fish is so rare here. If we bring home any fish after three days of labour, this cat immediately eats it up. She does not leave any milk, curd, butter or cream. That's why we are out to kill her."

He advised the people, "Why don't you treat her well and keep her in the home? She will then stop stealing. Or, just catch her and give her to me."

The people decided to catch her alive. All the young men and women caught her alive. Rokepoo paid them one silver coin and sent them away. He reached another village with the cat. There he found the people chasing a rat to kill it saying that it had destroyed their crops. He set the cat after the rat and it caught the rat and produced it before him. He paid the people a silver coin and marched off with the cat and the rat.

After a few days, Rokepoo, the cat and the rat reached another village and found the people chasing a dog saying that it had bitten a man. He bought the dog with the third silver coin and at last he arrived back home with the three animals.

When the villagers heard that Rokepoo was back from abroad, they crowded into his house to see what new things he had brought with him.

They broke into laughter on seeing what he had brought. They called him a trader in rats and made jokes. But he was unmoved.

His mother threw up her hands in desperation and mocked at him, "Tomorrow you should teach the rat how to plough and you should milk the cat and at night you should tie the dog in the field so he will provide manure to the ground with his dung."

Rokepoo calmly remarked, "Mother, I have done the right thing. These animals are bound to be found useful when the time comes. I have still enough money left to buy a pair of bullocks. I shall go out tomorrow to buy bullocks. But you will have to look after these three animals. They also have life in them. You feed them."

Early in the morning on the following day, he hit the road to buy cattle.

His way lay through a village. While going through that village, he saw that the villagers were chasing a huge snake to kill it. When he asked them why they wanted to kill the snake, they told him, "The snake lives in this wood. He bites our cattle and horses whenever they go there."

Rokepoo asked them, "But why do you let your cattle and horses go there at all? I think, you are going to commit a great sin, if you kill the snake. He would not have done any harm to others if they did not do any harm to him. You just let him go. I will take this." And so saying he gave them the last silver coin he had and sent them away.

The people let the snake go when they received the silver coin. In fact it was not a snake. It was Lee Deemee, daughter of the snake-king. One day she and her lover were playing in that wood. They were exhausted and they fell asleep. Cattle ran over her lover and crushed him to death. She swore that she would take revenge and since then remaining hidden behind the bush, she would bite any cow or horse in sight. That was the reason why the people were trying to kill her. When Rokepoo saved her, she was very pleased with him. She appeared before him in the form of a beautiful girl. Rokepoo got frightened. She said to him, "Let me have your hand."

Rokepoo offered his right hand. She took out a piece of "Norboo" (Diamond) from under her cloth and tucking it into his hand, she said, "May you be happy. Ask you mother to wear it on her neck. But for you, I would have died today. You call me any time you need help."

Rokepoo asked her who she was.

She told him everything. Then she took leave of him and vanished. Rokepoo tied the diamond in a piece of cloth and went home.

The Buddhist scriptures say: "You should help others if they are in difficulty. Buddha (Chaangee) will reward you."

Rokepoo's luck also turned for the better. From that day, his house began to be filled with riches. He became so rich that even Rajas and Maharajas did not dare to visit him. He led a happy and contented life. But he continued to have love and kindness for animals, and sympathy for the poor.

Rokepoo's reputation travelled far and wide. When thieves and robbers heard of his riches, they lost all sleep. They kept thinking how they could rob him of his riches.

Rokepoo put the diamond round his mother's neck just as the girl had told him to do. The thieves were on the lookout for an opportunity to swindle the old woman pretending that they wanted to buy or sell gold, silver, pearls and diamonds.

One day, three thieves, disguised as jewellers, called on her. When she saw the jewellery, she was fascinated. She offered to buy it with gold. But the three men demanded the piece of diamond as the price for the whole lot of their jewellery. The old woman was glad to think that she would be able to get gold ornaments worth lakhs of rupees in exchange for only one piece of diamond. She gladly took off the diamond from her neck and gave it away to the jewellers and put on a gold necklace. The jewellers felt very happy and saluting the woman, again and again, they went away. The cat was watching everything.

Since then Rokepoo's riches began to vanish. Rokepoo's family became poor. His hardship knew no bounds.

With Rokepoo and his mother, the rat, cat and the dog also had to starve for want of food.

One day at noon, the rat asked the cat, "In the past we used to get a variety of good food. Why aren't we getting it now?"

The cat replied, "The other day, I saw that three travellers came here and exchanged the diamond which our mother was wearing for the jewellery. We are getting less food to eat from that day. I think, that diamond is at the root of all these things."

When the rat heard this he called the dog also. They held a council under a tree and discussed how to teach the thieves a good lesson.

Yapped the dog, "I shall be able to trace those men's footsteps even if they have gone very far."

Mewed the cat, "I won't make any mistake in identifying those men. But, suppose they have kept the diamond in a wooden chest?"

As soon as he heard this the rat stuck out his chest and squeaked, "I take the responsibility for that."

After this, the three animals set out to get the diamond. The dog led the way and the other two followed him. As they were going, they talked about many things.

After walking for a few days, they became very hungry. The dog felt nervous fearing that the other two might kill and eat him. But, he kept mum.

When someone starves and he does not know from where his next meal would come, he does bad things. So, our three animals too were forced to take to stealing to save their lives.

One day, as the rat was hiding in a house to steal some rice, he overheard the houseowner saying to his wife, "The rich trader who lives across that river, bought a diamond from some wealthy person by paying him several lakh rupees, a year ago. From that day his riches have doubled. True, only riches beget riches."

When he heard this, the rat scurried back to see the cat and the dog and told them what he had heard. They immediately ran to the river bank. Fearing that the current of the river might sweep them away, the cat sat on the dog's back and the rat on top of the cat and in that formation, they crossed the river. After reaching the other bank of the river, they set out to find the thief's house.

By then, it was almost midnight. The trader and his wife had just returned. The rat quietly went under their cot and hid himself there. The cat kept mewing around so that the man would show up and she could make sure that he was the chap whom she had seen before.

Hearing the mews, the wife said to her husband, "Plenty of cats seem to have come to our house. I won't mind. But, God help us, should rats also come. Cats can't break into that wooden chest and steal the diamond from there. But a rat can."

When the rat overheard it, he was very happy. For, now he knew at once where the diamond lay. He quietly inched towards the wooden box and then began to gnaw it. He gnawed it away before daybreak and picked out the norboo (diamond) and held it with its teeth. But, as he was scurrying across the trader's cot with the diamond between its teeth, it dropped off from his mouth and fell on the bed. There was a big hue and cry in the house. Some said, "The rat which was seen scurrying off was not a real rat, it must have been some spirit."

Some others said that they thought it was a magician.

After some argument the man said, "Be it what it may, but from now on, I shall keep the norboo in my mouth. Then no one will be able to pinch it."

A man cannot be happy with ill-gotten riches. On the contrary, he asks for trouble at every step.

When the man hid the norboo in his mouth, the three animals again held a conference. The rat said, "I won't stop unless I have recovered the diamond. You too should keep yourself in readiness."

And so saying, the rat againt crept into the tradesman's house. He tucked the tip of his tail into the nostrils of the man and shook it hard. The man gave out a loud sneeze and the norboo flew out and fell near the dog. The dog was waiting for it. He picked it up in his mouth and dashed off.

The whole incident sparked off an uproar in the man's house. His people chased the dog. But they could not catch him. They consoled themselves with the thought that the dog and the rat must be two divine beings and gave up the chase.

The dog, the cat and the rat reached the riverbank and after taking a little rest, began crossing the river. The diamond was given to the rat and the three set out to cross the river in the same formation in which they had crossed before. Before they could reach the other bank, a huge fish leapt up and swallowed the rat. The dog and the cat found themselves in a great fix. They squatted on two stones and began to think of a plan to get out of it. Just at that time an otter who was their friend, and was passing by, saw them. He screeched out to them, "Hi, chums, what are you so deeply thinking about? Have you taken to doing chaam?*"

In reply, the dog laughed and told the otter all that had happened.

Out of fellow-feeling, the otter said he would help them. He set off catching every fish and eating it. At last he caught the fish which had swallowed the rat and set the rat free.

The three animals were very happy to be reunited. They placed the norboo on a stone and spread themselves out in the sun for a nap. But the rat could not sleep out of an unknown fear. He squatted near a small stone and rested there. Suddenly, a kite swooped down, grabbed the diamond and flew off to a tree. The rat watched the whole thing very closely. He woke up the dog and the cat and told them what he had seen. The cat said to the dog, "You should just lie in wait under the tree. I will push down the kite from above and you will finish him off as soon as he drops on the ground."

The cat kept a watch on the road.

Seeing a shining thing in the kite's beak, birds of all kinds kept flying around him. It made him feel mighty proud. He was cackling gayly all the while. The poor bird completely forgot all about the diamond. It was engrossed in its own thoughts.

In the meantime the cat stealthily crawled up to him and suddenly flung herself over the bird. The bird hurt its wings and rolled down onto the ground. The dog finished him off. The three animals then feasted on the kite's meat. After taking some rest, they returned to their master's house and gave him the diamond. Rokepoo was very happy to find the diamond which he had lost and also to meet the three animals. Riches again filled his house. From then on they lived happily.

---

* *Chaam* is meditation. The Sherdukpens are Buddhists and so they are quite familiar with meditation and prayer.

51
THE TWO BROTHERS

LONG ago there were two brothers, Asa and Munserung. Asa was the elder brother and intelligent. Munserung, the younger brother, was foolish.

They ran a wayside inn and passing travellers would often rest there and have some food. The two brothers made fair living.

One day Asa went out fishing while Munserung was left at the inn. Some travellers came. Instead of being helpful the foolish brother annoyed them and came to blows. The travellers caught hold of him as a captive and marched away.

Munserung was howling and weeping and shouting for his brother. The brother heard him and he saw from a distance that Munserung was being led away.

He made a plan. He ran by a short-cut and reached a jungle. He climbed up a tree and tied a number of fish to the different branches. He came down and met the travellers.

He implored them to free his captive brother. The leader of the travellers said, "Yes, we shall, but he has insulted us. You must pay a proper price for his foolishness."

The elder brother said, "Sir, I will take you to a jungle tree that bears fish as fruits. Whenever you want you could go and get fish." "What an absurd story," the leader said. The elder brother took the party and showed the tree from which a number of fish hung.

The younger brother was freed. The travellers plucked the fish and went away to return later and be disappointed.

The two brothers shifted their inn to another place. They did not want to face the travellers again.

52
WHY DO THE MYNAH BIRDS HAVE GOLDEN EARRINGS?*

THE mynah birds have an attractive pair of golden rings while Dorick pheasants have bloodshot eyes and ears. The Mikirs have a story for them.

King Tarkoping Recho and his queen had a very pretty and sweet-tempered daughter. She was a keen rider and would go out riding every morning.

One morning, however, on return from the ride she suddenly fell ill. Nothing could save her. She passed away. The king and queen were beside themselves with grief. They decided to observe the *shradh* (last rites for the dead) immediately without observing the usual gap of one month.

The Mynah and the Dorick pheasant were requisitioned to sing at the site of the *shradh,* lamenting the death. The king promised a pair of golden earrings to whosoever performed the best.

The Dorick pheasant started at a loud and shrill note. The pheasant's eyes and ears became bloodshot with the strain and after sometime she was exhausted and fell asleep.

The Mynah bird did not shriek hoarse like the pheasant. It sang intermittently but poured out melodious, plaintive notes throughout the day and the night. The king and the queen felt very pleased and presented the Mynah with a pair of golden earrings. The Mynah birds still have them.

The Dorick pheasant retained the bloodshot eyes and ears. They still have them.

---

* A folk tale from Tripura

53

LOVE AND LIGHTNING*

WHEN there are thunderous cloudbursts preceded by sheet-lightning changing into forked lightning, the young men and women of Tripura very fondly raise their fingers and shout, "There, you see Nagurai and Nakhapili, the two lovers, go to heaven." This is an impromptu homage to a folk tale that has held through centuries in Tripura, one of the tribal States of India where most of the people live in shifting villages by the hills and slopes and rushing brooks. They eke out an existence by *jhumming* a portion of the jungle or hill slope and when the soil is no more fertile they shift. They just burn a patch of forest and sow seeds in the ashes, that is known as *jhumming*. They lead a joyous and outdoor life, the men and women enjoy themselves with songs, dances, food and liquor and hunting or collecting jungle fruits and flowers.

Champrai Sardar was one of the important men in that small unnamed village by a rushing brook on the slope of a hill. His wife was Khulumati. Their son Nagurai was a remarkable youth with indomitable energy and physical strength. Very few youths would challenge him to wrestling. Did not Nagurai beat the professional *Pahalwan* (wrestler) from the north sometime back and get a reward of twenty rupees from the government official in the town?

Khulumati had gone for a bath in the brook while Nagurai was working in the *jhum* nearby. Suddenly the mother shouted for the son, "Nagu, Nagu, please rush, come at once." Hearing his mother's urgent call Nagurai leapt and was with her in a minute. The mother pointed at the body of a young girl being swept by the

* Probably the most popular story of the Tipras, the people of Tripura.

swirling river. The current was strong and swift as is usual with the hilly rivers, and swimming was hazardous. But Nagurai jumped in, swam and caught the body of the girl gently and with great skill brought her to the shore. Softly did he lift her and carefully stretch the body near his mother. By that time Khulumati had gathered a number of villagers by her shouts. Some said the girl was dead and others said she was not. There was a stampede near the girl but none knew what to do.

Where was Nagurai? He had gone into the hut and brought a bamboo *pati* (Just a few split bamboos held together with wild dried twigs) and put the girl on it and with the help of a few boys brought the girl to their hut. He had already sent for his uncle Chadarai Sardar who was an *Ojha* and knew many medicines. Chadarai was having his meal but he left it unfinished and gathering his small cloth bag of medicines rushed. He said the girl was still alive. He pushed in something through the mouth and swung the hands. The girl started bringing out water. The crowd yelled that the girl was alive. Nagurai cleared the small *angan* (Courtyard) of the crowd and ordered everybody to be quiet. His father Champrai and mother Khulumati were the only persons to look after the girl. Chaddarai Ojha gave some more medicines and said the girl would live but she should be allowed to have a long sleep.

There was a sensation in the village. Who was this beautiful damsel? None could recognise her as belonging to any of the nearby *jhums.* Was she trying to commit suicide? Did she slip while bathing? If she was bathing with others, why has not someone come following the river, enquiring for her? The village young girls told each other that their Naguda was a fine specimen of a youth who risked his life and saved the girl. The young men mostly envied their Naguda but would not give out anything as they were all afraid of Nagurai.

The girl was saved. Khulumati had no daughter and she poured her love for the daughter she always wanted on the one she had now got. Strangely, the girl would not give away anything about her. When asked she would burst into tears and Khulumati would draw her to her lap and fondle her. Her name was Nakhapili. (In Tripura, no one would give that name to any girl lest she has the misfortune of this girl). Champrai Sardar, Chadai and the seniors scouted within ten miles but got no clue as to who the girl was. Enquiries slowly ebbed, particularly because the family became very fond of Nakhapili. She became a part of the house and the apple of Khulumati's eye.

The village girls used to speak highly of Nagurai to Nakhapili and often told her how lovingly and softly he had carried her to the bank and how very bravely he had swam to save her. The girls often sighed as to who the lucky girl was who would nestle against the strong chest of Nagurai and be fondled by his strong arms. Nakhapili started looking askance at Nagurai. Young girls understand the secret throbs of a young man and the messages of the eyes that become soft and happy when a young girl is near. It did not take long for Nakhapili to know that Nagurai had a tender heart for her. Was she not also attracted to him. She was, but she strove hard to keep back her feelings. Who was she, an unknown castaway girl to aspire for the son of the Sardar of the village with that wonderful body and the cattle and the poultry that he would get from the father? And she was just nobody. The village girls would not leave Nakhapili and they often told her stories about Nagurai and made no secret that anyone of them would run away with Nagurai to a distant place and start a *jhum* there if only Nagurai gave a hint. Yes, they were anxious to know if Nagurai has had any secret talks with her. Nagurai had a fine *Langa* on his head with a figure of a boy in a jungle and a brook. A *Langa* is a small piece of cloth for the head. Did Nakhapili weave it? Nakhapili did not understand the hidden meaning of the question. She said she had done it. All the girls then started teasing her. The eldest of the spinsters warned her that she should not be foolish to think that Champrai Sardar would every marry his son to her even if the son wanted. Since then the poor Nakhapili was a target for teasing.

But Champrai Sardar and his wife Khulumati did not know what was slowly taking shape. They did not know that when Khulumati went for her bath and Nakhapili was alone at times, Nagurai would rush back home on the pretext of being in need of a drink from the field. Nakhapili would hand over the bamboo-funnel with the home brewn wine and their fingers would touch and involuntarily remain locked for few moments. Nagurai would gulp down the beverage and rush off again.

One day the young boys and girls gathered at the village open and started for the jungle to collect the *Muiah* (the young bamboo shoots.) The young bamboo shoots are a delicacy with the men and women of Tripura and collecting them from the thickest jungle was a sport. Nakhapili also went with the other young girls. Each of them, boys and girls, had a basket and a *langa*. The boys had a sharp *dao* (axe) to cut the bamboos. The *langa* that Nakhapili had was woven by Nagurai. The young girls wanted to know when and who had woven Nakhapili's *langa*. Nakhapili feebly answered she had done it herself but the way she gave this out was enough for the girls. The boys and girls would often burst out in some folk songs. Whenever there was an interlude, the girls would crack youthful jokes.

It was very usual for the crowd to break up in the jungle but remain near one another. The boys would cut the bamboos and put them in the baskets. The girls would collect the twigs, fruits and edible flowers. Occasionally the boys would give a shout and the girls would respond. They must be close to each other. Are there not wild animals that prowl and might attack? This is the usual manner by which the expeditions in the jungles are organised. If perchance any deer or rabbit was caught and knifed, there would be great outburst of joy. It is such raids that thrill the youths and bring them together. Other young people would close their eyes if a pair strayed away into seclusion. (They have a permissive society but after marriage the demands are very stringent.)

Was it deliberate that Nakhapili would be gathering fruits and flowers and twigs quite close to Nagurai? Or probably she did not know it. Suddenly, Nakhapili heard a hissing sound and was startled. It was a large python that was unwinding itself from a tree. The python was so large that the head was wound around one tree while the tail portion on another. The shining eyes were fixed on Nakhapili. The python's embrace was enough to break the bones of a person and the fangs were deadly. Nakhapili yelled and involuntarily shouted "Naguda, Naguda." Nagurai was cutting bamboo shoots nearby. He rushed with his *dao* (axe) in the hand. Nakhapili pointed her finger at the rushing python. No words could come out. Nagurai took in the situation. He rushed and pressed the python near the head. So the python's fangs could not do the deadly work but the python's tail went round Nagurai. Nakhapili yelled and several boys and girls rushed to them. They saw the deadly fight between Nagurai and the python. With his *dao* Nagurai impaled the snake's head and severed it. Blood spilled out and Nagurai's cloth became crimson. Slowly the tail slipped off the body. The body of the large python was still writhing although severed from the head. The twigs and branches were squashed. Nagurai came out of the embrace of the snake. Great was the rejoicing.

The snake's fleshy portion was chopped off to be carried to the village. Nakhapili was still panting with fright and gave a sidelong look of bashful love to Nagurai and the latter thought all his labour was worth its while.

Nagurai had a wash at a jungle spring and wiped off as much of the snake's blood as possible. The party returned and unwittingly Nakhapili walked a little distance behind Nagurai. Great was the rejoicing of the village elders when the party of the boys and girls came back. Nagurai's uncle, the *Ojha,* made a decoction of some leaves and made Nagurai drink it. He rubbed some leaves on his body to remove the effects of the snake's touch. He gave a strong dose of home-made liquor. (The older the brew the stronger it is and they keep a separate pail of them. The more respected person is given the stronger brew. For day-to-day use one-day-old brew is taken.)

That night there was a special feast at Nagurai's house. Two fat pigs were offered to God and sacrificed and the meat was cooked and distributed throughout the village. Some birds were also offered with particular kind of feathers which is obligatory for such occasions. At dead of the night two young hearts were throbbing in two different rooms under the same roof. No clear thoughts but the uppermost were what might have happened to the other. The boy was thinking of the girl and the girl's thought was for the boy. Neither of them could sleep. At dawn the pigs were snorting, indicating the presence of a wild animal near their pen. The girl and the boy rushed out to the pen, the pigs were quietened and their fingers touched while examining the door of the pen. They came back immediately before anyone else could arise. The old couple were snoring, the effect of taking too much liquor. The two young hearts were somehow soothed.

The old parents of Nagurai had already started looking for a suitable bride for Nagurai. In their society the boy has to prove worthy of the girl by passing some tests. One fine evening when the pigs were being put back in their pen and none was nearby,

Nagurai whispered to the girl: "Nakhapili, are you stone of that hill or the steel of the *dao*? Do you not understand? What more tests do you want me to go through to let me wed you?" She could not reply with words. But her eyes did. She just stretched her hand and Nagurai pulled her close to him. It was for a second but the betrothal was solemnised before God.

How to broach the matter with the old couple? They were still looking around for a bride from outside. Nagurai took courage and took his first cousin, the uncle's daughter, in confidence. She whispered to her aunt, "Auntie, why go on seeking a bride when the bride is in the house?" Nagurai's mother had already thought of it. But the want of knowledge of the parentage of Nakhapili was an obstacle. The girl should not be of prohibitive relationship. Otherwise she had loved her as her own daughter. Anyway, she told the Sardar. The Sardar had also thought of it but he was hesistant and wanted an opening. What about the boy? Was he agreeable? The old woman laughed and asked the old man to think of his younger days when he would move about near her under some pretext or other. Both laughed aloud. What about the girl? The mother was annoyed. Could there be any Tiprah young damsel who would not like to wed her son? But she wanted to be sure.

Nakhapili was sent for. Khulumati embraced her and said, "Child, we want to make you our real daughter by giving our son in marriage to you. What have you to say?" The bashful Nakhapili stooped and touched the parent's feet. That showed her willingness. No girl could be forced in that society to marry. The whole village was agog with joy. This is what they had all expected but none would dare suggest it lest the feelings of the older clan members are hurt as the girl's parentage was still a mystery. Nagurai was made much of wherever he would go. As for Nakhapili, her beauty had increased hundredfold since the parents' approval. Their betrothal by touching each other's hand was a sacred secret and they feigned bashfulness. Nagurai had to shift to his uncle's house till the marriage would take place. The *Kakchungmani* (the engagement) was held with pomp and gaiety.

The village priests were consulted and the marriage date was fixed. Extra feed was allowed to the pigs to fatten them for the great occasion. Messages were sent to all the *gotias* in the different *jhums* even fifty miles away that Nagurai's wedding was fixed. It was an occasion for the whole village to celebrate. Among the Tipra tribals forgetting a *gotia* on such an occasion means a tear in the clan life that will go down the generation. Even a poor relation shall not pardon the offence of being left out.

The day arrived. Dozens and dozens of Tipra men and women, young and old, came to join the wedding. Girls were gaily decorated with flowers and the men had sticks in their hands and colourful *langas* on their heads or shoulders. The *Haya* (platform on which the marriage was to be performed) had been raised three days before by the villagers and was decorated with leaves and flowers made out of bambooflakes. There was plenty of meat and drinks and songs and dances were going on from time to time. The whole village was present. Some were supervising the cooking of pigmeat, small crabs, bamboo-shoots and rice. Others were exchanging jokes. A group was fixing up the *bedi* (the raised place) where the bride and the groom were to be seated. The *Achai* (priest) was throwing his weight about. The *Chiklas* (the unmarried young men and girls) were making the most of these opportunities to cast sidelong looks of love at their lovers. The *pandah* (the particular spot where drinking takes place) was full of elders. The younger ones, not yet entitled to have a seat at the *pandah,* were occasionally dropping in and had a fill on the quiet while the elders looked away deliberately. Rejoicings were at their peak when a distant cousin of Champrai Sardar, living sixty miles away after shifting a few *jhums,* turned up with his second wife and a young daughter who were not known to Champrai or Khulumati. The two families had lost touch with each other for years. Champrai Sardar had only heard that his cousin had lost his first wife and had married another woman who was sharp-tongued and domineering.

The bride Nakhapili was sitting in another room surrounded by young gay girls singing and cracking jokes, looking resplendent with the flowers on her.

The newcomer Jumia sat at the site of *pandah* while his wife went straight to the cooking site where all the elderly women were working. Their young daughter went into the room where the bride was sitting and talking away gaily. On seeing the bride she felt that she knew her. She looked so much like her elder sister by her father's first wife who was supposed to have committed suicide by jumping into the river. The elder sister was ill-treated by the stepmother. She had to do all the domestic chores and got very little food to eat. Day and night she was abused and she could bear it no longer.

The girl did not accost Nakhapili but rushed to her mother who was in the kitchen and whispered. The mother came to the room of the bride and one look was enough. She gnashed her teeth and immediately told Khulumati that the bride was related to her son and there could be no marriage. The news spread immediately and the wedding house was turned into a mourning site. The bride tore off her bridal decorations and huddled into a corner and wept. Khulumati and Champrai inwardly cursed that Jumia should turn up at all but had to concede that there could be no marriage between Nagurai and Nakhapili as they belonged to one *gotra*.

Nagurai at the other house tore off his bridegroom's apparel and wiped off the sandal paste from his forehead. He was simply stunned and could not think of what to do. The guests departed one by one but Jumia, his wife and the daughter stayed on. Jumia's wife went on feeding the people with the concocted story of Nakhapili being a flippant girl for which she was severely abused and she had made an escape and they thought she had committed suicide. Some recalled that Nakhapili had persistently refused to tell her parentage and whereabout. They believed the false story. Not a word came out of Nakhapili. She was benumbed.

It was night. The cooked pigs' meat was untouched. The elders had been doing nothing but drinking to drown the sense of disaster and they fell asleep at the *pandah*. The women slept wherever they could. Nakhapili remained where she was. Not one young girl stayed back to comfort her. Some were envious of her beauty while others thought why she should pinch Nagurai, the doyen of the youths of the *jhum*. Strangely, after some bemoaning even Khulumati felt that Nakhapili had cheated her.

At dead of night Nakhapili heard a stealthy movement and someone touched her hands. It was Nagurai. Nagurai whispered, "Nakha, Let us run away from all these people to a far off place where no one would know us and let us have our own *jhum*, our own little hut by the brook where you shall be the queen. I have saved your life twice, now you save mine. If you do not come with me I shall commit suicide surely. Come Nakha, let us go just now. The night is still young and we can cover many miles." Nakhapili pressed the finger of Nagurai—that was enough.

In the still of the night the couple left with the stars above as their guide and witness. Quickly, they crossed the forest and a hill which the villagers of his *jhum* would not normally cross. By morning, they saw another jungle. They entered it. They ate some jungle fruits and drank the brook water. They snatched some sleep by turns and started walking again. In this way, they walked for three days and nights and then they stopped. They found a straggling village, met the Sardar and started their *jhum*. The other young men and women helped them raise their small nest. No one questioned as to who they were or where they came from. It was presumed their previous *jhum* had lost fertility and so they left. The fine physique of Nagurai and the supple body of Nakhapili and their behaviour at once captivated the villagers.

The couple sang and danced again. They gave their labour free as the other people had given theirs to them for making the jhum. In this way, Nagurai and Nakhapili were completely merged into the new village.

Champrai and Khulumati searched for Nagurai and Nakhapili in the morning and decided they had both committed suicide or had run away. Jhumia Sardar and his sharp-tongued wife went back not at all sorry that they had created all the havoc. Out of sheer grief the parents of Nagurai took to their bed.

Months passed. Champrai Sardar and his friends had to change their *jhum* as the patch had lost its fertility. They still yearned for their son although their love for Nakhapili got worn out. They started blaming Nakhapili for keeping back her past connections.

Chadarai's daughter Papti was married two years later. The bride had to walk with the groom three days to reach the groom's village. As was the custom, four young men were to accompany the couple, enjoy a feast there and return. Spending the night was no problem. They could knock at any door and they would be welcomed.

At last they reached the village of the father-in-law of Papti. On the way, they noticed a beautiful small *Tong* (hut on a *tillha*, top of a small hill). After some rest one of the party wanted to know who possessed the beautiful tong on the *tillha*. They were told that the couple had come there two years before and the name of the *jumia* was Nagurai. They were surprised and wanted to be sure if he was their Nagurai with Nakhapili in the lover's nest.

There was much merry-making, drinking and feasting on poultry and pigs. Nagurai got news of his parents and sent words of love through them, and so did Nakhapili.

The party went back and informed Champrai Sardar and Khulumati that Nagurai and Nakhapili were alive and happy. The young men were very joyous about it. The old couple immediately left for the new village of Nagurai with two of them to guide the way.

Nagurai and Nakhapili were returning home from the jungle. The *langa* of Nagurai was full of fuel and other titbits while the *langa* of Nakhapili was full of ripe fruits and tubers. They found their *tong* alive with people. They were surprised. They found Champrai Sardar and Khulumati, both grown very old and feeble, and their two young friends. Nagurai touched the feet of his parents as also did Nakhapili. They all wept.

After a little while the old man said, "Nagu, we have come to take you. We cannot live without you, do come. We shall marry you to some lovely young girl and we shall also have Nakha married well. We did want you both to marry. But as Nakha is your cousin, the marriage could not take place. God had intervened. Do not blame us."

The words were like a bombshell to Nagurai and Nakhapili. After a pause Nagurai slowly but firmly replied, "Father, my fate has led me away. God should not be blamed. I shall not return. I cannot live without Nakhapili. Without her I shall die. Please go back. Give us your blessings if you can. If not, give us your curses. We shall live with them." Khulumati then tried to win over her son. She wept and hugged her son and beseeched him to come back. She also turned to Nakha and told her, "We shall marry you to an equally good and strong young man. Please leave my son." Nakhapili wept bitterly but spoke not a word. Nagurai repeated to his mother that he could not leave his Nakhapili.

At this, Khulumati shouted at Nakhapili, "You wicked girl, you are a *daini* (she-demon), you have 'eaten up' my son. You were a bad girl. I mothered you and you could not do this for me. Die, die, die... a wicked woman like you deserves to die an unnatural death."

She did not reply immediately. She did her *pranam*, obeisance, to the elders by touching their feet and told Khulumati, "Mother, I did not know my own mother. You were my mother. Now that I have lost my mother's love and she has wanted me to die, die I shall. Do bless me that in my next birth I again get your son as my husband."

With these words Nakhapili ran down the hill slope. Nagurai had not heard all her words but had caught the last words. He ran after her. There was a deep ravine and a small winding stream ran down the slope. Nakha made for that ravine followed by Nagu. He shouted, "Nakhu, *Rangchak* (darling), where are you going? You cannot leave me like this. Let us go away, far away, where they cannot reach us." Nakha replied, "Love, do come, we shall go away and live an eternal life of love." She stood at the edge of the ravine and stretched her hand. A miracle happened. Nakhapili jumped from the precipice and so did Nagurai but instead of going down Nakhapili moved upwards. Nagurai also moved upwards. Both of them were transformed from their human form into lightning at first sheet and then forked lightning. Dark clouds suddenly enveloped the sky and thundered. The father, mother and the other people saw the strange happening. The mother shouted, beating her breast. "Nagu, my son, Nakha, my daughter, do come back, come back. I shall not say a word. Oh, do come back!" But the lightning had disappeared. The echo of the words rumbled and died away.

Even now whenever there is lightning and thunder, the villagers of Tripura fondly remember their Nagurai and Nakhapili and their abiding love. Their memory is evergreen in Tripura.

FOLK TALES
OF
ORISSA

Orissa

Orissa lies on the east coast of India. It is surrounded by West Bengal in the north-east, Bihar in the north, Andhra Pradesh in the south-east, Madhya Pradesh in the west and the Bay of Bengal in the east. The state has an area of 1,55,707 sq km, population 31,512,070, density 202 per sq km and literacy 48.65 per cent. Agriculture is the main occupation of the people but many industries, big and small, and cottage industries are coming up. Bhubaneshwar is the capital though Cuttack is the principal city.

Oriya is the language of the people with a rich legacy. Many of the folk tales have ancient origins. Often, these stories were narrated by pilgrims during their long journeys. Sometimes, they were retold in the temple courtyards, where the village-folk gathered in large numbers on festive occasions. But more often than not grandmothers have made these stories come alive for generations to come.

Orissa's civilisations and culture go back to very ancient times. Owing to many factors, this ancient land remained in comparative poverty and its glory was little known to modern civilisation. Misfortunes and sorrows were attributed to the wrath of the gods. The folk tales of Orissa project the hardships, fears, struggles, superstitions and poverty of the people.

54

WHY DHARMAPADA SACRIFICED HIS LIFE

ORISSA is a land of many splendid and attractive temples. Konarak is the finest temple which was built by Narasimha Deva, a great king who ruled in Utkal[1] long ago. It took twelve hundred artisans and twelve long years to build. The king had chosen the best artisans of the land for this work. He had ordered that none of the builders would be allowed to visit his home until the temple was completed.

The chief architect of the temple was Bisu Maharana. When Bisu left home to work on the temple, his wife was expecting a baby. Some months later a son was born, but the father was not allowed to leave his work and go home to see his newborn son.

Twelve years passed, yet Bisu could not see his son. In the meantime, the lovely baby grew up into a handsome boy. His mother adored him and bestowed great care on his upbringing. She named him Dharmapada and sometimes, lovingly called him Dharma. She took care to see that her son learned the craft of his forefathers. She taught him the art of temple-building. Even as a child, Dharmapada showed keen interest in this art. He spent hours building toy temples and forts in stone or wood. Those who saw his handiwork, wondered at his skill. They said that Dharma would one day become a great architect.

When he was five years old, he was sent to the village school. The boy had keen intellect and quickly learnt his lessons. His teachers liked him, his friends loved him, but there were some boys who were jealous of him.

---

1. Another name for Orissa.

One day, in the school, as the boys were writing, Dharma's chalk slipped from his fingers and rolled away from him. He asked one of his classmates to pick it up for him. The boy not only refused to pick it up but also insulted Dharma.

"Who are you to order me? Whose son do you think you are?" he asked rudely.

A few other boys joined him and said, "Yes, yes. Tell us your father's name. Have you ever seen him?"

Dharma was confused. He did not know what to say.

The boys teased him, "Oh, no, you have no father," and they laughed at him. Poor Dharmapada felt insulted and returned home sad.

His mother was worried to find her son in a sorrowful mood. "Why are you so sad, my child?" she asked. "Ever since your father left home to build the temple at Chandrabhaga[1] you have been the only joy in my life. Tell me truly, what grieves you?"

"Mother, I have never seen my father. Why does he not come home? Today my classmates insulted me by saying I have no father," replied Dharmapada in anguish.

"What! You have no father! Who dares say so? Believe me, your father is the chief architect of the finest temple that is being built. I have told you this before. You belong to a noted family of builders. They have built many temples and fortresses in this land of Utkal. Anyone should be proud of such ancestry," said his mother.

"Oh mother, I know the boys at school are jealous of me. Now I understand. But please tell me more about my forefathers."

"Listen, my child, your forefathers helped in the building of the great temple of Jagannath at 'Srikhetra'.[2] When the temple was completed, they were rewarded by King Indradyumna. Years later, when Emperor Kharavela had the beautiful caves at Khandagiri carved out of rocks, it was your forefathers who did the work. Again, King Lalatendu Deva engaged your ancestors to build the great temple of Shiva at 'Ekamrakanana[3]'. Years later your grandfather went to repair the 'Barabati[4]' fortress at 'Katak'.

---

1 The ancient name of the place Konarak. In olden times it was a famous place of pilgrimage.
2. Another name for Puri, the holy city of Jagannath.
3. Ancient name for Bhubaneswar, the present capital of Orissa.
4. An old fort at Cuttack, now in ruins.

He died there before the work was completed and he never returned home. You belong to the family of such famous builders, who have left their mark on all the beautiful temples and forts of Utkal."

"Oh mother, I wish to prove worthy of my ancestors," said Dharma, glowing with pride. "Now, tell me about my father and the work he is doing."

"Your father has been engaged by our great King Narasimha Deva. He is the chief among the artisans. The king has ordered that none of the builders should leave the temple area and visit their homes until the temple is completed. Your father, therefore, has not been able to see you. He is building a great temple dedicated to the Sun God at Chandrabhaga on the seacoast. Chandrabhaga is a holy place of pilgrimage. They say that the temple is nearing completion and I hope your father will soon return home."

Dharma became impatient. "Mother," he said, "I want to go to Chandrabhaga to see my father and the temple he is building. It will also be a pilgrimage for me to the holy place. I shall not stay there long. I shall bring news of father to you. Mother, won't you let me go?"

She, at first, would not consent to this. But when she found that he had set his heart on going, she could not refuse him. Before Dharma set out on his journey, his mother blessed him and said, "May the Gods protect you from all dangers and enable you to meet your father." She added, "Take these berries from our garden. Your father likes them. This will also be a token by which your father will know you. These berries grow only in our garden."

With his mother's blessings, Dharma set out on the journey towards Chandrabhaga. Though he was young and the way was unfamiliar, he travelled on bravely. As he neared the seacoast, he was thrilled with joy at the sight of the sand dunes and the tall casurina trees. When the wind blew, the leaves seemed to whisper to him words of welcome. He heard the roar of the breakers as they washed the sandy shore. The fishermen were busy unloading the day's catch. The sea-gulls hovered over the boats and the air was filled with the shrill cries of the birds and shouts of the fishermen. As he walked further, he got a glimpse of the magnificent temple from a distance. The blue sea with its mighty waves and the beautiful temple by its side filled him with wonder.

When he came nearer, he found the place bustling with activity. Workmen, with tools in their hands, were chiselling huge stones, carving out figures on them; others were lifting stones and fixing them; all were busy with their work. Dharmapada did not know anyone there. He did not know how to find his father in the crowd. He went about asking for Bisu Maharana. It did not, however, take him long to find his father. He introduced himself to his father, gave him the berries and gave him news from home also.

Bisu was delighted to meet his son whom he had longed to see during all those years. He took Dharma by his hand and showed him around the temple, describing to him the details of the work. Dharma saw the magnificent temple built in the shape of a chariot. The mighty wheels of the chariot were artistically carved with designs. The stone horses drawing the chariot looked so real. Every stone was adorned with beautiful carvings. The sculptured figures of men and women, of elephants and horses, of musicians and dancing girls, looked so lifelike to Dharmapada that he gaped at them with wonder.

His father explained to him, "This temple has been built to the Sun God. The king wants to make it a wonder of the world, so that many would come from far and near to offer worship to the Sun God and admire its beauty."

Bisu continued, "The building work has already taken twelve years and the temple is not yet complete. The king is anxious to have it finished soon. His dream has come true except for the crown stone which remains to be fixed on the temple. We have been working hard to fix it, but all our efforts have failed. Everytime it is placed on the top, it has fallen down. There must be some mistake somewhere. Yesterday, the king in his impatience and anger commanded that the temple should be completed within three days, or else, all the artisans would be put to death. Today, after sunset, the artisans are meeting to discuss what should be done. I don't see much hope and time is very short. We are at out wit's end."

Dharmapada felt sad to see his father and his kinsmen in distress. He begged his father for permission to be present at the meeting.

In the meeting various suggestions were made. They were discussed, but none seemed workable. At last, Dharmapada stood up and with folded hands addressed the gathering. "Sirs, I have something to say if you will hear me. I think I can be of service. Please do not spurn me for my young age. I hope to set aright the crown stone on the temple top. I only beg you to give me a chance."

They were all amazed to hear the boy speak thus. Some said, "What! Where we with all our skill and experience have failed, how can a mere lad succeed? He is boasting."

Some others said, "Let us not stand on our pride, but give the boy a chance. As it is, we have failed. We have nothing to lose by giving him a chance."

To this some others replied, "Why? We have everything to lose. When it is known that twelve hundred artisans failed to fix the crown stone, and a lad from nowhere came along and did the job, what will people say of us? Where will our dignity be? When this reaches the king's ears, you think he will spare our lives?"

At last an old artisan said, "In either case we stand in danger of our lives. Even if a boy from among us succeeds, our caste will still be held in esteem. But, if the temple remains incomplete, remember, this race of builders will forever remain in disgrace. Let us put aside our pride and leave the work in his hands." The old artisan's words appealed to all and they decided to let Dharmapada try.

Early the next day, Dharma went round the temple looking closely into the details of its structure. He spent hours studying the different parts of the temple. After a while, he climbed up to the temple top and worked on the capital far into the night. The twelve hundred artisans had no sleep that night. They were anxiously waiting for the result. At the first peep of day, to the amazement of all, the crown top became visible from its height. Dharmapada came down with his face beaming with joy. His father ran towards him and embraced him. The artisans soon surrounded him and showered blessings on him. Although they were happy to see the temple completed, their joy was not unmixed with sorrow. Sensing this, Dharmapada enquired why they still looked sad.

"May you live long, and may your deed be ever remembered. But your achievement will not remain a secret. The king will surely hear of it. You will be rewarded, but our fate is sealed," they replied.

Dharmapada was sad to hear this. "How does it profit me," he said, "when I am rewarded and my kinsmen suffer death? This wonderful temple is your creation. I only fixed the top stone at the very end. I am not worthy of any reward." So saying Dharmapada left the place.

He thought, 'Of what use is my life when my kinsmen suffer on my account? So let a single life be sacrificed for the good of many.' Before the first rays of the sun fell on the temple capital, Dharmapada climbed up to the temple top and from there jumped to his death.

Dharmapada is no more. The famous temple is still there, in ruins. The children of Orissa love to hear his story and cherish his memory. Dharmapada has become immortal.

55

THE KING WHO WAS CALLED A SWEEPER

ON THE coast of Orissa, where the waters of the Bay of Bengal wash its shores, there stands a great temple, which is known as the Temple of Jagannath. Pilgrims from far and near come to worship in this temple at Puri. But during the *Ratha Jatra*[1] festival, thousands of pilgrims crowd into the city to see the *Jatra*. This festival is held every year in the month of *Asadh*. The image of Jagannath and the image of Balabhadra and Subhadra, his brother and sister, are taken out in a procession. Three huge wooden chariots are built and colourfully decorated for this festival. The *pandas*[2] bring the idols from the temple and put them in the *rathas* or chariots. The pilgrims pull these chariots all the way along the wide *Bada Danda*,[3] a couple of miles away to the garden house. There the idols remain for a week, after which they are pulled back in the chariots to the main temple.

Some hundreds of years ago, there was a king named Purushottam Deva who ruled over Orissa. He was an ardent devotee of Jagannath. He was very humble and considered his kingdom as belonging to Jagannath and himself merely a servant ruling it.

At the *Ratha Jatra* festival, it was the custom for the king to take a broomstick with a golden handle and sweep the floors of the chariots of the deities. This was so, because King Purushottam regarded himself as a *sevaka*, a servant of the gods. Not until he performed this duty were the chariots allowed to be drawn by the people.

---

1. Chariot procession.
2. Priests
3. The Grand Road at Puri.

To the south of the land of Utakal, there lay the kingdom of Kanchi. King Purushottam, in his exploits in the southern regions, had seen Padmavati, the beautiful daughter of the king of Kanchi. He had fallen in love with her and wanted to make her his queen. He sent a proposal to the king of Kanchi for the hand of his daughter. Padmavati's father not only agreed to the proposal but at the invitation of Purushottam, came to Orissa to witness the *Ratha Jatra*.

During the *jatra*, the two kings sat on the terrace of the royal palace, close to the temple, and watched the ceremonies. The road from the temple to the garden house was thickly crowded with thousands of pilgrims. With the blowing of conchshells and the shouts of rejoicing by the vast crowd, the three images were brought out from the temple and put on the chariots reserved for each one of them. While all this was being done, the two kings were engaged in conversation. Purushottam was explaining the ceremonies to the ruler of Kanchi.

"Tell me, who built this temple and who started the worship of Jagannath here?" the king of Kanchi asked.

"This great temple that we see before us, was built by King Indradyumna," answered Purushottam Deva. He continued, "Indradyumna completed the building of the temple, but there was no God to be enshrined in it. Then, he saw in his dream, Nilamadhava, the God of the 'Savaras'[1]. King Indradyumna wanted to enshrine the god in the new temple. He sent Bidyapati, his minister, to the Savara village to get the image of Nilamadhava. Bidyapati went and stayed in the house of Biswabasu, the Savara chief, and married his daughter, Lalita. The Savaras worshipped Nilamadhava secretly, in a shrine hidden deep in the forest. No stranger was allowed there. So, Bidyapati did not know how to reach the shrine of Nilamadhava. He took the help of Lalita, who induced her father to take him to the shrine. But, Bidyapati was first blindfolded and then led to the secret shrine. The minister, however, was equal to the occasion and had secretly carried with him a handful of mustard seeds. These, he dropped, little by little, as he went along the way. At the shrine, in great excitement, he saw the image of Nilamadhava in the form of a deep blue stone. Again he was

1. An aboriginal tribe of Orissa.

blindfolded and brought back. Bidyapati returned and reported everything to king Indradyumna.

"Patiently, Indradyumna and his minister waited till the season came for the mustard seeds to blossom. Then, Bidyapati took the king with him to the Savara village. The golden flowers clearly pointed the way and they reached the hidden shrine."

The king of Kanchi, who was listening intently, became curious and enquired, "Now, tell me, is Nilamadhava the same God as Jagannath?"

"Yes," replied Purushottam, "He is the very same God, but now worshipped in a different form. This is how it happened."

He continued, "At the shrine, that night, Nilamadhava again appeared in a dream to king Indradyumna. He said, "Oh King! Hear my words and fail not to carry out my will. I am tired of this place. I do not desire to stay here any longer. The fruit offerings, made day after day, do not satisfy me. I long for cooked sweetmeats and food. Again, I do not desire to be worshipped here as Nilamadhava. I should hereafter be known as Jagannath. You will find a log of wood floating in the sea near Nilachala. My image should be cut out of this log and enshrined in the new temple you have built." The king woke up from his dream and strangely enough found that the blue stone had vanished.

"Indradyumna and his minister hastened to fulfil the will of the God. Sure enough they found, as indicated in the dream, the log of wood floating near the coast of Nilachala. The king had the log taken out of the water. He searched for a skilled carpenter who could fashion out an image of Jagannath. Many carpenters came but the moment they tried to cut the log, their chisels broke into pieces. At last an old carpenter, named Ananta Maharana, came and assured the king that he would get the image ready in twenty-one days. He made a condition that he should be locked up with the log in a room for twenty-one days. During this period he should not be disturbed and the doors should remain locked. This was done. Daily the curious king and others went near the locked room and heard the sound of wood-working going on inside. But a few days before the allotted time no sound was heard from within. The king grew anxious because he feared that the old carpenter who had taken no food and water must have died. In great anxiety the king got the doors opened and to his surprise found no carpenter inside. There were only three unfinished images.

"Therefore," Purushottam continued, "the images were enshrined in their unfinished form and are worshipped as such till now. This is how Jagannath, Balabhadra and Subhadra came to be worshipped here in the temple."

King Purushottam had just finished the long narrative when it was time for him to go down and sweep the floors of the chariots of the deities. As he swept them one after another, people loudly cheered him. But the sight of a king doing the work of a sweeper did not please the ruler of Kanchi. He was filled with contempt for king Purushottam.

Soon after the *Ratha Jatra,* the king of Kanchi returned to his country. He did not lose any time in sending word to the ruler of Utkal that he would not give his daughter in marriage to a *chandala.*[1]

Purushottam was enraged. He took it as an insult not only to himself but also to his God Jagannath, and he vowed to avenge it.

War was declared by Purushottam aginst Kanchi. In the war Purushottam was defeated. Next year he again declared war against Kanchi and this time he invoked the help of the gods. He marched with his hosts and before he had gone far, a milkmaid named Manika[2] met him in a village.

"Two of your men on horseback went ahead. One of them rode on a black horse and the other on a white horse. The men were thirsty and bought buttermilk from me. They had no money to pay and they gave me this ring to be shown to you and take money from you," she said.

The moment the king saw the ring, he knew that it belonged to Lord Jagannath. He was now sure that the riders were none other than Jagannath and Balabhadra who had gone ahead to fight for him. He took it as a sure sign of victory. Purushottam boldly marched forward with his army. This time, he defeated the king of Kanchi and brought Padmavati as a captive. In his anger, the king refused to marry her but resolved to teach her proud father a lesson.

"Her father had called me a *chandala.* Take her and marry her to a *chandala.* See that she becomes the wife of a low caste sweeper," he angrily ordered his minister.

---

1. Sweeper.
2. There is even today, a village called Manikapatna, named after the mikmaid, Manika, where this incident took place.

Though the minister was grieved to hear this, he humbly replied, "The king's order will be carried out."

But the kind minister did not marry Padmavati to a sweeper. Instead he took her to his own home where he and his wife took care of the princess as their own daughter. They were, of course, careful to keep it a secret from the king.

56

WHY A BRITISH CAPTAIN BOWED BEFORE A REBEL CHIEF

OVER two hundred years ago, the Marathas were rulers of Orissa. They appointed a local chief as Raja, but themselves lived far out in the west of the country. This Raja collected revenues on behalf of his masters, the Marathas. There were numerous *paikas*[1] under the Raja who fought the Raja's battles and in return got gifts of land for which they had to pay no revenue.

But when the Britishers came and conquered Orissa, the *paikas* lost their lands to the British. There was much discontent on this account. Soon this discontent spread like wildfire and the *paikas* banded together to fight the British.

At that time, there lived in the village of Naranagarh, Dalabehera, whose name is cherished even today by many in Orissa. He was the headman of the village, and had the heart of a prince. People called him the friend of the poor, and no needy person, whoever went to him, returned empty-handed.

When the *paikas* revolted, Dalabehera took the lead and fought against the British. In the beginning the *paikas* captured a number of places from the British, but soon fresh armies were brought against them and the revolt was firmly put down. Many were caught and hanged and many imprisoned. A number of *paikas* fled to the jungle for safety and refuge. Yet the anger of the British Captain was unmitigated. He wanted the head of Dalabehera. But Dalabehera was hiding in the jungle and he could not be traced. So a reward of one thousand rupees was offered to anyone who would capture Dalabehera. In spite of a search all over, Dalabehera could not be captured. He was living

1. Soldiers of Orissa in olden times.

in a thick jungle and lived on wild fruits and roots and water from the forest brooks. His clothes were tattered and with overgrown hair and beard he looked utterly miserable.

One day while roaming, Dalabehera met a man who looked deeply distressed. The man came up to Dalabehera and asked the way to Naranagarh.

"What makes you go to Naranagarh?" asked Dalabehera in surprise. "Whom do you want to see there?"

"I am going to Dalabehera of Naranagarh," replied the man.

"I know Dalabehera but tell me, why do you want to meet him?" asked Dalabehera.

"Sir, grave misfortune has fallen upon me. My home is in Ganjam. I was coming in a boat with all my merchandise and my boat sank in the *Chilka*[1]. I escaped only with the clothes I am wearing. I have a large family and I have lost everything. There is no one to help me. I have heard the name of Dalabehera. People say that he is a friend of the helpless. I am sure if I meet him he will not refuse to help," said the man.

Dalabehera was moved with the man's story and for a while remained speechless. His noble heart melted. The picture of the man's helplessness pained him and he made up his mind.

"Come along with me, my friend. I know your Dalabehera very well. He now lives in Khurda and I will take you to him. I also believe that he will help you," said Dalabehera.

But Dalabehera straightaway took the man to Khurda to the British Captain who was hunting for his life. Bravely, he stood before the Captain. The Captain, however, could not imagine that Dalabehera was standing before him.

Curiously he asked, "Who are you and what has brought you here?"

"Sir," boldly asked Dalabehera, "is it a fact that you have offered a reward of one thousand rupees for Dalabehera's head?"

"Yes, it is true. Do you know the whereabouts of this man?" enquired the Captain.

Dalabehera said, "Please listen, sir, I am Dalabehera, whom your men have not been able to track down. I myself have come to you. Arrest me, sir, and make good your promise. Please pay the reward of one thousand rupees to this unfortunate man."

---

1. A lake in Orissa. The crabs and lobsters of this large Chilka lake are famous for their taste.

Then in moving words he narrated the pitiful story of the man. "He has nothing now except the clothes on his body. I cannot bear his misery and therefore have come to you. Take me a prisoner and pay this man the promised reward."

In silent astonishment, the British Captain listened to the story of the man's great misfortune and Dalabehera's still greater sacrifice.

Uplifted in spirit, the British Captain confessed, "Dalabehera, I have long been utterly mistaken. I never knew you were so great in spirit! How could I be revengeful before such greatness? Take one thousand rupees for your friend and also your freedom with it."

The miserable man who was a witness to this amazing scene fell at the feet of Dalabehera, saying, "Sir, I had thought that you were only a rich man who helped the poor like many other rich men, but now I see that you are more like a god than man."

57

A RANI'S REVENGE

IN OLDEN times, there were a number of independent states in Orissa. Banki and Khurda were two such states which had a common boundary. There were frequent border disputes between the two states. Sometimes, these disputes even led to war.

Dhanurjaya, the Raja of Banki, was a renowned warrior who had fought many hard battles. He was a skilful archer and swordsman. His Rani, Shuka Dei, was no less a warrior than her husband. Her skill in horse-riding was well-known everywhere.

Banki was a smaller state than Khurda. Her resources in men and materials were poor. But Dhanurjaya's courage was such that he would yield to none and much less to the Raja of Khurda.

Once the Raja of Khurda forcibly occupied some villages on the border. Bravely, Dhanurjaya marched forward with his army to fight the invader. That day a severe battle was fought and many were killed. In the end, the small army of Banki could not resist the pressure of a heavy attack.

Dhanurjaya fought bravely, but fell into the hands of the enemy and was killed. When they found their ruler slain, the soldiers of Banki gave up the battle as lost and fled from the battlefield.

Soon report of the death of her husband reached Rani Shuka Dei. Her grief knew no bounds, yet her eyes had no tears but flashed fire.

Her counsellors came up to her and declared in one voice, "Our Raja is dead. Now there is no hope for us. Let us surrender to the enemy."

"Are we *Kshatriyas*[1] or cowards?" she cried out in anger.

---

1. Warrior class.

"No, madam," replied her minister, "we are not cowards. But our state is small and our army smaller. We can never expect to win against Khurda. Our Raja is no more and you, O Rani, are only a woman and Prince Dayanidhi is merely a lad. It is wise to give up now a bit of our territory rather than lose the entire state. This may satisfy the Raja of Khurda."

"What? Yield to the enemy! True, I am a woman but do not forget I am a *Kshatriya* and *Kshatriya* blood runs in my veins," cried the Rani in anger.

Turning to her *Senapati*[1] she continued, "I will fight, and if need be, die fighting like a *Kshatriya*, but never will I yield even a small strip of land to the enemy."

Feelingly she asked, "Did you not all run away from the battlefield? Tell me, did my husband run away? Bravely, he fought and died in the battlefield. If you are afraid, you may go and hide yourselves in your homes. I am going to the battlefield to fight again. If none of you comes with me, let it be known that I, a woman, will alone march forward and fight against Khurda."

Then she added, "Only those who are not afraid of death, need come with me. Let this be known, to my people."

These brave words of a woman put courage in their hearts and they declared, "If you are going to the battlefield, can we stay behind? We can't let you go alone."

They added, "We have asked the Raja of Badamda for help, and maybe, he will help us."

The Rani's undaunted courage encouraged the soldiers and soon a great army, with the Rani at the head, marched forward against Khurda.

In the meanwhile, the Raja of Khurda was celebrating the victory. When the news of this fresh attack reached him he could not believe it.

"Impossible!" he said. "The Rani of Banki attacking us? Dare she, a widow, take up such a foolish venture, and that too so soon after the death of her husband? Impossible!" However, he instructed his *Senapati* to make preparations for the war.

Great was the surprise of the Raja to see Shuka Dei leading an army against him. Soon a fierce battle raged near the boundary. The Rani's unusual courage gave spirit to her soliders and they fought bravely. Many deeds of courage were seen on the

1. General.

battlefield and in the end the *Senapati* of Khurda was caught and killed by the Banki army. Thereafter, panic prevailed in the Khurda camp and soon the Raja of Khurda was captured by the Rani's soldiers.

Bound with chains and guarded by the soldiers of Banki, the Raja was brought before Rani Shuka Dei. He was greatly ashamed when he was brought as a prisoner before a woman, and that too a woman whose husband he had so recently killed.

'Was not death in the battlefield thousand times better than this disgrace? Surely, revenge is in the Rani's heart and she will not spare my life,' thought the Raja.

The Rani looked at her soldiers and ordered, "Take off the chains and set free the Raja." Then looking at the Raja, she gently said, "You may now return to your own state. No one here will do you any harm."

The Raja was astonished at the unexpected turn of events. 'What,' he thought, 'she, whom I had taken to be my enemy seeking revenge, now orders my freedom!'

With his head bowed he humbly said, "I never imagined that you could show me such mercy."

The Rani replied, "Sir, you are my prisoner and if I like I can have your head cut off. But what good would such an act produce? I am a widow. I have a woman's heart. My husband is dead and my grief is too heavy to bear. How could I inflict such a suffering on another woman? No, no, I cannot do this to the Rani of Khurda! I fought with you only to bring back the lost prestige of Banki and not for revenge."

Deeply moved the Raja stood stunned. After a while, he humbly said, "Madam, you got victory over me in the battlefield today, and now you have won a second victory over me by showing such magnanimity. What could my grateful heart say or give you? I remain forever indebted to you and as a token of my gratitude, I surrender to you the entire Kusapala *pargana*[1] of Khurda. I vow, that never more shall the sword of Khurda be raised against Banki."

Later, a pillar was raised at Kusapala, to mark the heroism and magnanimity of Rani Shuka Dei. The pillar still stands.

---

1. A group of villages.

FOLK TALES OF PUNJAB

Punjab

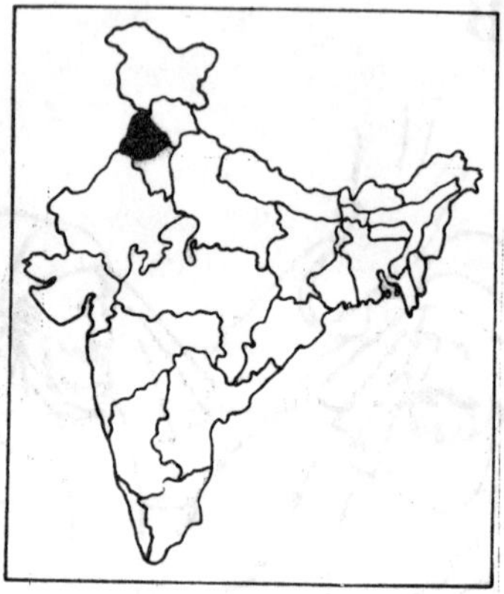

The word "Punjab" is made up of two Persian words, 'Panj' which means five and 'Aab' means water. This name was given to the land of five rivers when the region came in contact with Persia. It has an area of 50,362 sq km and 20,190,795 population with a density of 401 per sq km. The literacy is 57.14 per cent.

Punjab has Pakistan in the west, Jammu and Kashmir in the north, Himachal Pradesh in the north-east, Haryana in the south and Rajasthan in the south-west.

Punjab retains the old glory of being the land of a martial people. The main occupations of the people are agriculture, dairy farming and animal husbandry. The state language is Punjabi and Chandigarh is the capital city.

Punjabiat, the culture-complex of this "land of five rivers" is a mixture of progressiveness, faith in old traditions, loyalty almost to the point of fanaticism to religious ideas and a sense of humour.

Panjabi folklore has a vigour and liveliness of its own. The festivals, and dances, and colourful, music, is enthralling. Punjab has lost her professional folk tale narrators who with their *choga*, a dress, colourful turbans and a bag across the shoulders used to move about from village to village and regale the listeners.

58

THE ADVENTURES OF RAJA RASALU

ONCE upon a time there was a king of Sialkot named Salahan. He had two queens.

The elder of the two queens was Achala. She had a handsome young son called Puran.

The younger, Luna, had no children. So she was very jealous of Achala and her son. She plotted to poison the mind of Salahan against Achala and her son, Puran.

She told the king that Puran had fallen in love with her.

The king was angry when he heard this. He immediately ordered that Puran's hands and feet be cut off and he be thrown into a well.

2

Puran was innocent, but he took the punishment without protest. He sat at the bottom of the well and prayed.

And lo! in answer to his prayers, came Guru Gorakh Nath, the saint. The Guru took the prince out of the well, healed his hands and feet, and made him a handsome young prince again.

Puran put on the sacred earrings and followed the saint wherever he went. And, because of his devotion to the master, he came to be called Puran Bhagat, the worshipper.

For some years, Puran Bhagat wandered in different lands with Gorakh Nath. One day he was filled with the desire to see his mother.

Guru Gorakh Nath gave the young man permission to go to Sialkot.

Puran Bhagat went to his native city. And he sat down in a garden near the palace, where he had played as a child. The garden had become a wasteland. Puran Bhagat grew flowers and fruit trees. And soon the bare land became a lovely garden again.

The news of this miracle spread far and wide. People came from many parts of the kingdom to see the young sadhu.

The king and the queens also heard the news. They came and saw the miracle of the wasteland becoming green. What was more, Puran Bhagat touched the eyes of his mother, Achala, who had become blind through crying for him. And lo! he restored her eyesight.

3

As Luna saw the miracle, she thought she would ask the sadhu for the boon of a son she had so long desired. She fell at his feet and prayed, "Oh, holy man, give me the gift of a son, who may gladden the heart of Salahan in his old age."

'But Salahan has a son already," Puran Bhagat answered. "You have had him put out of your way. Tell me the truth if you want God to forgive you."

On hearing this, Luna felt humble. In the presence of king Salahan, she told the ascetic how she had told lies and got Puran's hands and feet cut, and had him thrown into the well.

Puran Bhagat, blessing Luna, said, "Rani, you thought you had killed Prince Puran. But here he is before you—I am Puran...."

She opened her eyes wide, to be sure, he was Puran. Only he had grown a beard and worn big earrings of the Sadhu. She fell at his feet and asked for forgiveness.

"*Acha,* take this grain of rice," said Puran. "If you eat it, you will have a son. The boy will be brave and good. But he will go away from you when he grows up, and you will suffer as my mother suffered."

4

As Puran Bhagat had said, a son was born to Luna. The priests wrote the horoscope of the child. The magic paper showed that the boy would live to be a great man. Only, for twelve years, he must not look either at king Salahan, or queen Luna. If he did so, they would die.

Luna asked the Brahmins if they could say some prayers, which might change her son's destiny.

They said, "Keep the child in a dark cell for twelve years. Do not see him during this time. Only thus can you avert the death of the king and yourself. After twelve years, the boy can come out.

Then he must bathe in the river to cast off the curse on him and come to see you."

Rani Luna had named her son, Rasalu, meaning full of *Rasa*, or the sap of life. He was a beautiful boy.

She had an underground palace built and put him there. And she appointed nurses and servants to look after him as he was growing up.

5

Rasalu lived in the underground palace for eleven years. He was fond of a parrot, which his mother gave him and he talked to the bird everyday. He rode on a colt who had been born on the same day as he.

Strong and beautiful, intelligent and brave, he wished to go and see the world as he entered his twelfth year.

The nurses told him, "According to the Brahmins you must not go out before the twelfth year is over."

Rasalu said, "I want to go and see the world and no one can keep me back."

So he put a saddle on his horse, put on his shining armour, and rode out of the palace.

The nurses wept seeing him go. But they blessed him and said, "Stop when you come to a river, bathe in the pure water, put on the new clothes and then go."

6

Not far from the palace, Rasalu found a stream. And he did what the nurses had told him to do. He dipped in the holy water. He put on the new clothes. Then he mounted his horse and reached the outer walls of Sialkot city.

Thirsty, he stopped near a well where women came to draw water and to fill their earthen pitchers. He asked them for water which they gave. Then they got busy with their chores.

He did not know how to send a message to his father, that he had come out of the underground palace. So he began to throw stones at the pitchers in which women carried water from the well.

The women were angry and went to complain to the king.

When king Salahan heard of this mischief, he thought it was Lord Krishna, who had come to life again. Then he thought it might be his son, Rasalu, in whom Krishna, the cowherd God, had been incarnated. But the boy may have come out of the underground palace before the end of his twelve years. And he dare not send his soldiers to bring him to the court. He remembered the words of the Brahmins, who had made the horoscope, "If the young prince saw his father or mother before the end of twelve years, they would die." So the king gave the women brass pitchers in place of the earthen pitchers to fetch water from the well.

But Rasalu was not to be defeated.

He shot sharp arrows at the brass pitchers of the women.

When the women told the king about this, he was still afraid to call him.

Rasalu could wait no longer. He mounted his horse and charged into his father's palace. And, facing the king, he said,

"I come to greet you, Raja Salahan, not to harm you.
What have I done that you turn me away?
Sceptre and crown for me have no charm
I go to seek a better prize, without harm."

After this he strode out of the court.

As he was galloping through the palace door, he heard his mother weeping on the terrace. He pulled up his horse and said:

"Oh! Rani filled with grief, have you nothing
But tears for your son.
Are you my mother?
If so, give a thought to my life just begun."

Rani Luna wept and answered,

"I am your mother, though I weep for the sight of you.
Go, for sure,
And rule over man,
But keep your heart good and pure."

Rasalu turned away from the terrace. And with his white horse under him and his parrot seated on his wrist, he went in search of his fate.

7

On the way, he met the son of a carpenter who wanted to join him. Then the son of a goldsmith who wanted to go with him.

Rasalu took them both and headed for the plains of Hindustan.

At the end of the day's march, they came to a thick forest. They sat down to rest. As the place was very lonely, they decided to keep watch in turn. The carpenter's son became the first watchman. He was to be followed by the goldsmith's son. Rasalu would be the third.

When the goldsmith's son was on watch, and the other two slept, a snake came towards the sleepers. The goldsmith's son asked the snake, "Why have you come here?"

The snake answered, "I have killed everyone within twelve miles. I am the king of this jungle. How dare you three come here?"

"Go away or I will wring your neck!" said the carpenter's son, waking up.

The cobra raised his hood threateningly.

Thereupon, the carpenter's son caught him by the tail, dashed him to the ground and killed him.

Then he hid the snake's body under his shield.

8

When it came to Rasalu's turn to keep watch, a terrible monster came out of the bush.

"Who are you?" Rasalu shouted.

"I have killed everything here within twelve miles around," replied the monster. "I am the emperor of this land. How dare you come into my kingdom?"

Rasalu shot an arrow into the heart of the monster and killed him.

At the end of the night, Rasalu woke his friends.

The carpenter's son immediately uncovered the serpent under the shield and showed his kill to Rasalu.

"Oh! just a snake!" said Rasalu. "It won't even hurt a sparrow. Come and look at the horror I have killed." And he showed his friends the dead body of the monster.

The two companions shuddered to think what would have happened to them if the prince had not killed the demon. They fell on their knees before Rasalu, saying, "We are not fit companions for a brave prince. Pray, let us go back home."

Rasalu was sad to think that he should lose them, but he did not want to drag them with him. He was sure that he would meet many dangers. So he bade them farewell.

9

After his friends had turned back, Rasalu went on his way towards the Ravi river. One day's ride and he arrived in the blue city of Lahore.

On entering the market, he was fascinated by the sight of an old woman, who was baking bread. She laughed and then she wept as she worked.

"Why do you laugh now and weep again?" Rasalu asked the woman.

'Go your way, young man, and don't ask silly questions. Why are you bothered whether I laugh or I weep?"

"I want to hear of your joys and your sorrows," answered Rasalu.

The old woman saw that the boy had a kind face. She had tears in her eyes and told him, "My son, I had seven handsome sons. Six of them were eaten by a demon, who comes to take the life of a young man, a buffalo, and a basket of *rotis* from our town everyday. My seventh son, the youngest and the most dearly beloved, will also have to go today, as it is my turn to pay the tribute to our enemy."

Rasalu's heart was touched by this story.

"The sons of kind mothers stay at home
Cowards they become all,
Brave princes alone can venture into the unknown
And come through dangers in strange lands.
Oh! kind mother do not weep.
Your son safe keep.
I fear neither life nor death.
I seek my fate everywhere, in struggle.
So calm yourself."

10

Rasalu got down from his horse. And he sat down beside the old woman, so that the demon may take him to be her son.

The monster's servants came.

Rasalu rose and offered himself to them. The demon's servants took away Rasalu, the buffalo they had taken, and the basket of *rotis*, they had collected. And they went towards their master's house in the jungle.

As Rasalu approached the demon's palace, he met a water-carrier, with a goatskin full of water.

The water-carrier spoke to Rasalu rudely, "Oh! what a wonderful horse you are riding? Where did you steal it, young rascal? It is too beautiful a steed for a tramp. Let me eat it!" And he advanced towards Rasalu to catch hold of the reins of the horse.

Rasalu drew his sword. And with one sweep he cut off the head of the water-carrier from his shoulders.

The monster saw this happen and ran for his life.

The giant's sister was passing by. Seeing him run in a panic, she shouted, "Brother,where are you running away?"

"Don't you see, silly woman, that the much awaited Raja Rasalu has come to destroy us all!" he answered. And he made for the darkest corner in the forest.

His sister followed him, as she had heard of the legendary Rasalu and how he would come and bring death to all demons.

The other demons of the jungle heard the uproar.

Seeing Rasalu advancing towards the jungle, they went to an astrologer to ask him if it was really Rasalu who had come.

"Come, all you evil demons!" Rasalu called as he galloped forward on his white horse. "Come I am Rasalu, son of king Salahan, born enemy of the demons!"

One of the monsters answered back, "Oh, you little finger of my hand! I have eaten many Rasalus like you. You are no Rasalu—when the real one will come, his horse will trample on us and his sword will cut us to pieces!"

Rasalu quietly lowered the heel ropes of his horse from his saddle. And he swung it as a lasso. And lo! he bound all the giants in his rope. Then he drew out his sword and cut the demons to pieces.

Rasalu went further and announced, "Come, all you demons. I am Rasalu, the promised killer of all giants."

Seven demons came out of their houses and shouted back, "Oh! little one, don't show off! You are a pigmy. And we are not afraid of you. When the real Rasalu comes, his arrow will pierce seven girdles placed one behind the other."

"*Achha*! you place the girdles then and stand behind them in a row!" challenged Rasalu. "And I shall show you!"

The demons did as Rasalu said.

Rasalu took aim at them and shot the arrow. And he pierced the girdles, as well as the demons, with his arrows.

After this, Rasalu made an image of himself and placed it on a pedestal near the jungle, to frighten the remaining demons. And it happened as he thought. The demons looked out of their holes, saw Rasalu's statue, and thought he himself was standing there, to kill them.

They were frightened. They dare not go out even to get their food. And they died of hunger. So this is how Rasalu killed the giants.

11

After some time, Rasalu reached the city of Hastinapura. One day, he was passing under the shadow of the palace of the famous beautiful queen Sundran. He saw an ash-smeared Sadhu, sitting by a log of smouldering wood.

"Why are you seated near the palace?" Rasalu asked the ascetic with folded hands.

"I have been waiting to have a look at the queen Sundran for the past twenty-two years," said the Sadhu.

"Take me as your disciple, Sadhuji!" Rasalu implored. "I too have heard of her beauty. And I want to see her."

"I can see that you have light in your eyes," said the Sadhu. "So why should you want to become a Sadhu?"

"No, no!" said Rasalu, "I did not know until now that beauty is God. I like your way. So let me be with you."

The holy man pierced the ears of the disciple to wear earrings. And he initiated him into the mysteries of his faith.

In the evening, the Sadhu went to beg for alms according to his custom. As he had to give half of the food to Rasalu, he remained hungry. This happened everyday.

Rasalu sat by the fire all the time, waiting to see a glimpse of queen Sundran.

The Sadhu became impatient and said, "I made you my disciple, hoping you would look after me. I thought you would go and beg for food, keep the fire burning, and fetch water in the pitcher for me to drink. Instead, I have to do everything for you."

"But, holy man, you gave me no orders," said Rasalu. "How can a disciple do anything without the master's bidding?"

"*Achha*, you can begin to serve me from now!" ordered the *Sadhu*.

Rasalu took the begging bowl and went off to the town to beg for alms.

12

He made straight for the palace. And, from under the shadow of the terrace, he called out:

"Alakh! Alakh!
O *Rani*
To your threshold I have come.
From a far off land
Fair Sundran
I have heard of your charm,
Give with a generous hand
Give to the earringed Sadhu
A gift of alms."

Rasalu's words seemed to melt Sundran's heart.

She sent her maidservant with a handful of rice to give to the Sadhu. She herself peeped out of the door, and as she saw Rasalu's beauty, she fainted.

Rasalu cried out:

"Alakh! Alakh!"

The sound again pierced Sundran's heart. She got up and asked another maidservant to give alms to the beggar.

The servant also fainted on seeing Rasalu's beauty.

Then Sundran herself went with a bowl of jewels in her hand. She poured these into Rasalu's bowl and asked, "Since when have you worn earrings! And how have you become a yogi? What arrow from Kamdev's bow has struck you? Who are you looking for here. Do you take your begging bowl to all the women you see? Or only to me, oh handsome yogi?"

Rasalu bent his head towards the Rani and replied, "Only a day since I assumed the earrings.[5]

"Only a day since I became a yogi,
Today Kamdev's arrow struck me.
And I look for my beloved here.
I don't need jewels of any kind.
Take back your jewels and give me food instead.
Your gifts are rich I find.
But too rich for a yogi's alms.
I beg for fair Sundran, no other I see.

From your palace, I seek only thee."

Sundran blushed and went into the palace.

Rasalu's Guru was surprised to see the pearls he had brought.

"These are of no use to me," he said. "I am hungry and want food."

Rasalu went back to the palace door and cried:

"*Alakh! Alakh!*
Oh Rani of Hastinapura!
To your threshold I have come.
Drawn by the fame of your charm.
Give with a generous hand.
Fair Sundran.
To the earringed ascetic
A gift of alms."

The queen came to the door and sang:

"Go beggar, you!
Your pearly teeth reveal
The curve of your mouth a bow of rubies!
The ashes do not hide your youth, beloved!
Your eyes quiver with mischief.
Pretend not to ask for the real alms.
Ask her the alms you seek!"

Rasalu smiled and sang:

"Oh! fair queen,
What if my lips were not rubies?
And my teeth were not pearls?
I don't need jewels of any kind.
Take back your pearls and give me food instead.
Your gifts are rich I find,
But too rich for a yogi's alms."

Rani Sundran took back the pearls. And she asked the handsome yogi to wait while the food was cooked.

Raja Rasalu waited patiently and did not speak as he did not want to reveal himself.

When he was going away with his alms bowl, full of good food, the queen asked him,

"Prince, what is your name?
And whence do you come?
Tell me, Oh yogi, of your real fame?"

Rasalu answered:

"I am queen Luna's son,
My father is Salahan the great by name,
My name is Rasalu,
And I have come for your beauty's fame.
To see if you are as fair as men say.
Now I have seen your face, I go away."

Rasalu returned to his Guru and put the food before him. Then fearing that queen Sundran might try to keep him in Hastinapura, he wandered away.

13

Sundran waited for Rasalu to come the next day. As he did not come, she went to the yogi's hut and asked him where his disciple was.

The yogi was angry. He thought he had sat there for twenty years and the queen never came to see him. But the disciple had become a favourite in a few days. So he said to her, "I have eaten my disciple. I was hungry and he did not bring enough food!"

"But I sent you pearls and food," Rani Sundran said. "Were you not satisfied that you ate him up?"

"I was hungry," said the yogi. "So I ate him up. His flesh tasted good."

"*Achha*! eat me also!" Sundran cried. And, saying this she threw herself on the fire and died for the love of the handsome Rasalu.

14

Rasalu journeyed on.

When he reached the valley where king Harish Chanda ruled, the soldiers tried to kill him.

He fought them all single-handed, dethroned the king and himself became the king.

After king Rasalu had ruled his new kingdom for a year, he was challenged to play dice by Sarkap, the king of the neighbouring country.

As he was halfway through there was a storm. And there was no way to take shelter from the thunder, lightning and rain, except a graveyard.

He saw a headless corpse and said to himself:

"There is none near me except this headless corpse
I wish to God his ghost would come
I would be less lonely with a friend."

And lo! his wish was fulfilled. The ghost of the headless corpse came into the body.

King Rasalu was surprised and said to the ghost, "The wind is strong and fierce, the clouds are thick. No shelter you have. So why not lie down in your grave."

The corpse replied,

"Once upon a time, I was like you.
A crown on my head.
As a king I rode on a white horse, fighting my foe.
I lived happy with my queens.
Sins lie heavy on my head! Now I am dead."

King Rasalu and the ghost of the dead king talked to each other all night.

When Rasalu was going to begin his journey, the ghost asked him where he was going.

King Rasalu said he was going to play a game of dice with king Sarkap.

The ghost said, "I am the brother of king Sarkap. He is an evil man. He kills two, three persons every morning just for fun. It is he who cut my head."

King Rasalu was not to be prevented from going to beat king Sarkap and play the game of dice.

"*Achha*!" said the dead king, "Take some bones from this graveyard. Make dice out of them. King Sarkap cannot defeat the magic dice made from the bones."

15

As king Rasalu rode along towards the kingdom of Sarkap, he heard a voice from a burning jungle.

"Save me from the flames, kind man! Save me!"

Rasalu saw he was a tiny cricket, calling out. He went and rescued him.

The little cricket was grateful. He pulled out one of his feelers and, giving it to his preserver said, "If you are ever in trouble, put this into fire. I will come to your help at once."

Rasalu smiled and said, "My little cricket, how can such a small thing as you help me?"

All the same, he took the feeler and went his way.

16

When Rasalu reached the capital of king Sarkap, he saw seventy fair girls, daughters of the king, come to greet him and to make fun of him. The youngest of them was so struck by his beauty that though she had come to laugh, she stayed to praise him.

As she knew what was in store for Rasalu in her father's palace, she said:

"Oh! fair prince,
On your white horse so gay! Turn back Oh prince!
Or lower your lance before the prey.
Or your head will be forfeited.
If you love life then, stranger, I pray
Turn back, turn back. Go away."

King Rasalu smiled at the young princess and answered:

"Oh! Fair maiden,
I come from afar,
Sworn conqueror in love and war.
King Sarkap will rue the day, when I cut his head away.
And then you will be my bride.
Young maiden, on my horse you will ride."

On hearing these brave words, the little princess had faith in his courage. And she loved him all the more.

The other sisters were jealous. They scoffed at Rasalu.

"Oh gallant warrior!
Your sword is rusty
Oh prince, your turban has no pearls.
Oh young man, if you wish to marry our sister
prove yourself first to be a good brother-in-law
And then look at the girl."

Rasalu answered:

"Oh! fair maids, I will do anything you desire.

You only have to ask,
And I shall bring all my fire."

The sixty-nine sisters-in-law were foul as they were fair. They mixed a hundred weight of millet seed with a hundredweight of sand. And they asked Rasalu to separate the two.

King Rasalu did not know what to do. He wanted to go and play dice with king Sarkap. The work which the girls had given him would have taken a long time. He racked his brain for some way out of the difficulty. Suddenly, he thought of the cricket, who had said he would help him.

He threw the feeler, which was given to him, into fire, and lo! the cricket stood before him.

"Separate the millet from the sand for me!" he asked the cricket.

"The job will be done in the twinkling of an eye," said the cricket. And he called the members of the cricket brotherhood and soon separated the seed from the sand.

The sixty-nine fair damsels saw that Rasalu had done the work, they gave him. So they put another test before him.

"Swing us all on the swing, one by one, till we are tired."

King Rasalu smiled and said, "This is not difficult. But it is more suited for a servant than for a prince. I can't spend my day swinging you here. I will swing all the sixty-nine of you together on the swing." The sixty-nine fair damsels agreed to climb on the swing together. Rasalu tied the bow to the fullest bend and then let it go.

The sixty-nine damsels shot into the air. And they laughed and giggled as they went up and down.

As the swing came near the ground, Rasalu cut the rope with one sweep of his sword. And all the maidens fell down and died.

17

The youngest princess survived, but was weeping for her sisters.

She told Rasalu not to play dice with her father. But as he insisted, she told him that he will have to get seventy drums beaten to announce his challenge to king Sarkap, as was the custom.

Rasalu wanted to break the custom. So he sounded the drums so hard that they all broke.

The princess told him that he would now have to strike seventy gongs with the hammer to announce his arrival.

Rasalu hammered the gongs, till the earth seemed to shake. Then he struck the gongs so hard, that they broke into pieces.

As the young princess saw the might of Rasalu, she went to her father and told him, "Father, a mighty prince has come on a white horse. He has swung my sisters on the swing and thrown them to their death. He broke all the drums outside the palace and all the gongs as well. And he wants to beat you at the game of dice and take me for his bride."

King Sarkap smiled and said, "Silly maiden, your words are of a lovelorn girl. For fear of me, his hand will tremble! As soon as I have beaten him, I will cut off his head! And you will wed another."

But as he said these words, king Sarkap was shaking in his shoes. He had heard of the deeds of king Rasalu. He thought of killing him, before the prince should come near. So he sent a tray of food as offering to the prince, having put poison in the sweets.

Rasalu threw the food to the dogs. The dogs died.

"Go and tell your king Sarkap, it is not brave to kill an enemy by fraud!" Rasalu told the attendants.

18

After that, king Rasalu set out for the palace.

On his way, he came across a cat near the pottery kiln, mewing in distress.

"What is the matter, little pussy cat?" Rasalu asked her.

"My kittens are in an unbaked pot in the kiln. And the potter is just going to set the kiln on fire to bake the pots. I fear that my little ones will die a fiery death!"

Rasalu was touched by this sad story. So he bought the whole kiln from the potter. Then he looked into every pot. At last he found the kittens in one and gave them to the cat.

Gratefully the cat presented him a kitten saying, "Good prince, keep it in your pocket. Perhaps it wil help you in your time of need."

Rasalu put the kitten in his pocket and went towards the palace.

19

The guards would not let him in. So he showed them his sword. And for fear of being killed, they took him to king Sarkap.

Greeting his enemy by lifting his sword, he put the sword in the scabbard.

King Sarkap wanted to cheat him by offering him wine, which he had poisoned.

Rasalu went towards the place, where the game of dice was laid.

Sarkap's kingdom was the first stake. The wealth of the whole world was the second stake and his head, the third stake.

Rasalu made the first move. He forgot the ghost's warning and played with Sarkap's dice.

Raja Sarkap let loose his notorious rat. The rat ran over the dice board and upset the pieces. So Rasalu lost the first game. And he had to give up his shining armour.

In the second game, the rat again upset the pieces. So Rasalu lost his horse.

The horse cried to his master,

"Fair prince I am the son of the frothing sea.
Come to serve you.
Don't give me away.
I will carry you swift as a bird.
But if you need must stay,
Put your hand in your pocket where you play."

King Sarkap was angry to hear the horse giving this advice to his master. He ordered his servants to take the horse away.

Rasalu's eyes filled with tears when he saw his white horse being led away. But the horse consoled him,

"Dear Prince, weep not for me
I shall not eat the grass from a stranger's hands,
Nor to strange stables shall I be led.
Put your hand in your pocket, as I said."

Rasalu now remembered the kitten that was in his pocket and also the dice of bones which the ghost had asked him to use.

So he told king Sarkap, "Do not take my armour, or my horse, till the last game is over."

As king Sarkap saw Rasalu talking in a firm voice, he called his queens to come and see the match from the terrace. He thought their beauty would distract the enemy from the game.

But Rasalu's eyes were on the game.

He said to king Sarkap, "We have played with your dice twice. Let us play with my dice the third time."

Rasalu emptied his pocket of the dice. The little kitten also emerged, and it went to sit near the hole from which king Sarkap's rat had come in.

Raja Sarkap saw Rasalu winning the game. He whistled to his rat. The rat did not come out of the hole, because it saw the kitten. So Rasalu won two stakes, one after another. And he took back his armour and his horse.

Sarkap prayed to his demons to help him. Then he thought his fate was in dice. So he prayed to the dice,

"Oh! dice favour me today.
For this prince is a clever man with whom I play.
No small risk-my life itself is at stake.
As Sarkap does, so do for king Sarkap's sake."

Rasalu matched the prayer of king Sarkap with his own incantation,

"Oh! dice of bone, given by the ghost
It is a man in whose hands you play.
No small risk but life or death are at stake.
As I do, you do for the honest game'sake."

The women on the terrace laughed. But Rasalu did not look at them. The rat was frightened of the kitten and did not appear.

The game went on and king Sarkap lost, first his kingdom, then all his wealth, and lastly his head.

20

Just then a servant came and told Raja Sarkap that a daughter was born to his youngest queen.

The defeated Sarkap was angry and shouted, "Go, kill her at once! She has come at an evil moment. She has brought bad luck to her father!"

Rasalu was shocked at Sarkap's speech.

"Spare your daughters, the seventieth and the seventy-first, oh cruel king! They have done nothing to deserve death. I will take them away and if you promise never to play for the stake of another's head, I shall spare you." King Sarkap fell at the feet of king Rasalu and asked to be forgiven.

"I will never play for another's head," he said. "And you will have my seventieth daughter for a queen and the seventy-first for her companion."

21

King Rasalu came back home with his beautiful bride and her sister. The whole town of Sialkot came out to meet him.

His father announced that he would give up the throne and make his son the king.

King Rasalu lived happily ever after and ruled as a just king.

FOLK TALES OF RAJASTHAN

Rajasthan

Rajasthan, the land of the Rajputs, is a land of chivalry, legend and a rich oral literature: a land full of gaiety and colour, of men and women to whom honour is dearer than life itself.

Jaipur, the "Pink City", is the capital of the state. It has an area of 3,42,239 sq km, population 43,880,640 and literacy 38.81 per cent. Haryana, Delhi and Uttar Pradesh lie to its north and north-east, Madhya Pradesh to the east and south-east, Gujarat to the south-west and Pakistan to the west. The principal languages of the State are Rajasthani and Hindi.

The State of Rajasthan is diamond-shaped lying to the north-west of Madhya Pradesh. The Aravalli range cuts across it from south-west to north-east. In the northern half is the desert and mountains with high cliffs.

Rajasthan has varied geographical features, the scorching noonday heat of the desert which may turn to frost at night. Also there are the lovely lakes and fertile valleys. The blue pottery, the tie and die and enamelled metal and glasswork of Rajasthan are some of the ancient village arts.

Rajasthan has a rich heritage of folklore. Folk literature was everywhere, initially, an oral literature but in Rajasthan it appeared in the written form at a relatively early date. And the inimitable storyteller, who later turned professional, has flourished through the ages. Storytelling became the hereditary occupation of the *Bhat*, the *Charan* and the *Bandi*. They devoted themselves mainly to stories, genealogies and proverbs. The religious customs, modes of dress, superstitions were skilfully woven into their tales which rendered them all the more interesting. Rajasthani folk tales abound in stories of heroes who sacrificed their life for their honour or honour of their women.

59
THE WILL

Amar Singh was a wise, old man. He had known days of dire poverty when he didn't have two coins to rub against each other. Probably that had hardened him and he vowed that he would work his way up the thorny ladder of success, but make his way up he would. The next decade saw him toiling his way up but never once did he lose heart and in the evening of his life, he was blessed. His savings through the years had grown steadily and there came a day when he dug it all up and looked at it with satisfaction. It was a big sum of money, bigger than he had ever imagined. He sold his field which was comparatively small and bought a large one, the most fertile field in the village. Then he went to a cattle fair and bought the best cows that he could spot. After that he never looked back. The field and the cattle brought him large returns and at last he could afford to relax.

Amar Singh had three sons. They were sturdy young men and much attached to one another but Amar Singh was a wise man and had seen much of the world. He was not a fool to rest assured that this love among brothers would last for all times. The sons would marry; children would be born. And it was but inevitable, thought the wise old man, that there would be frictions and the family and the wealth would split.

He gave a great deal of thought as to how he would divide his wealth, and when he was satisfied that he had arrived at a wise decision, he called his sons and said: "I am an old man now and have but a few more years to live. As long as you all work hard and share what you have, you will not need anything from me but when I am dead, a time may come when you may wish to live independently. I have made provision for that day. I have divided my property amongst you, according to age. Right here, under my bed, I have buried my will. Take it out and divide the property only when you are sure you need it."

The sons agreed. Amar Singh lived to a happy old age. After his death for a while all went well. The brothers worked more than their needs. They divided this equally amongst themselves. They married and by and by became fathers. The children quarrelled and the wives quarrelled.

The brothers feeling uncomfortable, said, "It is better that we set up separate establishments and put an end to all this. Father had once told us that he had made a fair distribution of wealth amongst us. Let us dig up the ground under his bed and see what he had left to each of us."

The sons carefully dug under the bed and brought out three brass vessels. On opening them they found that one contained earth, the second contained bones and the third contained coal. The brothers looked at one another in amazement. Whatever they may have expected, these items were surely not in their thoughts.

"Whatever did our revered father mean by this?" they wondered. "Each of these items stands for something but it's beyond our power to guess."

They thought and they discussed but they could neither solve the riddle nor could they come anywhere near to a suitable answer. At last they called a meeting of the elders of the village and laid the matter before them. Now these village elders were proud because they held the coveted post of village elders and they looked down their noses at the villagers, for they felt their wisdom somewhat akin to the wisdom of the great Vikramaditya himself. But when the problem of the old man's will was put before them, they were baffled. They coughed and they fidgeted, gulped down a few glasses of water but nothing helped to throw light on the meaning of the three items of the will. And at last, to their eternal embarrassment, they had to acknowledge defeat. The three brothers were not only disappointed; they were also greatly disillusioned. They had firm belief till now, as had all the other villagers, that there was no problem that their elders could not solve.

Anyway, the brothers were determined to solve the riddle. Each had to know what his share of the property was and so one day they bade goodbye to their families and set out in search of a wise man. After travelling for a number of days, they arrived at the beautiful city of lakes, Udaipur. They made inquiries at various places and they received the same answer—a wise old hermit lived in the northern part of the city.

"If anyone can solve your problem," said the men, "it is he."

The brothers went to his hut. They bowed before him and paid their respects.

"Holy father," said the eldest brother, "we have come a long way to seek the meaning of our father's will."

He told the old man about the unusual allocation of property that their father had made.

"What are we to infer from vessels full of earth, bones and coal?" he asked.

The hermit smiled and answered, "Son, if you had spent a little time in trying to understand the meaning of the three items, you would have saved yourselves this long journey."

"But we did think," replied the eldest brother. "Not only we but our wise village elders spent much of their precious time, trying to fathom the mystery."

"Your father was a very wise man. How is it that you, his sons, are unable to unravel the mystery of the will? This is the solution: To the eldest he gave earth, which means that he gave his fields and all that they produce; to the second he gave bones, that is, he gave his cattle, and to the youngest he gave coal or all the gold he had. This is the meaning of your wise father's will and I hope you are all satisfied with the fair division of property."

The brothers were satisfied. They returned to their village and lived happily.

60
THE CLEVER SETH

THE Sethani was in a very bad mood indeed. In the twelve months that she had been married, she could hardly remember a day when her husband had come home early. He left for his shop in the morning and it was usually midnight when he returned.

Whenever she pouted and grumbled, the Seth would say in exasperation, "You know that apart from my own work in the shop, I keep busy with all my social activities. There are gatherings which I have to address, the meetings of elders which I have to attend, and then there are the men in trouble who come to me for advice. Even the Rana seeks my advice and help. Anyway, I keep you in great comfort, so what you have to grumble about is more than I can understnad. There are half a dozen servants to do the work and a carriage is always at the door awaiting your pleasure."

It was true she had nothing to grumble about as far as comforts were concerned. She did not have to do any work at all. She had all the money at her disposal and recently the *patwa* or jeweller had made a *timniya* or collar studded with gems and a beautiful gold chain for her hips on which she now fastened her keys. But in spite of everything she grumbled and wondered how she could make the Seth spend more time at home. Fate played admirably into her hands as we shall see.

The morning after the Gangor festival which was celebrated worshipping Gauri, the goddess of bounty, the Seth was about to leave when he found his servants waiting expectantly for their *neg*—presents or cash which they expected as their right after every major festival. He paid them and left home.

He spent a very busy day. It was midnight when he took leave of his friends. One of them persuaded him to ride back on his horse as it was not safe to walk home at such a late hour. The Seth accepted the offer and mounting the animal, rode off homewards.

On the way he had to pass a road reputed to be a haven for thieves. He had but turned to this road when he found his path blocked by a drunkard. It was rather dark and the Seth could not see the man's features clearly nor did he even try. He felt sure it was a trap to rob him and so losing no time, he set his horse at a gallop, knocking off the man in the process. He heard a dull thud as the man's head fell on the cobbled road.

After riding some distance, the Seth felt he must go back and see how the man fared after the knock. The road was still deserted. Not a soul could be seen anywhere. The Seth went back and to his utter consternation saw that the man on the ground was none other than the youngest son of the Rana. The Seth nearly swooned when he discovered that the bump on the head had killed the prince. What was he to do now? If the news reached the Rana, he would be, without ceremony, hanged. The Seth could almost feel the noose around his neck and involuntarily lifted his hand to loosen it. He, who had always advised others and got them out of trouble, was now in need of his own wise counsel.

He lifted the body and slowly led his horse away. In one of the lanes, the Seth slung the body over his shoulders and tiptoed to a shop which now had its doors and shutters shut. It was a wine shop noted for its heady wine made from mahua flowers. The prince was a regular visitor to this shop.

The Seth propped the body against the door and rode away into the darkness. On reaching home, he went straight to bed. Not an hour had passed when there was a loud thumping at the door and a voice, full of fear, cried, "Sethji, Sethji, please help me."

"Go away," shouted the angry voice of the Seth. "Is this the time to distrub anyone?"

"Sethji, you must get up. I am in great trouble."

Grumbling, the Seth got up and opened the door. The man at the door was the very man he had expected to find. It was the owner of the wine shop. The man seemed half dead in fear. He cried, "Sethji, a terrible thing has happened. The youngest prince, obviously drunk, was standing against the door of my shop. Just by chance I opened it. The prince fell forward and banged his head on the floor. That bang killed him. If the king hears of it then I am as good as dead. Sethji, I will give you all my life's savings if you get me out of this mess."

The man placed a bag of coins in the Seth's hand. "It has Rs. 1,000 in it," he said.

After giving the matter some thought, the Seth went with the man. Once more he slung the dead prince over his shoulder and keeping to the shadows, he walked to the house of a minister. The Seth had definite news that the minister was plotting against the king. Still keeping to the shadows, the Seth approached the door.

"The youngest prince is the worst of the whole lot," said a voice from within. "If only I could get my hands on him, I would kill him."

The Seth waited to hear no more. He propped the prince against the door and raced back home. Within half an hour, he heard a loud pounding at his front door.

"Sethji, Sethji, please get up. We are in great trouble."

"Off with you," came the angry voice of the Seth. "I shall not get up at this ungodly hour."

"Sethji, you must. You must help us," pleaded the voice.

Reluctantly, the Seth left his bed and opened the door. The minister whose house he had just visited stood at the door with his two friends.

Holding out a bulging bag of coins, the Minister said, 'Sethji, here are Rs. 5,000. I was having a party at my house. When I opened the door to bid goodbye to my friends, the prince, who must have been drunk and who had been leaning against the door, fell down with a bang on the head. That bang has killed him. If the king hears of this, not only will I be hanged, but my whole family will be turned out into the streets. Sethji, you must help me out of this."

"This is a very delicate job you ask me to do," protested the Seth, gradually waking up. He locked the bag of coins and went with the men. For the third time that night he slung the dead body of the prince and keeping well to the shadows he walked off towards the palace. Luckily he found the guards dozing.

"Too much feasting and wining at Gangor festival," murmured the Seth.

He crept up to the door of the palace and propped the prince against it.

As he was coming away, the angry voice of the king came from within, "That young son of yours, Rani, is a shame to the entire family. I have always excused him for your sake, but if he gets into any trouble this time, he will get what he deserves and you well know what that means."

The Seth's feet took wings, when he heard the door being opened. Panting hard, he crept into his bed. Within fifteen minutes, there were loud knocks on the door. "Open immediately," shouted a loud voice.

"I will not be disturbed at such a late hour. Go away and come in the morning."

"Open in the Rana's name."

The Seth jumped out of bed and opened the door. Two royal guards stood there.

"The Rana has summoned you immediately."

The Seth went with them. At the palace, he found the Rana and the queen in tears. The dead prince lay on the royal bed.

The Rana cried out, "Seth, you are the only man in my whole kingdom who can tell me what I should do. I was wishing my son to be dead when I opened the door and he fell in and banged his head on the floor. He must have been badly drunk to have fallen so heavily. Any way, the bang on the head killed him. If news gets around, the whole kingdom will rise against me for bringing about his death. What can I do to make it seem that the prince died a natural death?"

The Seth was quick to rise to Rana's help. He said, "Sire, send out your drummers and have it proclaimed that the prince has been bitten by a snake and that everything is being done to draw out the poison."

Breaking the silence of the night the beating of the drums announced the sad news through the streets and lanes of the capital. Early in the morning another drummer went round to announce the death of the prince.

A bag of Rs. 10,000 was placed in the hands of the Seth for his wise advice. He returned home, a tired and rich man. The night had brought him much wealth no doubt, but it had nearly landed him in the hands of the hangman. He vowed never again to stay out late at night.

The Sethani had no further occasion to grumble.

FOLK TALES OF SIKKIM

Sikkim

Sikkim is a small mountain State in the eastern Himalayas. It is bounded by Tibet on the north, Nepal on the west and Bhutan on the east. West Bengal lies to its south.

The state has an area of 7,096 sq km, population, 403,612 and 56.53 per cent literacy. The capital is in Gangtok. The principal languages in use are Bhutia, Nepali, Lepcha and English.

The Lepchas, who are believed to have come from Assam, were the first settlers in Sikkim. They profess Buddhist faith.

Life in the village centres round the monastery of the Buddhist monks called the Lamas. The Lamas are highly respected in the community. In the olden days they were the only people in the village who knew how to read and write.

Like all tribal people in the world, the Lepchas enjoy nothing better than stories. On cold winter days they sit around the fire and retell these stories which tell about the creation of the world, the origin of the Lepcha people, the adventures of their heroes or just humorous anecdotes or fanciful fairy tales. Most of the tales in this collection come from the Lepchas.

61

LAMA LHATSUN CHHEMBO

LAMA Lhatsun Chhembo is the patron saint of Sikkim. Believed to have been an incarnation of the great Indian teacher, Bhim Mitra, he is said to have spread Buddhism in Sikkim. It was he who appointed the first Chogyal, Phuntshog Namgyal. Many monasteries in the country have been founded by the saint and many are the stories in the country about the heavenly powers of this holy monk.

Lama Lhatsun Chhembo was born in A.D. 1595 in south-eastern Tibet. When he was still very young he became a Lama and travelled all over Tibet, studying in many of the monasteries. He made a name for his great learning and wisdom and in a short time he had become famous all over Tibet. The grand Lama of Lhasa himself knew him and highly respected him for his scholarship and piety.

It is said that it was on the advice of Lama Lhatsun that the Grand Lama went to see the Chinese emperor, which really became an important event in the history of Tibet. The story is that before he reached Potala Palace, the headquarters of the Grand Lama in Lhasa, for his first meeting with him, the Grand Lama knew by inspiration that a great saint was to come to visit him. So he instructed the palace guards beforehand to receive the visitor with honours.

But the guards failed to recognise Lama Lhatsun Chhembo when he blew aloud his trumpet made of a human thigh bone as was his habit. The guards became angry, seized him and tied him to a rock in the neighbourood as a punishment for daring to blow his trumpet so close to the palace. The saint then shook the whole Potala hill, and it was in this way that he brought his arrival to the notice of the host.

On being admitted to the presence of the Grand Lama, Lama Lhatsun walked boldly up to him and struck him with his fist to the astonishment of all Lamas present. Then he vomited in everybody's presence, and said, "You are soon going to China; on the way you would face a great danger but by striking you as I did, I have rid you of that danger. In China you will find yourself in great danger some day! Read this paper I now give you and you will be all right."

Then he gave to the Grand Lama a scroll of paper, and said again, "My vomiting in your presence means that you will finally have great powers and riches through me."

This prophecy of the saint came true. Soon after, the Grand Lama visited China and was received by the Chinese emperor with great honour. But the heavenly emperor, to test his divine knowledge, asked him about the real meaning of the rainbow colours. This was the danger predicted by Lama Lhatsun, but the Grand Lama remembered the scroll given to him by Lama Lhatsun and gave a satisfactory answer. The answer pleased the emperor so much that he gave the Grand Lama great honour and many riches.

On his return to Tibet the Grand Lama offered to Lama Lhatsun in gratitude a great position in the Tibetan priesthood, but Lama Lhatsun was not interested in position of any kind. He had by now discovered the meaning of some hidden message left by Guru Rimpoche, the great Guru from India who had spread Buddhism in Tibet and established the Lama order of Buddhist monks. "I must go and open the northern gate of the hidden country of the rice valley, Sikkim," he said. "That is what Guru Rimpoche wants me to do and I must develop that country religiously."

Lama Lhatsun attempted to enter Sikkim by way of Jongri but he could not find a path there to cross over to Sikkim. So he stayed for the time being in a cave for meditation and prayer. Here, it is said, the Lord of Mount Kanchenjunga came to him in the form of a wild goose and spoke with the saint. Inspired by the majestic mountain, the holy Lama wrote a book of prayer for the proper worship of Lord Kangchenjunga.

However, the Himalayas could not be crossed. Finding no way through the south to reach his destination the determined saint flew over the peak, using his divine powers. Here he was met by two other lamas who had come from the south and west respectively. There they met at the foot of Kanchenjunga the Lepchas named *Yoksam,* meaning the meeting place of three superior ones.

The three holy lamas then spoke about the prophecy of Guru Rimpoche, who had said that four noble brothers from four directions would come to meet in this wild country to establish a kingdom in which the religion of the Buddha would flourish. Now the question was, where to find the fourth Lama, who was to come from the East?

Through divine grace they found Phuntshog Namgyal, perhaps of Chumbi valley. This fourth Lama was appointed Chogyal, meaning ruler, of the whole of Sikkim. In Dubdi monastery in Yoksam, the old capital of Sikkim, a stone seat is still preserved which is supposed to be the throne on which the first Chogyal was crowned.

FOLK TALES OF TAMIL NADU

Tamil Nadu

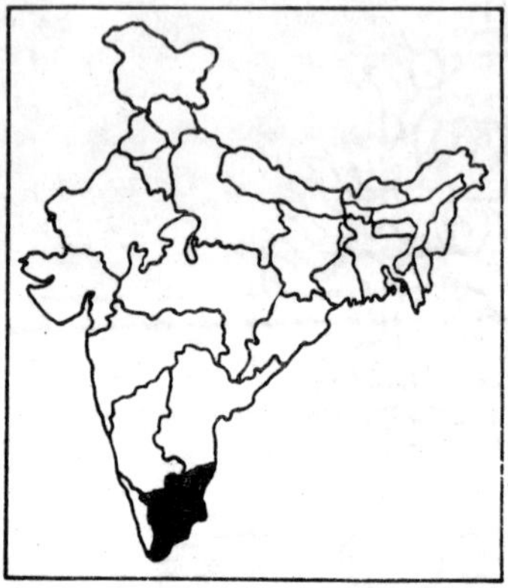

Tamil Nadu is situated on the eastern side of the southern tip of the Indian peninsula. It is bounded on the east by the Bay of Bengal, in the west by the Arabian Sea and the States of Kerala and Karnataka.

Madras is the State capital.

Tamil Nadu has an area of 130,058 sq km, a population of 55,638,318, with 63.72 per cent literacy. The State language is Tamil, but all the southern languages and their dialects and Hindi and English are spoken and understood by and large. Urdu and Gujarati are also spoken by a large section. Madras is a cosmopolitan city.

The people are highly intelligent, generally frugal, pragmatic and hardworking. They have a dogged perseverance if a cause is taken up. Highly patriotic, they are far too attached to their traditions, festivals, songs, dances, classical music, food, folklore and have given more to the surrounding regions than adopted. With a number of great rivers, and lakes, a highly developed language and literature and no Muslim invasions in the past, the Tamils are naturally proud of their culture.

62

VIDAMUNDAN AND KODAMUNDAN

IN A town called Thiruvela, there lived two persons, Vidamundan and Kodamundan. Surprisingly, their names were very appropriate to their behaviour and character, because a Vidamundan is always on the lookout to obtain things from people even if they don't wish to part with them, and Kodamundan is the type who is very stingy and niggardly and will go to any length to avoid giving.

Everyday, Kodamundan used to visit different houses and collect several *padis** of rice on the plea that he had to feed the Brahmins. Many charitable people were usually taken in by this false plea, since he staggered his visits to the donor's houses so as not to arouse any suspicion. In this way, he collected enough rice for him and his wife to pass their days in comfort. Kodamundan, however, very carefully avoided offering any food to a visitor. He would bluff that some Brahmins were eating at his house that very day and asked the person to come some other day. Thus, by making one excuse or another, he never parted with a single morsel of food.

Vidamundan had heard about Kodamundan and was aware of his tactics. One day he decided to have his meals at the house of Kodamundan. He was determined to make Kodamundan eat humble pie, no matter how hard he may have to try, or how long he may have to wait.

One fine morning he went to Kodamundan's house and told him of his desire to take food in his house that day.

Kodamundan said, "Today I have already invited ten Brahmins. Please come tomorrow."

---

* A kind of measure.

Vidamundan, who had decided to take food there, thought of coming the next day and left.

The next morning he reached at the same time and said, "As you asked me to come today, so have I come."

Kodamundan was now in a fix, and knew that ordinary excuses will not be enough to drive him away.

He went inside the house and consulted his wife. He asked her to lie down in bed and pretend as if she was having a severe headache.

He then came out and said to Vidamundan, "It is true that I invited you today. But as my wife has been suffering from severe headache since last night, there will not be any *Anna Dan*[1] to Brahmins till she gets well. As soon as she is well I shall send for you. You kindly come and take food that day."

Vidamundan said, "For such a small reason how can you refuse a Brahmin from taking food? I know cooking. Let me quickly tie my *dhoti*[2] and enter the kitchen. You also come. We both will cook and eat and prepare *Pongal*[3] for your wife."

Kodamundan did not know what to do. He thought that he would make Vidamundan cook and would drive him away without serving him food. He further thought that his wife would be saved from the botheration of cooking.

He said to Vidamundan, "Come, let us cook."

As soon as the food was ready, Kodamundan said, "I have only one plantain leaf to take food on. Please go and bring another." Vidamundan agreed and went out.

Kodamundan then went to his wife and said, "I have saved you from the botheration of cooking food. Now I have sent him to bring plantain leaf. As soon as he comes back you start quarrelling with me. I will beat you and you start weeping loudly. When he sees all this he will go away."

Vidamundan came at that time with a plaintain leaf. The husband and wife started quarrelling as planned. The wife said, "What is this? Whosoever comes to this house you give him food. We do not have anything left for tomorrow. Why do you not think about the house?"

1. Offering of food as charity.
2. A length of cloth worn below the waist.
3. *Pongal* is prepared by cooking rice and *moong dal* together and adding a little salt. Fried cuminseeds and black pepper are added for flavouring.

The husband then said, "If I feed the Brahmins why should you feel bad? I am spending only my hard earned money. I am not taking money from your father." Saying this he got up and started beating the wall with all his strength. The wife began to weep loudly.

Vidamundan who was hearing all this thought that it was not proper for him to go in at that time. He went to the storeroom near the kitchen and sat near the cowdung cakes. This went on for quite some time. When Kodamundan got tired of beating the wall, he came out and did not find Vidamundan there. He told his wife that the guest had left and that they should take the food. He served the cooked food in two plantain leaves.

When they were thus seated to take the food the husband said, "I beat you without hurting you."

The wife said, "I also wept constantly."

Vidamundan who was hiding himself near the kitchen said, "I also came back without going away."

Saying this he quickly jumped in and sat in front of the plantain leaf where food was already served. Kodamundan had no other way out but to serve him food.

Vidamundan thus had a hearty lunch in the house of Kodamundan.

63
THE IMPORTANCE OF LIGHTING

ONCE there was a big businessman. He had a son and a daughter. Both were happily married. The brother and the sister had great regard for each other. They decided that in case a daughter was born to one and a son to another, they would marry them to each other so that their family bonds continued. The son had three sons and the daughter had three daughters. The businessman became old and one day he passed away. As he was in debt, the creditors took away a large portion of his money, with the result that his son became poor.

The businessman's daughter was married to a rich man. He prospered in his business. He gave two of his daughters in marriage to two businessmen who were rolling in wealth and both the husband and wife were busy in settling the marriage of their third daughter. At that time, the third daughter reminded her parents of the promise they had made to her uncle. She also told that all her cousins were refusing to marry till she also got married and that she would marry one of her cousins only.

When her mother heard this she was stunned. She said, "Both of your sisters have married in rich families. If you marry a poor man, who will give you only *Kuya*,[1] how will they respect you?" She further said, "If you insist on marrying your cousin, I will push you in their house and will never think of you."

The girl did not give in. She had decided to marry one of her cousins only.

The girl's mother had no other way out. She sent word to her brother that she will give her youngest daughter in marriage to

---

1. *Kuya* is Ragee, powdered and cooked in water. A little salt is added to give taste. It is eaten along with red chillies.

one of his sons. When her brother heard this, his happiness knew no bounds. He made all arrangements and the marriage was celebrated. His other two sons were married in poor families. The youngest daughter's parents never came to see her or enquired about her welfare.

She was very happy in the poor man's family and never acted as if she was from a rich family. All the three brothers earned their living by stitching banyan leaves and selling them in the market. In this way they were passing their days in extreme poverty.

One day the king of that place was having his oil bath. He had taken off his ring and had kept it on the floor. Suddenly an eagle came and took away the ring and dropped it in the house of the businessman's son. At that time only the youngest daughter-in-law was in the house. She picked up the ring and tied it to the edge of her sari and did not tell anyone about it.

The king saw the eagle taking away his ring. He made an announcement by drumbeats that whosoever brought the ring it back to him would be rewarded with whatever he asked for. The youngest daughter came to know of this announcement. She went and told her husband about it and said, "Let us go and give it to the king. One thing I may tell you, that I will never ask for riches. Whatever I ask from the king, you must be satisfied with that and will never get angry with me." Her husband agreed, and both of them went to the palace and gave the ring to the king.

The King was happy to find his ring and he asked them what they wanted. The lady said, "Your majesty! I do not want riches. My only wish is that on one Friday, nobody should light lamps in their houses. Even in the palace there should be no lamp. Only I will light lamps in my house." The king agreed to this. An announcement was made throughout the town that no one should light his house on the following Friday, and if he did so their eyes would be plucked out.

The youngest daughter, as soon as she got permission from the king to light her house on the following Friday, told her brothers-in law to bring at least two *varakan*[1] on loan and that the whole house had to be lighted the next Friday. She also asked one brother-in-law to stand near the front door and the second one to stand near the back door. She told them that if anyone wanted to

---

1. One varakan is equal to nearly three and a half rupees.

enter the house they should let him do it only on the condition that he would not come out and in case anyone wanted to go out of the house they should let him go out only on the condition that he would not come in again.

All the three brothers went out to bring some money. Both the younger brothers kept their eldest brother in mortgage and borrowed two *varakan*. They bought oil, earthen lamps and cotton, to illuminate the whole house.

The long awaited Friday came. The youngest daughter with her two sisters-in-law observed a fast that day and during the night she lit the whole house.

The whole town was in complete darkness because of the king's order. Goddess Lakshmi[1] went from house to house but could not find even a ray of light anywhere. In the end she came to the youngest daughter's house. There she saw the brother-in-law standing in front of the house. She took his permission to go in. The brother-in-law enquired who she was, and let her go in only after being assured her that she would not come out.

As Goddess Lakshmi could not find light anywhere in the town, she accepted his condition and entered the house. No sooner had she entered the house than Poverty, Goddess Lakshmi's sister, could no longer continue to live in the same house and had to leave the place. She quickly came out and asked the brother-in-law's permission to leave the house. The brother-in-law then was reminded of his sister-in-law's words. He enquired who she was and secured her promise that if she left the house she would not enter it again, only then he would allow her to leave. She promised that she would not come back again and left the house through the back door.

The next morning when all the three brothers and their wives got up they found all the vessels, trunks, almirahs full of gold coins. Poverty had disappeared altogether and they became rich. The youngest daughter's parents and her sisters started visiting her house thereafter.

Do you know that from that day onwards people light their houses on Friday and perform *Pooja*[2] to invite Goddess Lakshmi.

---

1. The goddess of wealth.
2. Religious rites

FOLK TALES OF UTTAR PRADESH

Uttar Pradesh

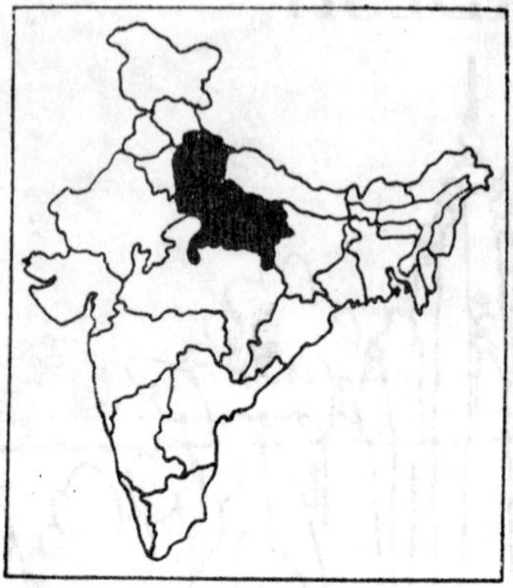

Uttar Pradesh is the most populated state in India with an area of 2,94,411 sq km, a population of 138,760,417, with density 471 per sq km but a low percentage of literacy at 41.7 per cent only. The state has gorgeous and mighty rivers, hills and dales, plains and snowbound tracts with a very large group of ethnic units in different stages of progress. Its capital is in Lucknow.

The boundary touches Tibet and Nepal in the north with an osmosis of culture and traditions, Himachal Pradesh, Haryana, Delhi and Rajasthan in the west and south-west. Madhya Pradesh joins it in the south and Bihar in the east. The regions are culturally and traditionally alike with a mixed Hindu-Muslim population and Hindi and Urdu as the languages. Uttar Pradesh has imbibed much from the regions beyond and has also given much to them.

A portion of the population from the poorer tracts is migratory. The people are proud and sensitive about their culture, ancient mooring in religions, traditions, faiths, superstitions, songs, dances and general heritage. With twenty universities and a large number of institutes for advanced studies and research in various disciplines one would have expected a higher rate of literacy.

The folklore of Uttar Pradesh is of mixed heritage. There is a strong influence of both Hindu and Muslim traditions. The dances, songs and folktales are of the type which one finds in the Hindi belt of Bihar, Rajasthan and Madhya Pradesh. The folktales of Uttar Pradesh are rich and varied.

The state is inhabited by many diverse races and people. Historical places like Agra with the Taj Mahal and Fatehpur Sikri, also give colour to the state. Bundelkhand, which forms the south-west corner, has a peculiar charm and tradition of its own.

64

SURAJMAL'S JOURNEY TO HEAVEN

It is said that in one of the towns of Barabanki district there once reigned a king whose minister Ajit Singh was very wise and able, and was his confidant. Due to this the other courtiers were envious of him, chief amongst whom was Surajmal.

One day they conspired against him, and going up to the King said, "Sire, Ajit Singh was boasting the other day that he can do what no one else can, Your Majesty not excepted. 'There is nothing impossible for Ajit Singh,' these were his exact words."

"Oh! ho!" excalimed the king. "So he has become so vain that he thinks himself even better than me!"

The courtiers were glad to hear the king speak thus, and they knew that their plan had succeeded.

So Surajmal said, "Sire, it is fit to make Ajit see who is the master. He seems to have forgotten. If your Majesty permits, I may say how this can be done."

The king said, "Go on, what do you suggest?"

Surajmal said, "Sire, set him some tasks, which will show him that there is something which even he can't do."

The king thought this to be a good idea and asked him to assign him such tasks.

Surajmal, and the other courtiers, conspired together, and filling a big room with cotton they said, "Sire, if it pleases you, order Ajit Singh to convert all this cotton into yarn by tomorrow."

The king called his minister and said, "Spin all this cotton into yarn by tomorrow, or else I will have you beheaded."

When he saw the room full of cotton, Ajit was filled with dismay, and went home crestfallen. The whole day he was weighed down with grief, and in the night he could not sleep. When it was morning he began to think that it would be better if he drowned himself in the river than suffer the dishonour of being beheaded.

So he left his home and proceeded through the forest towards the river. On the way he saw a hermit sitting beneath a shady banyan tree. He touched the hermit's feet and asked for his blessings.

The hermit knew the plight of the minister by means of his spiritual powers and said, "Man's life is a holy gift, my son, and it does not behove him to end it at will. I will help you to overcome your difficulties. Therefore go back and do as the king wishes."

Saying this he gave Ajit Singh a magic spinning wheel, a spade, and a scythe, and blessing him sent him back home.

Ajit Singh took the spinning wheel and went to the palace. As soon as he set it down on the floor of the room it began to revolve by itself so fast that in the twinkling of an eye a kilo of cotton had been spun! By noon the entire room was filled with yarn and the task was done.

Seeing this Surajmal and his companions were dumbfounded.

Still they said, "This knave of a minister has somehow managed to do this task, but we will soon get him."

Then going to the king they said, "Sire, having spun all the cotton, now Ajit Singh's vanity has risen all the more, and he says he can do tasks which even the king can't do; so if your majesty pleases he may be asked to harvest the grain in the royal farm by tomorrow."

The king was well pleased at this counsel, and calling Ajit Singh said, "The wheat has grown in the farm. See that it is harvested by tomorrow."

Now the farm was almost five hundred acres and it was impossible for a single man to harvest it even in a month. So Ajit Singh despaired. While he was musing over this he remembered the scythe that the hermit had given him. 'It might help, as his spinning wheel did,' he thought, and next morning he took it with him and went on the farm.

As soon as he started mowing, the scythe slipped from his hands and flying with the speed of lightning through the wheat stalks harvested an acre of land in a moment! Within a few hours the entire field had been done.

When Surajmal saw this he was wonderstruck but began to think of some other way in which he could harm Ajit.

So when the king came he said, " Sire, your wheat has been harvested but after the work had been done I heard Ajit Singh boast in triumph, 'What the king's labourers could not do in a week I have done in a few hours! Thus I have humbled the proud king!' The man's vanity, sire, has reached the limit."

The king asked, "Then, what other task do you wish him to do?"

Surajmal said, "Sire, you need more water for the sowing, so ask him to dig a dozen wells. That will benefit Your Majesty and at the same time humble his pride."

The king called his minister and said, "You have somehow managed to accomplish the two tasks given to you but now I want you to dig a dozen wells by tomorrow. If the wells are not ready by then, I will hand you over to the executioner."

Ajit was very sad because digging even one well was beyond his power, to say nothing of twelve. While he was lost in thought he remembered the hermit's spade and when he came early the next day he brought it along with him. As soon as he had dug the first spadeful of earth, the spade slipped from his hand and in a second it had dug through a foot. Ajit did nothing but watch and by noon all the wells had been dug.

The courtiers were amazed to see this and said, "Surely this man is possessed of the devil! But this time let us devise a plot to get rid of him."

They got together and after consulting each other their leader Surajmal went to the king and said, "Sire, this Ajit is very clever. Why don't you send him to heaven so that he may find out if Your Majesty's parents are living happily there?"

"How can he be sent to heaven?" the king asked, puzzled.

"It is easy, sire," Surajmal said. "Let faggots be placed and Ajit amidst them. Then let them be lighted, and ghee and aromatics poured and he will go to heaven riding upon the smoke!"

This idea pleased the king who thought that when his minister had done so many difficult tasks he might also succeed in finding about the welfare of his parents from heaven. So he ordered his men to start piling up faggots. Ajit protested in vain. When he saw no way out he arranged so that the faggots would be piled over him, and meanwhile with the help of the magic spade he dug a tunnel from his home to the place of burning. When the king's courtiers set fire to the faggots they danced with joy for they knew that Ajit would be reduced to ashes.

When the smoke began to rise they shouted lustily, "See, Ajit is going to heaven, riding on the smoke!"

Hearing their shouts Ajit smiled and lowered himself into the tunnel.

After a month Ajit Singh presented himself at the *durbar*. By this time everyone had forgotten him and his sight made Surajmal and the scheming courtiers tremble. They, along with the king and everyone present there, began to gaze at him speechless with their eyes transfixed.

Ajit said, "Sir, your parents are well and happy. Your revered father is the king in heaven also but he needs an able and a trustworthy minister. When I told him of the ingenious device by which Surajmal had conveyed me to heaven he expressed the desire that you should send him so that he could appoint him his chief minister and carry on his rule there with success."

Hearing this the king said, "Let Surajmal speedily be sent to heaven for my father is in great need of him."

Before he could collect his wits, the frightened Surajmal was put on a pile of faggots. The ghee was poured, and someone lighted the pyre.

The king's men began to shout, "See Surajmal goes to heaven, riding upon the smoke!"

The trip to heaven had indeed started for him, but this time there was no coming back!

65
THE MAGIC BEDSTEAD

ONCE upon a time there was a carpenter called Sital who would not work with the result that he and his family starved.

One day his mother said, "Son, you don't earn a single pice, how shall we live? As for me, I am old and I don't need any money, but what about your wife and your children? They have neither food to eat nor clothes to keep out the cold. At least for their sake you should do something worthwhile."

Sital was a sensitive man and his mother's words made him feel very much ashamed of himself. So he took out his tools and set to work on a bedstead. He was so engrossed in it that he forgot food and drink and kept making it day and night. Thus working on it for a few days he made a very beautiful bedstead which had four wooden soldiers, one on each side of it. What was wonderful about them was, that they could move about and talk like human beings! Sital took the bedstead to the king's palace and began to shout:

"Only he who wakes, gets anything;
He who sleeps, loses.
Buy a bedstead! a wonderful bedstead!"

Hearing this the king sent for the carpenter and had a look at the bedstead. He saw that it was well made and asked its price. Sital said, "Sire, I will take nothing for it. If it pleases your fancy, and it is to your liking, you may send for Sital carpenter who lives in *Barhai ki Gali!*" Saying this he bowed and departed.

Sital's mother was eagerly awaiting his return. She was imagining in her mind the riches and the rewards which he would be bringing with him. But when she saw him again return empty-handed she was greatly disappointed, and asked him, "Son, how did it happen that the king kept such a splendid bedstead without paying anything for it?"

Sital said, "Mother, the king was paying me its price, but I asked him to use it first, and then give me whatever he wished."

His mother laughed at his simplicity and said, "Son, you have done a foolish thing indeed! A king's mood is very uncertain. He can be pleased one moment and angry the next. God knows what he will finally decide about it. Besides, you know the saying 'A bird in hand is worth two in the bush.' "

Sital said, "Mother, now I have left the bedstead with the king I can't possibly bring it back. Let us hope for the best."

Meanwhile the king got the bedstead placed in his bedroom and lay on it. His mind was burdened with some affair of the state, so sleep eluded him, and he remained awake far into the night. When it was midnight the first soldier came out of the bedstead and said to the other three soldiers, "Now you look after the bedstead, tonight I will make a round of the kingdom and find out who is happy and who is not."

They replied, "Don't worry we will remain here and guard the bedstead."

The soldier went away. When he was out on the street he saw a demon wandering about roaring loudly.

The soldier asked him, "Where are you going?"

The demon frowned and said, "Mind your own business. I go wherever I please. I have eaten many human beings, today I go to devour the king."

The soldier said, "I am the king's guard. You will have to fight with me first if you want to kill him. Come on, let me see your strength!"

As soon as he heard the soldier's challenge, the demon pounced upon him but the soldier was ready for the move and jumped aside. The demon went sprawling on the ground, and drawing his sword, the soldier hacked him to pieces.

After having killed the demon the soldier returned and took his place on the bedstead.

One of the other soldiers said, "Friend, tell us what happened when you were on your round."

The soldier answered, "Today I killed the demon who had spread terror in the kingdom. He had devoured many men. I met him on the crossing and slew him with my sword. Now the king's subjects are rid of him forever!"

"Well done!" the other soldier said, "but what made you fight him? Did he challenge you?"

The first soldier said, "No, in fact it was I who challenged him. He was on his way to kill our king today!"

Hearing this the king rose and calling the watchmen of the palace sent them to verify what the soldier had said. The messengers returned and told him that indeed the demon was lying dead there.

Next morning as soon as the king awoke, he called Sital, the carpenter, and giving him a cartload of gold, pearls, and precious stones, said, "Take this! Your bedstead is priceless, and I am very happy to have bought it from you."

When it was night the king again went and lay down on the bed. This time he deliberately kept awake for the incident of the previous night had aroused his curiosity. As soon as it was midnight the second soldier took leave of his companions and got ready to go on his round. As he stepped down from the bedstead he was horrified to see a black cobra sitting on the king's slippers. The soldier drew his sword and hacked it into bits. Then he put the slippers back in their proper place, and went back to his position on the bedstead.

Seeing him back so soon, the first soldier said in an astonished voice, "Hello! you have come back very early!"

"Brothers," the second soldier said, "I haven't been out of the palace at all. As soon as I stepped down I saw a deadly cobra over the king's slippers. So I slew it and came back. I believe I have done as praiseworthy a work as you; have I not?"

"Certainly," the first soldier said, "you have saved the king's life!"

The king was very much surprised to hear this talk and getting up from the bed he took a lamp and flashed it on the floor. Sure enough, the bits of the slain cobra were lying near his slippers. Next morning he sent two cartloads of riches to the carpenter.

The third night it was the turn of the third soldier. He said, "Friends, now I am going on my round. Keep guarding the bedstead during my absence."

When the soldier reached the portion of the palace having the king's treasury he found four thieves breaking into the wall. He stood by silenly in the dark, and began to watch what they were doing. As soon as the wall was breached three of the thieves went inside, while one remained there on guard. The thieves collected all the wealth from the king's treasury and stuffed it into their bags. Meanwhile the soldier crept up to the thief who was on guard, and thrust his sword into his stomach. The thief fell dead without uttering a word. The soldier stationed himself near the breach which was big enough only to admit one man at a time. The thieves came out one by one. The soldier kept on hacking off their heads as soon as they stepped out of the breach, and killed all of them. Having done, so he put the bags inside, closed the hole in the wall, and went back to take his place on the bedstead.

Seeing him arrive so late, the other soldiers asked him, "Friend, where were you all this time? We had almost given you up for lost!"

The soldier said, "It is true I have been away for long and it is almost daybreak but I have done very useful work. Four thieves were looting the king's treasury. I killed all of them and put all the money and precious stones back."

The other soldiers were very happy to hear this and said, "Well done, comrade! You have indeed done wonderful work, having killed four thieves single-handed."

The king, who was listening spellbound to this talk, at once got up and went to see for himself. True enough, he saw the four thieves lying slain and all the wealth tied up in sacks, but safe.

Next morning he again called Sital, the carpenter, and said, "Your bedstead is really priceless. Whatever I gave you for it is little."

Saying this he gave him a necklace of diamonds and precious stones, and much gold.

On the fourth night the king lay awake again to see what happened. The carpenter's words, "Only he who wakes gets anything; he who sleeps loses", came to his mind. While he was thinking over this, he saw the fourth soldier leave the bedstead and go on his round. He came across a stranger fully armed, trying to jump through the window.

The soldier challenged him and said, "Who are you?"

The stranger replied in a haughty voice, "What is that to you? Keep out of the way or I shall make short work of you. I am going to kill the king for he is my mortal enemy."

"I see," the soldier said mockingly. "That's why you are entering like a thief. If you were a brave man you would not try to kill one who is asleep but meet him in open fight. What a coward you are!"

The stranger's face became red with anger and he said, "It seems your hour has come. If you speak a word I will kill you."

"Then let us see who kills whom," the soldier said, drawing his sword. The two flew at each other, and began to fight fiercely. Soon the stranger began to lose ground, and the soldier pushed him nearer the wall with each slash of his sword. He gave him no quarter and with one swift lunge pierced him through and through. The stranger fell on the ground and was dead. The valiant soldier wiped his sword and went back to the king's bedstead.

His companions said, "You look very happy, brother, what have you done this night?"

The soldier said, "I have reason to feel happy, for I have just now killed the king's mortal foe who was coming through the window to murder him."

The other soldiers exclaimed, "Well done! Now the king will have some peace."

Hearing this the king got up with a start and leaned out of the window. Sure enough he recognised his enemy lying dead in the lamplight. The sight gave him great joy, for now he need have no fear of him.

As soon as it was daybreak, the king called Sital again and said, "I can never pay you the price for this matchless bedstead, my friend. The four soliders you have placed upon it have saved not only my kingdom but my life as well. Therefore, I make you my chief minister, and shall ever count you as my friend."

Saying this, he embraced him and gave him many gifts. After staying sometime with the king, Sital went home and gave the good news to his mother and his wife.

FOLK TALES OF WEST BENGAL

West Bengal

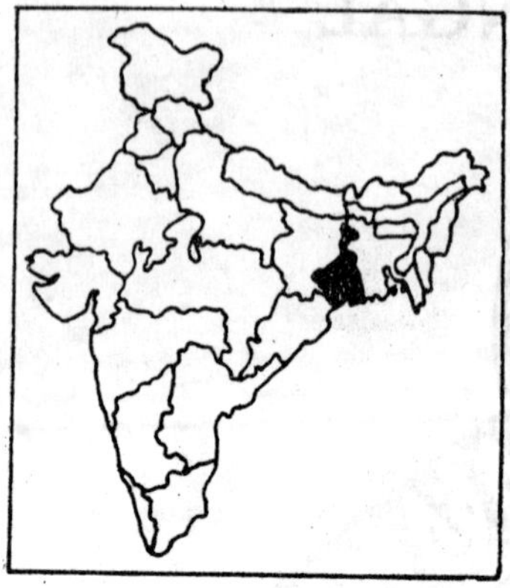

West Bengal has an area of 88,752 sq km and a population of 67,982,732. The literacy is 57.72 per cent. The capital is in Calcutta and is the focal point of the State. The State language is Bengali.

With Sikkim in the north, Assam and Bangladesh in the east, the Bay of Bengal in the south and Orissa, Bihar and Nepal in the west, West Bengal has a large number of ethnic units. The aborigines and the indigenous population have contributed largely to the religious faiths and culture of the State.

The main occupation of the people is agriculture and important crops are rice, jute (known as the golden fibre), and wheat. There is a good percentage of landless labourers and petty peasants.

West Bengal has folk tales, known as *Roop-Katha,* meaning 'beautiful imaginative stories'. *Roop-Katha* proceeds as an improvised narration which takes a vivid shape and creates a world of fantasy. The art of narration changes the shape and hue of a story and a clever storyteller, either a grandparent or the professional, keeps in mind the listeners' mood and occasion. In the past the professional male storyteller who walked from village to village, spread his mat under a shady tree and immediately attracted a crowd to hear his stories, often drawing from his imagination. There was another class of professionals known as the *alapinis,* the women-barbers, who would enter the inner apartments of the ladies, paint their toes with *alta* (a red liquid) and while doing it, keep the ladies engrossed in folk tales. Occasionally they sang parts of a story.

66

MAHUA

MAHUA was born of Brahmin parents. When she was six months old she was stolen by Homra, the leader of a gypsy gang. There are still a number of gypsy groups in Bengal who wander from place to place and earn a living by song and dance or by showing magic tricks. Some of them carry baskets of snakes. The snakes sway to the music of the flute. Mahua grew up with the gypsy gang under the strict control of Homra, the leader. She was a beautiful girl with lovely disposition. She is described by the poet Dvija Kanai as "a gem on a snake's hood". She danced well and was the star attraction of Homra's group.

In their tours the gypsy troupe arrived near the palace of Prince Naderchand. Naderchand had lost his father but had a loving mother. The queen mother was very keen that Naderchand should marry.

The gypsy troupe performed their magic tricks and other feats of skill before the prince. Mahua was in the troupe and a mere look at her was enough to strike the chord of love in the heart of the young prince.

The lovelorn prince was keen to meet Mahua who was also attracted towards the handsome prince. One evening Mahua had gone to fetch water in a pitcher. The prince was on the lookout and hastily went to the river bank and met Mahua.

The two lovers met secretly and both swore eternal love and faith to each other. But the love trysts were soon discovered by Homra, the leader of the gypsy gang. He shuddered at the idea of Mahua leaving the troupe as she was the star attraction. If Mahua did not dance how would the people come? After each dance of Mahua coins, big and small, were showered by the audience.

Homra chided the girl brought up by him and packed up the troupe. He wanted to leave Naderchand's area at once. But the two lovers managed to meet before the gypsy group moved away.

Naderchand swore eternal love and said that he was willing to take Mahua away from his kingdom and go to a distant land so that Homra could not reach them. The gypsy girl wept and "hung like a creeper round his neck" and replied, "Were you a flower my love I would hide you in my bosom. I love you so dearly that I cannot possibly think that you should leave your palace and mother for me. Please leave me and do not trouble yourself for my sake." The lovers parted but immediately afterwards Homra left the village. The gypsy troupe disappeared as if in air to avoid detection by Naderchand.

After a few days Naderchand also left his home in search of Mahua. The days were spent in search and nights in mental agony and sleeplessness. The search was made, far and wide, but Homra's gang could not be traced. The prince, Naderchand, grew more desolate but did not give up hope. He asked the birds, "Ye birds, you fly in the blue sky untethered and could see everything from a distance. Oh, tell me, please tell me, where have the gypsies gone? Tell me how is my Mahua?" He asked the gentle breeze if the breeze had passed Mahua and could give the direction. The prince was frantic and almost mad.

Long were the searches in the wood, in the forest, on the rivers and their banks, on the marshes, in the villages and in the cities. The journey was made by boats, on foot and on horseback; the prince did not know any rest. At last he met the gypsies and his Mahua.

The romance continued. The pair started meeting again through the help of a friend in the gang. But Homra put his foot down. He sternly rebuked Mahua and gave her a poisoned knife to stab Naderchand. Mahua took the knife. She was determined. She stepped forward and tried to stab herself but Naderchand snatched away the knife from her hand.

The pair, somehow, managed to escape and fled from place to place. At last they reach a far corner where the forest was deep and dense. The prince said, "Look there, Mahua, how the flowers are laughing, dressed in purple; and delicious fruits are hanging from the branches; the sweet water of the yonder stream is pleasant to the eyes." They spent the night in each other's arms. In the day they wandered hand in hand through the lonely forest.

Often the lovers would stay hidden in the hollow of the rocks with dead leaves. On occasions they would build a hut and pass a few days of anguish. Birds were their companions and sang to them their full-throated songs of love and bliss. The stars in the night were their friends. They spoke to the stars, birds, soft breeze, flowers and leaves. They knew not what fatigue was. They lived happily on jungle fruits and water of the springs.

Fate overtook them. One day the two lovers found that the big dog of the gypsy leader had discovered them. The dog ran back after trailing them and Mahua knew that the gang would find them soon. She embraced Naderchand with tears in her eyes and wished him farewell. Mahua knew that she would not be spared if she wanted to spare the life of Naderchand.

Within a short time the gang of the gypsy leader Homra overtook them. Homra gave the poisoned knife again to Mahua and ordered her to kill Naderchand. Mahua boldly took the knife and within a flash plunged the knife into her bosom and fell dead. But before that she uttered, "My husband, dearer than life, farewell. Bid me farewell, we shall meet again."

The gypsy gang fell on Naderchand and killed him at once. Thus the loving pair died leaving their love immortalised in a folk tale enshrined in a popular ballad.

67
MADHUMALA

THERE was a country where the king had lots of money and jewels, soldiers and servants, *Begums* or *Ranis*, courtiers, elephants and horses. He had no other want except that of a son and heir to the kingdom. People looked askance at the king. The *Ranis* or *Begums* were pitied and people would not like to meet the king or the queens at the crack of dawn. It is inauspicious to meet a married man or a woman in the early morning if he is without a son.

One early morning the king came out into the garden. The gardener who was working there turned his face away and disappeared. The insult was felt deeply by the monarch. The king got into the palace and locked himself up in a room. He would not eat or drink. Several nights and days passed without the king touching any food or drink and there was a deep gloom everywhere. The queens were praying hard and the faithful courtiers were wishing that some miracle should happen.

The miracle did happen. On the eighth day a mendicant with a long beard and ash all over his body and with big marks of his religious creed on the forehead came to the palace. Finding everyone in gloom he asked for the reason. He heard all about it, and that this was no problem. He sent for the king.

The king came out of the locked room and did his obeisance to the hermit. The hermit blessed the king and said, "Do not worry, I will give you two fruits. One you will take and the other will be eaten by the queen. You will get a son but on one condition. For twelve long years the son will have to be kept in an underground room (*Patalpuri*). He should not see the sun and the moon. If he comes out of the underground room and sees the world outside he might lose his life. Or he may have long ordeals to suffer but if he goes through them with a bold heart, he shall be happy." So saying and giving two fruits the sage melted in the air.

Happiness came to the palace and the country, when after sometime the news was broadcast that the queen was expecting. The queen shifted to a strongly built underground room where she bore a handsome boy. She never came out of the underground apartment and lived with the boy there. The boy did not know what the world outside was like. He was curious to know why one iron door was always locked and he was forbidden to go beyond it. Strict were the guards who watched the iron door day and night. But strange is the irony of fate. When only one day remained to complete the term of twelve years the guard of the iron door fell asleep at dawn after a night's vigil. The prince came near the door and finding the key lying near the watchman, took it, opened the gate and came out. He saw the world outside. He saw the sun and the palace. He was aglow with joy and ran about.

But there was consternation in the palace. The queen mother rushed out in search of the prince. The king left his court hearing the sad news and was frantic. The boy was found romping happily in the garden in bright sunshine and eating luscious fruits from the trees.

The king faced the future boldly. He declared by the beat of drum that the prince has to be given a suitable name and invited suggestions from the *pundits*. Many names were suggested. There was a dwarf Brahmin who stammered and had an ugly gait. He was goaded by his wife to go to the king's court and suggest the name Madan Kumar. She had dreamt that this name would be liked. The Brahmin took courage and came to the court.

He recited a verse composed by his wife in praise of the lovely prince and ended by suggesting that the prince should be called Madan Kumar. The prince shouted, "I like the name, I like the name." The queen nodded and the courtiers yelled in joy that his was a suitable name for the handsome prince. The dwarf Brahmin was given a bag of coins. He left the king's court bent with the weight of the bag.

The prince grew up and made friends with the son of the *Kotwal* (Police chief) and the son of the *Wazir* (minister). They met every day and spent hours together. One morning without the knowledge of the king this trio went out on a hunting expedition.

They spent the day hunting and rested in a tent at night. At the dead of the third night Madan Kumar heard two fairies, named *Kalpari* and *Nidrapari*,passing by and talking to each other. *Kalpari* said, 'Madhumala, the beautiful daughter of King Mahifal of Subarnadwip country should admirably be the wife of Madan Kumar.

Madan Kumar spoke to them, "Can you take me there and help me to meet Madhumala?"

The two fairies agreed and they whisked away the bedstead of Madan Kumar to Subarnadwip. The door of the bedroom of the princess Madhumala flung open by itself and the princess and the prince met. Both were charmed by each other and they exchanged their rings. They spent the night together in great happiness and swore eternal love to each other. In the early morning the bedstead of Madan Kumar was whisked back to the tent. Madan Kumar came back to the palace.

Since then Madan Kumar became a lovelorn and Madhumala at Subarnadwip also became a lovelorn. Both dreamt of each other and behaved in a strange manner. The two kings without knowing the facts were very anxious for their children and called a lot of *Hakims* and *Vaidyas* (physicians). But the physicians could not do anything.

At times Madan Kumar and the far away Madhumala used to think, 'Was it a dream, a sweet dream? Am I suffering from a hallucination?' But no sooner would their eyes would fall on their fingers than they would think, 'If it was a dream, a fancy of mine, whose ring is it that I am wearing?'

Nothing could cure Madan Kumar. The adventurous prince wanted to go out on a long voyage. The king agreed. He would do anything to soothe the prince's distracted mind. Fourteen large boats were decked up befitting the prince and his retinue. The captain of the boat was Gaurdhar. Gaurdhar behaved like a prince. He slept on a gold bedstead and stretched his feet on a silver one. His skill as a captain was unrivalled.

The boats set out. In the first boat was Prince Madan Kumar and was piloted by Gaurdhar. Distracted in mind he would come out on the deck, ask if Madhumala's country was visible and again go in.

At last after a long journey of months the captain sighted Subarnadwip and the prince was informed. Great was the excitement of the prince. But there was a terrible cyclone and the masts of the boats broke. The waves played havoc with the boats. The prince's boat was wrecked on a stretch of sand on the bed of the river. The prince was accosted by a brinjal plant that was a hundred and one years old. The brinjal plant told him that he had to marry a girl of that village before he could reach Madhumala. In this way the prince was tossed from place to place and he made several marriages as a prelude to meet Madhumala.

Ultimately the prince reached the country of Madhumala.

Madhumala was taken to be almost mad and *Ḥakims* and *Kaviraj* had advised that she must be married for a cure. But who would marry a mad woman who was talking to herself all the time and tearing her hair and weeping? At last a boy was found who had goitre and who was squint-eyed. He could only stammer and walk awkwardly. On top of that he had a hunchback and a flat nose. The father of the boy was paid money and was ordered by the king to bring the boy to the palace for the marriage. The father was trembling with fear. He was sure that the boy would be killed after marriage. On the way to the palace with his hunchbacked son he found Madan Kumar walking as if in a dream. He suggested to Madan Kumar that he should go and marry the princess in place of his son and for this he would be paid. Nothing was more welcome to Madan Kumar. He agreed.

Madan Kumar was married to Madhumala. She looked at her ring on Madan Kumar's finger and he saw his ring on Madhumala's finger. Both were overjoyed. The hunchbacked boy and his father were rewarded with bags of gold for finding Madan Kumar. Madan Kumar lived happily for ever thereafter with Madhumala. He got both the kingdoms.

68
BEHULA

Full of human pathos the story of Behula is well known in different parts of the Indian subcontinent like Bangladesh, Bhagalpur in Bihar and parts of western Bengal. It is the story of induction of Mansa Devi, the Snake goddess, in the higher echelon of the Gods of the Hindu pantheon. Mansa Devi is the presiding deity of the Bedia community, who catch snakes, train them and milk them for their poison. Usually the Bedias know herbal cures and *mantras, jhar-phunks* for snakebites and are in great demand in the rainy season when snakebites are a very common occurrence in the swampy villages. It is said that Mansa Devi was keen that she should find a place with the higher gods and goddesses, which was not possible unless an affluent devotee of Lord Siva, named Chand Saudagar, worshipped her. Chand Saudagar scoffed at Mansa Devi as she was the deity of the Bedias, a caste much lower in the hierarchy. But Mansa Devi stooped to conquer Chand Saudagar by clever machinations.

Mansa Devi did not find a place in the higher category of the Hindu gods and goddesses. This was a slur on her. The rich would propitiate her through a Mansa Devi priest who belonged to a lower caste. She was determined to put a stop to this. She had hit on a plan.

Chand Saudagar was a rich trader and his fleet of boats, large and small, laden with rich wares would go out sailing often to distant lands and come back with stuff from far off places. The large boats had a crew of more than two hundred men. Chand Saudagar (Saudagar means an affluent merchant) was a strong devotee of Lord Siva or Mahadev. Mansa Devi sent word to him that if he would worship her, his riches would multiply and she would make him the biggest merchant in the realm. But Chand

Saudagar scoffed at the idea. How could he worship Mansa Devi, the deity of the loathed snakes and the Bedias who were so low in caste-hierarchy? Mansa Devi would not give up. If Chand Saudagar even once worshipped her she would rise in status and would find her place along with Lord Siva, Parvati and Vishnu. A devious plan was hatched.

Even Gods have their revenge. She gave out that the beloved and only son of Chand Saudagar, Lakhindar or Lakhai, would be bitten on the day of his wedding. Chand Saudagar was not cowed down. He built a house of steel and saw that there was no space for even the tiniest snake to enter the bridal chamber. But Mansa Devi bribed one of the masons and he left a hair-breadth space in a joint which could not be seen even by the cleverest of the guards.

A very comely bride, Behula, was chosen and Lakhindar was married with great pomp but all the ceremonies were strictly within the steel house and all the men and women who participated were checked that they were not carrying any snake, not even the tiniest one. The couple retired for the night. Mansa Devi introduced a hair-like snake specially created for the occasion. The hair-like snake moved very silently when the couple were in the lap of sleep arm in arm. The venomous snake poured out on Lakhindar the choicest venom the snake goddess had endowed it with. The venom acted within a second. Lakhindar just could shout out that he was attacked by a snake and fell dead. The hair-wide viper slithered out unseen. Great consternation broke out. The merchant and his family were beside themselves with grief. Chand Saudagar hurled the choicest abuses on the snake goddess. But the mischief was done. Lakhindar, the apple of the eye of the merchant couple, lay dead. The beautiful young bride of the day was a widow on the wedding night.

The day broke and the funeral arrangements were taken in hand. A snake-bitten corpse is not cremated according to tradition and it was arranged that the body would be put in a traditional boat made out of plantain body (*Bhela*). The beloved son of the very rich merchant would be devoured by crocodiles and fish. The tragedy was too poignant and hundreds of mourners assembled silently. The mental agony was too acute for words.

The young bride-widow declared she would accompany the husband (dead he might be) in the *Bhela*. Chand Saudagar and his family were aghast. The mourners were smothered with more acute pain. The cruel crocodiles would also eat up the widow alive. No one knew where the *Bhela* would drift and there were wicked men to cast their evil eyes on the beautiful young widow, there could be storm and rain, the body would become putrid.All such thoughts were in the minds of the mourners and the household of Chand Saudagar. They tried to dissuade Behula, but she was adamant. If his beautiful body was meant for the cruel jaws of the crocodiles her body was also meant for them. Death could not separate her from her husband. All appeals failed. Behula was determined and touched the feet of Chand Saudagar and the other elders and told them they should leave her to her destiny.

In the presence of thousands of people and amidst the holy sound of conches Behula took her husband's dead body on her lap and the *Bhela* was pushed away from the bank. With favourable wind the *Bhela* quickly moved out into the midstream.

Days and nights passed. The *Sati Rani* (the chastest wife) Behula would not leave her husband. He was not dead to her. To her he was still living. She fanned the body to drive away the flies. Big crocodiles dashed against the boat but it would not capsize. Was not the halo of the bride-widow there? The crocodiles and the fish swam with the boat, made their obeisance and disappeared.

Storms and cyclones broke out, the boat was tossed and turned when the waves crashed. Behula was with her husband and prayed to God. The cyclones and storms melted away. There were cloudbursts and torrential rains and Behula and the body of Lakhindar were soaked. The boat started leaking. She was steadfast and did not flinch. The Rain God was ashamed and embarrassed and the Wind God sent a gentle breeze and they became dry.

The wicked men saw the beautiful lady and swam to the boat or went near the boat in other boats and tried to threaten her, cajole her to leave the body and come and live with them happily. She did not even listen. Waves, strong and swirling, drowned the wicked loafers and Behula's boat floated on. The body became putrid but Behula was unaware of the foul smell. Lakhindar was her husband and his body was sacred to her.

When the boat was near a bank some witches came and started dancing and said they were going to feast on both, the putrid body of Lakhindar and the soft and tender body of the foolish Behula. She heeded not. The wicked witches melted when they felt the heat of the bride's halo of chastity and love.

Came a damsel, beautiful and gaily decked, and cajoled Behula to give up her mad idea and said that very soon the putrid body of Lakhindar would disintegrate completely and she had better leave him now and stay with her. She was also a wicked girl. But her words were not even heard. The boat drifted on with Behula and Lakhai's dead body.

Weeks passed and the ordeal of Behula was not over. Her love for her husband and faith in God for her husband's revival stirred the *Dhrubolok*, the heavenly abode of the gods. Parvati, the consort of Siva, told her Lord that Behula's husband must be revived. She was afraid that Behula would supplant her as a more important goddess after her death. Lord Vishnu was moved and had a consultation with Lord Siva. Behula cannot be allowed to perish in this manner as she would carve out for herself a greater role in the heavens. Her steadfast love, loyalty and devotion to her husband and her unflinching faith in God for the life of her husband must be rewarded.

Both Lords, Siva and Vishnu, rode in their divine chariots to Brahma, the Supreme Lord and the Creator. Brahma asked them what had brought them to *Brahmalok*, the abode of Brahma. The incident of Behula was narrated. Brahma said that lately he was being disturbed in his *Tapasya* very frequently and now he understood the reason. The aura of Behula was disturbing him but he wanted to be sure.

The three gods held a consultation and sent for Mansa Devi. Mansa Devi, a much smaller deity in importance, came trembling to the court of the Holy Trinity, Brahma, Vishnu and Siva. She was told that Behula's husband must be restored to life and peace be brought back to the earth and the heaven. Mansa had no other option but made a humble request that Chand Saudagar be induced to worship her once so that her prestige was also maintained.

The Lords were very pragmatic and agreed. Lord Siva told Chand Saudagar in a dream that his son was being restored to life and all his boats that had sunk with merchandise were being resurrected by Mansa Devi and in return he should just once worship Mansa Devi as she was a deity. Chand Saudagar agreed and with great devotion worshipped Mansa Devi.

Just at that moment cyclone, lightning and thunder burst on Behula who sat faithfully with the putrid and disintegrating body of her husband on the *Bhela* which was being tossed about by mighty waves. She prayed devoutly. Soon it was calm. Lakhindar sat up resplendent and smiling and the boat was anchored back in Chand Saudagar's village. Shouts of joy broke out. The parents rushed to meet Behula and Lakhindar. There was joy in the air. Everyone sang about the steadfast love and implicit faith of Behula. Mansa Devi was also happy. Her *puja* established her status among the elite too.

69

SEVEN CHAMPA BROTHERS AND SISTER PARUL

THERE was a king who had seven queens. The first six queens had a very annoying air of superiority about them but the youngest, the seventh queen, was demure and sweet natured. Naturally the royal household liked her. The king was also very fond of her and spent more time in her palace. This caused great jealousy among the other six queens.

The youngest queen became pregnant and this made the other queens very resentful as they did not bear any children. The six elder queens hatched a conspiracy against the youngest queen.

They were very sweet to the youngest queen and fussed over her when the king was in the queens' palace. They told the king that they would take care of the youngest queen when she delivered the baby. They also said that all indications were that a prince would be born to the queen and an outsider may cast an evil eye on him. The king was convinced by the arguments of the six queens though the youngest queen was not very happy about it.

The important day came. The king had a golden chain with a bell at the end, tied, from the youngest queen's chamber to the royal court and told the elder queens that as soon as the child was born they should pull the chain and from the tinkle he would know and come to see the royal baby.

The youngest queen almost fainted with the labour pains but she gave birth to seven handsome sons and one lovely daughter. The elder queens quickly smothered them and buried them in the nearby garbage heap and substituted a few puppies and a kitten.

The mother was shocked when she was told by the queens that she had given birth to seven puppies and a kitten and swooned. The elder queens pulled the chain and the king rushed to the harem. With tears in their eyes the elder queens told him that some puppies and a kitten were born. They hinted that the youngest queen was a witch. The king was aghast. He immediately ordered the puppies and kitten to be killed and the youngest queen to be banished with dirty clothes and given the task of cleansing the cowshed.

The order was immediately carried out by the elder queens. The youngest queen was thrown out of the palace and made to lead a miserable life. The elder queens were very happy that they were successful in their plan.

At the garbage heap where the newly born babies were buried seven *Champak* or *Champa* flower trees and one *Parul* flower creeper grew. The trees quickly bore very sweet-smelling flowers. The gardener watched the trees bloom and at the right time went to pluck the flowers. As soon as he stretched the bamboo pole to pluck the flowers the flowers moved up quickly.

The Parul flower sang out, "My seven Champa brothers, wake up."

The Champa flowers responded, "Sister Parul, why are you calling us? What has gone wrong?"

Parul replied, "The king's gardener has come. Should we allow him to pluck the flowers?"

The brothers sang in unison, "No, no, sister, we shall not allow the gardener to get the flowers. Let the queens come."

One by one the six queens came but were rebuffed and then the Champa flowers sang, "Let the King come and we shall see what is to be done."

By that time the gardener had rushed to the royal court and had acquainted the king of the strange happenings. The king went to the garbage heap and found the six queens standing and learnt from them that they had also failed to get the flowers. Then the king took the bamboo pole, absolutely sure that he could get the flowers. But, no.

The Parul flower sang out, "My Seven Champa brothers, the king has himself come. Shall we allow him to pluck the flowers?"

The brothers replied, "No, no. Let the poor banished queen who is a beggar now and cleanses the cowshed come and we shall give her the flowers."

The banished queen in tatters and lean with starvation and misery came and wanted to pluck the flowers. The seven Champa and the Parul flowers immediately came down and out of the flowers came out seven lovely boys and a sweet looking girl. They addressed the banished queen, "Mother, mother darling, take us into your lap. We are your children, buried under the garbage heap."

The banished queen was overwhelmed with joy. The king wept in happiness. The six wicked queens tried to run away. The king ordered that they should be buried alive in huge pits which would have the most poisonous prickly thorns at the base and above and the pits be filled up with earth. The king's order was carried out then and there.

The youngest queen, the seven princes and the daughter were taken to the palace by the king amidst gaiety, music and songs. There was great happiness and rejoicing and the king and the queen reigned long and happy.

70
MALANCHAMALA

In the days of yore there was a king who was unhappy because there was no heir to the throne. The king and the queen did many *Yajnas*, observed scores of fasts on auspicious days, wore amulets to no end. The king convened a very large *Yajna* in the course of which thousands of maunds of butter were poured into the sacrificial fire and *sadhus* and *sanyasis* (holy hermits) and other dedicated devotees of God got together and recited *mantras*.

On the last night of the Yajna both the king and the queen had a dream. A holy figure appeared in the dream and asked the king to observe fast for three days without even a drop of water and on the fourth day to go to the *malancha* (garden) and he would find two golden-coloured mangoes. The mango on the left of the king should be eaten by the queen and the fruit on the right was to be taken by the king.

For full three days and nights complete silence prevailed in the palace. The king's *Bhat* (a singer who wakes up the king with a song in the mornings) sang not, the chirping birds in the golden cages did not murmur and the horses in the royal stable did not neigh. The servants moved silently. The king had shut himself in the innermost room of the harem and not even the queen could go there. No food or water was touched by the king. The royal court did not meet and all the court affairs went by default.

On the fouth morning the *Pakshiraj* (the royal horse that could fly) stood at the threshold of the palace. The king said his morning prayers and performed his ablutions and wore the *Prasadi* (the flower that had been given as a homage to the God in the temple and had come back to the king with His blessings) flower-garland round his neck. The king uttered the names of his gods and rode on the horse and it flew towards the garden at some distance.

Yes, there were two fully ripe golden mangoes. The king aimed his arrow at the branch that held the couple of mangoes, tried thrice but the arrow missed. The king's mind was filled with consternation. He controlled himself and asked the gardener for the bamboo pole with which fruits are plucked. As soon as the pole touched the mango tree it broke into pieces. The king tried with another pole and the result was the same.

The king Chandra Raja, was desperate and sent for the *Kotwal* and ordered him to climb up the tree and get the two mangoes intact. The *Kotwal*, the police chief, had to swallow his pride before the crowd and climbed the tree and plucked the fruits. In his anxiety the monarch forgot to tell the *Kotwal* that he should keep the two fruits separate so that the hermit's behest be carried out, the king eating the fruit on the right and the queen the one on the left. The fruits got mixed up.

Collecting the fruits, the king whipped the horse and flew back to the palace where the queen was waiting anxiously. The fruits were eaten by the royal couple with reverence and prayers.

But unknown to them and to everyone else the mischief had been done by the interchange of fruits. There was great rejoicing throughout the kingdom because the queen was going to have a child. Ten months passed, regularly marked by *pujas* (worship) and offerings to the deities.

The Rani gave birth to a beautiful male child. Money and sweets were given to the poor, shawls and silk sheets were presented to the *pandits* and the Brahmins were fed sumptuously and each given a gold piece. The king made promises to dig several tanks.

The sixth day was an ominous day as it is on that night after birth God's agent Dhara comes to the newborn babe and unknown and unseen writes the lines on the forehead of the babe that determines his destiny. The *angina* (courtyard) of the palace was lit up with earthen lamps fed by clarified butter. *Shamianas* were hung with trappings of gold, there was gaiety all round. Strict vigilance was maintained and a woman with supernatural powers was engaged to keep special watch for God's agent and to intercept and enquire the lifespan of the royal heir.

The queen-mother was entertained by the recital of folksongs and folk tales as was customary so that she could also keep awake. It was believed that if the newly born baby was guarded by watchful persons the God's agent could not but write favourable lines on the child's forehead.

But by midnight everyone started feeling drowsy. The queen-mother with her hand on the baby fell asleep first. The maids reciting stories and singing songs had to stop lest the sleep of the queen was disturbed and they too started dozing and fell asleep. The last to doze off was the woman with supernatural powers, specially engaged to keep vigil. Finding everything and everywhere unusually silent she at first felt uneasy and then yawned and started dozing and fell asleep. When everyone was deep in slumber Dhara, the agent of God, stealthily crept in and let the pen move on the forehead. The tradition is that even Dhara has no control on the pen which moves by divine dispensation and she is only the means for the *likhan* (writing of the fatelines).

After Dhara finished her work she was slipping out when the woman with the supernatural powers woke up, caught hold of Dhara and asked her what she had written. Dhara said she had not even read the fatelines she had inscribed or rather the divine pen in her hand had inscribed. But she would not let her go and forced her to come back. Though Dhara was not inclined first, she went over the lines and was shocked. She found wealth, learning, fame and glory but the child would live only for twelve days.

She had to tell this and at once there was consternation and loud weeping everywhere. The palace guards shrieked in agony and terror without knowing why they were doing so. The queen-mother got up and yelled in some unknown terror. The king woke up and found he was perspiring and shivering and he ran to the queen and asked her what was the matter. The woman who was told by Dhara pointed at the prince and wept bitterly and gave out what she had heard from the agent of God, who had disappeared into the air after doing her job. It was a cruel shock, a tragedy for which no one was prepared. Only 12 day's life for the prince!

The queen-mother fainted, the king was dazed. The watchmen, the maids of the queen and others howled in grief. The elephants and the horses left their stables and ran amuck, maddened with grief. Many men and women swooned. The whole palace was benumbed with sorrow. The news went round and the entire townsmen came out and rushed to the palace weeping.

The king along with the *mantris* (ministers) and the *Rajguru Purohits* (royal priests) rushed to the *malancha* (the garden) from where the two fruits were obtained. They found a Brahmin praying under the mango tree and from the halo around his face the party could see that he was a holy man. When the man opened his eyes the king humbly spoke to him about his woes and wanted him to examine the prince's palm and suggest some remedy. The Brahmin agreed and walked to the palace, refusing the conveyance offered by the king.

The Brahmin examined the palm of the prince very carefully and after deep contemplation said, "My king, there is only one remedy, someone has to do penance besides the parents as both of you ate the wrong mangoes. The prince can only live beyond twelve days if he is married to a girl twelve years old. I can see there is one such girl in your town." So saying the Brahmin melted into the air like a true *Yogi*.

At the crack of dawn a vigorous search started for a girl of twelve years for the one-week-old royal prince. People were aghast, mothers were taken aback and fathers were seized with terror. But the royal guards would not spare anyone. Did not the holy man predict there was a twelve-year-old girl in the town? The king went to the *malancha* again and started an indefinite fast till a twelve-year-old girl was found.

Suddenly the king's eyes fell on a young girl who had come for a wash in the tank nearby. She looked twelve years old. The king felt that this was the damsel who could save his dear child. He directed his guards towards the girl who was innocently playing with the lotus flowers in the tank. The guards found out she was Malanchamala the daughter of the *Kotwal*, the Police Chief, and strangely enough she was just twelve years of age. A beautiful slim girl, but the only snag was that she was not of royal blood.

The *Kotwal* was at once brought to the king and the king ordered that he had to marry his daughter to the prince that very day to save the life of the prince. The queen suggested that the *Kotwal* be given a quarter of the kingdom and be purified by the royal priests to make him royal. The mother of three daughters, the *Kotwal's* wife, raised a hue and cry against the idea and said she would commit suicide if Malanchamala, the apple of her eye, will be married to a babe of seven days. The *Kotwal* was keen as he wanted to grab the quarter of the kingdom and the rich presents that would follow the marriage.

Malanchamala smiled and told her mother, "Do not grieve, my destiny is mine, I have to work it out. But ask the king to make three promises."

The king was too anxious to have the wedding performed and asked what were the promises.

Malanchamala asked, "Will you, Oh king, allow my father's son-in-law to come to our house?"

The king replied, "Yes, I do promise that."

Then Malanchamala said, "Would you, king, agree to have rice cooked by me along with the queen after I become your daughter-in-law?"

The king replied, "Yes, I do promise to eat the food cooked by you."

"My third question is," said the girl, "would all the articles usually given in the *Basar Ghar* (bridal chamber) be given and allowed to be brought to my father's house along with the groom and me?"

"Yes, I do solemnly promise," said the king.

The girl again repeated, "King, with the sun on the sky as our witness you do promise the three things as that alone would show to the world that you have truly and solemnly married me to the prince and have taken me into your family."

The king had no other option but to reply in the affirmative.

Then Malanchamala gravely turned to her mother and said, "Mother darling, grieve not, if I am a true wife I shall restore the prince to life even if death claims him on the twelfth day of his life. Please deck me up as a bride and send for the priest and make the arrangements."

She was no longer a sprightly child of twelve years but a mature Hindu bride going to be married with full sense of responsibility. From the heavens fragrant flowers fell on her and a sad but solemn music from afar floated to her and other people's ears.

The marriage took place. But destiny, as ordained, took over. The prince died on the twelfth day and the royal household was furious. The king and the queen blamed Malanchamala for it. The bride was assaulted and turned out. She was given torn and dirty clothes. All her ornaments were taken away. She did not protest.

Her eyes were fixed on the dead husband, a mere 12-day-old child in eternal sleep with a smile on his face.

Malanchamala told her father-in-law and mother-in-law, "Do whatever you like to me, but give me the *dan* (gift) of my husband and forget us for twelve years."

Was she mad to suggest this? That was the feeling. Was she a witch and wanted to eat away the dead body? Her fingers and earlobes were cut off and blood streamed out but she felt no pain.

The girl repeated, "King, you had given me before the sacred wedding fire my husband to me, do you want to break your promise?"

The king was furious and shouted, "Take away this witch and put her in the jungles. Pull out her eyes, cut off her hands for the affront she dares to the king."

The soldiers tried to rush but a strong unseen force smothered them and the king felt the impact of the force too.

The prince was taken to the funeral pyre. The fire was lit. The bride was also forced into the fire. Was there a smile on her face? The fire engulfed the pyre. There was a terrific heat and the assembly of mourners had to move a considerable distance away.

Unexpectedly, there was torrential rain, a cloudburst and a cyclone. The men including the king who had gone to the funeral had to rush back to a safe place. Witches and evil spirits floated above their heads and drove them away. Malancha took the dead body of her husband in her arms and came out of the pyre. Witches and evil spirits surrounded her and menaced, "Leave, leave the body to us, you wretch, for a long time we have not tasted the soft flesh of a tender baby, let us eat him up and you go away from this place at once," they shouted.

Malancha did not flinch. She said, "If I am a true wife none of you would be able to come near me and take away my dear husband who is eternally and truly mine."

The witches and evil spirits melted away. Came bigger and more threatening evil figures with protruding, fierce and fiery eyes and they howled, "Mala, you are now in our zone. You cannot go away with your husband. Your husband had died and you cannot hold him back from us. Be sensible, unless you also want to be killed. Go away from here leaving your dead husband."

But Malancha was not afraid. She held her husband in her arms and started moving. The figures melted away.

Malancha went to a forest nearby and rested under a tree.

A young beautiful girl came and said, "Mala, do you remember me? We used to play together. But what is that? The dead body of a baby? Throw it away. In a few days it would be putrid emanating a terrible stench and then you will have to throw it away. Be sensible now. Throw it away and have a bath in the yonder pond and I will take you home. You shall be happy. Listen to me."

Mala told her, "Sister, if you have played with me you are my friend. Do you not realise he is my husband?"

The girl replied, "I am going to snatch away the dead body. I cannot let you keep the body of a dead child."

She came nearer. Mala held the baby's body tighter and gently replied, "Sister, if I am a true wife, no man or woman could take him away from me. Try if you like."

There was a gust of wind and lightning. The eyes of Malanchamala were blinded for a second. This was followed by a gentle breeze carrying sweet fragrance of flowers. Malancha found her baby-husband steadfastly looking towards her and the girl had vanished. Malancha understood that she was a *Devi* who had come to test her and made her obeisance to the *Devi* who had revived her husband.

She looked round and found she was in a lovely small cottage in the midst of the forest and all the articles—a small velvet bed, a quilt, a tiny pillow of white mustard, a piece of white sandalwood, silver pales for keeping milk, silver spoons for feeding the baby-husband, *ghee* (clarified butter), etc.—kept ready for her use for the baby. There was also some milk. She heated a small quantity of milk and fed the child-husband with the spoon.

During the night a tiger and a tigress came to the hut, smelt human flesh and started scratching the door. Malancha opened the door and the tiger saw the baby. He told her that the child would be tasty for the cubs and she would make a good meal for him and his wife. Mala told the tiger that the child was her husband and narrated the story. The tiger and the tigress were moved beyond words and told her to remain absolutely fearless as his whole family would be with her day and night and guard her and her husband. The tigress had spare milk as her cubs were now eating small animals and she agreed to give it to Mala. From that day the tiger family lived in that part of the jungle and Mala felt she had genuine friends.

The child grew into a boy and the tigress's milk made him lovely and strong. He was now five years old and Mala knew that at this age a boy should start his lessons with the *Guru* (teacher) in the village *pathshala* (school). But how could there be a school in the jungle?

Malanchamala spoke of her problem to the tiger and tigress, that she has to go to a village where there would be a *pathshala*. The tiger suggested he would go and pounce on the *Guru* (teacher) and carry him in his jaws to the forest and force him to stay here and teach the child. Mala smiled at the suggestion and told the tiger that it would not do as the teacher also had his family. It was difficult for the tiger family to understand why their idea was not good. They had to bid a sad farewell to Mala and the child-husband. The tiger promised to appear whenever remembered.

Malanchamala boldly started with the child-husband on her journey with a few things in a bundle. After a few hours they came to the fringe of a village where there was a much neglected garden. The flower trees had withered, no birds chirped, there was tall grass and jungle weeds all round. Mala found a deserted hut also. Evidently no one had stayed there for quite sometime. Malanchamala decided to make her home there.

A miracle occurred. As soon as Mala put down her small bundle and the boy started playing with a small dry stick, the withered trees were covered with lovely foliage, flowers bloomed and birds chirped. Bees hummed on flowers. The weeds and the tall unkempt grass disappeared. The well nearby filled with water. The dried up stream had a glistening flow of crystal-clear water. The doors of the hut flung open as if in welcome. A woman, the gardner's wife rushed to Mala and asked her, "Who are you? Are you a *Devi* in human shape? This garden had become barren years ago in spite of our best efforts. Nothing grew here. The fruit trees bore no fruits. The *champak* and *kadamba* trees had dried up. The *parul* and *aparajita* creepers withered although we tried hard to keep them alive. My husband, the *Mali* (gardener), and his brother and I, had worked so hard but to no effect. Not even a bird would sit on these trees. When you set your foot here everything changed. What a lovely boy! We must not allow you to go away. You have to stay here. Take pity on us. We have fallen from the king's grace as we cannot supply the royal household with flowers and garlands. Do take pity on us and make your home here. We shall do everything possible to make you comfortable."

The boy came back with a handful of sweet-smelling *bakul* flowers and gave them to Mala. Mala agreed to stay there and the *malini* (gardener's wife) said she would come and live with her. The hut was immediately repaired and another room added. Mala did not tell the woman that the boy was her husband.

The boy-husband had been named Chandramanik, the bright jewel on the moon. The *malini* informed Malanchamala that there was a *Raj Pathshala* (school) nearby where the seven sons of the king and his lovely daughter Kanchi studied. The *malini* took the boy Chandramanik and admitted him in the school.

Immediately Chandramanik made his mark in the school and within few months he was far ahead of other boys. His memory was sharp. Kanchi, the king's daughter, could make no progress. Her brothers, the seven princes, chided her and asked her why she was lagging behind. She said, "Brothers, to tell you the truth, half of my time in the school goes in looking at the very charming and comely face of the *mali's* son and hearing the learned words of the Vedas and Puranas that come out of his lips. What a marvellous boy and how very handsome. How come he is a *mali's* son? He has beaten you all. Fie on you." The king's sons were shocked. They had also noticed the marvellous progress Chandramanik had made in the school and how the *Gurus* loved him. They were jealous of him.

One day they warned the boy, Chandramanik, after school-break, "Look, you lowly son of the *mali*, if you want to come to this school where we read, you must not come in such ordinary and torn clothes. You have to dress properly. Or we shall give you a thrashing and your feet and hands would be twisted and dislocated. Better be out of the school."

Chandramanik went home weeping. Malanchamala told the *malini*, "*Mashi* (aunt), do see why he is weeping. My heart breaks if I see him weeping."

The *malini* replied, "What are you saying? Does not my heart break too if my *manik* (Jewel) weeps?"

Both of them rushed to the boy. With tears in his eyes, Chandramanik repeated all that had occurred in the school. Malancha thought of the tiger friend and within a few minutes the tiger and the tigress followed by the cubs came. The tiger laughed at the problem and in one leap disappeared. The tiger visited the cloth shop and terrorised the cloth dealer, who immediately gave the choicest clothes to the tiger.

Clothed in the best, Chadramanik attended the school next day, and became the envy of the seven princes. Kanchi loved him all the more as he looked very charming in his fine clothes. She taunted her brothers and said she was in love with him and wanted to marry him. The brothers were aghast at the sister's infatuation and thought of another plan to outwit Chandramanik. They told Chandramanik that it ill behove him if he came on foot with all the fine clothes. So he had to come on a horse and win a race with them, or he would lose his head for trying to compete with the princes and beating them in studies. Chandramanik returned home morose and weeping and told his problem to Malanchamala and the aunt.

Malanchamala told him, "Do not worry. I shall get you a horse with the help of your Tiger maternal uncle."

She thought of the tiger and the tiger appeared. Malanchamala asked the tiger to take her on his back and go to the kingdom where she had lived as a child. With a grunt of satisfaction that he could do something, the tiger with Malanchamala on his back, went in a jiffy to the capital where Malanchamala was a bride. They found all the houses closed and the doors shut. The market was deserted. The royal palace looked haunted, there were no guards in front and the lofty gates were tightly closed. She came to know that the *Pakshiraj*, the horse of the monarch, had gone mad and was prowling about and killing any man it met and ate him up. That is why the palace and the area looked deserted.

Malanchamala recognised the *Pakshiraj* horse and knew that the horse had gone mad grieving for her.

She boldly went towards the royal stable and shouted the horse's name, "Harikali, where are you? I am Malanchamala the daughter of the *Kotwal*, who used to feed you with *dub* grass when I was a child."

The horse neighed from afar, rushed to Malanchamala and put his face in her hands and expressed his joy with grunts and nods. Malanchamala told her problem to the horse and it at once neighed and wanted her to ride on her.

The tiger and the horse, who was perfectly normal then, played for a minute by brushing their bodies against each other. People were amazed to see Malanchamala as a young woman of great beauty and dignity. They had all taken her to be dead. They were also surprised to see that Harikali, the *Pakshiraj* horse, that had gone mad and killed scores of people, had become normal on seeing Malanchamala. While going Malanchamala sang a song.

My king, it is Malanchamala that goes with Harikali,
It is that Kotwalkanya
....who you got as bride to the prince,
To whom you gave promises and broke them,
Wait, king, wait for twelve years to complete, a few days more.
You get the full story then, my king, do not be sore.

The song was heard by the king, the queen and the royal household. News spread like wildfire that Malanchamala had come seated on a tiger that played with the mad horse who became normal at Malanchamala's touch. They all rushed to the royal stable to see Malanchamala. But she had flown away seated on *Pakshiraj*.

The king sent out his messengers far and wide to trace Malanchamala and his son, the prince. The Kotwal's wife was again greeted and feted at the palace by the queen. Was not her daughter the prince's wife?

Malanchmala brought the horse to her hut and fed him with milk and *dub* grass and sugarcane. Chandramanik was afraid to ride on the fiery and foaming horse when the horse was ready to go. Malanchamala entrusted her husband, the boy Chandramanik, to Harikali and enjoined the steed to bring him back safely. She touched the feet of Chandramanik who was much surprised as he did not know the relationship. Malanchamala pulled out a hair from her head and put it as a garland round the horse and told the horse to win the race and bring back Chandramanik. The horse neighed in consent and trotted away.

The *Pakshiraj* horse flew with Chandramanik to the *Pathshala* and the princes got the shock of their life. They had only heard of a *Pakshiraj* horse and never seen one. They could not dream that

Chandramanik who they knew as the *mali's* son could get a *pakshiraj* horse. But a bet was a bet. They stood in a line and enjoined that Chandramanik's steed will not fly but run as a normal horse. Chandramanik agreed to this. His horse neighed and gave consent. The princes imposed another term. Since he was a *pakshiraj* horse there be a very big gap. This term was also agreed to. Four races in the four directions—east, west, south and north—were proposed and agreed to. The seven princes were defeated by a very great margin each time. Kanchi was full of joy. The other students backed Chandramanik and they were overjoyed.

The seven princes then proposed that the *mali's* son should come to the palace with the *Pakshiraj* horse so that the royal household including the king would see the horse. Harikali, the *Pakshiraj* horse, neighed harshly disapproving the idea and wanted to take back Chandramanik to Malanchamala who was waiting for them. But overjoyed with the victory in the races, Chandramanik wanted to visit the palace and whipped the horse round the neck. The hair of Malanchamala that was tied round his neck as a garland broke and fell on the ground. The horse neighed his disapproval again. But Chandramanik did not understand the hint.

The horse flew and stopped at the royal palace gates. The gates were flung open and the musicians at the portals unasked, started playing a joyous tune. As soon as Chandramanik dismounted, Kanchi, the princess, put the *jayamala* (the garland of marriage) round Chandramanik's neck. Kanchi was a bashful bride then and Chandramanik also blushed as he had seen the girl so many times and liked her a lot. Love that was lying dormant in his heart, and Mala had never told him of her relationship with him, blossomed and he gently touched the soft fingers of Kanchi. Cupid did the mischief and chose to break the heart of Malanchamala.

Everyone was surprised at the greeting with *jayamala* by Kanchi. There was no way out. The seven princes took Chandramanik to the royal court and the king agreed to marry Kanchi provided the *mali's* son was in prison for twelve years with a chain round his neck and thereby earn the princess and wash away the slur of the low caste of the *mali*. There was no escape for Chandramanik either. The marriage was immediately performed with great pomp. Immediately after the marriage the bridegroom was enchained and imprisoned.

The *Pakshiraj* horse, Harikali, came back to Malanchamala crestfallen and started rolling in the dust, shedding profuse tears when he narrated to Malanchamala and *malini* what had happened. Malancha swooned. She got up and wept bitterly as to why she had carefully hidden her relationship from her husband. Many a time Chandramanik had asked her who she was and where they came from. She had fondled the child-husband but not as the spouse. She wanted to wait for the completion of the period of self-imposed twelve years and then tell him all that had happened and go to his father and return the prince to his royal parents. The *malini* was also stunned when she came to know the story. She, of course, said Malancha was responsible for the tragedy as she had not taken the husband into her confidence. Tears, heart-rending tears, welled in Mala's eyes.

She swooned again but did not utter a word to condemn her husband. She felt it was destiny again that was working unseen but inexorable.

"What is fated has to happen," she told her aunt, the *malini*, and said, "Aunt, I have my duty to my husband which is still unfulfilled." She rubbed her eyes with her *anchal* (edge of her long apparel) and pulled up Harikali.

To Harikali she said, "Grieve not, Harikali, you are not responsible. Today the twelve years' period shall be over and it is my destiny which has worked. I shall give you a letter which you have to carry to my father-in-law, the king."

She wrote:

My Father, the period of twelve years is over. Your son Chandramanik, my husband, is in the prison of Raja Dudhbarna after being given the *jayamala* by his fortunate daughter, Kanchi. Your chagrin at me—the daughter of the *Kotwal*—is now washed away. Dear father, whatever was destined has happened. Once do visit the tank of the garden where you had seen me playing with the flowers of the tank. Mala.

To the *malini* she said, "Aunt, do not blame my husband. He is innocent. I have to fulfil my destiny, that is God's behest. You have been a mother to me, if I am born seven times and get an opportunity to serve you my debt to you shall remain unpaid."

Malancha left for her place where she had been born and married and wanted to drown herself in the cool waters of the tank where she had been chosen as the prince's bride. On the way she met the tiger family and the tiger wanted to know why she was so morose and where she was going. Malancha told the tiger, "Uncle, you have come at the right time. I want you and *mamima* (aunt) to feed on me and let the cubs have a good meal out of me. Today is one of my happiest days."

The tigress asked, "Where is my son who I had nursed with my own milk? Why are you all alone today and without proper clothes? You look as if you have been weeping and you say today is one of your happiest days? What is this riddle?"

Malancha narrated all that had happened. She said that the princess Kanchi has given the garland of marriage to Chandramanik.

But when the story was completed the tiger uncle said, "You call this the garland, it is a chain which our darling son will have to wear for twelve long years."

Malanchamala replied, "Uncle, but you are forgetting that a princess of high caste cannot live as the wife of a *mali's* son or anyone lower in caste unless he has expiated his sin by going through some ordeal."

"Rubbish!" the tiger yelled. "Fie to your mankind if this be the decision for love for a lower caste man. Come, let us go and see what can be done to our Chandramanik."

The tiger family with Malanchamala flew to the kingdom of the king Dudhbarna.

Earlier, the *pakshiraj* horse, Harikali, had delivered the letter of Malanchamala to Chandramanik's father, the king. He immediately sent for his army chief and with his army left to conquer Dudhbarna. He did not know the exact direction but had a vague idea of the country. He came to the fringe of the town and found the *malini* who was almost mad at what had happened and was crying day and night.

The king heard her bemoan,

My Chandramanik is in chains,
My niece is in the forest losing her husband,
This is the hut where they lived,
This is the path they trod.
My God, how shall I live without them?

Hearing the moans of the *malini* and the story he had heard from Harikali the king stopped and the army pitched their tents. There was a fierce fight after King Dudhbarna refused to release Chandramanik and let him go with his bride. He said to the messenger that if Chandramanik was really his son let him fight and win him and his daughter back.

The king lost the battle and was also put in chains and lodged separately from Chandramanik. Thousands of his soldiers died and the loss on Dudhbarna's side was also heavy. Then Malanchamala arrived with the tiger family—tired but full of eagerness to rescue Chandramanik.

At dead of night the party went to the prison and the tiger ate up the guards and those who were left quickly threw open the prison doors to escape death. But the cubs did not spare them either and all the guards were killed. Malanchamala found Chandramanik lying on the ground as his neck and feet were chained and clamped to a wooden post and he could not even stand. With her own teeth Malanchamala broke open the links of the chain. All her teeth came out. Due to intense pain and the bleeding from the gums Malanchamala fainted away.

Chandramanik suddenly felt that the chains had snapped. In the dark he could not make out who had brought about his release. He came out and met the tiger family. The family greeted him and at once started killing the people in the royal household. They ate away the king, the seven princes, and the royal guards. The animals, elephants and horses were killed. Hundreds died of sheer fright. They got into the ladies' apartment in the house and were getting ready to kill Kanchi, the princess, when Malancha regained her senses and rushed to see what the tigers were doing.

The tiger told her, "Malanchamala we have finished all those who had tormented you and Chandramanik. Only Princess Kanchi remains and we are going to kill her there on her bed."

Mala shuddered and cried out, "Do not, oh! do not crush out the line of progeny of my husband. Oh, do not kill my husband's wife, his father-in-law, his mother-in-law or brothers-in-law or their men. They have not sinned against me. Spare them. If you have killed them, revive them, do revive them. Kanchi is my darling husband's darling, could I entertain any other feeling but sisterly love for her?"

The tiger family was amazed. Anyway they wanted to drink water as they were feeling very thirsty after their feast and orgy. Mala went with a pitcher to the nearby tank for fetching water. At that moment the king, father-in-law of Malanchamala, had come out from the prison and had come to the tank for a wash. Malancha saw him and took the dust of his feet by touching them with her hands and the king asked her who she was as she had not uncovered her face.

She replied, "I am that very unfortunate woman Malanchamala."

The king flared up and wanted her to go away or come to him in a proper manner with palanquins, and men. The king left for his kingdom with Chandramanik and his bride Kanchi and there was great rejoicing at the palace. The tiger arranged for a large escort for Malanchamala and with bands and music the tiger family also reached the palace but the king would not allow her to go in. Again he broke his promise.

The tiger family was furious and told Malanchamala that they were not going to listen to her anymore and were going to kill the king along with all the other household members. Again Malanchamala prevented them and told them that destiny would work out a solution and not to worry. She said the palace doors might be closed for her but the space outside the doors could not be denied to her. She would rather starve and stay in the place which rightfully belonged to her and where her husband lived. She sent away the tiger family and all her escorts, the band and the musicians called by the tiger.

Malanchamala went to drown herself in the water of the tank and found the tank was well protected by steel wires and thorns. She tried other tanks too but found the king had made them also unapproachable. Malancha smiled. She thought, so the king does not want her to die: is he cruel or is he kind? Oh yes, kind he is, who else do I have in the world to hurt me more so that I could burn and purify myself more other than my father-in-law, she thought.

Malancha stayed on unknown to her husband Chandramanik, and kept herself away from the portals of the palace. But every night when the midnight gong struck and the guards changed at the palace gates, Malanchamala slipped in and came out when the guards changed again at the crack of dawn.

She visited the bedroom of her husband and feasted her eyes on the beauty of the sleeping prince and his bride, Kanchi. There was not the slightest rancour in her mind.

On the fourth day while she was humming a tune that she hummed everyday and feasting her eyes on the sleeping couple the prince woke up and asked her who she was. She said she was the maidservant of the palace and begged pardon for waking him up. But Chandramanik had recognised her and told her, "I have known you all my life. Do not give me an untruth, tell me how are you related to me? I feel my blood surging within me, mislead me not." She said the sun had dawned and she could only give the answer some other day and quietly slipped out.

But that morning the minarets of the palace started crumbling one by one. Chadramanik had a son who died, epidemics broke out and people died of famine. The king said to Chandramanik that this was the work of that witch, the daughter of the *Kotwal*. Chandramanik protested and said that she revived dead persons. The king taunted that if she could do that she would have revived her father the *Kotwal* and his wife, her mother, and left for the court.

The first person to greet the king was the *Kotwal*, the dead Kotwal now alive with smiles. The *Kotwal's* wife came to the palace and greeted the queen and said she had come to see the new daughter-in-law.

The king was bewildered and decided to go out hunting and relax. He lost his way, his horse slipped and became lame and the king's followers lost their way. Somehow dragging his tired body he searched for a spring or stream as he was very thirsty. He could not find any. He felt giddy and he started seeing circles in front of his eyes. Just then there appeared a woman with a veil on her face.

The king cried out, "My Daughter, give me some water, I am dying of thirst!"

The woman said, "I could give you milk but no water."

The king replied, "My Daughter, could thirst be quenched by drinking milk? I am dying for some water."

The woman smiled and gave out cool refreshing water in a pail pouring it out of the pitcher.

The king quenched his thirst and gave his blessings saying, "My Daughter, whoever ye be, you shall adorn your father-in-law's house. You will bring fragrance to the household by your smiles and make everyone cool and happy."

The woman stooped low and did her *pranam* to the king and touched his feet and said, "Father, you have poured cool refreshing water into my troubled soul. You have made me happy beyond words, oh father, by once calling me your daughter. Give me, oh give me your blessings. I am Malanchamala."

The king was overjoyed. Remorse had been eating into him for sometime though he did not admit it; the king touched the Mother Earth and took out some soil and rubbed it on his forehead and said, "My Daughter, I make a promise now with Earth as my witness. I shall not break my promise again. If I do, let death gather me and let lightning hit me at once. Come, come to my house."

Malancha said, "Father, it is enough that you have called me as your daughter, it is enough that you have desired me to go to your house. I am happy, very happy and do not want to go to your palace."

But the king would not leave her and said, "My Daughter, if you do not come to my palace I shall take it that you, my daughter, have not pardoned me and I shall commit suicide to atone my sins."

Malanchamala relented and replied, "Father, let me stay on my own for a few days and then I shall surely come. How can I refuse to be with you when you want me? These few days I shall be visiting the *malini*, my tiger uncle and his family and look up Dudhbarna king's kingdom and then I shall come to you. The king consented. Immediately his limping horse became fit, his followers turned up and the forest guide appeared. The king left, again blessing Malanchamala.

On his way the king ordered for the digging of large tanks, renovating the old ones, digging wells and distributing alms. Happy tidings spread throughout his kingdom and all the people were happy and gay. Chandramanik and Kanchi were full of joy. Chandramanik had already come to know of his relationship with Malanchamala. Everyone was happy at the coming of Malanchamala.

Malanchamala could not forget her old friends and well-wishers. She first went to the *malini*, the wife of the gardener who had given her shelter. The *malini* had lost her eyesight with constant weeping for her. Her husband had become feeble and decrepit. Both revived on seeing her and felt strong and happy.

She then went to see the tiger and his family with her. The cubs had all become huge and started rubbing their noses against Malanchamala and they accompanied her to the kingdom of Dudhbarna, the king and father of Kanchi. The tiger revived the families they had killed, the king, his queen, the seven princes and all the men of the king.

Everywhere there were shouts of joy and happiness by hundreds of men and women, when flanked by the tiger and his family and Harikali, the *Pakshiraj* horse, Malanchamala arrived at her father-in-law's capital. Harikali flew and circuited the capital neighing loudly and all the horses and the people he had killed were revived. The tiger revived all those whom it had killed. The welcome was joyous and tumultuous.

The *Kotwal* and his wife, Dhara, the agent of God who had written the fatelines on the forehead of Chandramanik came, and all the gods and goddesses from the heavens showered flowers in blessing, and the whole palace was enlivened with music.

Malancha told Kanchi, "Sister, do make a garland for me."

Kanchi made one. Malanchamala put it around the neck of her husband Chandramanik and touched his feet in obeisance. She touched the feet of her father-in-law and all the elders and kissed all the younger ones.

Milk, honey and sweets were distributed in the capital and everyone had their fill. The tiger family ate vegetarian meals and drank pails of thickened milk and slept on golden cots for the first time in their life. The people made Malanchamala *Thakurani* and Malanchamala made Kanchi the *Patarani*. By calling her *Thakurani* the people recognised her greatness, her spiritual background, her faith in God, the king, her husband and the elders and affection for others, and her love for birds and animals. All the gods and goddesses were happy and pleased with Malanchamala's sacrifice and blessed her. Chandra Raja, her son, Chandramanik, Kanchi and all others lived happily and the subjects prospered. The *malini* became the constant companion of the *Thakurani* Malanchamala.

71
THE STORY OF SHREEMANTA

MANY years ago, there lived a merchant named Dhanapati in Sripur. He had no child by his first wife, Lahona. So he married again. The second wife was called Khullana.

It was surprising that though they were co-wives, they never fought with each other. In fact they were very fond of each other and lived like two sisters. Lahona prayed to the Goddess Mangal Chandi to bless Khullana with a son. To achieve this heartfelt desire, she undertook many types of worship.

At last Lahona's prayer was answered. "Chotaban" (Younger sister) Khullana was expecting. Lahona was very happy. She constantly looked after Khullana's health and comfort.

One day the merchant called Lahona and said, "Look, I have decided to start sailing for purposes of my trade. My boats are ready for departure. I shall start early tomorrow morning."

Lahona hesitated a bit, and then answered, "But why do you not wait a little more? Would you not like to see the face of your newborn baby before you start?"

The merchant replied, "No, I think I cannot delay any longer. My trade will suffer. You are here, so I know you will be in charge of everything. *Chotaban* will surely be well looked after. I have nothing to worry and no cause to postpone the voyage and let my business suffer."

Next day at the crack of dawn the merchant sailed for Ceylon with seven boats full of merchandise.

Some days later a bonny baby was born to Khullana. It was a boy. Lahona was the first person to rejoice at the happy event. She named the boy Shreemanta, the handsome one.

Though both the wives waited eagerly for the return of their husband, there was no news of the merchant. At last people started speculating various things concerning him. Some feared that he may have been drowned. Some others said that possibly he had been killed by robbers. The wives felt miserable, but did not know what to do. They looked at each other helplessly and prayed to God for the merchant's welfare.

At last news came that Shalibahan, the King of Lanka (Ceylon), had imprisoned the merchant.

When Shreemanta was five years old, the ceremony to start learning *(Hate-Khari)* was observed. It was *Basanta-Panchami*, the spring festival day in Bengal. The goddess of learning, Saraswati, is worshipped on that day.

Boys and girls wore dhoties and saris dyed yellow. An earthen image of Saraswati was placed on a wooden *Jal-Chouki* (a square wooden stool) heavily decorated with *alpana*. Children who were already studying, put their books, pen and inkpot at the feet of the goddess. Some placed their musical instruments, like sitar. The beginners appeared full of excitement, each with a new slate and long thick chalk in his hand. They were taught how to write their first alphabet by a learned Brahmin. Then, together they recited verses of the prayer, offered a handful of flowers. Shreemanta also learned his first alphabet in this conventional way.

Then he was admitted to the village primary school, the *Pathsala*. Lahona and Khullana sent him to the school and then eagerly awaited his return.

One day, after sometime the boy came back with tears in his eyes. Lahona took him on her lap, dried the tears tenderly from his face, and asked affectionately what was the trouble.

Shreemanta said, "Mother, tell me the name of my father and where he has gone. My friends said such bitter things to me today. They insulted me badly."

Lahona caressed him and wept. Then she told him the whole story of the merchant who was supposed to be a captive in Ceylon.

Shreemanta heard every word with attention. Then he heaved a sigh. At last he said, "Mother, you must permit me to start at once to meet my father. Unless you agree, I will neither touch any food nor sleep."

Lahona and Khullana were so shocked by the little boy's resolution that they did not know what to say. How could they allow a small boy like Shreemanta, who was the apple of their eyes, to start on such a perilous journey? They tried their best to dissuade him, argued long about the dangers on the way, but could not make Shreemanta change his mind.

At last, finding no other way, Lahona had to agree. As a measure of safety and precaution, she called a faithful boatman and put him in charge of the sailing expedition. Seven boats were fitted out as trading vessels. Shreemanta was a trader's son, so he must travel as a trader himself.

On the morning of his departure, Lahona, Khullana and all the village women gathered on the bank of the river Poorna where the boats were waiting for Shreemanta to bring good luck. Lahona put a mark of sandal paste and *dali* on Shreemanta's forehead. The sound of conchshells and loud *dhwani* filled the place. These were the traditional ways of expressing best wishes for a *Shubhayatra* (safe journey).

As Shreemanta touched the feet of his mother before taking leave, Lahona wept and embraced him. Then she said, "My son, never forget to pray to the goddess Mangal-Chandi daily. God forbid, if you ever see any trace of danger at any time, call out her name, and I am sure, she will come to your rescue."

Shreemanta agreed and said, "Yes, elder mother, I shall always remember your wish."

Then the boats started. The boatmen sang aloud to the goddess of the rivers and the sea, and the Lord of winds so that through their blessings, the voyage could be safe and prosperous. Lahona and Khullana gazed at the boats till they were out of sight. Then both of them turned back to the house weeping.

On that very night they dreamt that the goddess, Mangal Chandi, was saying to them, "Do not be worried for Shreemanta unnecessarily. He will come to no harm."

Shreemanta was proceeding smoothly. One day he forgot to say his prayers. And it happened that, that very day one of the boats ran into treacherous currents and was in danger.

Another day, the sky became pitch dark with clouds. A severe storm started. It looked as if Shreemanta, with all his boats, cargo, and boatmen, would be swept away by the gale. A thought flashed into his mind and Shreemanta started praying to the goddess Mangal-Chandi aloud. Gradually the storm stopped, the sky became clear, a rainbow appeared in the sky and all were saved from imminent danger.

When they came close to the shore of Ceylon, Shreemanta suddenly observed an amazing sight. A beautiful girl was sitting on a lotus on the surface of the water. She was holding two elephants one in each hand swallowing them whole, and again bringing them out whole, alternately.

Shreemanta bowed to the girl, thinking her to be a symbol of the goddess Mangal-Chandi. The boatmen also looked puzzled at such an unusual sight.

Embarking at Ceylon, Shreemanta went to the king's court. The king asked him to sit down. Then he asked Shreemanta, "Have you come across any unusual sight on the sea?" Shreemanta, answering the king's question, described the scene of the beautiful girl on the lotus.

The king was furious to hear this. He said angrily, "It seems that this boy is also trying to make a fool of me. You better put the prisoner's handcuffs on his hands." He looked at his guards.

Then he addressed Shreemanta, "Can you show me this sight which you have witnessed yourself?"

Shreemanta answered at once, "Yes, Maharaj, I can. Why do you not come out with me?"

So Shreemanta accompanied the king to the seashore. But it was surprising that the king could see nothing. He called Shreemanta a liar and a fraud and ordered him to be killed immediately.

Poor Shreemanta's young heart sank at this brutal order. He had come in the hope of finding his long lost father. Now, there was no question of meeting his father. Perhaps he would never even be able to meet his beloved mother again. He felt miserable. Suddenly he saw a ray of hope. He would pray to the goddess Mangal-Chandi to get him out of this danger.

So he requested the hangman that he should be givn a little time to say his last prayers before he was killed. The hangman agreed and Shreemanta prayed with all devotion to the goddess.

The goddess was moved by little Shreemanta's sincere prayers. She took pity on him and resolved to save him. She appeared, disguised as an old woman and said, "Why, my poor boy, why are you weeping so much? Come and sit on my lap."

When the hangman struck the head of Shreemanta with his axe, he observed to his surprise, that the victim's head remained unhurt while the axe broke into two parts. He ran to the king to give this extraordinary news.

The king was very annoyed. He started with a band of his soldiers to see personally.

Just as the party reached the place, the old woman uttered something angrily. Immediately a number of ghosts appeared on the spot and started killing the king's men.

The king now became frightened and sensed something supernatural dominating the place. So he pleaded with the old woman.

The old woman said, "Oh king, why did you want to kill that poor boy?"

The king replied, "The boy told me a lie, so I wanted to punish him."

The old woman said again, "No, the boy told you the truth, you are a sinner—a great sinner. So you could not see the sight which the boy had actually seen. Now, I order you to go back and release this boy's father at once. Not only his father but release all the other kings whom you have kept as prisoners. Then I would like you to get your daughter Sushila married to this boy Shreemanta. He is a very good boy and deserves the hand of your daughter."

The king remained dumbfounded for a while. Gradually he understood that this person in the disguise of an old woman must be none other than the goddess herself.

So he sat down at the woman's feet and pleaded, "Oh, my dear mother! I would obey you in everything. But I beg of you for only one kindness. Please, Goddess, be kind to me, and let me see you in your true form as *Kamale-kamini* (the woman in a lotus) just once as you had appeared before this boy."

The old woman said, "All right, go to the same place and you will be able to see the same sight as Shreemanta did."

She disappeared immediately after saying this.

The king rushed to the seashore again with Shreemanta. This time, also, the king could see nothing of the glorious sight. He felt very upset, when suddenly an idea struck him. Why did he not make Shreemanta, the goddess's favourite boy, sit on his lap? Perhaps then he would be able to have a glimpse of the goddess. So he asked Shreemanta to sit on his lap and as he did so, the king could see the goddess on the lotus at long last!

The king was overjoyed. His happiness knew no bounds.

He felt very thankful to Shreemanta and said, "My son, but

for you I would never have been able to achieve this wonderful experience."

He brought Shreemanta to his palace and ordered immediate release of his father, the merchant, and all other kings whom he had kept prisoners for a long time. The merchant could hardly believe his eyes when he was told that this was his son. He hugged Shreemanta affectionately and blessed him heartily.

Shreemanta was married to the king's daughter, Princess Sushila. The ceremony was observed with pomp and show. There was illumination for one whole week and a continuous banquet for ten days. Each and every citizen took part in the merry-making.

When the time came for the young couple to take leave, the king arranged several boats, all full of gorgeous presents for them, for the bride's in-laws and especially for the two mothers-in-law. So the merchant, Dhanapati, started the return journey, at last accompanied by his son and daughter-in-law.

As the boats touched the shore of Dhanapati's village, Sripur in Bengal, people stared curiously. They were astonished to see the merchant alive, along with the young son, Shreemanta. Some ran to Lohana and Khullana at once, carrying the happy news of their arrival.

Lahona and Khullana rushed to the ghat. Their happiness was beyond measure when they saw their long-lost husband back with dear Shreemanta, the apple of their eyes. They greeted the bride most warmly.

The ceremony to welcome the bride, *Baran*, was performed meticulously. Conchshells from almost every house started sounding loudly. Along with that the sound of *hullu* mingled and gave a warm reception to the bride.

Then Khullana walked ahead of the couple, and went on sprinkling water from a silver pitcher all the way along that path. Shreemanta with his bride went ahead with Lahona. The merchant came behind them.

Lahona performed a thanksgiving ceremony to the goddess Mangal-Chandi. All the villagefolk were invited to take part in the worship and then to have *prasad*, a share of the food offered to the goddess. Everyone came to know the story of Shreemanta and his father being saved from danger by the mercy of the goddess.

Thereafter, the merchant lived happily with his two wives, son Shreemanta and daughter-in-law Sushila.